INROCK

INROCK

Desmond Morris

JONATHAN CAPE
THIRTY BEDFORD SQUARE LONDON

First published 1983
Copyright © 1983 by Desmond Morris
Jonathan Cape Ltd, 30 Bedford Square, London WC1

British Library Cataloguing in Publication Data

Morris, Desmond
Inrock.
1. Title
823'.914[F] P27

ISBN 0-224-02950-9

Printed in Great Britain by
Hazell, Watson & Viney Ltd

Contents

1 The Deserted Village 7
2 The Golden Worms 17
3 The Display Prison 25
4 The Ten-chin Banquet 36
5 The Niar-storm 48
6 The Dream-stalk 61
7 The Flag Ceremony 70
8 The Ludo Attack 79
9 The Root Forest 87
10 The Skin Tomb 99
11 The Long Lake Port 111
12 The Island of Feathered Dwarfs 120
13 The Strummer Invasion 129
14 The Pacification Orchestra 137
15 The Deadly Alternative 148
16 The Battle of the Snowcocks 158
17 The Rock Arena 169
18 The Bonefire Race 183
19 The School of Unlearning 195

Contents

20 The Sculptor's Den 203
21 The Censor's Whiskers 213
22 The Journey to the Gateway 223
23 The Zoobore Collection 234
24 The Valley of the Hearties 246
25 The Tunnel of Joy-poloy 257
26 The Tricorn Herd 266
27 The Muzzleking's Sacrifice 278
Postscript 287

CHAPTER ONE
The Deserted Village

The village chimneys were quietly smoking in the yellow-grey half-light of evening. It was already spring, but the long winter habit of lighting fires was slow to die. Jason left the farmhouse and wandered down to the road. The cluster of cottages at the centre of the village, not far away, looked sleepy and friendly. Nothing moved.

For a moment he pretended that he was the only human being left alive. As he walked along the side of the road, he tried to think what he would do when he came to the village and found no one there. There would be plenty of food in the kitchens and he could go anywhere he liked, through the gardens, into the houses, and do whatever he wanted. After a while it might be rather lonely, but it would be exciting to be completely free, with nobody in the way. He would own the entire village.

Just as he paused to pull a long grass out of its stem to suck the tender end, there was a dull roaring sound behind him. He swung round but could see nothing. The noise grew and became harsher. Staring hard at the orange part of the sky where the sun had glowed an hour before, he thought he could make out a vague shape.

Inrock

Suddenly it was over him, a great black shadow, ploughing through the darkening sky. It throbbed overhead and disappeared in a rush beyond a clump of trees.

Jason had been living in the village of Avebury all his life, but he had never witnessed anything like it before. It was strange that no one in the village had dashed out to see what it was. Perhaps the place really was deserted. Perhaps, earlier in the day, the great black shadow had landed nearby and taken all the villagers off to a secret destination, leaving him behind by mistake.

He had been lying in the old barn all afternoon, watching one of the farm cats feeding its new litter of kittens up in the hay-loft. That must have been when they came and took everyone away.

Any minute now, he thought, as he neared the village, someone will look out of a door, or a cart will come rumbling round the corner, and I shall be back to earth with a bump. Daydreams are exciting, but they never last, something always breaks into them.

All the same, he told himself, Avebury is a strange kind of village and you can't help thinking odd thoughts here. Some places are so ordinary that it is hard to imagine anything weird ever happening in them. But here it is different. As soon as you get to the edge of the village you can feel it, for all around, circling the cottages in a vast, perfect ring, are the mysterious standing stones, the biggest over fifteen feet high and weighing more than sixty tons. Jason had often asked about them, but nobody could give him a sensible answer. All he could ever find out was that they had been put there in ancient times, thousands of years ago, and were supposed to be magical, but what sort of magic no one would say. Today people often came from far away to look at them and left as puzzled as when they arrived.

He could see the dark outlines of some of the stones now, as he came nearer to the village, but at that moment something made him stop and look down. As he stared at the surface of the road, he thought he saw it glow. It seemed to go pale for a few seconds and then darken again.

'Fantastic!' he said out loud, but the word was drowned by a deep thundering noise. Everything pulsated and then went very

The Deserted Village

still. It was even quieter than before.

Jason listened, not moving, waiting. After a while, when nothing further happened, he spun round quickly, almost expecting to see someone standing right behind him, but the road stretching back towards the farm was empty. Then he heard a pattering sound, a friendly, familiar noise of heavy raindrops falling on big leaves. So that was it — a thunderstorm. How disappointing, just as he was beginning to feel certain that something unusual was going to happen.

But his disappointment faded as he looked up at the tree above him. Its leaves were dry, completely dry, and the pattering sound was getting louder. It was behind him, coming from the direction of the village. He looked over his shoulder and stared in amazement. Every dog from the village was on the narrow road. They were bunched together in a huge pack and were running as fast as their pounding legs would carry them. Their paws beat a tattoo on the hard surface of the road and they were all racing in his direction. There was no yelping or barking, only the pattering of their feet. They were all there, the mongrels, the terriers, the hounds, all the dogs he knew so well.

There, at the very front, leading the pack, Jason could make out the shape of his favourite dog, Satan, the vicar's grizzled old boxer. On his face he wore a heavy leather muzzle, not to stop him biting — he was the friendliest dog in the village — but to prevent him from burying his bones in the cemetery. His undoing had come one evening when the baker's widow, carrying a bunch of white flowers to place on her husband's grave, had come face to face with him there, standing over a freshly dug hole right next to the tombstone and with what appeared to her to be one of the dead baker's bones clamped between his teeth. She had dropped the flowers, screamed, and gone on screaming until she lost her voice three hours later. Even the idea that the dog was burying the bone in the grave rather than digging it up did not console her and from that point onwards the unhappy boxer had been forced to wear a muzzle whenever he went out of doors. Everyone had promptly nicknamed the dog Satan — everyone, that is, except the vicar, who confused the poor brute by continuing to call him Rex.

Jason loved the ugly, leather-bound old Satan and was astonished to see him running so fast and with such a fixed, determined look in his eyes. As he came closer, Jason whistled and called out to him, shouting his name several times, louder each time, but the dog ignored him completely and the whole pack rushed past his legs without pausing. Up the roadway they went, beyond the farmhouse path and into the distance, disappearing around the bend by the copse.

'Fantastic!' he said again, but now his voice was the only sound to be heard. He was alone once more.

What did it all mean? Where were they all going so intently, so seriously? He started walking towards the village again, more quickly this time. He didn't want to miss anything.

Before Jason could reach the centre of Avebury he had to pass through the great circle of standing stones, rearing up like frozen sentinels around the cluster of houses. Most of them were so massive that they towered over him. One in particular was huge, bigger than all the rest, and his uncle had once told him that it was a growing-stone and that some people called it the ninth wonder of the world. The older villagers swore that it used to be smaller and that each year it grew a few more inches, but no one had ever bothered to measure it to find out.

Jason glanced back at the giant growing-stone as he entered the village and thought that for a fleeting moment he saw it shudder very slightly. It was probably only a trick of the fading light, he told himself, and kept moving, heading towards the square.

Nothing. Absolutely nothing. No one to be seen, no animals, no movement anywhere. He ran across to a friend's door and knocked. No answer. He peered through the window and called out. Still no answer. The whole place seemed to be deserted.

After wandering around for a few moments and trying other cottages with the same result, he decided the only thing to do was to go straight back to the farm and report what he had seen. In his daydream he had strolled gaily from kitchen to kitchen, feasting on the abandoned food. But this was no daydream, it was

The Deserted Village

happening, and he set off without delay.

As he came out of the village, he glanced again at the growing-stone, now almost black in the advancing dusk. He stopped dead. This time he was certain. It really was moving, visibly trembling, and there was a soft hissing noise coming from it.

Treading very gently, he opened a small gate in the fence at the side of the road, slipped quietly through, and crouched down on the grass. He was about thirty feet from the stone and could see it clearly. It was shuddering more violently now. He watched, motionless. Then it gave three or four powerful jerks, one after the other, very quickly, and was still. The hissing had stopped as well.

Jason waited, but nothing happened. After a while he stood up slowly and as softly as possible came nearer. When he was only ten feet away, a tapping sound began inside the stone and a long crack appeared on its surface. He touched the crack with his fingertips and felt it growing wider. Spreading like a moving snake across the face of the tall stone, the dark line became longer and longer until it reached the ground. Jason watched it as it disappeared below the grass and then looked up quickly just in time to see the other end of the crack rising and disappearing over the top of the stone. Now this line began to shoot downwards on the far side until it too vanished beneath the ground.

'It's splitting open, like an egg hatching,' Jason gasped, and leapt back in case part of it fell on him.

With a groan, the split halves began to move apart, and as they did so there was a violent rushing of wind. Leaves and strands of grass were torn loose and sucked in a thrashing flurry towards the black space in the centre of the great stone. The air hissed and whistled and Jason found himself being pulled little by little in the same direction. He tried to lie down and grab hold of the turf beneath his feet, but it was useless. In a flash he was gone.

Inside the growing-stone he bumped into something soft and warm and clung on to it with both arms. Whatever it was started to struggle with him, pushing and shoving and grunting as it fought against the howling current of air. It managed to break free and dragged itself out through the gaping hole, round the side of the stone and away.

Jason felt himself being sucked down onto a firm surface and flattened there by the wind. He could hardly breathe. Then, with a sigh, the gale dropped to a whisper and he was able to clamber out on to the soft grass. Lying there panting, he realized that, for the first time since the dogs had left so hurriedly, he was not alone. Somewhere in the half-darkness he had a strange and unknown companion.

He got to his feet and started to pull the grass and leaves from his clothes and hair. Then he heard it.

'Tonk, tonk, tonk. Tonk. Tonk, tonk.'

'Who are you?' he called out. 'Where are you?'

'Tonk-tonk-tonk-tonk.'

'What do you want?' he asked firmly.

'Tonk-tonk. Tonk.'

'Is that the only noise you can make?'

There was a soft, mumbling sound. It seemed to be coming from behind one of the other stones that stood in the great circle. The mumbling became a gurgle and the gurgle became a sad, low voice which said:

'Are you going to hurt me?'

'No, of course not,' Jason replied. 'Come out where I can see you.'

'They said you would hurt me,' mumbled the voice.

'I never hurt animals – or people,' he added quickly, not knowing what it was and not wanting to offend it.

'Will you help me?' it asked in a doubtful tone.

'Why are you so suspicious? Of course I'll help you. Come over here.'

Slowly, very slowly, a shape emerged from behind the next stone and began to move towards him. As it did so, the tonking noise began again.

'Tonk, tonk, tonk. Tonk. Tonk-tonk.'

As it came closer he saw its face clearly in the moonlight. It was large, round and very sad, with big eyes and a heavy, flat, whiskered nose. Its soft lips sagged down at the corners. Beneath its heavy head were two short arms, bent double so that the hands were held close together just below the chin. Instead of fingers there were long, curved claws with blunt ends.

The creature was standing on two long, tapering legs with bird-like feet. As far as Jason could see, the limbs came straight out of the huge, rounded head. There seemed to be hardly any body at all. Both the head and the limbs were covered in a soft, dense coat of brown fur, except at the back of the head, where the hair gave way to a cluster of sharp spikes that flapped up and down with each step the creature took. In amongst the broad spikes were some thinner tubes, each with a small swelling at its tip.

'What is your name?' asked Jason. There was no reply, only a forlorn, baleful stare from the huge black eyes.

'My name is Jason. Please tell me yours.'

Instead of answering, the creature suddenly walked off, tonking as it did so. It moved in a circle and in a few seconds was back exactly where it had begun, staring at Jason. He asked his question again, several times, but on each occasion the creature made the same response, turning away from him and walking off as if to leave him, only to loop back again to stand glumly in front of him.

Obviously, he was getting nowhere. He decided to try another approach. Noticing that it kept its mouth shut when it made the tonking noise, he said, in as friendly a way as possible:

'You must be a ventriloquist.'

The big eyes became even bigger.

'No,' it said, 'I can't be.'

'Why not?'

'Because I don't know what the word means.'

'That's ridiculous,' said Jason 'When you were born you must have cried, but you didn't know the word "cry" then, did you?'

The creature's reaction to this was extraordinary. As soon as it heard the word 'born' it began to shake all over and in a few moments had collapsed quivering to the ground.

'What on earth's the matter?' asked Jason, horrified by the effect his words had had.

'That word, that word,' gurgled the creature.

'What word? You mean "born"?'

At this, the quivering became more violent and the creature's arms and legs started flailing about. It staggered up and began to run round and round in small circles, like a moth singed on a lamp, mumbling and gurgling and tonking faster and faster.

'Warrgh. Gurrgh. Warrgh,' it shouted, and plunged head down into a bank of earth.

With its sharp spikes sticking up and its face hidden, it began scrabbling in the ground, digging as fast as it could go, kicking the earth out backwards with its bird-like feet. Bit by bit it began to sink out of sight until all that was visible was a great clump of spikes and tubes, looking like some strange, prickly kind of plant.

Jason ran over to it and tried to reassure it, but all he could hear was a muffled mumbling sound. When he leant over to touch one of the spikes, they all started twitching and twisting and, as they did so, the tonking sound started up again.

'So that's how you tonk. It's your spikes. Well, if you won't tell me your name I shall call you Tonk. Hey, Tonk, come out. I won't harm you.' But the Tonk stayed put, mumbling.

He tried tugging at one of the spikes, carefully avoiding the sharp tip. The Tonk let out a great gurgle:

'Wuuggle. Warrgh. Wuuggle. Gerrough,' and there was more scrabbling.

As it began to sink further into the ground, Jason noticed a change in the thin tubes that were mixed in with the spikes. The small swellings at the tips of the tubes were growing rapidly in size and at the same time were changing colour, becoming brighter and brighter. As they expanded they became red and yellow, glowing vividly in the dim light. When they were swollen to ten times their original size, they began to look like magnificent, gaudy flowers.

'Hey, Tonk,' called Jason, 'you are sprouting flowers.'

The Tonk mumbled sadly to itself from beneath the earth. By

The Deserted Village

now the flowers were really beautiful and in full bloom. Jason could not resist the temptation to pick one. As he did so, the spikes twisted and tonked frantically and there was a wild gurgle from down below.

'Warrgh! Gooarrgh!' shrieked the Tonk, and rose unsteadily to its feet.

Jason leapt back to avoid being stabbed by the sharp spikes and then looked down at the flower in his hand. As he went to sniff it, it collapsed and shrivelled up. In a few seconds it was as limp and dull as a pricked balloon.

'You see, you see,' roared the Tonk, slashing its front claws against one another, as if it were sharpening a carving knife. 'I knew you would hurt me. They told me you would hurt me. They were right, they were right. I'm a disaster, a disaster. I should never have broken through, never, never, never, never,' and with a great moan the creature sat down quivering on the grass.

'I'm terribly sorry. I didn't mean to hurt you. It was stupid of me, but I simply couldn't resist picking one of those fantastic flowers.'

'Exactly, exactly, you couldn't help it — just what they told me, just what they said. A disaster, a disaster.' The Tonk looked even sadder than when he had first appeared.

'But you're safe now. I wouldn't dream of doing it again,' said Jason reassuringly.

'There are others — everyone will want to pick on me when they see me for the first time. It will kill me. Slowly and painfully, it will destroy me. I know it now, I should have believed them.'

'Nonsense, I shall tell everyone not to touch you.'

'Easy to say,' snorted the Tonk, 'but I am much too tempting when my flowers are out. No one can resist me the first time.'

'They will be sensible,' said Jason, 'they'll learn.'

'By that time I shall be dead — plucked to death, bloom by bloom,' gurgled the Tonk.

'Then I will hide you from them. If you come with me, I'll put you in the old barn. No one has been in there since the new barn was finished last winter. You can stay there and I'll bring you food and water. What do you eat, by the way?'

'Worms,' said the Tonk.

'Oh,' said Jason. 'Oh well, I'll do the best I can for you. Come on.'

CHAPTER TWO

The Golden Worms

As they walked to the farm Jason was silent, thinking. The Tonk mumbled softly and licked its lips at the thought of the promised worms, tonking noisily as it plodded along. Its flowers had shrunk back into their tubes again.

'Why won't you tell me your real name?' Jason asked suddenly.

'Because that would put me in your debt,' mumbled the Tonk.

'But that's ridiculous,' said Jason, 'I've told you *my* name and I'm not in *your* debt.'

'Then why are you going to hide me and feed me?' asked the Tonk.

'Because I want to help you.'

'Exactly,' said the Tonk. 'That's what I mean. You have burdened me with your name so now you have to burden yourself with helping me. But remember that's *your* game, not mine. I'm not playing.'

Jason decided not to argue and they walked on in a silence broken only by the tonking noise and an occasional mumble. He wanted to ask about the panic he had caused by using the word 'born', but he was afraid of starting it all off again, so he kept quiet until they reached the farm.

'The barn is over there,' he said, pointing the way, and led the Tonk to the large battered door at the end of the building.

Inside, the creature tonked itself down on a pile of hay and promptly went to sleep, snuffling and snoring loudly within seconds of closing its heavy eyelids over its huge black eyes. Jason was surprised to see that there was a large, dark spot on each eyelid, so that it still seemed to be staring at him even with its eyes completely shut. It would certainly fool anyone who didn't look too closely, thought Jason, and they'd think twice about creeping up on the Tonk and trying to take it unawares. But the trick was spoiled by that terrible snoring. Yes, the poor old Tonk really was a bit of a disaster. It certainly needed help from someone.

Taking a lamp from a hook on the wall and picking up an old, dented bucket, Jason went off in search of worms. He found them easily, large juicy ones that had ventured up on to the cool night surface of the lawn at the back of the farm. They were there in their hundreds, round and plump and glistening, lying half in and half out of the earth. He had to grab them before they could shoot down into their holes, then pull them out slowly, the way a blackbird does, so that they didn't break in two.

Setting to work energetically, crawling this way and that, he threw worm after worm into the ancient bucket. After ten minutes he wiped his hands on the grass and shone the lamp on to his catch. Satisfied with the writhing mass of Tonk-fodder that he saw there, he returned to the barn and quietly opened the door. He could not see the creature anywhere, but then, over in a far corner, he heard a scrabbling and a snuffling accompanied by an occasional 'Tonk-tonk'.

'What on earth are you doing?' he called out. 'You can't go digging up the barn floor like that.'

'Worms,' mumbled the Tonk. 'Must have worms.'

'I'm sure you're hungry, but there's no need to wreck the place. I've brought you a whole pile of worms. Fresh, farmhouse worms, home-grown.'

The Tonk scrabbled out of the hole and flung itself on the bucket. It pushed its enormous mouth down on to the rim and

The Golden Worms

started to make flobbering noises. A few moments later it sank back, pulled itself over to the hay and sagged wearily down on to the soft bed where it had slept briefly before.

'It's the moment, the moment, the moment of truth,' it gurgled. 'I'll know any second now. I must find out. I must find out. May snackers protect me and all who worm with me,' and, crossing his front paws, he closed his eyes and waited as if expecting something terrible to happen.

Jason became impatient. 'What moment?' he asked. 'What are you talking about?'

'Watch me very closely,' said the Tonk, its eyes still shut tight. 'Bring the lamp nearer – tell me if you see any change, anything odd.'

'Are you afraid the worms may make you sick or something? Are you going to go green?' But Jason got no answer. The Tonk was breathing deeply now and appeared to be concentrating very hard.

After a few minutes it opened its eyes and looked down at itself. 'Did I change? Did you see any change?'

'Not really, except that perhaps you grew a little, but then I suppose you would, with all those worms inside you.'

'Warrgh! Glurrgh! Warrgh!' shrieked the Tonk. 'I have failed. I have failed. I am going to die. Horribly. Warrgh! Hideously. Gorarrgh! Unspeakably. Glurarrgh!' and it thrashed about on the hay, gurgling and dribbling.

Jason waited. There was no point in interrupting. The Tonk was in full gurgle and the only thing to do was sit it out. Eventually the creature subsided into a sad, sagging lump. They looked at one another quietly.

'Right,' said Jason in a business-like way, 'now, if you will explain, I will try to help.'

'It's too late, there's nothing you can do.'

'Stop looking like a baked apple. You're not dead yet.'

'I will be before long. We were all warned what would happen if we broke the rule. I should never have risked it.'

'How will you die?' asked Jason sternly. 'What exactly do you imagine is going to kill you? And who are "they"?'

'They are the rulers and they told us that if we tried to break through without permission — without the golden ceremony — we would . . . we would . . . '

'Go on, go on.'

'We would . . . *put on weight.*'

Jason snorted. 'How ridiculous! *That* won't kill you.'

'You stupid, twiddle-toed, quarter-brained, idiotic . . .' The Tonk was flailing and quivering again, thrashing its arms and legs about and shaking with fear and rage. Once more Jason had to wait patiently for it to subside.

'I will die,' said the Tonk sadly, after a long pause, 'because I shall grow and grow and become so heavy that I shall not be able to support my own weight. I shall suffocate. If I had managed to get away with it, to beat the rule, then I would not have started to swell after that meal of worms. That was the moment of truth. And I failed. I started growing straight away and it will go on and on now, quicker and quicker, until I fill this whole barn.'

'Why don't you go back where you came from, then?' suggested Jason helpfully.

'Look at me, look at me. Shine that light all over me.'

'I see what you mean,' said Jason, rather taken aback by what he saw. The Tonk was already twice its original size. 'You are too big to get through the hole in the growing-stone.'

The Tonk gurgled and sagged even more sadly on to the hay.

'But wait a minute!' cried Jason. 'It *is* a growing-stone. If *it* is getting bigger, too, perhaps . . . ' but the Tonk cut him short.

'No no no — that's all nonsense. Who told you that? The stone doesn't grow itself. It's called a growing-stone because *we* grow if we break through without permission. Grow until we die. Warrgh! Grrough! Painfully, excruciatingly, odiously . . . '

'So *that's* what the name means. I didn't understand before.'

' . . . agonizingly, nauseatingly, pitiably . . . '

'Tonk!'

' . . . wretchedly, disgustingly, appallingly . . . '

'Tonk!' shouted Jason. 'Shut up and let me think.'

The Golden Worms

They were both silent. Time passed, but no useful thoughts came to mind and the Tonk was definitely growing faster now, puffing up like a blister. Jason didn't much like the idea of having a barn-sized Tonk on his hands. And the creature's quaking fear about its swollen future was beginning to worry him. Perhaps it really would die in terrible agony, suffocated by its own weight, like a stranded whale, and that would be too awful to watch. He would have to do something. There must be a way out.

'Is there nothing that could stop the growing?' he asked hopefully.

'Only the Golden Worms,' muttered the Tonk.

Jason sprang to his feet. 'Why on earth didn't you say so before, you stupid great Tonk. I'll go and get some for you. Where are they?'

'They're in the Inrock and you would never find them anyway. I've been searching for them for as long as I can remember. They are only found in one special place and no one knows where it is. Or, at least, if they do, they won't tell me.'

'They'll tell me. I'll worm it out of them!'

'If you think this is a subject for joking, then I hope the Sculptor gets hold of you, that's all,' muttered the Tonk, kicking savagely at the empty bucket with a huge, swollen foot.

'Who's the Sculptor?'

'It doesn't matter. You can't go anyway. No one has ever been *into* the Inrock from the outside. Never. Only the other way round.'

'Why can't I simply go into that hole in the growing-stone and down to wherever it is you come from? You left the stone open when you . . . '

'WHAT!' screamed the Tonk. 'I did *what?*'

'Yes, I frightened you and you rushed off and left it open.'

'This is a catastrophe, a calamity. I must go now, go and shut it . . . there will be a massacre if I don't. The Sculptor will go insane. My friends will suffer. I have betrayed them, I have betrayed them.'

The Tonk struggled desperately to get to its feet, but already its weight was too much for them and they splayed out on either side of its great balloon shape.

'Relax. I'll go. You try and sleep.' Jason reached out and touched the soft fur on the giant face. 'Poor old Tonk, you really are in a mess, aren't you. Don't worry, you are under my personal protection now. I'll think of something.'

The Tonk looked at him for a long moment, blinked slowly and gulped. Then it sighed and closed its eyes. Jason left it mumbling and burbling to itself and walked thoughtfully across to the barn door. He paused there, trying to make up his mind. He had a feeling that, for him, it would not be too difficult to find the Golden Worms. The Tonk had obviously been hopeless at it. Surely all it needed was a little intelligence and a little cunning? But supposing he was wrong, supposing it took a long time, would it be worth it? He might be too late to save the swelling Tonk. On the other hand, if he didn't go, the Tonk's fate was certain. So there was nothing to lose, and anyway, if he was honest, he needed an adventure, and here was the perfect excuse for one. He *had* to go! Slapping the barn door with his hand, he turned and ran back to the now slumbering hulk on the hay.

'Tonk! Wake up!' he hissed.

'Warrgh?'

'Wake up and listen. There is something I must ask before I go. Trust me and tell me your real name — and anything else about yourself that may help me. Tonk, please!' and he shook the bulging shape.

'Oh dear, must I, oh dear — well — if it will help. I suppose. Oh dear. Where to begin?'

'Your name.'

'Well — they call me the Meggamole. My friends — Ha! — my friends say that I am mad — they call me the Mad Meggamole. I was a reject, but I wouldn't listen. Now look at me! I came from the Silver Swamp. Lots of lovely, luscious worms, done to a turn — lovely worms . . .' and the heavy eyelids sank down again.

'Keep awake — just a minute longer, that's all. Tell me what happened when you came here, when you broke through. There

The Golden Worms

was a great roar and the dogs all panicked.'

'Magworks . . . magnetworks . . . mag . . . can't remember the word . . . magnets all upset . . . everything throbbing . . . bad time . . . sleep now . . . sleeeep . . . '

'This is hopeless. Is that all you can tell me? Tonk?'

'Worms. Must have the Golden Worms. Golden . . . '

'Tonk!'

'Watch out for the Sculptor . . . Wurrrgh . . . '

Jason gave up. He took one last look at his strange, sleep-heavy visitor and set off again for the barn door. This time he did not turn back.

Outside the air was so still you could hear the silence humming, as if it were waiting for a sharp noise to break the monotony. As he reached the road, he jumped. There *was* a noise — the single, frantic yelp of a dog. Then silence again and the gentle humming.

'Satan! Satan, is that you?' For a moment Jason thought the yelp had sounded like his old friend the vicar's boxer. But perhaps he was mistaken. He couldn't be sure. Anyway, there was no reply and no further sound as he went swiftly down the road towards the village and the growing-stone.

The hole where the Tonk had broken through was still there, gaping in the rock-face, and without hesitating he struggled inside.

'There must be a way to make it close,' he said out loud, 'because the Tonk's arms aren't as strong as all that. How did he manage to open it?'

He tapped and pressed everywhere, but nothing happened. Then he tried jumping hard on the ground beneath his feet. After the fourth jump he felt a slight vibration. This was followed by a shudder and the two great slabs of stone groaned, hissed, and slowly slid back towards one another. With a snap they shut tight and at that moment the inside of the rock appeared to light up. Where was the light coming from? He twisted round in the small cavity inside the stone and, looking up over his shoulder, he saw the answer. To his amazement it was the full moon. The moment the two halves had snapped shut, the whole of the growing-stone had become completely transparent. He could see out of it as if he were in a glass dome.

'Fantastic!' he cried. 'So they can see us but we can't see them. I wonder if all the rocks are like this inside. Perhaps that is what Tonk meant when he said he came from the Inrock.'

He looked down at the floor of the cavity again. 'Now what do I do?' he wondered. He tried stamping again, but this time nothing happened. He jumped harder. Nothing. Then a soft whirring noise began. It grew into a roar. In a few seconds it was so deafening that he had to cover his ears. The whole stone started to tremble.

As he stood there, his body tensed, he felt the ground beneath him becoming softer. His feet started to sink into it. It was as if all the grains of earth were becoming looser and looser, and they were moving like sand shaken in a sieve.

He was sinking fast now. His legs were gone and his body was slipping down after them. He covered his eyes with one hand and his nose and mouth with the other . . . and under he went.

It was warm and soft and he felt himself sliding down, his speed increasing every second. He held his breath and kept his body rigid. His clothes were being dragged upwards and were almost torn from him. To his relief, his passage downwards through the shifting, dancing, vibrating grains of earth seemed to leave him unharmed. He felt no pain.

Suddenly he sensed himself curving round to one side. The descent was flattening out. Rolling over and over, he threw out his hands to steady himself, and heard the hissing sound again, only much louder this time. Then with a roar it was all over. He skidded to a stop and everything was quiet and still.

CHAPTER THREE
The Display Prison

For a moment Jason lay where he was without moving. Then he stretched the toes on his left foot. Next, his right foot. They still worked. He could feel them wiggle. Taking a deep breath he opened his eyes and sat up. He was sprawled at the base of a huge pile of loose earth. In front of him he could make out the contours of a great cavern. Looking down he saw to his surprise that his clothes had been torn to shreds, but they were still clinging to him.

'Somehow,' he told himself, 'I will have to get back up there again eventually and it's not going to be easy. But first I must do some exploring and find the Golden Worms before the Tonk bursts the roof off the old barn.'

The cavern was warm and dry. In the distance he could see that it curved to the right. The light was stronger there and he picked his way carefully along the rough floor, making for the brightness. At one point he thought he heard a soft whining sound and called out, 'Satan, Satan, is that you?' but there was no answer. Peering into dark corners he could find no trace of his old friend. The whine had sounded strangely familiar, but he must have been mistaken. Perhaps the noise was in his head. He certainly felt most peculiar. The only thing to do was to struggle on towards the light. The walls began to broaden out until he found himself entering a vast under-rock arena.

'Papers, please,' snapped a sharp voice at his elbow. It came from a narrow slit in the wall at his side. Jason approached it and was startled to see twenty or thirty small eyes staring at him from the gloom. They seemed to be floating about in the darkness inside the slit, each one moving in its own special way, quite independent of the movements of the others.

'Who are you?' he enquired. 'Can you help me please, I am looking for the Gol . . . '

He was interrupted by an angry rattling noise. A long, armoured spike, vibrating so fast that it was almost a blur, shot out of the slit and hovered menacingly in front of his face. Still rattling, the spike started to wander over him, always keeping an inch or so away from the surface of his body. It appeared to be examining him closely, but without actually touching him. When it had finished, the eyes slowly emerged from the darkness of the slit in the wall and Jason could now see that they were on long stalks, like waving tentacles. They weaved this way and that, each one looking at a different part of his tattered clothing.

'Who are you?' he demanded again. At the harshness in his voice, the eye-stalks shrank back a little and bunched together, facing him, dancing back and forth in front of his nose.

'Polizesti. Now hand over your papers. You know the rules. No one may enter the main assembly area from a side-tunnel without showing love-papers and name-papers. You have been told the penalty for breaking this rule.'

'I had a bad fall. You can see my clothes are torn. I have no papers, nothing.'

'You realize I shall have to spike you, then?'

'Will that be painful?' asked Jason, frowning at the armoured point, still vibrating slightly in front of his stomach.

The question seemed to worry the Polizesti, who emerged slowly from his slit and stood stiffly in front of the tattered figure. Jason was now able to see him clearly. He was tall and thin and his eye-tentacles emerged straight out of the top of his slender,

The Display Prison

upright body. His armoured spike, also on a long stalk, grew out of the middle of his stomach. His legs were long and tapering, with bird-like feet, reminding Jason of the legs of the Tonk.

He repeated his question: 'Will it be painful? Will it hurt me?'

'I suppose so,' said the Polizesti, 'or it wouldn't be much use, would it? The truth is I've never had to use it, so I'm not sure. I'd much rather you showed me your papers. Love-papers first, and then name-papers, please.' His voice had slipped into its official tone again.

'What are love-papers?' asked Jason innocently. All the eyes began to dance and blink and the spike rattled furiously.

'Stop playing games with me. You know perfectly well what they are. They list all persons you love and state reasons for loving them. Your name-papers give all the names you have had during your various shape-stages. Now hurry up and hand them over. The Interviewer will be coming soon and I shall have to report.'

'I can't. I would if I could, but I can't. Don't you understand? I have no papers. I'm sorry, but I must go now. I have an urgent job to do. There is something I must find.' He had decided not to ask about the Golden Worms at this point in case it got him into more trouble.

'I am a Polizesti and I have no choice.' The tentacles stiffened and reared up to their full height. 'In the name of the Sculptor, I spike you,' and he thrust out his armoured point. As it touched Jason's body it hissed and rattled more violently than ever. He felt himself begin to shake with it. His arms and legs shot out straight and stiff and his teeth started to chatter. He was quivering all over now, uncontrollably. Everything became brighter and brighter until the whole place was an intense white glare. He shook more and more, great shudders going right through him from head to toe. Then the light began to fade and a jet black darkness descended. He collapsed to the ground.

As he lay there a large, soft shape slid round the corner and sniffed at him. The Polizesti bowed to the new arrival, his now drooping tentacles almost touching the ground.

'Report. Report. Report,' boomed the soft shape.

Inrock

'Ready to report, Interviewer, ready to report,' rasped the Polizesti. And the Interviewer listened silently to his story.

When Jason awoke he found he had been moved. The Polizesti had gone. At first he thought he was alone, but when his eyes had grown used to the harsh light, he realized that he was in fact surrounded by a large crowd, all watching him intently.

He was lying on a smooth slab of rock on a slightly raised platform, like a bandstand. When he got up, the crowd pulled back a little and then pushed forward more eagerly. Near the edge of the platform he could see several figures that looked rather like the Polizesti, except that they were taller and had several armoured spikes each instead of a single one. They were facing the crowd as if they were guarding the platform, but occasionally one or two of their eye-stalks would twist round to peer at Jason for a moment, then swing back again.

The crowd itself was made up of all kinds of strange creatures, some large, some small, some thin and spindly and some fat and stumpy. Their heads, bodies and limbs were unlike anything Jason had seen before. Weird shapes and colours were everywhere, with tubes, horns, scales, lobes of flesh and tufts of hair sticking out in all directions. The crowd was pressed so tightly together that it was difficult to sort out exactly which bits belonged to which creature. It was all too confusing and Jason soon gave up staring at them and concentrated instead on examining his platform. It was a perfect circle, about twenty feet across, and was completely smooth except for a circular crack about three feet wide, near to the slab. Looking upwards, all he could see was an unbroken glare of bright yellow light.

Remembering what had happened inside the growing-stone, he got up again and stamped on the circular crack with his foot. All the eye-stalks of the guards turned swiftly to stare at him, blinking rapidly. He ignored them and stamped once more, using both feet this time, with all the strength he could muster.

There was a grating noise from below and the circular patch began to move. He had expected it to fall down, like a trap-door, but instead it rose, a tall column of rock sliding upwards into his

The Display Prison

enclosure. Part of the column was hollow and out of the cavity stepped a young girl.

She looked frightened, but shouted out boldly in a high-pitched voice: 'Sit! Sit! Sit! Lie down on your slab. Lie down, down. Lie down,' and she began to prod at him with a long stick.

Jason obeyed and the girl seemed to relax a little. She waved to the crowd and walked slowly round the slab like a lion-tamer.

'I'm not a wild beast, you know,' ventured Jason, sitting up as the girl came close to study his face.

'Down! Down!' she screamed, leaping back. 'Lie down,' and she pressed her stick against his throat, pushing him backwards.

'Have it your own way,' muttered Jason. 'I suppose you just want to show off.'

The girl went on stalking round the platform, pretending to ignore Jason, but glancing at him from time to time to make sure he was not moving. He took the opportunity to study her more closely. She was slightly smaller than he was and covered in short, dense fur of a pale brown colour. Out of the hair on top of her head grew two short curved horns. Otherwise, she appeared to be a normal girl, the first even remotely familiar shape he had seen since he entered the Inrock.

'Where am I?' he asked softly. 'Tell me where I am, please.'

'You are in the Display Prison,' she said, stopping to gaze down at him, 'and you will soon be examined, but I have to tame you first to prevent a scene when your turn comes.'

'I *am* tame,' said Jason. 'Try me out.'

'All right. Stand up. Now walk backwards in front of me. Now turn round. Again. Sit on the floor. Good. Lie flat. Now open your arms and legs. Close them. Open them. Close them. Open them. Good. Stand up. Turn to me. Touch my face with your hand. Now your other hand. Kneel. Both knees. Head forward. Press your face on the ground. Stop there.' And she walked slowly round him while the crowd hissed and rattled approvingly.

'Right, you can join the others now,' and she gestured him to the hole in the pillar.

As the column sank into the ground, Jason heaved a sigh of

relief. He had followed her orders exactly, hoping it would help in some way, and it had worked. True, he was not free yet, but at least he was no longer on display, watched incessantly by a sea of curious eyes.

Beneath the platform was a tunnel and, when the column had risen again and collected the horned girl, they set off together along its winding path.

'In there,' she ordered, pointing to an open door in the wall.

Leaving her standing in the tunnel, Jason passed through the opening and heard the door snap shut behind him, plunging him into sudden darkness. He groped his way forward until a flap dropped in front of him and he felt himself sliding down a chute into the bright light again.

This time he was in a vast dome, surrounded by curved, raised seats packed with even weirder creatures than before, of many different kinds. Inside the great space of the dome were four other figures and they rushed to greet him. Two of them took one leg each while the other two grabbed his arms. They all pulled in different directions and carried him to the centre of the space, where they lifted him on to a huge coloured ball and began to tug him this way and that, making the ball roll back and forth beneath him.

Suddenly, a light flashed and they all let go at the same moment, so that Jason, spread-eagled on the ball, began to roll over with it. It came to rest on top of him and he could hardly breathe. Twisting his head round he could see them scrambling about at the bottom of the chute, picking up small pellets and eating them hungrily.

'Help me,' he called out, but they ignored him. He felt dizzy. The weight of the ball was becoming unbearable.

The four gobbling figures relaxed, having eaten all the pellets. They sprawled contentedly on the floor. Two of them were blue, with four stumpy legs and trumpet-shaped heads. One of the others had two very long legs, with a black, crescent-moon-shaped body and two pop-eyes on the ends of thin, spindly tubes. The fourth one had a fat, round, warty body, deep red in colour,

The Display Prison

with big, sleepy eyes, bushy whiskers and short, pointed ears. His bird-like feet were splayed on the ground.

'I think he's dying,' said Red Warty, smacking his lips. 'Someone had better shift him, or we'll be in trouble again.'

'Can't we watch him die?' asked Black Moon, hopefully. 'I want to see if he rattles when he's dried out, like that stupid Twitching Punti we had in the other day.'

The two Blue Trumpets looked at one another, shrugged their backs, and wandered off.

Jason moaned slightly and Black Moon pranced over and sat down by his head.

'Are you konking out?' he asked excitedly. 'I love konking-outs. Or is it konkings-out? I never can remember.'

Jason tried hard to think of something frightening to say. 'Polizesti!' he hissed.

'Not in here, ducky, not a hope. Konk, go on, konk, I want a new rattle.'

Jason tried the only other name he had heard: 'The Sculptor will get you for this,' he wheezed, with what felt like his last breath.

The words worked like magic. Black Moon leapt to his feet and Red Warty rushed over. They collided heavily and fell against the ball, which began to move. The Blue Trumpets pelted towards him and started shoving against it. In a moment he was free.

Gasping for air, he heaved himself up and faced them angrily: 'You didn't know I was a spy for the Sculptor, did you? Now what have you to say?'

Red Warty's legs gave out and his fat body plopped to the floor. He began to hiss loudly, yellow steam coming out of his warts. His spherical body slowly shrank and his eyes closed.

'You've killed him!' shrilled Black Moon. 'You've konked him, he's a dead Warty. Marvellous, wonderful, the first shock-death I've ever seen. Pure shock. Instantaneous. Exquisite. You are quite, quite brilliant. I salute you.'

'You're disgusting,' said Jason. 'I didn't mean to kill him.'

'Never mind, never mind,' soothed the Blue Trumpets in

unison. 'It was a clear case of self-defence, we will support you, never fear. And how *is* the dear Sculptor these days? Haven't seen the Great One for . . . '

'Shut up!' shouted Jason, and their high, flute-like voices trailed off into a whisper. They looked at one another uneasily.

Jason was bending and stretching his body, trying to get the blood circulating again. He glared at the shuffling Trumpets:

'Try and help Red Warty. Try and blow him up again, or mend his puncture. Do *something*! Don't just stand around chattering as if nothing has happened.'

'Are you out of your spiny, shredded mind?' sneered Black Moon. 'Old Warty is better off than we are. We were doing you a favour just now. If I didn't dislike those dribbling Trumpets over there so much, I'd have konked them out long ago. It's the only way to avoid you-know-what.'

'What?' demanded Jason. 'What's this you-know-what nonsense?'

'The examinations,' hissed Black Moon. 'The examinations. Now do you understand, you shredded, shrivelling idiot?'

'Frankly, no,' insisted Jason. 'What's so terrible about the examinations? I am told I have one coming up at any moment.'

'Eeeeahh! Don't touch him, it might be catching,' screeched Black Moon, and they all withdrew to the far side of the dome.

Jason took a deep breath and walked over to the soggy shape of the dead Warty. At that instant the floor to his left rose and four small Polizesti rushed out and surrounded him. Then what looked like a double green apple on legs sauntered forward, looked down at Red Warty's body, nudged it with his purple foot, and boomed with laughter.

'Oh, this is going to be *fun*!' he bellowed. 'This-is-going-to-be-fun. My favourite grade of examination. The fiftieth. Splendid, splendid. Simply splendid. Take the stranger away and prepare him. I can hardly wait.'

Jason was taken beneath the floor to a long, low water-room where slender, pink, soft-tentacled creatures gently removed his tattered clothes and soaked his skin. He let himself dream that he

The Display Prison

was home again, lying in a steaming bath-tub after a hot day in the fields chasing hares with Satan.

The tentacles of the Soft-pinks stroked him and caressed him, soaping his body and smoothing his hair. Then they wrapped him in what appeared to be a huge roll of blue wool and carried him up some steps and into a scenting-and-oiling room. The air was misty with heavy perfumes. Jason was placed on a long bench and massaged with warm oils. The Soft-pinks used their smooth body-lobes for this, flickering them deftly over Jason's skin with such skill that he began to feel more and more relaxed and dreamy. He forgot all about his quest for the Golden Worms, and all about the ever-swelling Tonk and his terrible predicament.

'I've never felt like this before,' he murmured.

'Shhh!' whispered the Soft-pinks. 'Let your body go limp, blank. We will soothe you into condition.' They began to fan different scents, some cool, some deliciously warm, over different parts of Jason's body and he felt himself floating away into a tingling haze. His arms, his legs, his whole body went loose and limp and he sprawled there in the misty, scent-laden room, all his tensions gone, completely at peace. The Soft-pinks nodded slowly to one another and silently withdrew.

Jason dozed and dreamed. The dream was vague and confused – pale colours rippled and changed direction. Dimly outlined shapes swirled around him. Nothing came into focus. He drifted through a world of melting light and shade.

When he woke up he found himself in a new room, about the same size as the scenting-and-oiling room, but with an entirely different atmosphere. He was wrapped in a long, blue sheet and all around him there was frantic activity. Everything was busy, agitated and bustling. A spindly, blue-striped creature was fussing and arguing in a squeaky, high-pitched voice.

'No, no, no. *Not* the yellow. I told you yellow was out. How many times do I have to . . . Ah! Hallo, darling.' He squinted at Jason. 'You must have been exhausted. How you can have slept through all this noise, I simply can't imagine. You must have the most wonderful body-control. I wish *I* had it, but look at me, a quivering, jibbering wreck. It's all *their* fault, stupid, clumsy, incompetent poofilators.'

He paused for breath and peered closely at Jason's face. 'Now. *What* are we going to do with you? What *are* we going to do with you? What are we going to *do* with you? What are we going to do with *you*?'

'I'm all right, thank you,' said Jason, 'but I am rather thirsty.'

'Later, later,' intoned Blue-Stripe. 'First things first, I always say. Now, the hair, what about the hair? Can't let you go out looking like that, can we? I've got it — fabulous — brilliant. I don't know how I do it. Where *do* my creations come from? It's like some kind of magic. I reach up with my mind, pluck them down and there they are, ready for immediate sale. Now listen, darling, you are going to be a sensation. A sensation. They'll talk about you for weeks. Well, days, anyway. Well, perhaps for only a few minutes, but it's worth it, it's worth it. You never know who'll be there, do you, or where things may lead. You've always got to be ready, I always say, don't you always say, darling?'

'I . . .'

'Now. I'll tell you what I'm going to do for you. Black and white — it's just come to me this instant, this very instant. Attention, everyone. I am going to transform this darling creature. *Black* and *white*. Black and white. Half and half. Short tunic, black on the left, white on the right. Hair long — keep it long — no crafty snipping behind my back now — black on the right, white on the left. Parting dead centre, dead, mind you, *dead* centre. Right shoe — very plain — jet black. Left shoe — pure white. Got it, everyone? Got it? All right — off you go then. Quick as you like. Quick as *I* like. Hmm, hmm, hmmm,' and he started humming and whistling and fidgeting with a tray of strange instruments.

For the next hour they fussed and fiddled, until a shrill bell sounded and a door opened. A small, orange tube-creature, with one tired eye, poked its body round the door and called:

'Examinations, examinations. Five minutes, please,' and was gone.

The Display Prison

'Oh dear me, how times fly. Now, up you get. Look in the mirror and tell me what you think. There!'

Jason gasped. He hardly recognized himself. One side of his hair had been bleached white and the other half dyed jet black. His short tunic reversed the pattern. His face was a deep brown with several black and white spots dotted about on it. His lips were white and his eyebrows black.

'I don't know *what* to say!' he exclaimed.

'Speechless. I knew you'd be speechless. They all are. Now off you go. Enjoy yourself. You'll have a wonderful time. But watch out for old Chinny. He's a bit of a lad, or so they tell me. Goodbye, darling, goodbye, goodbye,' and he ushered Jason through the door.

Outside, in a brilliantly lit corridor, he was escorted by two silver and green Polizesti, with their armoured spikes shimmering in gold. At the end of the passage they came to a great archway draped with a heavy, mauve curtain.

'Thumbs,' hissed one of the Polizesti. 'Thumbs.'

'What?' asked Jason, looking at his thumbs. 'What about my thumbs?'

'Cross them,' hissed the guard. 'Quickly, before the curtain rises.' Jason did as he was told and waited. Beyond the curtain he could hear a murmuring sound, as though a large crowd was waiting. As if on a signal, the murmuring died away and a voice he recognized as belonging to the double green-apple creature boomed out:

'My Lord Ten-chin, Grannits, Gentleladies and Men. May I present . . . The Young Spy.'

CHAPTER FOUR
The Ten-chin Banquet

The mauve curtain rose with a swish and Jason stepped forward into an enormous banqueting hall. Green-apple was standing beside a heavy red-and-black throne on which was sitting a bulky figure. All heads turned towards Jason as he was led along, past the tables groaning with a rich variety of strange foods and bottles.

'No ceremony, no ceremony. Can't stand ceremony,' said the bulky figure on the throne. 'Come and sit on my left, my dear chap, no fussing now. Eat, everyone, eat.'

At this the great crowd of gaily dressed creatures, all shapes and sizes, stamped their feet rhythmically on the floor, making the whole place shake.

'Long live Lord Ten-chin!' shouted a voice from the back of the hall.

'Oh, you are too kind. Really. Too kind,' murmured Ten-chin. 'Now eat, I say, eat.' And they all fell on the food, slurping and gobbling and spitting out the pips.

'Three new guests for you to taste, My Lord,' boomed Green-apple.

'Ah yes, thank you, thank you,' sighed Ten-chin as the first new

The Ten-chin Banquet

guest was hustled forward, grovelling and whining.

The Great Lord sniffed thoughtfully at the outstretched hand and then licked it with his long, rough tongue.

'Not bad, not bad,' he murmured. 'A good year for Scrufflepoms. Admit him to the benches. Next!' The process was repeated, but Ten-chin could hardly conceal his lack of interest. He yawned wearily.

'I believe this is your first examination?' he said, clearing his throat and leaning his huge bulk in Jason's direction.

'Yes, it is, but I'm not quite sure what I . . . '

'Please, please, don't give it a moment's thought,' interrupted His Lordship. 'In your case, my dear chap, it's a mere formality. As soon as we learned that you were a friend of the Sculptor, we, er, well, we adjusted our sights accordingly, you might say. How is the dear Sculptor, by the way?'

'Very well,' said Jason, realizing he had to keep up the act. 'But rather angry about something lately.'

'Really? Really?' His Lordship shot a quick glance at Green-apple, who was sitting on his other side. 'What seems to be the cause of the Great One's wrath?' he asked in a casual tone, popping rather too many small, orange cubes into his mouth at once and munching them thoughtfully. 'Or perhaps you are not at liberty to . . . ' He waited. 'To . . . ' He gestured expansively. 'To pass on this information at the present time?'

'It has to do with the Golden Worms,' said Jason in a quiet, firm voice, hoping for a clue.

'Aaaah,' said Lord Ten-chin with great relief. 'I'm not surprised. Very nasty situation. Very delicate. Yes.'

'What do you mean by "nasty"?' asked Jason. 'In what way "nasty"?'

'Well, all these rumours, you know. Stories that the GWs don't really exist at all — that they are just an invention of the Great One's to scotch any attempt to break through up there' — he raised his eyes briefly to the ceiling — 'without permission. Of course, it's all a bit outside my line, but I'm sorry to hear the Great One's having trouble with it. I expect it will all blow over, these things usually do after a while.'

'Yes, I suppose so,' said Jason thoughtfully, trying hard to think of some way of extracting some more worm-news.

But His Lordship was eating hard, grinding and snuffling and spilling grease all down his ten great hanging chins. They reached right down to his lap, roll after roll of them, wobbling gently as he chewed and swallowed. His heavy head was completely naked, not a hair to be seen anywhere, except on the tips of his small, pointed ears. His purple robe hid his wide body from view, immersing it in folds of rich cloth, only the ends of his hairy paws protruding. Each finger had a large, round pad at the tip and with these he picked up morsels of food. Each morsel he touched stuck to his finger-pads as if by suction and he then jammed his food-laden paws into his mouth and sucked noisily.

'Delicious spread, don't you think?' He smiled briefly in Jason's direction. 'Of course, I don't much care for this sort of thing myself. Too much ceremony, too much ritual. But in my position I have to go through the motions.' He snapped his fingers at Green-apple who leapt to his feet and boomed:

'Chin-wipers!'

Two shrivelled, grey forms emerged from the side of the hall. They had lumpy, barrel-shaped bodies with long arms and very hairy hands. They leant around the throne, one on each side, and started wiping the backs of their hands carefully back and forth across His Lordship's greasy chins. One began at the top, the other at the bottom, taking a chin at a time until they met in the middle. Then, with their hairy hands dripping grease, they withdrew screeching softly and bowing. As they reached the archway through which Jason had entered, they were spiked by two Polizesti and stuffed into a large bin.

'What happens to the Chin-wipers now?' asked Jason. 'They haven't killed them, have they?'

'Of course,' yawned His Lordship. 'We're very up to date here. They are completely at my disposal. We used to use the old-fashioned washable ones, but nowadays we've turned over completely to the disposable variety. Much safer, more hygienic.

The Ten-chin Banquet

With the other sort, well, you never knew who they'd been wiping, did you?'

Jason wanted to complain to his gross host about the cruel treatment of the harmless Chin-wipers, but he was afraid this might seem out of character. He was, after all, supposed to be a spy for the Sculptor and he had to avoid arousing even the slightest suspicion. In any case, it was too late to help the unfortunate creatures now.

The food was disappearing rapidly from the tables.

'Those filter-feeders over there,' observed Lord Ten-chin to Green-apple. 'They really are too messy at table. Remind me to do something about it next time they come up for election. Look into their backbones, find something, a scandal, a disease, anything. You know what I mean.'

Green-apple nodded the two lobes of his head-body knowingly, took out a pencil and scribbled something hurriedly on one of his nose-fins. He had a very finny nose.

Ten-chin suddenly heaved himself to his feet. He raised his glass. Silence fell on the crowd.

'To the Sculptor, the memory of Grannits past, and to the unity of the Inrock. Death to all climbers.' He emptied his glass and sank back. The crowd rose and solemnly repeated the toast. Jason followed suit.

'Gentleladies and Men,' boomed Green-apple. 'You may laugh,' and the crowd began to titter and guffaw amongst themselves.

'Pathetic, aren't they,' observed Ten-chin. 'Pathetic. I suppose it's because of my fatuous habit of granting favours, I should never have started it.'

'But that should please them, surely, and make them less of a trouble for you?' said Jason.

'You *are* a sweet, innocent young thing, aren't you,' murmured Ten-chin, stroking him gently under his ear. 'You don't understand favours at all, do you? Obviously never been bothered with them. The problem is, you see, that you can't make them *all* happy with favours. A favour is not so much something you give to one, as something you don't give to the others. Once you've grasped that, you've got the basic essentials. It doesn't matter a Grannit's Cuss what the favours are, it's the horror of not having them that's the spur.'

He fumbled in the folds of his robe and pulled out some blunt red pins.

'See these? They're my latest favours. Nothing but stupid little studs, but they'll do anything to get them. Then they have them hammered into their flesh — terribly painful process, horrible, ugh! — and parade them around as though it's made them better in some way,' and he began to chortle to himself, his ten fat chins wobbling and flopping about like water-filled balloons. 'It really is pathetic, and do you know, they can't see through it. Utterly fooled by it, they are, completely taken in. And here I sit with the poor scrabblers hanging on my every wobble. It's ridiculous. And, of course, it does waste a great deal of my time, when there's so much I ought to be getting on with.'

'What sort of things?' asked Jason.

'My Grannit research,' explained the Fat Lord, sounding interested for the first time. 'Are you interested in research, by any chance?'

'Very.'

'Very?'

'Very interested.'

'Splendid chap. Splendid. Isn't he splendid, Green-apple? What, what?'

'Splendid, as you say, sir.'

'Green-apple, change places with him. I'm bored by his black side. I feel like talking to a blond for a change. Don't get enough of them, these days, and they are so much brighter, usually.'

Jason and Green-apple changed places.

'Now, if you would really like to hear about my research, I'll give you a brief summary of things as they stand at the moment.'

'Thank you,' said Jason. 'I am always interested in new ideas.'

'Ah, yes, well, er, of course, so am I, but I was going to tell you about my research.'

The Ten-chin Banquet

'Surely that involves new ideas, doesn't it?'

'No, no, my dear chap, you are muddling it up with search. You search for new ideas, but you re-search old ones. You take other people's ideas and re-work them. Nothing original, really, just shuffling the pack — re-sorting — that's what research is.'

'I see. I must have got it wrong.'

'Yes, you've obviously been listening to people who don't actually do it themselves. They have some funny attitudes sometimes. But let me tell you about the Grannits. We felt it was about time we analysed them to see how they do it.'

'Do what?' asked Jason. 'I'm sorry, but I don't understand.'

Ten-chin looked suspicious.

'Exactly how can it be that an Inrock citizen, especially a personal friend of the Sculptor's, has failed to learn the basic facts of Grannit life?' he demanded.

Sensing danger, Jason replied quickly: 'Ah, yes, I forgot to tell you I had a bad fall recently and it has robbed me of certain parts of my memory.'

'Hmmm. I'm sorry to hear that. Most unusual. Well, as even a sub-gumf knows, the Grannits are vitally important to our survival. While living, they provide us with our light — that sea of white above our heads is a mass of floating Grannits, thousands of them, all glowing down on us. Then, whenever there is a Break-in Alert, the Grannit alarm is given and millions of them swarm off to deal with it. It goes rather dim locally for a while, but they soon breed back to maximum numbers again and restore the light supply.'

'What sort of break-ins give you the most trouble?' asked Jason, trying tactfully to find out what a break-in was.

'Ah, now that is an interesting and, if I may say so, an intelligent question. I have recently carried out a survey — that is, my technicians have — I wear white overalls occasionally to give the right impression, but I leave all the details to them. I simply save them the trouble of presenting the results of what they find out. Where was I? Oh yes, well, my recent survey shows that 80 per cent of all break-ins today are caused by human interference from upstairs. Rock-blasting, bomb-dropping, drilling, and that sort of thing. Only 20 per cent are the result of natural upheaval — cliff erosion, subsidence, earthquakes and so forth. The human break-ins are less predictable, we find, and the speed of the Grannits is severely taxed sometimes. If we are not careful, we'll have a severe breach in our defences one day and once all those monsters up there have some solid evidence of our existence, well, I'm afraid it may be the beginning of the end for the Inrock way of life. That is why my research is so important. You see, it is vital that we should find ways of increasing the speed of Grannits to keep up with the scale of the more explosive human break-ins. That is why I am having so many Grannits caught and cut up, to study the way they move. They're ugly little creatures, so no one minds a bit about them being treated in this way,' he added confidentially.

Jason was rather upset by this news, but was determined to find out as much as he could.

'How exactly do they stop the break-ins?' he enquired.

'You really *have* had a nasty fall, haven't you,' said Ten-chin in a puzzled tone. 'Well, as everyone knows, the pressure change caused by a break-in affects the Grannits' sensitive pressure cells — those little white spots on their wings — and the splendid creatures go rushing off to the source of the trouble. Millions of them go buzzing along like a stream of light and smash headlong into the break. Wave after wave of them crash in on top of one another with incredible force, fossilizing themselves instantly and sealing it off. Their bodies, as you know, or rather you don't know, are made up largely of hard, brittle stuff — like living shells they are — with one pair of wings at the front end, another at the rear, and a row of tiny eyes all down the middle. Their bellies glow white, and under normal conditions they simply hover high up overhead, like a ceiling of light, making their food from the particles of goo that rise up from us here below. They also absorb the bad air and give off clean air. Remarkable little creatures they are, really, and the very devil of a job to catch. We've had a lot of difficulty with that. You see, if one gets wounded, the others immediately eat it — they swarm round it and suck it dry — so we hardly ever get one grounded. I am not at liberty to disclose the precise method we do use to trap them — it's still top secret. In fact, I think I've really said rather too much already, but I get carried away. It's my pet topic. I think, though, if you'll forgive me, it is time to start the examinations.'

'One last question,' ventured Jason. 'What happens if, when they are crashing into the break, they hit it so hard that they go right through and come out the other side, out into the . . . the upstairs?'

'Horrible, horrible,' burbled Ten-chin. 'Awful mess. They overheat and melt and great masses of them spew out all over the Outrock. When this happens it has to be recorded with the Sculptor as a volcanic disaster area, and there's hell to pay afterwards. But happily volcanoes are pretty rare these days. Now we really must get on with these examinations.' He signalled to Green-apple who boomed for silence.

'Bring in the first sub-gumf,' ordered His Lordship. Turning to Jason, he murmured privately: 'Just to remind you, there are four classes — sub-gumfs, gumfs, super-gumfs and great gumfs. Nearly all the guests here are at the ordinary gumf level. Green-apple and I and one or two others have been elected super-gumfs. Great-gumfs are, of course, extremely rare and in the whole of the Inrock I doubt if there are more than five or six of them. If sub-gumfs are successful in their examination, they become ordinary gumfs, as you may see in a moment, although I have my doubts about the ones we are being offered today.'

The curtain rose and through the archway came the two Blue Trumpets that Jason had encountered so painfully at the Display Prison. As they wended their way through the tables they were pinched and slapped by the guests. They halted in front of Lord Ten-chin, who nodded to Green-apple.

'Answer the following three questions,' boomed Green-apple. 'One. Why do the Grannits light our way?'

'My favourite question,' confided Ten-chin.

'Answer!' boomed Green-apple.

'Because the Sculptor willed it so,' chanted the Blue Trumpets in unison.

'Correct,' replied Green-apple, and the guests stamped their feet. 'Two. Why do we obey the Polizesti?'

'Because the Sculptor willed it so,' repeated the Blue Trumpets.

'Correct.' There was more foot-stamping, until Green-apple held up his hand. 'Three. Why are you standing there quivering while we are sitting in comfort?'

'This will fox them,' murmured Ten-chin, with a slow wink in Jason's direction.

'Because the Sculptor willed it so,' trilled the Blue Trumpets nervously.

'In-corr-ect,' boomed Green-apple heavily. A long hiss rose from the guests. The Trumpets shook violently.

'Your verdict, My Lord?' enquired Green-apple smugly. Ten-chin turned to him and they pressed their heads close together. It sounded to Jason as though they were saying 'Wuffle wuffle wuffle' to one another, over and over again, but he thought he must be mistaken. Then Ten-chin nodded grimly to Green-apple and swung across to Jason, thrusting his great head uncomfortably close.

'Wuffle wuffle wuffle,' he intoned.

'What?'

'Wuffle wuffle wuffle,' he repeated and then, under his breath: 'Just say the same thing. It makes no sense, but it saves the trouble of discussing the case. I am supposed to take advice, you see – it's in the old rules. Of course I never bother – there's no point – but I like to go through the motions. Puts a good face on it for the gumfs,' and he gave another of his slow-motion, overblown winks. 'Wuffle wuffle wuffle,' he said, out loud.

'Wuffle wuffle,' replied Jason, feeling rather self-conscious.

'Good, good,' said Ten-chin. 'So we are all agreed then?' Green-apple nodded and gazed into the distance. Ten-chin laboriously stood up. 'Blue Trumpets, you have failed. This is your seventh examination and I therefore have no choice.' He fingered his fifth chin, fondling and caressing the bulbous roll of fat flesh. 'I sentence you to permanent exhibition in the Display Prison.'

To Jason's surprise, the Blue Trumpets perked up and trotted briskly from the banquet hall.

There was a short pause and then Black Moon was brought in. He failed miserably and Ten-chin became more and more angry. His chins began to change colour, rippling with reds, blues and yellows. Leaping to his feet, he stormed at the cowering figure:

'You crackling, sloppy-eyed, boggle-kneed climber! You grout, you pomerated fig-tongue, you are unfit for habitation, a disgrace to the ancient and honoured order of gumfs. I sentence you to be fossilized at the next Grannit alarm.'

The guests stamped and hissed. Black Moon shrieked and started rushing round in small circles. He was quickly surrounded and spiked by Polizesti and his rigid body was then carried slowly from the hall.

'Thank goodness that's over,' sighed Ten-chin, relaxing. 'Now, my dear chap, it's your turn. A mere formality in your case, of course. Would you mind standing over there? Thank you.'

Jason moved around the table and stood in front of the throne. The hall was quieter than it had ever been before.

'First question,' boomed Green-apple in a bored voice. He was obviously disappointed not to have a more exciting examination. He had been sure that his next victim would get the full Fiftieth Grade treatment for causing Red Warty's death, but because this wretched Jason knew the Sculptor personally he was to be treated gently. 'Typical!' he muttered to himself, while he leafed through the questions. 'Would never have happened in *my* young day – rules were rules then – oh, well, never mind, let's get it over and done with,' and his formal boom rang out:

'One. Have you enjoyed your meal?'

'Yes. Every second of it.'

'Correct. Two. Do you care about the fate of the Blue Trumpets?'

'No. That's their problem.'

'Correct. Three. Do you care about the forthcoming forcible

fossilization of Black Moon?'

'No. That's his problem.'

'Correct.'

'Congratulations, my dear chap,' beamed Lord Ten-chin. 'Beautifully done, if I may say so. I am sure the Sculptor would have been proud of you. Come and sit here again. You are a fully-fledged gumf now.'

Jason took his seat and the Fat Lord leaned over confidentially:

'I must say,' he whispered from behind his cupped paw, 'you lie magnificently. Such verve, such assurance. Splendid, splendid.'

'How did you know I was lying?' asked Jason, rather taken aback.

'Well, it's obvious, my dear chap. I mean, you wouldn't have passed the exam otherwise, would you? That's what it's all about, as I am sure you know perfectly well. Still, your show of innocence is charming, quite charming, and I am grateful for it. So many simply don't bother nowadays. Takes all the fun out of it. Now, where's that young female with the horns? Ah, there she is. Get her over here, will you. What's her name, Green-apple?'

'Ludo, My Lord.'

'Ah, yes, Ludo. Ludo, come over here and take the Young Spy off to his new quarters. Goodbye, my dear chap, great pleasure examining you. Hope we meet again soon. My regards to the Sculptor. Goodbye, goodbye.'

Jason was led from the hall, accompanied by the fur-covered girl-with-horns that he had first encountered in the Display Prison. She was silent and stared rather sullenly at the ground as she walked along in front of him.

'I suppose you are sulking because you can't tame me with your stick any more?' he asked dryly.

'No, sir. I was just wondering what will happen to me when you report me to the Sculptor,' she mumbled.

'Forget it. Let's start off fresh, as from now,' smiled Jason, having had time to realize that he badly needed a friend and ally. 'You can call me Jason and I shall call you Ludo. That is your name, isn't it?'

'Yes, thank you.' She brightened up considerably. 'Er . . . follow me, we go this way.'

They turned into a side-tunnel and then out into a broad open space.

CHAPTER FIVE
The Niar-storm

It was a wonderful sensation to be free again and Jason found it difficult to conceal his immense relief. As Ludo led him away from the complicated buildings and out into the surrounding countryside, he took several deep breaths, filling his lungs to bursting and then sighing noisily as he let each breath escape. The furry, horned girl, walking bolt upright and slightly ahead of him, made no comment. After they had walked some distance she announced in a flat, even voice:

'My village is about eight miles away. I have been assigned to you until the Sculptor's next visit. Perhaps, then, if I have pleased you, you will put in a good word for me?'

When that day comes, thought Jason, I am going to be in real trouble. Until then I must learn all I can and try to find out something about the Golden Worms.

The girl looked at him enquiringly and he realized she was waiting for an answer.

'Yes, of course. By the way, I have never travelled with the Sculptor in these parts. What is the routine here? When do you next expect a visit?' He tried to sound off-hand, as if the question had little importance to him.

The Niar-storm

'That we never know. There is never any warning. It may happen any day. We all fly our body-flags from the tops of our cells as a sign that we are waiting. But the visits are becoming rare. We do not know why. It is very worrying.'

'What is a body-flag? We have flags where I come from, but they show designs, not bodies.'

'Body-flags show designs, too, but the design is always related to the special features of our bodies. Mine is a pair of short, curved horns, for example. Yours, when you get one, will show your black and white hair. When the Sculptor works on us and alters us in some way, we get a new body-flag showing the latest improvements that have been made, and there is a great celebration in the village to mark the occasion. Everyone dances around the cell where the new flag flies, and we drink and wash one another and touch feet all night.'

'Sounds exciting, but where I come from a cell is a place in a prison.'

'Not here, not here. For us it is the place where we sleep and have our taste-eggs. It is our home, our safe place. No strangers are allowed in. We only meet strangers outside our cell walls.'

'But I am a stranger,' said Jason.

'No, no. You have passed the examination. There will have been an announcement about you already. You are no longer a stranger. You will share my cell. Now, we must ride. It is too far to walk, or we shall not arrive before the Grannits are screened for the night. Come on, there's a Flummel over there. He will take us to the village.'

A tall creature with six humps, a triangular head and four lanky legs sauntered up and crouched on the ground in front of them. Ludo helped Jason to climb up between the second and third hump and then settled herself between the third and fourth. The Flummel grunted, heaved itself to its feet and set off at a steady trot.

As they thumped along, Jason was able to study the strange landscape. The pink sand over which they were passing was studded with small clusters of glinting colours – yellows, pale greens and deep blues. They twinkled and sparkled like jewels. Here and there he saw a tall white spike sticking up out of the ground, with tiny purple spheres grouped near the tip. Glistening, lizard-like creatures scuttled out of the Flummel's way as they approached and Jason noticed that near some dark zig-zag cracks there were long, thin, hovering objects, flashing brilliant emerald and gold in the intense light of the Grannits. They buzzed and dashed wildly about as the Flummel skirted round the cracks and then they settled back again to their quiet hovering as the huge six-humped beast moved ponderously on.

From the distance a faint rumbling sound was heard.

'Now we are in for it!' called Ludo. 'There's a niar-storm ahead. I am afraid we shall have to go straight through it. There won't be time to go round.' The rumbling grew louder. 'Hold tight to your hump, here we go!' She kicked wildly at the Flummel's flanks.

Its mouth twitching and its long, curved eyelashes flickering, the lanky creature lowered its neck and took off at a gangling, lop-sided gallop. Jason clung desperately to the quivering hump in front of him and waited for the storm to break.

'Listen to that rednuth!' shouted Ludo above the rumbling. 'It'll be pouring up any minute.'

'Up?' yelled Jason. 'What do you mean, up?' But Ludo's answer was drowned as the rumble became a roar and the storm burst upon them.

Just before the Flummel plunged bravely into it, spurred on by Ludo's heels, Jason managed to see what the girl had meant. The storm water, unlike the rain Jason was used to at home, was shooting upwards from the sand, instead of down from the sky. The desert, which, until a few moments ago, had been so dry and parched, was suddenly heaving and spurting with countless jets of water. They sprang out of the earth and climbed many feet into the air before cascading down again. The Flummel was heading straight into what was virtually a sea of fountains, a million jets strong, as far as the eye could see.

With a crash they were into it and Jason soon found he could hardly breathe for the pressure of water. Hugging the now

The Niar-storm

slippery hump tightly with one arm, he cupped his free hand over his nose and mouth to stop the water splashing in. He did not dare to look round to see how Ludo was faring, but he could see the poor Flummel's head shaking and spluttering in front of him.

Somehow the ungainly beast managed to slither its way through the tallest part of the storm until the jets of niar-water were only about six feet high. Even now, as they jogged along, their three heads — the Flummel's, Jason's and Ludo's — and the creature's six humps were all that could be seen, sticking up above the sea of niar-jets. It was almost as if they were bumping along on the surface of a shallow lake, the Flummel looking for all the world like a great sea-serpent.

'We're through the worst of it,' yelled Ludo. 'No, we're not! I forgot. Hang on, hang on!' Her voice rose to a scream as the Flummel began bucking and rearing and giggling inanely, in a manner quite unsuited to its ponderous bulk.

'Heeh, heeh, ooo, ahh, heeh, heeh, heeh!' shrieked the Flummel, cavorting more and more wildly, kicking out its legs and trying to arch its back.

'What's happening?' called Jason, as he was flung this way and that between the waggling humps.

'The jets have sunk to belly-level,' called back Ludo, 'and Flummels are ticklish — they can't stand it. I forgot to strap on its belly-cover before we started out. I'm sorry. Hold on!'

But it was too late. The hysterical Flummel skidded over and crashed to the ground, still giggling helplessly. Jason and Ludo were thrown on to the wet sand, the powerful jets shooting up all around them. Ludo rushed over to the panting, struggling beast and grabbed a heavy, rolled sheet from between its fifth and sixth humps, dragged it open and, with Jason's help, managed to fasten it around the creature's soaking belly. Slowly, it began to quieten down.

With the water streaming up over their bodies, gulping and coughing, and hardly able to breathe, they started pushing and shoving the Flummel to its feet. It stood shakily for a moment, twitching its skin, and then obediently crouched down so that they could remount.

Taking deep breaths of air, they set off once more, heading away from the worst of the storm and towards the distant village. Their progress was less eventful now, with the Flummel its old, docile self again. Ludo began to laugh.

'What is it?' called Jason.

'The Decorator would be furious,' she shouted back. 'Your colours have run. His creation has been ruined. You're no longer black and white. The storm has washed your pattern clean away.'

Jason looked down at his tunic. It was plain white now and so were both his shoes. He felt his face.

'Yes, that too,' she called. 'It's back to its old colour, *and* your hair.'

'It didn't last long, did it,' laughed Jason, who was glad to be rid of the crazy black and white design.

'It wasn't meant to. If the Decorator's fashions lasted, he'd be out of business in no time. But I think this would be a little too short-lived, even for him. He'll have to dream up a new body-flag for you now.'

'Thank goodness for that,' yelled Jason and, feeling strangely happy, he gave the Flummel a playful kick with his feet that sent it careering off at a lively canter, spitting in all directions.

'Does it ever take aim, or does it spit anywhere?' he called back to Ludo.

'It's only warming up at the moment. Wait until we reach the tail of the storm and then you'll see if it can aim or not.'

The jets of rising water were thinning out now and were no more than four or five feet high. Further ahead Jason could pick out small red blobs on the tops of some of the stronger jets. He pointed them out to Ludo.

'Yes, here they come – we call them Floating Moters. They are nasty little pests – tiny hairy bags of blood that fling themselves at you, burst all over you, and then drip themselves to the ground, taking bits of skin and flesh with them, dissolving it as they go. Once they're down, they roll over to a new jet and up they go to the top to wait for their next victim. Luckily they can't fling

The Niar-storm

themselves very far and, as you'll find out, Flummels are crack-shots with sand-pellets.'

'How do they fire them?'

'They swallow a lot of sand when they're resting, then shoot it up their long throats in small pellets, on to the back of the tongue. The tongue is rolled up into a tube and with a single puff they can shoot a sand-pellet as far as twenty feet. The range of the Moters' fling is only about eight feet, so we're not in much danger. Watch!'

Sand-pellets began to fly at bewildering speed as the Flummel charged the Moter patch, head down and tail high. Shiny red spheres, with long, straggling hairs hanging down all round them, were leaping and curving through the air, each one trying its hardest to reach the flanks of the galloping, spitting beast.

Here and there, there were small explosions as the sand-pellets found their mark and burst the bloated pest-bags, splattering them down their columns of water. One large one that the Flummel had somehow missed made a gigantic effort and sailed a record eight-and-a-half feet through the shot-torn air to land on the great beast's heaving rump.

'Walla-walla-walla-walla!' bellowed the wounded Flummel, leaping into the air like a kangaroo with a porcupine in its pouch. Sand-pellets spewed from its mouth as fast as machine-gun bullets, its long neck twisting this way and that and its baleful eyes blazing with panic and pain.

'Take cover!' yelled Ludo from behind number three hump, as the demented Flummel's head craned round and began firing at its own rump.

'Walla-walla-walla!' screamed the Flummel as, in its terror, it hit its number one hump with three large pellets.

Jason ducked and prayed that the humps were pellet-proof. Then with a lurch the nightmare was over and they were through the Moter patch and out of the storm zone, back on to dry, warm, welcoming, desert sand. The Flummel sank to its knees, panting and moaning, and its shaken passengers dismounted. They walked unsteadily around the poor beast, patting and soothing it, and laughing nervously at their escape.

'Wow!' said Ludo finally. 'That was a bad one. The worst I've ever known. Are you all right?'

'Yes, I seem to be in one piece, but what about him?'

'Oh, he'll patch up in no time. It's more shock than anything. He'll heal over in a few days – be as good as new. Flummels are like that, tough old brutes. But we'd better give him a few minutes to calm down.'

The Flummel was angrily reloading, gulping down mouthfuls of sand, scowling over his humps every so often in the direction of the Moter patch, as if contemplating a return bout. Ludo and Jason sprawled on the hot sand to dry out.

'Where does all that water come from, in the middle of a desert?' asked Jason, idly picking up a few coloured crystals that were lying nearby and popping them into the leather pouch at the side of his belt.

'It used to be much damper in the old days and there was a bog here, called the Silver Swamp. It used to be a favourite hunting ground for some of the villagers. Then the whole area began to dry out and there was a powerful sand-storm. It blew millions of tons of this sand across the top of the swamp and submerged it, but the pressure down there is terrific and every so often the water bursts through and we get one of these niar-storms pouring up. Unfortunately, some of the swamp-pests get forced up as well and one kind has managed to turn the situation to its advantage. I don't need to tell you which kind that is. Come on, I think the Flummel's rested now.'

They remounted and rode quietly on. Before long, Jason spotted a blur of orange in the distance.

'That is my village,' said Ludo proudly. 'We shall be there very soon.'

The land was bone-dry again and open, with a feeling of great space. The surface was broken now with only an occasional cluster of the brilliantly coloured crystals, winking and sparkling on the bright pink sand.

'Do you ever collect any of these jewels, these crystals, and take them back to your cells?' Jason enquired.

The Niar-storm

'No. Never. They are said to bring bad luck,' replied Ludo casually, not having seen Jason pocket a few of them when they were resting after the storm.

'But do you believe that?'

'I'm not sure. But why risk it? We can see them out here whenever we wish.'

'You don't want to own them, then?'

'No, of course not. You can own *people*, but you can't own *things*.'

'I don't understand.'

'Well,' said Ludo, frowning slightly, 'you can't own something unless it knows it is owned. Objects can't know anything, so they can't be owned. People can, so they can.'

Jason gave up and decided to keep the crystals anyway. The landscape was far too beautiful to argue in and they rode on in silence. At one point, far away to the left, he thought he saw the distant figure of a running dog, but by the time he had drawn Ludo's attention to it, it had vanished. Perhaps he had imagined it.

Ahead of them, the village was clearer now. He could make out the small circular houses, like smooth windowless turrets. As they approached the outskirts, the pink sand became whiter and then a very pale blue. The Flummel skidded slightly and Jason realized that the blue surface was made up of square tiles, so carefully fitted together that the lines where they joined could hardly be seen. At first, the tiles were washed with white sand, but as they moved into the middle of the village the sand thinned out and vanished, leaving only the perfectly flat, blue floor.

'That is my cell, over there,' said Ludo, pointing to a bright orange turret near an open square. 'That brown and white flag with horns on – that's my personal body-flag.'

Jason noticed that every one of the turrets was flying a solitary flag, each with a different design on it.

'Judging by the single flag on each turret – or cell, I should say – you must all live alone?'

'In one sense, yes, because we have no families. Being rejects, we are not repeated, but the whole village is like one large family.

It's not too bad, really, when you get used to it. Your cell won't be ready for some weeks yet. In the meantime you will share with me.'

'Oh. I see,' said Jason quietly. It was beginning to dawn on him that he was about to become the house-mate of this strange, furry, horned girl, and he was not yet sure whether the idea appealed to him. 'There will be no one else in your cell – just the two of us?' he asked, as she got off the Flummel, which had crouched down in the centre of the square.

'Just the two of us,' replied Ludo reassuringly. 'No complications, thank goodness,' and she led the way across the square to the door of her turret.

The circular wall was extremely thick and full of passages. They led to small doors or curtained archways, but Ludo offered no explanations. The two of them were climbing steadily up a curved slope. Ludo seemed relieved to be home and her body lost some of its tenseness. She took Jason past a red screen and on to an open walkway that ran like a wide parapet around the top of the turret.

'What do you think of it?' she asked confidently.

'Fantastic,' said Jason. 'What a view – all these flags and the tops of the turrets and the desert out there in the distance. And what are those two big towers over there – the ones with a whole ring of flags?'

'The one on the left belongs to the village Cook and the other one houses the local Polizesti. It's the same in all the villages near here.'

'Why is the Cook considered so important?' asked Jason.

'Because he controls the taste-eggs for the entire village. It's a highly skilled task. The whole population depends on him. You won't be hungry after the banquet, but later, when we have slept, I will show you my taste-egg. It's a new model, very sensitive, you'll enjoy it.'

'Thank you, I'd like that,' said Jason, smiling, but not really having the faintest idea what she was talking about.

A bell began to ring at the top of the tall Polizesti tower and

The Niar-storm

Ludo whistled.

'It's much later than I thought. We only just made it. Five minutes to Grannit-screening. Come on, jump!'

'Jump?'

'Yes, down there, in the centre of the cell. That's our dip — our sleep-dip.'

'But it's twenty feet down. I'll break a leg, if not a neck.'

'Nonsense, the whole floor is five-padded. Wherever you lie, you sink in. It's like floating on a flossle. Watch me, I'll go first,' and she leapt wildly from the parapet, waving her arms and legs about in mock-panic.

She landed without a sound and lay there laughing up at him. He counted to two and jumped. Ludo gave a yelp and scrambled to one side in the nick of time as he landed with a sigh in the very centre of the circular sleep-dip. Bouncing around happily for a few minutes, as if trying out a new mattress, he finally flipped out flat on his back, with his arms and legs flung wide, gazing up at the top of the wall and the sky of blazing Grannits beyond. Ludo propped herself up on a furry elbow and stared at him, smiling.

'The Sculptor has done a good job on you,' she said. 'You are very well made. I am surprised you were rejected.'

Jason closed his eyes. It was all so confusing.

'I wasn't rejected,' he murmured. 'I passed the examination. You were there. You saw.'

'No, no. You don't seem to understand anything. Of course you passed the examination. That has nothing to do with being rejected. We are *all* rejects here. All of us. Every single villager. We wouldn't be here if we weren't. We'd be up there — upstairs — living on the Outrock. You follow? The examinations simply decide what class of reject we each belong to. Sub-gumfs have a rough time of it and so they try to become gumfs, but if they fail seven times they are condemned. It's the end of the story for them. You witnessed that yourself. But as I said, we are all rejects. The Sculptor visits us from time to time and tries out something new here and there — adds a bit to someone, or takes a bit off, alters something — and then, if the Great One likes the result, the improved reject is selected for passing on to the Testing Grounds. I'm not sure what happens there, but I gather it's pretty tough, and only if you pass the Test do you get a through-rock ticket. If you are successful, then you wait your turn and one day — zip — you're through and out of the rocks — you're upstairs and free.'

'I see,' said Jason, who was beginning to get a glimmer of what she meant. 'So the Sculptor remodels you, and passes you on for testing. And you are all rejects. That, I suppose, is why you are all different, hardly any two the same.'

'Of course, there's no point in making a whole family of rejects — I thought I explained that already — we might start breeding. There'd be no point in that, would there? It would only give the Sculptor more work. We are all prototypes, really. Later, when we have been allowed through to the Testing Grounds, we are duplicated to produce a small colony, before we get our through tickets to the Outrock. Then we can start breeding as soon as we get above rock. It's quite a sensible system, you must agree. I don't see how else it could be done, really, do you?'

'No,' said Jason quickly, not wanting to start an argument. 'No, it's all very logical.'

'Of course, there are a lot of non-gumfs living here, too, all over the Inrock. But they aren't like us. They're not singletons, there are lots of each kind. They live and breed here and stay here forever. They don't count. The Sculptor never touches them. Mostly they are a nuisance, but some we can eat, and others, like the Flummels, are quite useful.'

'What about the Blue Trumpets? There were two of those, and *they* were gumfs, well, sub-gumfs, anyway.'

'Oh, yes, I know, but they weren't a *pair*, they were only twins. One of the Sculptor's nastier little jokes. Ugh! I wouldn't want to be two of me, would you?'

'I've never really thought about it. Thank you for explaining it all to me. You have been very patient.'

'It must be awful to have forgotten so much. They told me you had a bad fall and can remember very little. I am supposed to retrain you. Ask anything you like.'

The Niar-storm

Jason was trying to find the right words for an innocent-sounding question about the Golden Worms, when the light began to fade. It happened so suddenly that he sat up, startled, and looked anxiously at Ludo.

'Grannit-screening,' she said calmly. 'Your eyes will soon adjust. There is enough light left to see your way about in an emergency, but we rarely need it. Look up again.' As Jason did so, he saw that there were tiny dashes of bright, twinkling light. The sky was filled with long, thin stars.

'Those are cracks in the Grannit-screen,' Ludo explained. 'They started out as an error, but proved to be so useful that they have been left. We call this "slit-light". It's a romantic time, when rejects lie and dream of the day they will be passed as fit for Testing and will eventually be duplicated so that they can fall in love with one of their own kind. Some are sad at this hour, but I have got used to the idea. Anyway, I have a feeling I am going to be lucky soon.'

'I'm sure you will, but perhaps we ought to try and get some sleep now,' said Jason firmly.

'Yes, you must be tired. I'll lend you my dream-stalk. Here, give me your hand.'

'What is it?' asked Jason, as Ludo pressed a small tube with a silver tassel into his palm.

'I'll show you.' She got up and leant over him. 'Give it back to me and I'll fit it in for you.' She slid it gently into his right ear, spreading the tassel out on the soft bed-surface. 'Now, when you go to sleep you will have a marvellous dream. It's a new invention of the Cook's. I've only had it a week. I didn't know what I'd been missing. It's as if you are taken off to another world.'

'That should be novel,' said Jason, sinking back into the deliciously soft bedding, but the sarcasm of his remark was lost on Ludo, who grinned happily and stroked his face. Her short, dense fur was pleasing to the touch, as he had imagined it would be, but he was surprised at its warmth.

'You feel hot, are you all right?' he asked sleepily.

'Yes, I'm fine. I was just thinking how cool your skin is. I suppose it's your lack of fur. I don't *mind* you being without hair,' she added hurriedly. 'I must admit I can't imagine what the Sculptor had in mind, but it doesn't worry me, or put me off, or anything like that.' She leant over so that her face was only an inch or so above his, taking a deep breath as she did so. He opened his eyes and they stared quietly at one another.

'I'm sorry, I shouldn't have breathed from you like that. Forgive me, but you smell so golden.'

'Goodnight, Ludo, and thank you for everything.'

'Goodnight, Jason. Dream well.'

And dream he did.

CHAPTER SIX
The Dream-stalk

Jason's dream began the moment he fell asleep. He felt himself becoming lighter and lighter until he began to float above the great circular bed. He glanced down and could see Ludo sprawled out below him. His body floated higher and higher, rising gently through the air, past the top of the turret walls. Now the flags of the village were sinking out of sight beneath him and he was soaring up and up towards the sky of long, thin stars.

He passed magically through the Grannit-screen and on into the blaze of light from the millions of tiny Grannit bodies. He was dazzled by the glare and was forced to cover his face with his hands. As he floated higher and higher, he could feel the beating of small wings all around him, brushing against his skin. He was rising through the seething mass of Grannits now and right up to the great ceiling of rock that separated his new world from his old one. With a slight bump he arrived and opened his eyes.

He was pressed lightly against the rocky roof, bouncing gently at it, like a trapped balloon. He reached out and touched it with his fingers. It was warm and smooth and made up of many colours. By pushing against it he could make himself float sideways. It was almost like swimming, and soon he was travelling fast across its surface.

A sudden gust of wind struck him, catching him unawares, so that he began to spin round and round. The wind became stronger, swirling him along faster and faster. He felt himself rising again in a wild gasp of rushing air. The ceiling began to curve upwards. He had stopped spinning and was zooming straight up, head first into a vast hollow tube of rock. The walls were covered with white and green crystals, glinting and glistening as he sped past. Slowly the walls of the tube grew closer together until he was shooting up through a narrow, vertical tunnel. The rock surfaces were changing, darker now and streaked with crimson and orange. It was almost pitch dark and he could feel soft grains of sand sliding over his body.

With a loud hissing noise he burst out into the light again and came to rest on a rippling floor of yellow-brown earth. Dusting himself down, he looked around. He was in a beautiful cave hung with tall, snake-like columns of blue and purple. Threading his way through them, he came to the edge of an underground river. On the other side he could see steps and a small path. At the far end of the winding tunnel a disc of light grew larger and brighter and in a moment he was outside.

To his amazement, he was standing on a tiny ledge, high up on a mountain. All around were snow-tipped peaks and tall pine trees. In the distance he could hear the tinkling of cow-bells. Clambering down the mountainside, he came to a rough roadway, little more than a donkey-path, and there, a few hundred paces along it, where it curved sharply, stood a low hut, with smoke coming from its stone chimney. Sitting in the doorway was a frail old woman with long black hair. Her skin was wrinkled and shrivelled, but she held herself with dignity as if remembering the days when she had once been beautiful and had broken the hearts of all the young men in her village.

'You have come a long way,' said the old woman, without looking up. Her hands were busy, tearing up tough, green leaves and dropping them into a wide earthenware pot at her feet.

'Yes, it has been a tiring journey,' Jason replied, 'and it is so

The Dream-stalk

peaceful here, I would like to rest for a while if I may.'

'Sit down,' said the old woman, 'and recover your strength. There is clear mountain water in that jug over there. Drink and you will feel refreshed.'

Jason took the jug and drank and they squatted on the ground, leaning their backs against the wall of the hut.

'If I lived here I would never want to leave. It is so beautiful. Already I feel I would like to stay here the rest of my life.'

'Drink some more of the mountain water,' ordered the old woman, 'and I will tell you a story. Do you know the legend of the Princess and the Sea-eagle?'

Jason shook his head and drank again from the black jug. The old woman stopped her leaf-tearing, gazed into the distance, and began her story:

'The Sea-eagle is the most handsome of all the eagles. His body is a rich, chestnut brown, but his head and neck are pure, pure white. He is a powerful and savage bird, feared by everyone in the land, but secretly he is very sad. Whenever his sadness becomes more than he can bear, he throws back his head and utters a haunting, plaintive cry, asking a lonely, desperate question. None of the other animals can answer him because they cannot understand what the question is. Even strong and clever men are unable to fathom its meaning. Only a beautiful girl in search of love can tell what the great bird is asking, and when she hears the question she smiles a private smile and answers softly. But the mighty eagle in turn cannot understand her words and so he throws back his head again and again, calling and calling, crying out his passionate message.

'And this was the tragedy of the Sea-eagle until, one day, a beautiful Princess came walking alone to his riverside home. She had wandered far from her valley in search of water for her people, who were dying from a terrible drought. Her heart was full of love for them, for she was their Princess, and she prayed that in the great eagle's home she might find good water that would save them.

'Her love made her face so radiant that she could answer any question without the help of words. The lonely, white-necked bird, seeing her, threw back his head, calling out his eternal question. Their eyes met and, although she did not utter a word, the mighty eagle at last knew the answer. With outstretched wings he hovered above her, grasped her gently in his powerful talons, and flew slowly up into the sky. He did not stop until he came to rest on the top of a very green mountain, and there they lay down side by side.

'Soon they came to understand one another's words and were able to talk happily together. At last, the Sea-eagle stared hard at the Princess and said: "Tell me what deed I must perform to prove myself before you." The Princess thought for a long time, to find a task great enough. The love for her people still burned inside her and she knew that unless the Sea-eagle could quench this fire with a truly great deed, she would have to climb alone down the mountain and return to her dry valley, to die honourably with her subjects. After many hours she replied: "You are a lordly Sea-eagle, but the drought has made the waters of your river stagnant and evil, so that you must fly many miles out to the seas to find fish that you may eat. To prove yourself before me, you must fly to the centre of the largest ocean, catch the biggest whale you can find, and bring it back here to me. When you have set it down before me, only then will I know your true feeling for me. Only then will I be able to stay with you and forget the suffering of my people."

'The Sea-eagle flew off with a heavy heart, knowing that even his massive claws could not hold a whale, but unable to tell her the truth because he loved her with every feather of his being.

'After many terrible adventures, the great bird flew wearily back to the mountain with only a small fish clasped in his talons. Several times he had nearly drowned, pulled under the giant waves as he clung desperately to the backs of huge whales, but they had always escaped and the puny fish was all he could catch. He had failed in his task and now he must tell the Princess, losing her forever.

'She was lying asleep, stretched out in the sun, on the very top of the mountain peak. When he landed nearby he could not believe his eyes, for she was even more beautiful than before. As he looked at her, his love welled up inside him and he felt he was going to split in two. He threw back his head to ask his plaintive question for the last time, but then, staring up at the sky, he remained silent. No sound broke from his gaping beak because, as he stood there outlined against the sky, he felt a strange sensation moving through his body. Looking down he let out a startled gasp for there, between his legs, as if by magic, the small fish was growing into a great, glistening whale.

'It grew and grew, writhing to escape from him, until it was bigger than any of the whales he had seen in the sea. At this moment the Princess awoke and smiled up at him. "Ah! You have returned and you have brought me my beautiful whale." The Sea-eagle began to stammer out the truth, but the Princess placed her soft hand lightly over his beak. With her other hand she caressed the whale. She was surprised to find that there was a hole in the top of its head. A fish does not have a hole here, she thought, perhaps the whale was already killed by a hunter before my Sea-eagle found it.

'Reading the doubt in the Princess's mind, the Sea-eagle said: "No hunter has made this hole, it is natural to the whale and through it he spouts a great jet of water." So saying, the Sea-eagle squeezed his legs together against the body of the glistening whale, which spouted a great spout. The water shot into the air like a fountain and drenched the Sea-eagle and the Princess, who clung tightly to one another.

'The fountain became a flood and they felt themselves being swept down the side of the mountain and into the valley on a great torrent of rushing water. The people in the valley saw them coming and cheered and waved. Borne along by the flood, the Sea-eagle and the Princess were carried right into the heart of the valley, until at last they came to rest in a strong tree.

'The water soaked into the land and the valley soon became fertile again. Seeing their crops grow and their lands prosper, the people gave thanks to their Princess. "We know we have lost your heart," they said, "but you have saved us from a lingering death in a dry, cracked land, and we forgive you." Whereupon they declared the Sea-eagle to be a great Prince and carried him and his Princess back up to the top of their domain, where the two of them lived happily together, breathing deeply the cold, thin, mountain air.'

The old woman sighed and became silent.

'That is a beautiful story,' said Jason quietly.

'Yes,' replied the old woman sadly. 'A beautiful story.'

'Then why does it make you so sad? It ended happily.'

The old woman was silent.

'That was the end of the story, wasn't it?'

Still the old woman said nothing, but continued staring out at the distant mountain peaks. After some moments she slowly stood up and walked to the other side of the path. There she leant against one of the tall pine trees. Jason waited. Nothing happened. After several minutes had passed, he pulled himself up and went over to see if she was ill. She looked so frail and sad, leaning forlornly against the great tree.

Walking round in front of the slender figure, he was upset to see that she was quietly crying, long rivulets of tears streaming down her face and splashing on to her shawl. No sound came from her lips. Her eyes were wide open, staring, but not seeing.

'Can I help you? Is there anything I can do? Please let me help.'

'It is nothing. I am being stupid. Just a stupid old woman. Take no notice of me.'

'But I can't leave you like this.'

'I thought you were going to stay here forever,' replied the old woman, smiling through her tears.

'I would love to, but the truth is I have a rather urgent errand to do for a friend and I must get back soon or he will be in serious difficulties. I wish I could stay, but I can't, not now. Perhaps I will be able to come back here one day and live with you on the mountain.'

'People never come back, do they,' said the old woman. 'Something else always happens. People never return. At least, not as themselves.'

'I will, I promise. And when I do I'll still be me. I won't have changed.'

'Yes you will. You'll be someone else by then. And never make promises,' snapped the old woman, turning sharply. 'Promises get broken and hearts with them. It is wrong to make promises, dangerous and wrong.' Her head sank and she stared at the ground.

'Before I go,' said Jason determinedly, 'I would like to hear the end of the story. What happened to the Sea-eagle and the Princess? Were they always happy together? Why does it make you so very sad?'

'You are so young. Be content with the story as it is. It is a good story.'

'But how can I rest now without hearing the end of it?' pleaded Jason. 'Please, or I shall think the worst.'

'Very well, but there is little more to tell. They lived together for a long time in perfect contentment, but the Sea-eagle's passion for the Princess was so strong and his claws so powerful that one day he accidentally hurt her. She loved him still, but could not help being frightened by his uncontrollable strength. As time went on, he hurt her more and more. His love was so painful for her that she began to shrink away from him until one morning she fled from the top of the mountain and hid in a cave. He could not follow her there because of his broad wings, and stood outside the entrance to the cave, screaming and calling to her. She covered her ears and wept. Eventually she was exhausted and fell asleep inside the cave.

'The next day, she crept out and looked around for the giant bird, but he was nowhere to be seen. She built herself a small hut on the mountainside and began to live a quiet, solitary life. She had lost both her people and her Prince and remained there alone, staring out at the mountain peaks and the pine trees, half-hoping, half-fearing, that the great Sea-eagle would one day return to her.'

There was a long pause, the silence broken only by the old woman's breathing and the faint tinkling of cow-bells in the far distance. With a sigh, she continued:

'But he has never been seen again. That is the end of the story. You should not have asked me to tell it. Now go. I do not want you here. I have told you too much. You must leave me. Leave me alone,' and she walked heavily back to her wooden log-hut, entered, and closed the door.

Jason knocked and called to her repeatedly, but there was no reply and the door remained firmly bolted. He was so concerned about the old woman and her great sadness that he tried to climb around the side of the hut to look in at the window. As he clung to the rough pine walls, he glanced down at the sheer drop beneath him and gasped. The hut was perched on the very edge of a deep ravine and there was only an inch or two of rock beneath his feet. He edged along it, step by step, until a loose stone shifted beneath his weight. As he lost his balance he saw the old woman come to the window and stare down at him. There was no expression on the wrinkled, white face. It stared blankly out at him as he began to fall.

'Help me!' he yelled. 'Help me!' But the mask-like face continued to stare. The window did not open.

Tipping backwards, Jason hurtled down into the ravine. As trees and rocks flashed by, he grabbed out at them, but it was useless and he gave up, closing his eyes and letting himself fall freely through the rushing, hissing air. He began to feel cold, then hot. Lights flashed through his closed eyelids. Suddenly, it was pitch dark and there was a soft humming sound. Feeling his descent become less violent, he opened his eyes again and saw above him the long, thin stars of the Grannit-screen. He was sinking slowly now and gently came to rest on a soft, warm surface.

Sitting up, he looked around and saw the sprawled, sleeping form of Ludo by his side, her short, curved horns pressing lightly into his left leg. When he moved it away, she woke up, mumbling:

'What's the matter?'

'I had the most peculiar dream I have ever . . .'

'I told you you would,' she interrupted, and turned over.

The Dream-stalk

In a moment she was sleeping again, and Jason lay back, staring at the stars and thinking about the dream. But it was fading already. All he could remember was the blank, staring face looking down at him. He shuddered and stretched. Propping himself up again, he pulled the dream-stalk from his ear and then settled back to try to get some less exhausting rest.

CHAPTER SEVEN
The Flag Ceremony

When Jason opened his eyes again, Ludo was missing. He must have been sleeping for some time because the hard, bright light was once more blazing down from the Grannit sky. He stood up and tried to walk to the edge of the sleep-dip, but the bedding was too soft and he tripped over. Crawling the rest of the way, he pushed through a curtain and climbed the stairs to the top of the cell wall. There he found Ludo, lying inside a large crystal egg. Her eyes were closed and, above her, hanging from the roof of the egg, was a mass of thin, pulsating tubes. They stretched down like soft white roots and seemed to have attached themselves all over Ludo's reclining form. Every so often, her fingers twitched and fluttered and then relaxed again, but otherwise her body hardly moved except for the regular rise and fall of her furry chest.

He tapped on the transparent shell. Ludo opened her eyes, smiled at him and stretched herself. Her sudden movement sent all the slender tubes shrinking back to become little stumpy blobs drooping limply from the roof of the egg. She tapped on the side of the shell, it opened and she stepped out.

'You were tired. I did not want to disturb you, but now you are awake you will be hungry. This is my personal taste-egg, but you

The Flag Ceremony

may use it while you are here.'

She helped him into the capsule and told him to lie very still. Before she closed the shell again, she explained:

'There is nothing to do and nothing to fear. The tubes will attach themselves so gently that you will hardly feel them. They will send tiny connections through to your blood and pump you a delicious feast. The tubes that find your mouth and nose give you all the flavour you need. Oh, and if you close your eyes and breathe deeply it is better. We have a really good Cook in this village. He controls the master-egg in that large tower you saw yesterday. Now I will shut the dome and leave you to your meal.'

Ludo watched for a moment as the blobs began to stretch down towards Jason's body and attach themselves to his skin, then she turned slowly and started down the tiled steps. As she descended, her face looked worried. She had a difficult question to ask him, but it would have to wait. She lay down in a shallow cup in one of the cell wall's side-cavities, thinking. Would he help her? Could she trust him?

'That was fantastic! I have never had a meal like that in my whole life. I don't know how I am ever going to repay you for your kindness in looking after me like this.' Jason was smiling down at her with an expression of complete contentment.

It was too soon to ask him yet, but he was in such a good mood . . . could she risk it?

'If there is ever anything I can do for you,' Jason insisted, 'you will tell me, won't you?'

It was too good a chance to miss . . .

'I wonder . . .' she began. 'I . . . er . . . did you close the dome of the taste-egg?'

'Yes, I think it's all right.'

'There is something, but I am not sure if I should ask you,' she said, frowning down at her furry hands.

'Try me.'

'Well, the village has a problem. It may get you into trouble if you help, but the risk is slight.'

'What do I have to do?'

'One of the inhabitants, a crazy, sad character named Meggamole — we call him the Mad Meggamole — has gone. He has tried to break through — up there — without permission. We told him he was insane, but he refused to listen. We warned him he couldn't do it without the sacred meal of the Golden Worms, but he ignored us. He said the Sculptor would never complete him, would never let him go to the Testing Grounds. He wouldn't wait. He was so impatient. It's not a bad life here, but he became so bored, so restless, especially after the Silver Swamp dried up and he was robbed of his hunting grounds. He lived for his hunting. Now the Cook suspects something. We go to his empty cell from time to time to use his taste-egg, to cover up for him as best we can, but we seem to have failed. Any moment now the Polizesti will be alerted for a flag ceremony and then the game will be up. We shall all be punished. It's in the rules. The whole village will be found guilty.'

'What is the flag ceremony?'

'It's what they do when they want to check that all the villagers are present. Each one of us goes, on a signal — the ringing of a bell — to the top of our cell. On another signal — the beating of a drum — we lower our personal flags. Then they look to see if any are still flying, check them against the official travel-permits, and in that way they can tell if anyone is missing. If someone has gone without permission, they wait for three Grannit-screenings and then they strike. They take ten inhabitants at random and scramble them. It's . . . it's horrible to watch. I have only seen it once, a long time ago, but I shall never forget it.' She fell silent.

'I think I can guess what you want me to do,' said Jason. Ludo turned to look at him, but did not speak. 'You want me to go to Tonk's . . . I mean the Meggamole's cell and lower his flag when the signal goes.'

'It will save the village.'

'Then of course I'll do it. Show me the way. I'll stay in his cell until it's all clear.'

'Thank you,' said Ludo. 'The village will remember you and what you have done. Come on.'

The Flag Ceremony

'What happens if I am caught?' asked Jason, as they made for the deserted cell of the Mad Meggamole.

'I am not sure. They'd do something to your body, but it's best not to think about it.'

As they reached the empty cell, a bell began to ring out slowly over the village.

'It's the flag ceremony signal. Quick, hurry. Go straight up to the flag-mast. Stand there and when the bell stops, take hold of the handle. Give one full turn for each beat of the drum. When the drum stops, do nothing. Nothing, you understand? Don't move. Stay absolutely still. Then, when the bell starts again you can wind the handle the other way, to put the flag up again. After that, jump down into the Meggamole's sleep-dip. Lie there until I come for you. Good luck . . . and thank you.' And she dashed off, back in the direction of her own cell.

By the time Jason had climbed up to the Meggamole's flag-mast, the bell had stopped. He barely had time to notice that the design on the flag was a fan of sharp spines, like the ones he had seen back at home on the Tonk's body, when a drum began to beat out rhythmically in the distance. He grasped a silver handle at the bottom of the mast and turned it. Instead of dropping, the flag shot up to the tip of the mast and jammed there.

'The wrong way,' he gasped, 'I've turned it the wrong way.' He tried hard to reverse it, but the flag was entangled in the hook at the top of the pole, and refused to budge.

There was only one solution. He grasped the pole and began to clamber up it. From her nearby turret, Ludo groaned in horror as she saw him heaving himself up the Meggamole's mast. She tugged at her fur and stamped her foot in anguish. Jason slipped back and almost lost his grasp, then struggled on again and at last reached the top. Swaying dangerously, he pulled at the flag and tore it loose. Then, sliding down, he twisted awkwardly and his feet flew out into space. His hands were dragged from the pole and he fell headlong into the Meggamole's sleep-pit.

Landing softly on the bedding, he scrambled across to the side-curtain and pelted up the curved stairway in the circular wall. By the time he had reached the handle once more, all the other flags in the village were two-thirds of the way down their masts. If only there had been a few official travellers, their flags might have hidden his mistake, but the entire village seemed to be in residence. Only the Meggamole's emblem remained at the top of its mast. Panting for breath, he spun the handle round and round — correctly this time — and quickly caught up with the others. Then he followed them in their downward movement at the proper, slow pace — one turn for each beat of the drum, until the drum stopped.

Still breathing hard, he crouched on the floor of the parapet and waited. After a long, tense pause, the bell began to peal out again and he wound the flag back into place against the top of the mast.

With a deep sigh of relief, he leapt down into the sleep-dip and sprawled out happily on the warm, smooth bedding. A moment later there was a sound of running feet and Ludo clambered in beside him.

'What happened? What went wrong?'

'I wound it the wrong way. It jammed. Do you think they noticed?'

'We can't be sure. We can only wait and see.'

They lay very still, listening. Minutes passed. Nothing happened. Then heavy steps approached the cell and stopped outside the door. There was a loud knocking.

'Meggamole, called Mad Meggamole,' rasped a sharp, nasal tone. 'This is a Polizesti order. Come to your cell door. Immediately.'

Ludo crept across and squatted down just inside the door. The voice repeated the message.

'I am here,' said Ludo in a strange voice. 'What do you want? What have I done?'

'Open the door.'

'No. I am frightened. And how do I know that you are Polizesti? It may be a trap. I want proof.'

'Stop this nonsense. We cannot give you proof unless you open the door. Obey the order. We command it.'

The Flag Ceremony

'But once I have opened the door, it will be too late, and I have no way of knowing who you are.'

There was a hissing noise from outside and then a pause.

'You are a fool, Meggamole. A stupid, grottless fool. The Cook is displeased with you. Nothing escapes him. He saw that you were late in lowering your flag. You spoiled the flag ceremony. Do not let it happen again. This is a final warning to you. You have caused difficulties before. You will not do so again. You are confined to your cell for three days. That is all.'

There was a grinding noise outside the cell door and then the muffled footsteps again, this time receding. They grew faint. Ludo climbed back into the sleep-dip and looked at Jason with grateful eyes.

'We are safe. We have carried it off. The whole village will thank you.'

'Have they locked us in?'

'Yes, there is a sand-flow time-lock in each cell wall. They will have set the sand to run through in three days. Then the door will open automatically. Provided there is no further trouble — no more flag ceremonies — and provided we are not asked for by anyone at my own cell, all should be well.'

'What are we going to do for three days, shut up in here?' asked Jason.

'We can relax — sleep, dream, taste, and clean one another's fur. The time will pass soon enough.'

Jason smiled to himself and lay back. It could be worse, he thought, and perhaps this will give me time to find out more about the Golden Worms.

That night he used the Mad Meggamole's dream-stalk and once again experienced a vivid hallucination.

This time, as he started to dream, he felt himself transported to a strange, hot land where he came to rest at the foot of a tall, prickly tree. A hungry she-goat had climbed the tree and was munching away merrily at the tough, green leaves. Balancing precariously on the high branches, she was startled to see the huge face of a giraffe only a few inches away from her nose. The giraffe's eyes were misty and white and he had obviously lost his sight completely. His long tongue was flicking out in all directions, tearing off leaves whenever it managed to make contact with a branch.

'Werrrgh!' spluttered the she-goat, as the great, sticky tongue sloshed across her left ear.

'Who are you?' demanded the blind giraffe, somewhat taken aback. 'I thought I was alone.'

'I am a friend,' gasped the she-goat, struggling to keep her balance as the blind giraffe sniffed and licked her face. 'Please be careful, I am not as strong as you are and I may lose my footing.'

'You are very tall,' said the blind giraffe. 'I am sixteen feet, four and three-quarter inches high and you must be almost as much yourself.'

'That depends on how you measure it,' replied the she-goat. 'At the moment I suppose it is true, but it is not always so.'

'That matters little to me,' said the blind giraffe sadly. 'I live for the moment. Ever since I was struck blind by a drunken tree-snake — I curled my tongue round him to prop him up and he panicked and spat poison in my face, wretched thing — I have given no thought to the future. I exist from second to second and at this particular second I find you here and I adore you. I can feel that you have a beautiful face and I am in love with you already. Say you will be my mate and I shall be happy for the first time in many seasons. You will bring some light into my dark life and I shall once again be able to face this cruel world without wanting to curl up my neck and die.'

'I am very flattered . . . er . . . touched. Deeply touched,' replied the she-goat, 'but I fear I would make a poor mate for you. My legs are far too short, not to mention my neck.'

'What the eye does not see . . . ' murmured the blind giraffe, slurping his tongue over the she-goat's snout. The she-goat was tipped backwards and crashed to the ground.

'Where are you?' called the blind giraffe, searching wildly through the branches. 'Don't leave me. All the other giraffes have deserted me. I am alone and desperate. I will kill myself if you go.

The Flag Ceremony

Come back. Come back.'

The she-goat hid behind the trunk of the tree and waited, nursing her bruises.

The wailing of the blind giraffe woke up an elderly leopard, who staggered out of a nearby clump of bushes. Seeing the huge giraffe thrashing about in the branches of the tall tree, the leopard groaned. He had managed to avoid a really vigorous kill for several years and was enjoying a peaceful retirement pouncing on snoozing conies and three-legged hares, but now it looked as though he was face to face with a serious challenge. He glanced over his shoulder to see if any lions were watching. He did not want to lose his membership of the Hunt Club, but this giraffe really was too much of a good thing. Indigestible, too.

Just then he spotted the she-goat, whose attention was completely taken up with the frantic movements of her sightless suitor. She-goats are usually very alert, but this one was so absorbed with the problem of what to do with an amorous blind giraffe that she failed to notice the aged leopard creeping up from behind.

Summoning all his energy, the old cat leapt on the she-goat and felled her silently with a single blow. Then, as leopards will, he took her body in his jaws and dragged her up into the branches of the tall tree. Wedging his prey into a fork, he paused for a much needed rest. He was breathing so heavily by this time that the blind giraffe heard him and mistook his gasps for goatly passion.

'Ah, beloved, you are still there. I can hear you panting with pleasure. You sound as excited as I am,' called the great, blind, long-neck. 'Say you will be mine and I will make your days hum with happiness,' and he once again began slurping his over-sized tongue across the she-goat's face.

'Go away and leave me alone, you indigestible idiot,' roared the leopard, wheezing badly, and placing a paw firmly on his booty.

'Yaaargh!' screamed the giraffe. 'I have been making love to a lousy leopard,' and he fled in terror, crashing into bushes and trees as he went.

The noise, helped by the vigorous slurping, revived the

she-goat who, as luck would have it, had only been stunned by the old leopard's blow. The ancient feline was just on the point of taking a bite out of his hard-won prey, when their eyes met. They were both so surprised that they fell out of the tree and rolled together on the ground. The she-goat took off at full speed, with the wheezing leopard in hot pursuit. He was gaining on her rapidly and about to pounce for a second time when Jason woke up with a start.

CHAPTER EIGHT
The Ludo Attack

As Jason lay there, gazing up at the long, thin stars, he was puzzled. He had never had dreams like this before. Was it him, or was it the dream-stalk putting ideas into his brain? Did the dream-stalk invent dreams, or merely make them more vivid? He could not be sure. But it frightened him.

'What in earth's the matter with you?' asked Ludo. 'You're shaking all over.'

'I had another bad dream,' murmured Jason. 'It's nothing. I'm sorry.'

'Was it the same kind as before?'

'Not really. It had some things in common. But the setting was so different.'

'Yes, well, you *are* using Meggamole's dream-stalk, so I'm afraid you'll find your own dreams taking place in *his* dream-space. I bet it's all jungly? He loved jungles.'

On the next night the dream was as real and intense as before. And, sure enough, the setting was the same. Jason found himself back again in Meggamole's dream-space, the strange, hot land, among the tall, prickly trees. He saw the old leopard limping along, spitting and coughing and wheezing and cursing and swishing his moth-eaten tail.

'Stinking goats,' flubbered the fat old cat. 'Bone-headed goats. Solid bone. Can't knock 'em out. Not worth trying. Overrated dog-meat, the lot of 'em,' and he sloped off in search of a crippled, pygmy field-rat he had overheard some cubs talking about at the last Hunt Club meeting.

'Great udders of fire!' gasped a voice right above Jason's head. 'Thank my horns he's gone. Dirty old louse-bag. Ooh, my back is killing me.'

High on a branch was the quivering form of the she-goat, nostrils flapping. Gingerly she stretched out one of her back legs and nearly slipped. The branch creaked ominously.

'Ah-ha! My dove!' It was, of course, the blind giraffe, who had tiptoed up from nowhere and was now intently murmuring sweet nothings at the wrong end of the goat. 'At last we are together again. Now we shall never be parted. Our necks will twine and thump forever. My faithful one.'

'Cut it out, you great slobber-tongue,' screamed the she-goat, terrified of being knocked to the ground again. But nothing could stop the love-crazy long-neck. Following the sound of her agitated, goatly screechings, he moved steadily round to the she-goat's front end and began rubbing horns in a showy, virile fashion. Unhappily the horns of the two animals were different shapes — the giraffe's short and stumpy, and the goat's long and curved — and when they locked together they jammed tight.

'How passionate, how clinging you are, my only true love,' purred the blind giraffe, as the she-goat struggled desperately to free herself, twisting her head this way and that until, at last, she lost her balance.

Closing her eyes and bracing her legs for the fall, the she-goat was surprised to find herself dangling in mid-air. She half-opened her left eye and peered down. The ground was far below her, moving fast. Opening both eyes fully now, she saw to her horror that she was being carried aloft, locked to the giraffe's horns, as he strode dreamily along towards the watering-hole.

'Come, my love, dip necks and drink with me. We will toast our

The Ludo Attack

betrothal in lovely, bubbly, tatsi-water.'

'I'm a nanny, you old fool, let me down,' shrieked the she-goat, flailing her airborne legs helplessly.

'Forget the past,' murmured the giraffe, 'I'll give you children of your own.'

'Rubber-necked imbecile!' yelled the she-goat, but it was to no avail. The blind giraffe was already dreaming of the thunder of tiny hooves and the happy herd to come.

Reaching the watering-hole, which was a broad side-pool of a great river, he spread his long front legs and swung neck down with a flourish, crying:

'To us, my angel, to us!'

'Amen,' moaned the goat as, still hooked horn-to-horn, she disappeared beneath the surface of the pool.

The giraffe drank long and deep as bubbles rose from below his nose.

'Bubbly, oh, so beautifully bubbly,' he spluttered, flinging his neck high at last. 'Where are you, my darling, come close so I can snuffle you.' He sniffed this way and that. 'Dearest one, where are you?'

The she-goat, whose wet horns had slipped free as the giant head pulled up from the water, was floating upside-down, hooves to heaven, towards the edge of the pool, bubbles still trickling from her nose.

Arriving at the water's edge, her body bumped into a sleeping crocodile who snapped his jaws angrily and woke up just in time to see a huge hoof descending on his skull from the sky above.

'There you are, my angel, light of my life,' squealed the giraffe, stumbling around in the shallow water, pinning down the raging reptile. 'Come, we'll run together across the plains and into the piffle-grass.'

'Crocodile!' spluttered the she-goat, who had been thrown on to the bank by the reptile's thrashing tail. 'Crocodile!'

'Yeeoowh!' roared the giraffe and took off fast in the wrong direction, crashing into a parked zebra.

'Look where you're going, you long-necked lout,' rumbled the zebra, only to be struck in mid-stripes by the dripping body of a fear-maddened she-goat.

'Get away, you soggy slob,' cried the zebra. 'My stripes will run and then those filthy horses will be after me again. Get away.'

Leaving the outraged zebra rolling her stripes dry in the dust, the blind giraffe and the she-goat turned their tails on the watering-hole and accelerated to full gallop.

'Free at last, my love,' panted the giraffe. 'And I smell trees. Over there,' and he pointed his neck to the left, tripping over a large, dozing lion as he did so.

The she-goat would have left him then and there, but she had already spotted the rest of the pride of lions, closing in rapidly. It's no good, she thought, I'm stuck with this blundering giraffe. There's only one thing for it.

'Back to the river,' she shouted. 'It's our only escape.'

Together they plunged through the shallow side-pool, trampling once again over the wretched crocodile, and out into the swirling waters of the main river.

'Have no fear, angelic one, I know this river well. Even in the middle it is no more than ten feet deep. We'll walk it across easily,' said the giraffe proudly, nose up and ears erect. 'Here we go!'

Only his long neck was showing now above the surface of the water, as the little she-goat struggled along valiantly by his side.

'I'll make you happy, so very happy. You'll see . . . '

But the she-goat could no longer hear him. The current had dragged her further and further away towards the roar of a great waterfall. Over the edge she slipped, kicking and struggling to the last, down, down, deep into the thundering spray . . .

Jason groaned and sat bolt upright, bathed in sweat. Ludo was sleeping peacefully by his side. He tossed his head, trying to shake the pictures from his mind, and wiped his damp face with his hand. These dreams would have to stop — they were too exhausting. It was as if they were trying to tell him something — something he did not want to know. He lay back, frowning to himself, and slowly dragged the dream-stalk from his ear.

On the third night in the Meggamole's cell, he decided not to

The Ludo Attack

use the stalk and after Ludo had fallen asleep, he took it out and placed it near his head to make it look as though it had fallen out accidentally. Ludo had been so insistent that he wear it each night and he did not wish to offend her.

On the morning of the final day, after a blissfully dreamless night, he awoke fully refreshed and ready for anything.

I am bored, he told himself. I have been stuck here for three precious days and I have learnt virtually nothing about the Golden Worms. Ludo either can't or won't answer my questions, and I have wasted too many valuable hours. When the time-lock opens the cell door, I am off!

'Good-morning, Jason.' Ludo was smiling. 'We have done it! We are free to go. Come on.'

Eagerly he followed her outside.

'Let's get back to my cell.'

'No. You have been very kind, but I must leave. I can't afford to delay.'

'Don't be silly. It's fun here really, if you don't ask too many questions. You'll see. I know it's been difficult so far, but . . . '

'I'm sorry,' said Jason firmly. 'It's no good. I *must* set off at once.'

'But the Sculptor may come soon and we would stand a good chance of being chosen for remodelling. Then we could go together to the Testing Grounds.'

'You can wait if you want to, but I can't. It may be ages before the next visit. It's time for me to go. Now! My mind is made up.'

'No. Listen. Please wait.' Ludo ran after him and grabbed his arm. 'I am sure the Great One will come soon. I feel it, deep inside my fur.'

'When was the last visit to the village?'

'I can't remember exactly. It was . . . '

'Of course you can't remember. I doubt if there's ever been one. In fact, I am beginning to wonder if the Sculptor exists at all! It's probably just a trick to keep you all in order – to keep you waiting.'

Jason had spoken without thinking. His mind was already on

the journey ahead. Ludo had stiffened and remained stock still. Her eyes were blinking rapidly and her tongue flicked out repeatedly to lick her lips. She gave a soft moan. Then, to Jason's surprise, she sank to the ground and crouched there, squatting on her haunches.

'I'm sorry,' grunted Jason, still not realizing what he had said. 'I didn't mean to cast any doubts.'

'Keep quiet!' hissed Ludo, getting slowly to her feet. 'Keep quiet and come with me.'

She looked so serious that Jason followed her without further argument. When they were back at her own cell, she slammed the door and made straight for the sleep-dip. There, without warning, she turned and charged him with her horns, knocking the breath out of him and sending him reeling backwards so violently that he lost his balance. Standing over him, glaring down at his startled face, she hissed:

'Explain. Explain what you said. Explain, if you can, what you said out there.'

'What do you mean,' asked a bewildered Jason, rubbing his smarting chest. 'I've said I'm sorry.'

'You know perfectly well what I mean. How can a personal friend, a per-son-al friend of the Sculptor's have doubts about the Great One's existence? You are a fraud, a complete fraud. Who are you? Where do you come from and what are you doing here?' With each word Ludo was becoming more and more enraged and Jason, realizing now what he had done, had to think quickly.

'I was only testing you out,' he spluttered. 'Just testing you to see if . . . ' but he could not finish.

'Liar!' roared Ludo, lowering her head as if to make a second charge. Jason bunched up his body and covered his face with his arms to protect it from the sharp, curved horns. He waited, immobile, but no blow came. Uncovering his eyes, he found that he was alone.

She's gone to tell them, he thought, and scrambled hurriedly across to the edge of the pit. Rushing down to the door of the cell, he nearly tripped over the crouched figure of Ludo, sitting

The Ludo Attack

hunched up on one of the steps. She was hugging her body with her arms and rocking gently back and forth. Her anger had subsided and she looked sad, almost desperate. Jason paused in the doorway.

'I'm sorry,' he said. 'Truly sorry. I am very fond of you. You have been good to me. The last thing I wanted was to make you angry. Forgive me – and wish me luck. I must go now.' He turned to open the door.

'Wait,' said Ludo in a hoarse voice. 'Don't go, it's too dangerous. I will help you, but first you must help me.'

'How?'

'You must tell me the truth. Then we shall see. I shall probably be scrambled for this, but I can't – I can't let you go off alone. I . . . I have come to feel for you. I have breathed from you and you have groomed my fur. I cannot let you go out there alone.'

Jason slid down to the floor and rested the back of his head against the smooth, orange wall.

'All right, I'll tell you. Where do you want me to begin?'

An hour later they were still sitting there. Neither had moved. Ludo rubbed her hands over her eyes.

'And then,' Jason was saying, 'you brought me here to the village. The rest you know.' Ludo shut her eyes and tugged at her throat.

'It is hard to believe,' she said at last. 'But I suppose it must be true. You could never have made it up.'

'No.'

'And now you want me to help you to find the Golden Worms?'

'I never asked that. Why should you? You are happy here. I'll manage somehow. I'd soon get bored here, anyway. But you stay. It's the life you are used to. It would be wrong to leave it for a search that doesn't concern you.'

'But it does. Now it does. That's the trouble. I want to be with you and to help you. I don't know why. I admit it doesn't make sense. We normally keep pretty much to ourselves, but with you it's different. I don't understand it, but there it is.'

'Promise me you won't try to hold me back'.

'I promise. I realize it would be impossible for me to do so. But it is stupid to set out now, in broad Grannit-light. We'll start tonight, as soon as the screens have been drawn. We'll find a Night-slopper and steal a ride to the Root Forest. That should be a good starting-point. I remember the Meggamole was planning to hunt there after the Silver Swamp disappeared beneath the sand. At the time we thought it was to be nothing more than an ordinary hunting trip, but perhaps he was on to something. Anyway, it's the only lead we've got. Today we must get as much rest as possible — we shall need all the muscles we can muster — the Root Forest has a bad reputation.'

As they lay side by side in the sleep-dip, Ludo stared into the distance.

'It's incredible,' she murmured. 'You have actually been up there, on the Outrock. We long for it, wait for it, pray for it, and you risk it all, throw it all away, and come down here to help a stupid, headstrong, Mad Meggamole. A dim, bobbling twit like that. You must be either extremely kind, or extremely foolish.'

'Or both,' sighed Jason, and closed his eyes.

CHAPTER NINE
The Root Forest

'Wake up! Wake up! It's dark,' hissed an urgent voice in Jason's ear. 'Come on, we must go now. Now. Come on.'

Ludo was shaking his arm. He must have been dozing for at least an hour and felt that muzzy vagueness that a short sleep leaves. They had spent the day busily planning their trip and exchanging information about their two different worlds. It had been a tremendous relief for Jason to be able to tell the truth at last. Keeping up his earlier pretence and the supposed loss of memory had proved a severe strain. But that was all behind him and his friendship with Ludo had somehow survived.

Waiting for dark, with nothing to do and all their words talked out of them, they had finally lain down again in Ludo's sleep-dip and drifted off into sleep. But now it was time for action. The Grannit-screens had been drawn and it was slit-light once more.

'Right. All right. I'm with you. Give me a moment.'

They crept silently through the village and out beyond the tiled pavements to the soft sands of the desert.

'This way,' whispered Ludo. 'Keep close to me.'

There was a strange humming in the air, a throbbing that grew stronger as the village shrank behind them. Ludo did not speak, but Jason could see that she was cautiously making for a distant cluster of glistening spikes. The tall, pointed shapes glinted and twinkled in the dimness. They looked like long, thin, white crystals, but appeared to be pushing up from the ground as if they were some sort of weird plants.

As they came nearer, the throbbing developed a powerful regular pulse, like a frightened heart-beat, and Jason had to press his lips tightly together to stop himself from crying out. A searing pain was burning through his skull. He touched Ludo's arm and she looked round at him in alarm.

'I am going mad,' he whispered. 'The throbbing — my brain is going to burst.' Ludo appeared to be totally unaffected and was obviously puzzled by Jason's state of distress.

'We can't stop now. There's bound to be at least one Night-slopper hiding here. You'll soon get used to the noise of the Singing Rods.'

'Singing!' groaned Jason. 'Singing! I can't stand it much longer. I . . .' and his words faded. His mouth went on moving but no sound came out. His legs seemed to be miles away. There was no feeling in them. He sank to the sand and collapsed writhing on the ground. By the time Ludo had crouched by his side, he was unconscious. She glanced frantically around, then darted off into the darkness.

When he opened his eyes, Jason saw the Grannit-stars swaying above him. The throbbing had stopped, but his whole body seemed to be rocking from side to side. He propped himself up and peered about him. It was not his imagination, he really was swaying about. Then he heard Ludo's voice calling softly.

'Don't get up. Lie where you are. I managed to grab a Slopper. You're in one of her back-pouches. I'm in another, just behind you. We'll be all right. Don't worry. We are nearly at the edge of the Root Forest. Stay put and relax.'

Jason did as he was told, but by twisting his head this way and that, he was able to make out the shape of the bizarre creature on which they were travelling. It was something like a giant slug, with four large eye-tentacles at its head end and what looked like a

The Root Forest

vast, curved thorn at the rear. All over its long, low back were soft pits, like shallow basins. Ludo was lying in one, Jason in another, and miniature versions of the Slopper were peering at them out of the remaining nine or ten.

'I had to remove two of her young to make places for us,' whispered Ludo. 'It was the only way. I didn't like doing it, but there was no alternative.'

'Does she always carry her young ones around with her on her back like this?'

'Yes, all the time, while they are at the helpless stage.'

'But what will become of the ones you threw out, if they are so helpless?'

'I am afraid the Sabenites will get them when daylight comes. It can't be helped. They will have no protection.'

'Ludo, you can't *do* that! Tell her to go back. I won't go on. Tell her to turn round. We'll pick them up.'

'It's no good, Jason. If she doesn't reach the Root Forest before dawn, she will be killed herself and all her other offspring with her. It's too late. Look, you can see the edge of the forest already. Over there.'

Jason did not reply. He slumped down into the pouch and stared up at the Grannit sky. Was it worth it? Was the Mad Meggamole worth all this effort? To save the fat fool, he had already uprooted Ludo and caused the death of two infant Night-sloppers, not to mention the wretched Red Warty back in the Display Prison. But the quest for the Golden Worms had become important to him by now. He was too involved and, if he was honest, he was no longer thinking only of old Tonk, back in the barn. He was also trying to prove something to himself. Once, he had been accused of never finishing things that he had started, and it had made him angry. This time, he would prove that he *could* finish something. The search had become a personal challenge.

Something brushed across his face. His thoughts evaporated and he sat up with a start. In doing so, he thrust his head into the middle of a mass of tiny, hanging fronds, which clung to his cheeks and his hair like sticky cobwebs.

'Keep down,' shouted Ludo. 'We're entering the forest. If you sit up you'll be swept away.'

Shrinking into the pouch, Jason brushed wildly at the clinging tendrils, desperately trying to disentangle himself, but they were too strong for him.

As the Night-slopper slithered on, he felt himself being dragged out of the pit and along the smooth, slimy back of the giant, slug-like creature. Just in time, he saw the huge, curved thorn at her tail-end looming up towards him and pushing off as hard as he could, swung to one side.

Swaying wildly in mid-air, he dangled free, held tight by a mass of strong tendrils. A few feet below, he could see the forest floor, but he was helpless, powerless to touch it.

'Ludo,' he shouted, as the squat bulk of the Slopper disappeared into the undergrowth. 'Ludo, Ludo! Come back. I'm stuck. Help me.' But his voice was muffled by the dense mass of sticky vegetation all around him.

A few moments later he was quite alone, hanging limply in the tenacious grip of the root-tendrils. When he struggled, all that happened was that he bobbed gently up and down, like a puppet on an elastic cord. He could do nothing but wait for Ludo to rescue him. Soon she would discover that he was missing and then she would come looking for him. He would keep still, save his strength, and wait.

Minutes passed. More minutes. There was no sign of Ludo. Then a faint rustling sound started somewhere below his feet. He peered down, twisting his head first to one side and then to the other, but in the profusion of vegetation he could make out nothing with any distinct animal shape.

The rustling stopped. Then, to his horror, he felt something undoing his shoes. Tiny hands began to move up his legs. He kicked out hard and there was a frightened scurrying noise. Then silence. After a pause, the rustling started up again. This time it was stronger, as though reinforcements had been brought in to help. In a few seconds, he felt a whole mass of small fingers

The Root Forest

clasping hold of his feet and his legs, pulling him down. Above him, the twisted tendrils strained and stretched and the weaker ones began to snap. He shivered in mid-air, caught between the two forces. Slowly but surely, the hands began to win and with a crackling and twanging of roots, he crashed to the ground.

As he lay there he felt himself covered with exploring fingers, all busily probing his clothing and tugging at his hair. He tried to get up, but all that he managed to do was to roll over. As he did so, he saw them for the first time. Hundreds of them. They were swarming all over him and under him. Together they lifted him up and began to carry him slowly along, inch by inch, across the forest floor.

With a sudden grab he managed to snatch one up and bring it round to a point where he could study it more closely. It squeaked and squirmed, but he held it tight. It was very small, about the size of a monkey's hand, or a baby's. And a hand was all it was! It had four fingers, a thumb, a single eye in the middle of its palm, and two small, clawed feet where its wrist should have been. That was all. A bodiless hand. A seeing, walking, claw-footed, baby hand. He dropped it and it scampered off.

Like a ship gliding down a launching ramp, he was borne along by the great swarm of hands. They were descending a slight slope now and entered a shallow cave. He tried to struggle free, but it was useless. They only swarmed more densely around him and over him. He gave up. After passing down a long tunnel, they laid him down on a soft bed of pink earth and began dashing frantically around in all directions. At first, it was not clear what they were doing. Then, in a flash, it dawned on him. They were building a cage – a strong root-cage – and he was to be the animal it would contain.

He leapt up into a crouching position under the low roof, but instantly they flung themselves at him. Wave after wave covered him, blinding him and nearly stifling him. They began tearing at his clothes and the more he struggled, the more they ripped and tore. Soon his tunic was in shreds and he lay back exhausted. They immediately retreated, carrying off fragments of clothing as they went. He lay on his stomach and covered his head with his arms. The clatter and noise grew all around him, then it stopped and there was the sound of clapping. He looked up. The cage was complete. He was trapped. Outside the root-bars, as far as the eye could see, there was a vast army of little hands. They were squeaking and jumping for joy. Some were snapping their fingers at him. Others, in pairs, were clapping themselves together. Then, as if on a signal, they rushed towards him, lifted up the cage and began to carry it off, deeper and deeper into the tunnel.

After about an hour of hand-borne travel the tunnel became lighter. Broad, flat fronds of some rubbery brown substance hung from the roof and Jason's cage pushed through these tattered curtains of vegetation with increasing difficulty. The struggling hands were sweating profusely now, but despite their efforts the pace was slackening. Just as it seemed that the impetus was going to be lost completely, there was a flash of light and the cage shot out of the overgrown tangle of the tunnel and into a wide, root-lined avenue. The pathway dipped slightly and the hands could hardly keep up with their heavy burden, which threatened to slide on ahead of them. Dashing along as fast as they could go, they swept Jason down the slope at such speed that he could scarcely make out the details of the scene on either side of him. He could just pick out the shapes of many different kinds of scaly, sharp-toothed creatures, some with frills and others with sharp spines, or armoured warts. Beady eyes glinted and long pointed tongues flicked in and out. There was a strong smell, a cross between a laundry and a cowshed, or was it a kitchen and a rubbish-dump? He could not make up his mind, but whatever it was, it was rather unpleasant and oppressive. At the end of the avenue he could see a heavy door and he hoped that, once through there, the humid, steamy smell would be left behind.

When they reached the huge door it was obvious that the hands were not going to be able to reach up to the handle to open it. A few of the stronger ones made a leap at it, but failed to come anywhere near. While some of the lazier, podgier hands amused themselves by prodding at Jason through the bars, the more sinewy ones held a hurried conference. Then, with an excited clicking and snapping of fingers, they formed themselves into a long line. The hand nearest the door braced himself and, as soon as he was ready, the next one ran up to him and leapt up on to the tips of his fingers. The third followed suit, ending up on the tips of the second. The rest followed, clambering up their companions until there was a tall column of hands reaching right up to the door-handle. The top hand bowed like a circus acrobat to the swarm below, waved its fingers to them, then turned and grasped the handle. The column weaved and wobbled as the upper hand twisted, but it managed to take the strain. With a deep grinding noise the door began to open inwards. The column of hands collapsed and scattered.

A strong blast of hot, damp air shot out of the doorway from the steamy interior, nearly suffocating Jason. The heat was almost unbearable and the stench was worse than ever. Swarming round the cage, the great crowd of little hands triumphantly lifted their heavy burden and marched through into the palatial chamber beyond, pushing the door shut behind them.

'At last, at last,' hissed a savage, spine-tingling voice. 'The hand-luggage is here at last. I have been made to wait too long. I shall secrete a sharp revenge for this.'

The hands became abject and desperate, wringing themselves together. They set the cage down carefully in the centre of the ornately decorated floor and formed themselves into pairs. Flattening their palms together, each pair began to bow, while at the same time they shuffled backwards, retreating humbly from the room.

Jason looked up. He could not believe his eyes. There, reclining regally on a mound of brightly coloured cushions, was Ludo. Could it have been *her* voice that he had heard a moment ago? She was lying lazily on one elbow, nonchalantly nibbling small blue fruits which she selected from a bowl that grew out of the yellow and green shell of a two-headed, two-tailed turtle. The turtle was wandering about amongst the cushions with great difficulty. As Jason watched, it tripped and spilled a few of the fruits. There was a sharp hiss and a long, pointed tongue shot out and slapped it hard. It rolled over and disappeared with a crash beyond the edge of the cushions, scattering the blue fruit in all directions.

The owner of the tongue gave vent to a nasty, panting laugh and stretched himself luxuriously. From where Jason was crouching inside his cage he could see little of the long-tongued creature's body. All that was visible, to the right of Ludo, was a hideous paw and part of a scaly arm, the bulge of a scaly belly and a thin, whip-like tail that curled round on itself at its tip. Ludo appeared to be fascinated by her new companion and was smiling in his direction.

'Ludo!' shouted Jason. 'Ludo, thank goodness you're here. Tell your friend to let me out of this contraption. My legs are twisted. Hurry, *please.*'

Ludo turned and gazed at him, then burst out laughing.

'Listen, it talks, it is trying to say something,' she said, smiling at the monster next to her.

A slender, vicious-looking face rose from behind the mountain of cushions at Ludo's side. Its round, glass-hard, lemon yellow eyes fixed Jason with an unblinking stare. From under a scaly nose-shield it uncurled a long, spindly proboscis and held it out, quivering, in his direction. As it weaved back and forth in the steaming air, testing Jason's scent, the heavy, hinged scales covering the creature's head began to rise and fall like the feathers of a parrot's crest. The needle-thin teeth protruding from the hard line of its expressionless mouth clicked against one another in a frightening way. Jason shrank back as far as the bars of his cage would allow.

'So it does,' hissed the monster. '*So* it does. It speaks. Say something, you slag, you scaleless slime, you piece of indescribable dirt,' and he heaved himself up into a better position to study his newly acquired pet.

Jason could see the rest of him now, but in a way he wished he couldn't. The creature was covered in scales and spines and bony frills and appeared to have the body of a fat, pot-bellied serpent, with bloated alligator limbs. The grotesquely swollen trunk and

The Root Forest

limbs made a sharp contrast with his slender head, his whip-like tail and his long, thin paws. He seemed to be a hopelessly misshapen being and Jason wondered if he was ever able to leave the soft support of the mound of cushions.

'Let me out of this cage,' Jason shouted. The monster hissed and spluttered with delight.

'Go on, go on,' he panted. 'Don't stop. This is delicious.' But Jason remained silent, thinking hard.

'An intriguing specimen,' said Ludo, leaning forward with feigned interest. 'Rare, I would say.'

'Medium rare for me,' hissed the monster, cackling inanely and writhing his tail. 'Look, look, it's going to speak again.'

'I have a message for you from the Sculptor,' called Jason, hoping that the magic name would have some effect. But Ludo leant nearer to the scaly head and Jason just managed to hear her whisper:

'It is only a trick. Take no notice.'

'Ludo,' he cried. 'What are you doing? What has happened? Why are you pretending not to know me? Help me, please, help me.'

'Another trick,' murmured Ludo and the monster nodded knowingly. Breathing heavily, he slithered himself forward to the edge of the cushions and stared hard at the cage.

'Show me your hands,' he gasped, panting for breath.

Ludo watched with an amused expression. Jason hesitated, then reluctantly pushed his arms out through the bars towards the scaly head. The long proboscis uncurled again and the slender tip nosed around, over his outstretched fingers.

'Good, firm hands, yes. They will do very well indeed. We will lop them off tonight. We haven't had a hand-out ceremony for ages. Makes my scales curl to think of it. Delicious, delicious.'

Jason found it hard to take in what the monster was saying. His brain had frozen.

'Don't like his feet much, though. No grasp there. No good for fetching and carrying. Shan't bother with those. Mustn't lower our standards.'

Inrock

Jason's brain cleared. Ludo had betrayed him. He was trapped and soon he was to be sacrificed or, at the very least, mutilated to provide more hand-servants for this grotesque monster. Something had to be done and done quickly. Without thinking further, he grabbed out suddenly and took hold of the twitching proboscis. The monster screeched with pain as he felt his sensitive nose being dragged through the bars and into the cage. Working swiftly with his fingers, Jason tied the proboscis into a tight knot around one of the bars.

'Hi, you, hairy one, what's-your-name, Ludo, get me out of this,' screamed the monster, lashing his whip-like tail wildly across the ornately patterned floor.

Ludo clambered down from the cushions and surveyed the scene.

'My dear Mha-kee,' she said seriously, 'O lofty and powerful one, O ruler of a million scales, I fear you are caught.'

'Now's your chance,' shouted Jason. 'Open the cage. Hurry up before he calls for help. Stop fooling around.'

Ludo appeared to take no notice. She examined the monster's twisted nose closely.

'If I try to loosen you, O merciless one, O prince of all the forest, it will trap me, too. I dare not reach towards your regal nasal organ, or we shall both become the victims of this noxious, naked-skinned thing.'

The monster roared and writhed. His proboscis was turning pale green and fraying at the knotted edges.

'Ludo, please,' begged Jason. 'Don't just stand there!'

'I have an idea,' said Ludo suddenly, kneeling down beside the hissing body, whose blunt claws were working clumsily at his trapped nose without success. 'I will call the hand-servants back. They will rescue you from the clutches of this insolent, scaleless trash.'

'Ludo,' roared Jason. 'Come back!' But she was already walking towards the huge door and turning the heavy green handle. Peering out through the open doorway, she stamped her foot several times.

The Root Forest

The hand-servants swarmed in, squeaking and clicking their nails. They rushed over to the cage and began tearing at it with their fingers. In a few minutes the bars lay scattered on the floor and the groaning monster clambered painfully back on to his great pile of cushions, clutching his aching nose. Jason scrambled free of the shell of the cage and tried to drag himself towards the open door, but the hands swarmed over him and held him down. They pulled at his arms and legs until he was stretched out, spread-eagled on the ground. He heaved and twisted, but they held firm. As soon as one group of hands became exhausted and sank to the floor with limply curled fingers, another wave pushed eagerly forward to take their place.

'Hold it up,' hissed the monster. 'I want to see its face.' The hands stiffened and went to work, straining and shoving until Jason's body was dragged across to a wooden screen between two pillars, heaved up, and held securely in place. Stretched out tightly on the lattice-work, he was once again a helpless prisoner. The bright, glassy eyes of the Mha-kee of the Root Forest glinted at him. There was a long, dank, steamy silence. The swarm of hands waited expectantly for some new order from their master. Eventually, Ludo spoke:

'My dear Mha-kee,' she asked, 'how do you deal with cases of this sort?'

'They are not common,' hissed the monster. 'We have no set procedure. I shall have to devise something special to suit the occasion.' He fell silent again. After what seemed to Jason like an eternity, he hissed:

'Usually we simply cut off their hands and send them to the Hand-stitcher. He tests the fingers and, if he approves, he sews up the wrists and moulds on a pair of claws. Where these fit on to the wrist he inserts a small mouth and onto the centre of the palm he grafts an eye. After about a week they have recovered and can be put to work. I have about seven hundred hands at present, but some are getting old and weak and rather wrinkled. I am always on the look-out for new specimens.'

'After you have sliced off the hands,' asked Ludo casually,

'what do you do with the rest of the body?'

'We feed it to the old hands,' replied the Mha-kee, sinking back into the cushions and popping a blue fruit into his toothy mouth. 'It's very economical. No waste. No mess. All very neat and convenient.'

'You only use naked hands?' asked Ludo.

'Of course! We Scalies are not barbarians. It would be unthinkable to touch another Scaly. Hideous, disgusting. We are far too sensitive for that. And as for furry ones, like yourself, well you, of course, are our honoured guests.'

'Naturally, naturally,' murmured Ludo. 'I quite understand.'

'It is only the lowly, naked things that can be treated in this way without distressing our finer feelings,' hissed the Mha-kee, munching some more of the fruits. 'They have very poorly developed systems, you know. They hardly feel any pain at all. Or so the Stitcher assures us.'

'But this one has caused pain, even if it cannot feel it,' Ludo reminded him, smiling blandly.

'Yesssss,' hissed the Mha-kee in a long-drawn-out breath. 'I have not forgotten that. There will be a special ceremony tonight. Something you will not forget in a hurry, my dear Ludo. An exquisite experience, I promise you. But now I must rest. This has been so fatiguing. We will retire to the steam-rocks for a hand-massage and then sleep and digest our food. Come.'

They withdrew beyond the mound of cushions and Jason was left alone, except for the swarm of clutching hands. So Ludo was not his friend after all. She had deliberately brought him here to his death. The Root Forest was to be his final destination, where only his hands would live on, slaving and struggling for this hideous, scaly tyrant. He sighed and let his body sag against the wooden framework. There was no point in struggling. All he could do was wait.

CHAPTER TEN
The Skin Tomb

Exhausted, Jason dozed fitfully. As if in a dream he saw Ludo gliding noiselessly towards him, smiling.

'Jason,' she whispered, 'keep your voice low. Don't call out.' He jerked his head up with a start. He was not dreaming. It really *was* Ludo. 'Listen carefully. The Mha-kee is asleep and I managed to slip away. I couldn't speak before. If he had even the slightest suspicion that we are together, he would kill both of us. I'm sorry, I seem to have got us into rather a mess, but I'll do something, somehow. I don't know what. We'll have to wait and take our chance later. The whole place is guarded by seven-headed snakes. Trust me. I'll find a way out. Forgive me.'

'And forgive me.'

'Forgive you? What for?'

'For thinking that . . . oh, it doesn't matter. Just forgive me, that's all.'

Ludo shrugged. 'Whatever you thought, I more than deserved it.'

'Why can't we try and get away now?' whispered Jason urgently. 'Together we could overpower these hands, couldn't we?'

'I doubt it, and anyway he has left a heavy guard around the palace while he is sleeping. They may come in at any moment and inspect you. If we tried anything now, we'd lose our advantage. We must wait until later tonight.'

'But what about the ceremony? . . . I shall be punished and then killed, eaten by these revolting hands that keep swarming over me. We can't wait.'

'Trust me,' urged Ludo. 'Trust me. I'll think of something before then,' and she was gone. An agonizing doubt swept across Jason's mind. Could he really trust Ludo? Should he try to get away now, on his own? He was on the verge of making one last, gargantuan effort to twist an arm free, when he heard a slithering noise behind him. He froze and waited.

Something was passing slowly between his legs, brushing against his skin. Then, as it reared up in front of him, he saw it and cried out. The seven heads of the great serpent waved gently before his face. Seven tongues, each with a three-pronged, forked tip, flickered out and fluttered against him.

His cry echoed around the palace. As she lay down quietly on her steam-rock alongside the slumbering bulk of the scaly Mha-kee, Ludo shuddered at the sound. Should she go to him again now? What were they doing to him? The monster stirred and Ludo quickly closed her eyes. Jason's distant cry seared into her fur. She grasped her horns in her hands, screwed up her face and clenched her teeth. Tonight. She must save him tonight.

Ludo lost all sense of time. It seemed hours before the Mha-kee roused himself and stretched.

'Ssssss-ou-arrrgh,' yawned the great reptile. 'Food. Bring me food!' As if by magic, tall, crested lizards appeared, hopping on their hind legs. Balancing on their spiky tails, they held out flat stones crawling with insects. The Mha-kee flicked his tongue over the surface of the stones, scooping up the seething mass of bugs. In a few moments they had all vanished and the crested lizards quietly withdrew.

'Appetizing. Most appetizing. Cloak me!' he shouted, and two of the lizards reappeared bearing a huge, multi-coloured cape.

The Skin Tomb

Hurriedly, but with experienced care, they draped it around his steaming body. Others then came forward carrying what looked like a portable hammock and heaved the monster into it. Forming a procession, they set off, hissing in unison, one hiss per step.

Ludo followed them in the direction of the main throne room. As they entered, she looked anxiously around. Jason was still in the same position, but his face was drawn and haggard.

'His face,' Ludo gasped.

'What about his face?' snapped the Mha-kee.

'Nothing, really. It is different. That is all.'

'Hmmm. Strange. Now I wonder why you should care about a small thing like that?' hissed the Mha-kee, slithering out of the hammock and on to the mountain of cushions.

'I don't *care* about his face. I was simply making an observation. Nothing more,' objected Ludo, realizing that she could easily land herself in difficulty if her thoughts became too transparent.

'Rubbish, we only observe those things that have special meaning for us. No one *ever* studies *anything* unless, in some way or other, they are deeply emotionally involved with it. Don't you agree, my dear Ludo?'

'Yes, of course, you are right as always, O glorious one, and I see that I must confess. In truth . . . I . . . I am looking forward perhaps too greedily to making a meal of that face before the night is out, provided, of course, that the hands can spare it when they come to divide up the body after the hand-lopping is over. It is the tastiest, juiciest face I have seen for many a season, and my concern was simply that you may have had it hanging for too long, so that it is beginning to shrink and become withered and dried up. That, I confess, was my true interest, but, as your humble guest, I felt it was impertinent of me to mention it.'

'Not at all, not at all. So you feed on faces, do you? Quite remarkable. Do you prefer them smiling or frowning?' asked the Mha-kee, now completely at his ease again.

'Contorted. But then, when it comes to the crunch, one has little choice.'

'You eat them alive, then?'

'Of course, they lose their blush so quickly.'

'Extraordinary. You really must visit me more often. I am quite starved of sophisticated, civilized company these days. But enough of this chatter. Let us proceed. We are wasting valuable time.'

The crested lizards hopped over to the great doors and flung them wide. A waiting crowd burst in. They were all Scalies of varying designs and proportions. Slipping, hissing and pushing, they scattered into the corners of the throne room and poised themselves expectantly.

'Punishment!' screeched the Mha-kee. 'Punishment is the great cleanser. Punishment makes pure again.' Without looking at Jason, he went on: 'You slimy, scaleless skin-bag, you have dared to inflict grievous nasal harm on this royal and godly person. You shall suffer the highest penalty known to my court, prior to your ceremonial handing-over. I condemn you to a Static Whirl, the sentence to be carried out forthwith and with force. Summon the musicians.'

Excited hissing and gasping filled the throne room. Slender bodies began to undulate and convulse in agitated anticipation.

'O slithery and wondrous one, O awesome and astounding one,' said Ludo, speaking as calmly as she could . . .

'Yes, yes. Go on, go on. Don't stop! I love it, I love it,' hissed the Mha-kee, settling himself regally amongst his cushions to await the court musicians.

'O fearsome figurehead, O sumptuous sultan, O noble nabob, O majestic monarch, O . . . '

'More! More! It's curling my scales. More!'

'O glorious grand-vizier, O stately sovereign, O princely potentate, O dreaded dictator, O magnificent mikado, O opulent overlord, O . . . '

'I am dying of pride. More, more, more!'

'O tsar of all the forests, rajah of the reptiles, caesar of the cold-blooded, slide-ruler of the serpents, chancellor of the crocodilians, doyen of the dinosaurs, leader of the lizards, O supreme highness of the steaming world of scalies, O despot, O

The Skin Tomb

beloved Mha-kee . . . '

'Oh! What delight! What poetry! Pure, pure poetry. I am so moved I think I may shed a skin. Silence, everyone. Our honoured visitor has a question to put to my royal person. Well, go on, spit it out.'

'I . . . I've forgotten what it was. Oh yes, I remember . . . can you tell me, what, exactly, is a Static Whirl?'

'Yes, of course, you are unfamiliar with this type of sentence. It takes the form of a dance, performed by the royal, seven-headed serpents — here they are now — and what a dance! They are hypnotic, you know, quite fascinating.'

'But how will this punish the offender? I don't see that . . . '

'He will be held firm by the hand-servants. He will be unable to move.' The whole court groaned at the Mha-kee's words, but Ludo was still puzzled. 'The prisoner will be compelled to join them but will be unable to move a muscle. The agony this will cause him is beyond description.'

'I see,' nodded Ludo, beginning to understand at last.

'It is a sentence of denial, the worst sort. Here in the Root Forest our greatest punishment is not being able to do something we want to do. There is no stronger pain. It is fitting, particularly fitting in the present case. I am ready. Is he facing the music? Good, good. Let the dance begin.'

Sinuous sounds whined and hummed through the great hall of the palace and from the dark corners slid the glistening shapes of the long, muscular serpents. They reared up rhythmically and slowly began to curve and twist their powerful bodies to the beat of the music. As the pace quickened, their undulations became more and more frenzied until they were whirling round and weaving back and forth with such hypnotic force that Ludo felt herself being drawn on to the floor with them. All the other members of the court were swaying too, helplessly swinging their bodies in time with the mesmeric music.

Suddenly, a scaly, shell-less turtle screamed and started to spin round and round. Other reptilian shapes followed suit, whirling and twisting faster and faster until they lost control. Ludo was caught up in the pulsating rhythm now, with all thoughts of Jason's plight spun from her mind. She felt herself flinging her body round, laughing and shouting and screaming and chanting with the beat. Even the Mha-kee himself was heaving and rolling, turning over and over on his soft mound of cushions.

As she spun like a wobbling top, Ludo heard through the haze of her hypnosis a great roaring cry of pain. Struggling desperately to collect her thoughts, a memory of Jason flashed through her brain.

'Jason!' she shouted, risking everything. 'Jason, I can't stop, I can't stop. Where are you?' His blurred shape was flickering by as she continued to spin, but she could make out no details, only a vague image of a writhing body held firmly in place by a sea of hands.

With a crash the music stopped and the entire court collapsed, twitching and jerking, to the ground. For a moment Ludo lay there panting in the steamy heat, then raised herself painfully on one elbow. Jason was not moving. His body was unnaturally twisted and his head had fallen forwards, half-hiding his contorted face. As she watched, he went limp and fainted. She scrambled over to his side.

'Oh, that was good,' murmured the Mha-kee's voice from beneath a confused jumble of cushions. 'That was *gooood*.'

Luckily for Ludo, no one seemed to have noticed her cry to Jason during the dance. She was still safe, but there was no time to lose. Jason was still in one piece, but it was hard to say how much damage the Static Whirl had done him. She should have acted before, not waited and waited. But what could she have done? More important, what could she do now?

'I think I am game for another,' hissed the Mha-kee, struggling up to survey his sprawling court. 'Another Whirl, everyone? Good, good. Let's step up the heat-bugs and then we'll all go out of our steamy little minds.'

'But it's boiling already,' protested Ludo, whose face was lathered in sweat.

'Switch on the stand-by heat-bugs,' roared the Mha-kee,

The Skin Tomb

ignoring her. 'We must have more heat if we are to dance faster.'

This gave Ludo an idea. If the hotter air would speed up their reptilian bodies, then it followed that the cold night air of the forest outside the palace would slow them down. Glancing up, she could see that the dome of the throne room was made up of clear crystal panes. Dragging herself over to a low slab, she picked up a heavy stone cup and, without hesitating for a second, hurled it upwards with all her force. It smashed a jagged hole in the crystal roof and immediately there was a tremendous inrush of what, by contrast to the steamy interior, felt like icy-cold air.

'Temperature alarm!' shrieked the courtiers, struggling to their scaly feet. 'Temperature alarm! All hands to the roof!' But it was too late. Even as the army of hands scrambled into action, the giant reptilian figure of the Mha-kee and the stumbling bodies of his followers were sinking rapidly into a sagging, torpid condition, their movements becoming increasingly sluggish until they stopped altogether.

Stepping over the immobile figures scattered around the floor, unheeded by the frantically busy hands, Ludo quickly reached Jason's now collapsed form and dragged him outside into a corridor. The cool air that had helped to quell the reptiles had the opposite effect on Jason, and he soon revived, helped along by slaps from Ludo's furry hands.

'Come on, wake up, wake up. Now's our chance, while the hands are all working on the roof. Oh, wake up, please.'

Jason staggered to his feet and was half-dragged and half-carried by Ludo into a curved side-passage with branches going in all directions.

'Which way, which way?' gasped Jason, finding his voice for the first time since the ordeal of the Static Whirl.

'Down there, quick. It leads to the Skin Tomb, the place where the Mha-kee's old skins are kept.'

They ran, as fast as Jason could manage, down a winding tunnel. At the far end was a massive bronze door, studded with coloured jewels fashioned to look like reptilian scales. In the centre of the door was a heavy knocker carved in the shape of the

Mha-kee's head. Ludo knocked four times and the door swung open slowly, creaking and groaning.

'I'll oil it tomorrow, I'll oil it tomorrow. I know I've said that before, but this time I will. I promise. I promise faithfully. Just a minute . . . ' The Skin Tomb-keeper blinked at them, realizing for the first time that they were strangers. 'Who are you? What do you want?' He was a small, sleepy-looking creature with white scales and pink, bleary eyes.

'Don't worry,' whispered Ludo to Jason. 'The Mha-kee told me about this place. I know what to do.' Turning to the Tomb-keeper, she said in an urgent tone: 'The Mha-kee is shedding his skin . . . sooner than expected . . . he has been over-eating . . . we have been sent as special envoys to start making preparations for the burial. Are the burrowing snakes ready?'

'Oh, lawd, no. Nothing's ready. Shedding now, is he? Oh, lawd. But . . . but he *can't* be. He's not due for at least another week. Oh, lawd.'

'Stop fussing, we know that. That's why we're here, to give you some help. Show us the way to the new chamber.'

'Oh, lawd. Oh, my lawd. It'll never be ready. You'd better come and look,' complained the bleary Tomb-keeper, shuffling off down a side corridor.

Jason and Ludo exchanged glances, rapidly entered the main hall of the Skin Tomb, and heaved the massive door back into position. Catching up with the Tomb-keeper and following him through the maze of passages, they kept silent, each trying frantically to remember the number of turns, to left and to right, which they had taken. They passed many doors, each one decorated with an image of the Mha-kee, carved in snake-stone and encrusted with scale-shaped jewels.

'Fifty-one, fifty-two, here we are . . . fifty-three,' said the Tomb-keeper. 'It's his fifty-third shedding coming up, and if he goes on gorging himself like this and splitting at the seams before he's due, he'll simply have to give me a new set of burrowers. These are nearly worn out.'

The Skin Tomb

He flung open the door and a hissing grumble started up inside. The fifty-third chamber was only half-dug and loose rubble lay scattered across the uneven floor. A bunch of burrowing snakes, twined together in the corner, lazily uncoiled themselves and began thrusting half-heartedly at the jagged walls.

'You see what I mean?' moaned the Tomb-keeper. 'They don't even bother to corkscrew any longer. Get on with it, you dozy twisters!'

The snakes reluctantly spiralled themselves up and pressed more vigorously into the walls, spinning round like drills.

'That's better! That's more like it.' He wiped his nose with a black lace handkerchief. 'Got to keep them at it. Can't take my smarting eyes off them for a second.'

'We'll watch them for you. You go and get some rest. You look as though you could do with it,' said Ludo in a friendly voice.

'Oh, yes, I could, I could. That's most civil of you. Thank you. Thank you. You know where to find me if you want me,' and he shuffled gratefully away.

'Now what?' asked Jason, swaying slightly on his legs.

'You look terrible. Stay here and watch them. I'll be back in a moment,' and Ludo darted out into the corridor. Jason heard noises coming from outside and hoped they would not alert the Tomb-keeper. Before long Ludo reappeared, dragging a huge, dried skin with her.

'It's his last shedding,' she explained, 'so it's reasonably fresh. If we wrap it around ourselves and walk straight out of here we should look enough like the Mha-kee to be able to escape.'

'We'll never get away with it.'

'It's the best I can do, Jason,' said Ludo desperately. 'It's our only hope. I know you are exhausted, but there's no other way. You take the back legs. Bend forward, hold on to me, come on, hurry.'

The Tomb-keeper was snoring contentedly as they passed through the main hall, dragged open the tall entrance door, and stepped boldly outside. To their relief, the air in the palace was still cool and its inhabitants remained dazed and inert.

They heard a scrabbling sound coming from the throne room, where an army of tired hands, some of them wearing gloves against the cold, were still struggling to repair the hole in the roof.

'This way,' whispered Ludo, and dragged the half-conscious Jason behind her towards the source of the sound.

The hands froze in astonishment at the sight of their master, glowering at them from the throne room doorway.

'Stop that immediately!' hissed Ludo. 'Conduct me to the edge of the forest. Hurry, or I will bite your nails to the quick.'

The hands hesitated, looking first at the real Mha-kee, sprawled torpid on his cushions, and then at this new apparition that was threatening them from the doorway. Some of them began to strum nervously.

'If you disobey, your knuckles will be skinned, your thumbs screwed and your fingers broken. Now move!'

With a shudder, the hands snapped into action, scampering off as fast as they could go and leaving the gaping hole in the roof unattended, the cold air pouring in.

'That should give us a good start,' said Ludo confidently, as they struck out into the forest, the sea of hands clearing the path before them and guiding them down a safe hollow, free from the clinging root-tendrils.

At the edge of the forest the false Mha-kee turned to the assembled hands and Ludo spoke to them.

'Now listen carefully. I have an announcement to make. You have worked well and I will grant a free pardon to all hands if one of you — any one of you — can direct me to the place of the Golden Worms. Before the Stitcher converted you, you belonged to many owners and you came from many lands. Among you there must be one who knows the place I speak of. If he comes forward, without delay, you will all be free to do as you wish and you need never work for me again. If he stays silent, your slavery will continue forever.'

Ludo and Jason held their breath, while the hands fidgeted and whispered. Then, from the back of the throng, a gnarled old fist pushed his way out, spat and bowed.

The Skin Tomb

'I heard long ago,' said the fist, 'of an island out in the Long Lake, where the head-hunters live. On it, so they said, there was a golden box full of Golden Worms, and on special days the islanders wore the Golden Worms around their necks and . . . but that was long ago . . . and . . . that's all I can tell you.'

'No one else?' hissed Ludo. 'Can no one add to that?'

The throng was silent until a tiny, chubby hand piped up:

'I was told that the Golden Worms live inside the Sculptor's helmet,' and everyone tittered nervously.

An even smaller hand, little more than a midget monkey-paw, then stepped forward and squeaked:

'*I* was told that the Golden Worms live in the Mha-kee's pillows,' and the sea of hands rippled with high-pitched giggles.

'I *am* the Mha-kee, you foolish paw, and if the Golden Worms were in the Root Forest I would certainly know about it. Now stop this nonsense or I shall have you squeezed until the sweat pours from the pores of your poor paw. Silence, and listen, all of you. You have little to tell me, but I am lenient. You have shown willing. You have tried your best and that is enough. You are all granted a free pardon. Now go . . . the Root Forest is yours.'

There was wild cheering. The great throng of hands formed into pairs and clapped loudly. The false Mha-kee nodded, turned and walked regally off into the distance. The hands shook one another warmly, waved happily to the departing figure, and then began to scatter into the undergrowth.

When they were well out of sight of the forest, Jason and Ludo threw off the Mha-kee's skin, buried it under the pink sand and struck off into the desert. After several miles they came to a dried-up river-bed and slid down into it. Jason was feeling much stronger, the exercise having relieved the cramps his limbs had suffered during the ordeal of the Static Whirl. Ludo, however, was worn out. The strain of the escape from the palace was beginning to show. They rested in the shade of a curved rock.

'What do you think about the answers the hands gave?' asked Jason. 'Do they mean anything to you?'

'Well, I'm not sure. No one took the last two seriously for a minute, but that old fist may be on to something. There *is* a Long Lake and there *are* some islands on it, but nobody I know has ever been there. One end of the lake is quite near here, but they say no one has ever found the other end. It must be, oh, a hundred miles away, at least. So the islands could be any distance, anything from one mile to a hundred.'

'Are there any boats?'

'Yes, there is a small fishing port at this end of the lake. We could try there, if you think it's worth it.'

'We have nothing better to go on.'

'That's true. Right. The lake it is then. But I must warn you, I can't swim very far. My fur gets waterlogged and I start sinking.'

'Then we'll have to find a good strong boat.'

'Or make one,' said Ludo. 'We'll see. But I think we'd better spend the night here and make a move in the morning. It's sheltered and there are some logs over there covered in soft twigs.'

They tried to break off the twigs for bedding, but found that they refused to snap. In the end they gave up the struggle, lay down on top of the logs and were soon sleeping soundly. As they dreamt of boats and islands and golden boxes full of Golden Worms, a trickle of water snaked around the curve of the dusty river-bed and crawled noiselessly in their direction.

CHAPTER ELEVEN
The Long Lake Port

'Dee dum dee dum-dummmmmm.'

Jason and Ludo awoke to the sound of a deep, singing voice.

'Dee dum dee dum-dummmmmm,' sang the voice. 'Dee dum dee dum-dummmmmm. *Good* morning, good morning. Can I sell you any luck on this bright, lovely day?'

They sat up, squinting against the bright light. Their sleeping-logs were slipping gently along on the surface of the now swollen river, which had mysteriously flooded during the night. Floating beside them on his back was a large brown beast with two heads and a tray of pebbles on his belly.

'Where are we?' asked Ludo, clinging nervously to her log, 'and where did all this water come from?'

'You are not far from Lo-la-po,' replied the brown beast in a friendly tone, 'and the water is here because of the crack in the dam. I know, because I cracked it. With one of these lucky pebbles, actually. Want to buy one?'

'But there are pebbles everywhere,' said Jason sleepily. 'We only have to pick them up off the ground. Why should we want to buy one from you?'

'Because *these* are lucky pebbles, that's why. *These* aren't just any old pebbles. Oh dear me no. I had to dive two thousand feet into Long Lake to dredge these up. They're special. What colour would you like? Puce? That's flea-coloured. Pale Sludge? Or perhaps this one in Off-mud?'

'What do they do?' asked Ludo, sniffing in their direction.

'They bring bad luck,' said the brown beast. 'Not to you, of course, silly, to your enemies. You throw one of these and *crack*! Can I interest you in this dark green one? Very strong material, very bad luck indeed, this one.'

'How much?' asked Jason, hoping that, if he bought it, he could get the over-friendly creature to go away and leave them in peace.

'What have you got?'

'I'll give you one of these,' said Jason, feeling inside the pouch on his belt for a desert crystal. He pulled out a small yellow one and handed it over.

'But . . . but this is merely common-or-desert sweat-glass. There are thousands of bits like this, all over the pink desert,' complained the brown beast.

'Oh no,' retorted Jason, 'that one came from the site of the greatest niar-storm the Inrock has ever witnessed. I have been offered great riches for that crystal. Why, only the other day, the Mha-kee of the Root Forest offered to exchange all his hand-servants for it, so that he could have it embedded in the centre of the main door to his Royal Skin Tomb.'

'*That* old rogue! I heard someone had frozen his assets. Still, he knows his crystals. Oh, all right, very well,' and, grumbling to himself, the brown beast reluctantly handed over the green pebble. His two heads both squinted closely at the small, yellow object. 'I suppose it's a fair exchange.'

'Unbelievably fair,' replied Jason, studying the rather dull-looking pebble for a moment and then pushing it into his belt-pouch.

Throughout the transaction, he had been talking only to the brown beast's left head. The one on the creature's right side had remained silent, apparently uninterested, except for a brief glance at the crystal.

The Long Lake Port

'Does your right head ever speak?' asked Jason, trying to make polite conversation, since their companion showed no sign of departing.

'Very little. I'm left-headed. Always have been. But he thinks a lot for me, and when I'm alone he's someone to talk to, even if he doesn't reply very often.'

'Are you a full-time pebble-diver, or is it only a hobby?'

'By profession I am a Disruptor and Disorganizer – and much in demand, I may say. The pebbles are merely a side-line. They come in very handy for smashing and cracking – like the dam. Oh, that was beautiful, beautiful – there's going to be chaos at Lo-la-po when this flood reaches there.'

'Where is Lo-la-po?'

'Lo-la-po? Didn't I tell you? It's my home town. Oh, yes, of course, you won't know the code. Well, the full name is Long Lake Port, but it's a local custom to shorten all the names. We take the first two letters of each word and put them together. Long becomes Lo, Lake becomes la, and Port becomes po – making Lo-la-po. Simple. Try it on your own name and see what you get. It's fun.'

'But what's wrong with Long Lake Port? It's a good name,' insisted Jason, 'and it doesn't really take much longer to say it. I can't see the point.'

'It's because there was never enough room on the forms.'

'What forms?'

'Oh, you know. Pebble permits, Water-knot licences, things like that. There are hundreds of them. We are always being given new forms to fill in, fill out, or fill up, and there was never, never enough space on them for the names, professions or addresses. The Form-makers do it on purpose, of course. It's their only tiny little taste of power, you see, but we fooled them by shortening the names of everything. They were furious, naturally, but they knew it was useless to retaliate – making the spaces even smaller – because we'd only go to initials if they did. Several of them have gone and jumped into the lake and drowned themselves. Very satisfying. So now, instead of people having to call out to me:

"Hallo there, Disruptor and Disorganizer" — what a terrible mouthful that was! — they can shout: "Hallo there, Di-di." Much nicer. And now I welcome you to Lo-la-po. You must be my guests and tonight we'll celebrate the cracking of the dam.'

'But won't you be attacked for flooding the town?'

'Attacked! Attacked? Whatever for? I shall be given a hero's welcome. They *live* for my exploits. How would they survive without them? They would die of boredom. If it weren't for me, life in Lo-la-po would be perfect — calm, peaceful, serene, and utterly, utterly boring. They'd go out of their conventional minds. Every go-ahead community has its Di-di. We are idols! They put up statues to us, write songs about us. Attacked, indeed!'

'How do you go about it? I mean, apart from cracking dams?'

'Well, there are two methods: the indirect and the direct. The indirect is safer, but less fun, decidedly less fun. I start rumours, for instance, stir up trouble between rivals, that kind of thing. One of my specialities is what I call "up-the-losers". I find some small band of rebels — a protest group, strikers, do-gooders, mutineers, reformers, or what-have-you. Then I secretly give them my support, back them up in any way I can. They are usually poorly organized and, of course, they don't really want to win at all, because intuitively they know that, if they do, they will have ruined their way of life — you can't go on protesting after you have won, can you? So I move in and put some fire and drive into their movement until I have stirred them up into a frenzy. Then, at last, they become a *real* nuisance and have to be put down with force by everyone else. There are terrible demonstrations and counter-demonstrations, leading to rioting, looting, brutality and lots of lovely blood. Everyone *adores* it. It's like a carnival, only with more pepper in it. I get a lot of praise in such cases and, if I'm lucky, I even become a cult figure for a time.'

'What's that?'

'I'm not sure, but they put up lots of posters showing my faces. Most gratifying. All the same, I prefer the direct method personally. There's more style in it, more immediate satisfaction. Let me give you a demonstration . . .' and, without even turning his heads to watch, he hurled a large, flat pebble at the river-bank. It struck the base of a tall, rickety-looking, wooden tower they happened to be passing. The tower groaned, swayed and then collapsed in a splintering mass, scattering its occupants on the ground and bursting into flames.

'You're crazy!' shouted Jason. 'They'll be furious. You can't tell me they are going to thank you for *that*?'

'Oh, no, not them. *They* will be too . . . involved, you might say.'

'Yes, I might.'

'But think of the fun their neighbours will have. They'll have the cheap thrill of putting out the flames, the pious joy of being helpful to the homeless, and the superior pleasure of feeling more secure and better off themselves. I can just hear them now: "Quick, quick, there's a fire. Whoopee!" And then, "Oh you poor dears, you're half-dead, how dreadful for you, how simply simply awful!" And then, "Thank *goodness* it wasn't us. I always said their scruffy old house was a fire-risk, and an eye-sore, too, although I don't like to speak ill of the afflicted!" . . . and so on. They'll *love* me for it, the lousy spinks. *And* they'll be able to talk about it for weeks. Do you realize that, if it weren't for me, there would be no startling news, no spicy gossip, no awful scandals, no juicy chit-chat. It's unthinkable! Of course, it's a dangerous job. I mean, it needs care and cunning. If I were to go too far – to cause disasters instead of mere disruptions – they'd hang me by the necks with rope as joyfully as they now hang me with garlands. But I am an expert. If I do say so myself, I am . . . I . . . I . . . Oh!'

'What is it?' asked Jason, seeing the brown beast's expressions change suddenly to two of terror.

'Where did you say you were going?' was all he replied.

'We didn't,' said Ludo, 'but if you must know, we are making for one of the islands in the lake.'

'Which one? There are several.'

Ludo and Jason exchanged glances.

'The important one,' said Ludo.

'Ah, that will be Goffland,' muttered Di-di. 'Do you have a boat?'

'No, we . . . '

'Never mind, we'll use mine. I'll take you myself — for a fee, of course. We'll set sail immediately.'

'But I thought we were going to celebrate? I thought you were . . .'

'Change of plan — change of plan. No time like today. Procrastination is the thief of time, and all that. Never put off . . . never put off until tomorrow . . . You see those spires and towers sticking out of the water, there, up ahead, in the distance, with small figures clinging to them? That, er, that is, er, was Lo-la-po.'

'What he means,' snapped the right head, speaking for the first time, 'is that his latest little disruption has become a fully fledged disaster. The town is submerged. Everything is destroyed. I told him, but he wouldn't listen to me. Idiot!'

'Er, yes, well, it can't be helped. At least I had the good sense to anchor the boat well out in the lake. I *knew* there was a risk, but they were *so* bored. I had to do something spectacular.'

'Spectacular!' snorted right-head. 'Spectacular! We'll be lucky if they don't lynch us.'

Left-head's reply was to burst into song:

'The rainy day you're saving for is near, Oh, the rainy day you are saving for is here, I disrupt and I dismay, I destroy when I am at play, and my halo becomes a noose when it slips a *lit*tle way. Dum-dee-dumm dee-dum, oh, dum-dee-dumm dee-dum . . . dee-dum . . . dee-dum.'

'Raving lunatic!' spat right-head.

'Take no notice of him,' said left-head, 'he's always like this.' Then, turning to his better half, he boomed, 'Hold your breath, old sour-puss, we're going under.'

The river was widening out now and the swirling waters were muddy and full of floating debris, including accordions and archilutes, banjos and bassoons, cellos and castanets, drumsticks and doodlesacks, euphoniums and eagle-organs, flageolets and fipple-flutes, guitars and glockenspiels, harmonicas and horn-pipes, ilk-harps and instrument-cases, jenny-gongs and jambo-bases, kettle-drums and keyboards, lyres and lyrichords, marimbas and mandolins, nagaras and nota-fifes, oboes and ocarinas, pianos and piccolos, quitch-pipes and quaver-horns, recorders and rattlebones, sackbuts and spinets, tom-toms and tambourines, ukeleles and uniphones, violins and virginals, whistles and washboards, xylophones and xenochords, yodel-boxes and yardstick-tubas, zithers and zundle-cymbals, to mention only the musical detritus. Di-di was just about to duck his two heads beneath the water when he noticed the predominantly orchestral nature of the debris.

'Oh no!' groaned left-head.

'Oh yes!' snapped right-head, now visibly alarmed. 'You've done it this time. Trust you. You didn't know the Strummers were in town, did you? Eh? You didn't reckon on that, did you? Imbecile!'

'The Strummers? Who are the Strummers?' shouted Jason.

'They must have moved in last night,' moaned left-head. 'They are a band of wandering brigands, the scourge of the countryside. They are vicious, merciless, wanton. They stop at nothing. They strum everyone to death, without pity, and they smile, they never stop smiling, it's terrible, terrible. They must have swooped down in darkness and caught the town unawares. These things floating by, they are the Strummer's weapons. I am finished. They'll burst my ear-drums, they'll strum me to little pieces. Oh, wet is me!' And, as the sunken town sped past, Di-di grabbed the two logs to which Jason and Ludo were clinging, and disappeared beneath the murky surface of the swiftly moving water.

The tips of the submerged buildings flashed past, one by one, and Jason could see the stranded inhabitants of the town quite clearly, clinging to any handhold they could find, shouting and cursing and screaming for help. The brown beast remained completely submerged and Jason began to wonder whether perhaps he had lost his grip and been carried away, but as the logs swished through the town and spun out on to the choppy waters of the lake, two gasping heads popped up, gulped air greedily, and disappeared again.

When they were completely clear of the town, Di-di resurfaced and started looking frantically for the boat.

'There it is! Over there. The anchor's held and we are drifting straight towards it. Yippee! Jump, you two, when we get nearer, but watch out for the current. Jump this side of the boat, then you'll be carried to it.'

'But it's only a raft,' shouted Ludo. 'It's not a boat all.'

'That is a five-knot vessel, I'll have you know,' spluttered left-head. 'The fastest boat in Lo-la-po. Now jump. *Jump!*'

Clambering aboard the raft, the three of them watched as the two logs went careering off in the powerful drag of the flood waters.

'Make ready at the anchor,' bellowed Di-di, and both heads let out a piercing whistle. There was a flurry in the water at the front of the raft as he tugged ferociously at five lines that were attached there. Five glistening snouts appeared close by and began to give answering whistles. Then they turned and pointed out into the centre of the lake.

'Up anchor!' shouted Di-di. 'The Water-knots are standing by. Hurry, hurry. And once we are moving, keep well away from the stern of the raft there, or, with those flood-waters following us, you may be pooped. Now lift, lift, lift!'

With great difficulty Jason and Ludo heaved the anchor up. It was a huge shell and nearly rolled off again as soon as they had it on board, but at last they managed to make it secure and Di-di's two heads roared in unison:

'Full ahead five!'

The raft started to move forward, slowly at first and then faster and faster, until it was throwing up a foaming white wake.

'Splendid beasts,' yelled Di-di. 'Look at them go! What a team! Best on the lake. Nothing to stop us now.'

The five Water-knots, which looked to Jason like miniature whales with long frills of joined fins down their backs, were beating their tails wildly and heaving the makeshift vessel through the increasingly rough waters at terrifying speed. The striken port of Lo-la-po was already receding rapidly behind them.

The Long Lake Port

'I'm glad we have seen the last of the Strummers,' called Jason. 'They sounded rather unpleasant.'

'Sounded? Sounded? But you haven't even heard them. They are vile, hideous, diabolic, triabolic. May Grannits protect you from their wrath,' roared left-head.

'And what makes you think we have seen the last of them?' asked right-head dryly. 'What gives you that sweet, innocent little idea, eh? You're fools, all of you, all fools,' and, at this, both Di-di's heads subsided in a long, horizon-staring silence.

For hours they sped over the featureless expanse of the great lake, the Water-knots untiring in their efforts, until eventually night fell. After eating an unappetizing meal of things resembling limpets and barnacles, scraped from the bottom of the raft and carefully shelled, they settled down to await the dawn. Lulled by the gentle swaying of the raft, they slept soundly until, with a crash, they were awoken by a violent storm. The winds hissed and the waters raged around them. The anchor slipped overboard and was torn loose. As they clung on for their lives, they heard the Water-knots' lines snap, one by one.

The raft was spinning now and bucking like a tickled Flummel. Jason saw Ludo losing her grasp and struggled to move closer, but in doing so he was swept away into the darkness by a giant wave. As he began to sink, he felt his belt being grabbed from behind by a powerful snout and his body thrust upward to the surface. The last sensation he remembered was a gulp for air and spray dashing in his face.

CHAPTER TWELVE

The Island of Feathered Dwarfs

In the distance was a sound of hammering. At first, it seemed to be coming from behind and below Jason's throbbing ears, but, as he sat up, it slowly became clear that someone really *was* hammering and that it *was* in the distance and not inside him.

He was on dry land — well, wet land, but land for all that. Gentle waves were lapping around his hips. Only his legs were still immersed in the cruel waters of the Long Lake. As he dragged himself further up the white, sandy slope on which he had been lying — for who knows how long — he heard a whistling sound behind him and turned just in time to see a grinning Water-knot clapping its jaws, wiggling its frills and slapping its broad tail on the water in what appeared to be a signal of farewell.

'Thank you!' called Jason, as the now contented creature flipped gracefully out into the lake. 'Thank you, you saved my life.' A few more squeaks, a crackle, and a strange noise like a creaking door were the creature's only reply. It dived and vanished.

Jason surveyed the coastline. He appeared to be on a small,

rocky, and rather barren island. He looked around for Ludo and Di-di and called their names, but there was no answer and nothing stirred. In fact, there were no signs of life at all except for the distant hammering and he staggered soggily in that direction.

Skirting a rock, he came upon a feathered dwarf nailing a large notice on to a broken-down old notice-board. It read: 'Warning! Anyone wearing an undressed head on this beach will be arrested.'

Standing back to admire his handiwork, the feathered dwarf crashed into Jason and screamed. Ruffling his plumage and crouching low, he swivelled round, brandishing his hammer. Seeing Jason's bedraggled form, he lowered his arm and straightened up, settling his feathers, once again, sleekly against his body.

'Your head!' he screeched. 'Look at your head. It's a disgrace, a public disgrace. Read that notice. See what it says? Have you no shame, no sense of public decency, coming out here with your head undressed in that filthy, obscene manner?'

'I was nearly drowned. I . . . '

'That's what they all say, but it's no excuse. I shall have to arrest you, unless . . . '

'Unless?'

'Unless — oh dear — I shouldn't do this, but you do look rather sorry for yourself. Come over here,' and he led the way to a large bag he had left on the sand near the signpost. Snapping it open, he rummaged inside for a moment and produced a gaudy, decorated head topped with a fussy, flowered swimming-cap. 'You may not be my size, but we might as well try. Must help one another when we can, I suppose. Here, give me your old head and put this one on.' He glanced nervously up and down the deserted beach. 'It's strictly against regulations, but there's no one about and it will save me a long walk to the arresting station.'

'Put it on?'

'Yes, hurry up, give me your old head.'

'*Give* it to you?'

'Don't be dense. Hold on a minute, you're not a tourist from the mainland by any chance are you?'

'In a way, yes. I do come from the mainland.'

'Ah, well, that explains it. Then it is my duty to inform you that, as a visitor to Headland, you are required whilst here to abide by our local laws and customs. They include severe penalties for appearing in public places improperly headed – as *you* are at this moment, my dear sir. I suppose you're one of these new-fangled uni-heads?'

'Uni-heads?'

'Yes, these foul-mouthed young filthies who think they can go through life with a single head on their shoulders. It's revolting! Do you have any idea – any idea at all – even the remotest, dimmest glimmer of the pain and anguish which this behaviour causes to some of our older inhabitants? They can hardly bear to go out of doors – afraid to show their feathers on the street – in case they are accosted by one of your disgusting uni-heads. It's appalling, quite appalling. I don't know what Headland is coming to.'

'I am sorry if I have offended you and I apologize for having only one head. A friend of mine, out there in the lake, has two heads if that is any help?'

'Two! Two! Why even the lowliest, scurviest politician can't make do with fewer than seven, and even the most savage and scabby little priest has five. Our great social leaders – our sewer-sorters and barnacle-scrapers, our flea-dusters and oyster-stringers, our hole-fillers and rope-coilers, not to mention our crack-tappers and sand-sifters – *they* have as many as thirty or forty heads apiece.'

'It must be rather a strain on their shoulders.'

'Oh, you imbecilic mainlanders make me sick. You are so ignorant and so cocky with it. Sit down and let me explain. In Headland, long ago, the islanders lived quietly and peacefully, mending their nets and carving their great stone temples to the all-seeing, all-whistling, all-wise Knot-god. His name was Codpuss and he was a benign and playful deity who watched over us and protected us until, one black and terrible day, the island

The Island of Feathered Dwarfs

was overrun by plundering invaders from the mainland.

'They were the Gyles, a terrifying race of glaring-eyed fiends who destroyed the temples, chopped up the holy statues of the One True Codpuss, and sacked the towns and villages. But worse was to come. No sooner had the islanders learnt how to please their new masters, the Gyles, than a second invasion of blood-thirsty marauders set foot on our shores. These were the Schefs, great, bearded giants who were so tall they had to eat sitting on the floor.'

'Why?'

'I don't know. Why does anybody want to invade anywhere? Swollen preening-glands, I shouldn't wonder. Makes them irritable, makes their friends hate them, that makes them hate their friends, and their friends' friends, then their friends' friends start hating *them*, and that's too much, so they look around for someone to take it out on and invade some poor, inoffensive little colony like Headland. Does that answer your question?'

'No. I wanted to know why the Schefs had to eat sitting on the floor.'

'Oh. Well, that's simple. If they had eaten standing up like the rest of us, they wouldn't have been able to reach the food. Their arms were too short and if they had tried to bend over and pick it up with their mouths, they'd have toppled over. They were top-heavy as well as tall, you see. It was those armoured beards, mainly. Ugly things. Anyway, after the Schefs came the Ecks, dark, swarthy villains from far away on the west coast of the lake. *They* were feather-collectors and we suffered terribly. Imagine having to stand by and watch your friends being plucked alive! Finally, came the Goffs, small beings with sad faces who, despite their size, were the strongest of all and completely without mercy. I'd rather not talk about them, if you don't mind. It's too fresh in the memory. They renamed the island Goffland and . . . '

'Goffland! This is Goffland?'

'Not any more it isn't. Their reign is over, thank goodness, and now, at last, we are our own masters. This is Headland, please remember that, and never refer to the Goffs again. Headland!'

Inrock

'I see. That's because of all your heads?'

'Yes. You must understand that each new wave of invaders brought their own laws and customs and each time the islanders — those that survived the terrible battles — tried to change their ways to please their new masters. Eventually they realized that their position was hopeless and they resolved to take a drastic step to deal with the situation. As you can see, we have feathered bodies and, in the old days, we had feathered heads to match. But it was decided that a single head was a handicap and that only if we could become multi-headed — one head at a time, of course — changing heads to suit each occasion — could we hope to survive the whims of our various masters.

'A head-office was established and a factory built which could turn out a hundred heads a day, of every shape, colour and design. Then, at a great ceremony, we all lost our heads — our old, feathered ones, that is — and the factory's head-foreman fitted us out with neck-sockets. As a special introductory offer, we were given a set of four free heads in a commemorative hand-case. We each fitted one on and carried the other three. But those were early days. The original set of four had been designed to give us the chance to look like any one of the four invaders — you must understand that they had all retained strongholds in the island and were still ordering our lives. With our four removable heads — a glaring Gyle, a bearded Schef, a swarthy Eck, and a sad-faced Goff — we could now move about from one part of the island to another with ease, changing heads as we went, to please the tyrants.

'As time passed, however, we were able to buy new heads from the head-office whenever we could afford them and build up our collections. We could try out new fashions, new moods, new profiles, anything that took our fancy. Some of the older families have a most impressive head-room, with all their ancestors' heads arranged in glass cases, and on special holidays they take them out and wear them to fancy-head balls.

'Now, in modern times, we have strict rules about the wearing of proper heads for proper occasions. No one, for instance, would be seen in public with a head like yours! That, if I may say so, is a strictly private sleeping head and, if it is the only one you have, I fear you may provoke serious public hostility.'

'But I can change my expressions and wash my face and smooth my hair and wear a hat too, if necessary. You won't recognize me then. If this is the island that some call Goffland — incorrectly, of course, I appreciate that now — then I have an important task to perform here and I will do anything you ask so long as I may be permitted to stay here a little while. But first . . . I don't like to mention this . . . but I am very, very hungry . . . do you think . . . is there anywhere I could find some food?'

'Food. Food? Oh, yes, I suppose so. What kind of seed do you take?'

'Seed?'

'Yes, we are all seed-eaters here. As it is the only thing we can grow on the island, it's just as well. Here, try some of these,' and he scattered a handful of black and yellow seed-pods on the ground. Jason ran round, picking them up and stuffing them into his mouth. They tasted revolting, but he munched them down.

'In exchange for that seed, you will please show me your expressions. Ours, I fear, are rather fixed. If we wish to be in a laughing mood, we have to wear a happy face, then take it off afterwards.'

'Oh, that's easy. Watch,' and Jason ran through as many expressions as he could think of, clowning a mood to go with each one. The feathered dwarf watched intently.

'Remarkable, quite remarkable. You may be single-headed, but you have certainly been issued with a most versatile model. I have a suggestion. When you meet other islanders and it becomes necessary to change face, simply turn round, pretend to switch heads, and then you can reappear with a new expression. Say you are a head-conjuror and do it by sleight of hand. Some of us have become very quick at making the changeover and you should be able to get away with it. Now, I must take you to the Head-waiter. Follow me.'

They marched together across the rocky surface of the island.

Whenever they encountered other feathered islanders of some importance, the dwarf fumbled in his shoulder-bag and put on an appropriate head to greet the passers-by. Jason noticed that if they met a more lowly inhabitant, the dwarf kept his head and it was the other islander who had to make the change. There was one hilarious moment when they met another dwarf looking exactly like Jason's companion, except for the head he was wearing. Both dwarfs plunged into their bags and changed heads, only to find that they were still unmatched, but now the other way around. They plunged in again, made a quick change back, and found themselves face to face as they had been when they first met, and still, of course, unmatched. They went back and forth through this routine several times before finally they managed to get the same heads on at the same moment. With sighs of relief, they embraced one another and immediately went their separate ways.

Eventually Jason and his strange companion came to a curious town of rock-burrows, plastered with lake-shells and mud. In a large, curved hollow they noticed an angry group of islanders, all wearing hate-faces and screaming, their ruffled feathers rising and falling in great agitation. In the centre of the group Jason spotted a splintered raft and on it, to his great relief, the crouching and bedraggled figures of Ludo and Di-di. As he and the dwarf approached the scene, a tall, scrawny islander with black plumage jumped on to a rock, fitted on a solemn, I-am-about-to-be-pompous-so-shut-up head, and called for silence. He pointed at Di-di, and three large, feathered Polizesti surrounded him. Reluctantly, the brown beast got to his feet and stood, dripping lake-water on to the battered remains of the raft.

'This creature, this obscene brown beast, has dared to venture to our sacred island, our beloved and revered Headland, wearing two heads at one and the same time. Two heads at once, brothers, two heads *at once!*' There was a screeching and fluttering of feathers. 'We have no choice. This act of gross indecency compels us to take the strictest measures. He has claimed tourist immunity, but public morality *must* be satisfied and he must be

The Island of Feathered Dwarfs

made to lose face. We cannot allow these mainland standards to penetrate our shores, or our whole code of conduct will be undermined. Brothers, as you can plainly see, this despicable intruder in our midst is *two-faced*! You will be relieved to hear that the Head-waiter has already put in hand the construction of a double chopping block, and the offending organs will be severed tomorrow by the deputy Beheader. The beheading is set for Grannit-plus-one and light refreshments will be served. Black-heads will be worn. Please tell your friends. The Grand-Goff has promised to honour us with his presence.'

With a rapid change of hate-heads, some loud clapping, the smoothing of ruffled feathers, and an odd shout of 'Jolly good show, well done, good show', the crowd dispersed to spread the glad news.

'What a stroke of luck,' clucked the dwarf. 'Tomorrow is Sculptor Day, and this beheading will be a fine start to the celebrations. It's a special day for us, the day we commemorate the occasion when the Sculptor was shipwrecked here, many years ago. That reminds me, I must look out my Golden Worms. Mustn't forget those.'

Jason could hardly suppress his excitement.

'Your Golden Worms?'

'Yes, it is the only time we are allowed to wear them, on Sculptor Day.'

'I have heard about them but I have never seen them. I shall look forward to that. Will I be permitted to wear some, do you think?'

'I'm not sure about that. Strictly speaking they are for islanders only, but I'll see what can be done.'

'Thank you. By the way, what will happen to the other intruder, the furry one, the one with a single head and horns?'

'She will have a choice.'

'Between what and what?'

'Between the left side of the chopping block or the right. She is an accomplice – probably the two-faced beast's agent or promoter. We get quite a few of these filthy exhibitions here – ever since those poor Water-knots were harnessed for lake travel – but we stamp on them with both claws, tourists or no tourists. Now, come with me, and I'll see if I can find you some Golden Worms to wear tomorrow.'

CHAPTER THIRTEEN
The Strummer Invasion

Jason and the dwarf had just entered a smelly underground cave, hung with rotting fish and head-racks, when there was an enormous explosion. Feathered islanders began tearing in and out of tunnels, screaming and shrieking. One of them rushed up to the dwarf and panted:

'The Strummers are coming, the Strummers are coming. It's a full-scale invasion. To the dug-outs – take shelter! Take shelter!'

'This way!' shouted the dwarf. 'We are under siege again. We have been expecting it, and for once I have taken precautions – I have a brand-new Strummer's head ready. I must get to my nest and find it. Won't do to be caught without it. Keep close behind me or you'll get lost.'

'But what about the Golden Worms? You were going to find me some to wear tomorrow.'

'Tomorrow! What do you think this place will be like tomorrow, after the Strummers have finished with it? There won't be much celebrating tomorrow, Sculptor's Day or no Sculptor's Day.'

'But supposing you win? Supposing you rout the Strummers?'

'That's a thought! I mustn't put my Strummer head on too

soon. Have to wait and see. But I don't think there's much hope. The Strummers will be too strong for us.'

They reached the dwarf's nest and he scrabbled around, tipping over head-racks and undoing bags until he found his new Strummer's head. He paused to admire it for a moment before popping it into his hand-case and, in that second, Jason acted. He snatched it from the dwarf and held it high in the air.

'I'm sorry to have to do this, but I have an urgent task to perform. You must give me the Golden Worms, or I will smash your new head to the ground. Quickly. I mean it!'

'Careful! Be careful with it!' squawked the dwarf, his feathers flickering with anxiety.

'I'll be careful, but hurry. Listen. Listen to the Strummers.' There were more explosions outside getting louder and closer. 'You don't have much time.'

The dwarf hesitated briefly, then dashed over to a large box in the corner of the nest. Wrenching it open, he dragged out the contents and scattered them on the floor.

'Must be here somewhere,' he kept muttering. 'Must be. I put them here last year. Can't have lost them. Ah! Here they are. Now, give me my Strummer and let's get to the dug-outs.'

They made the exchange and Jason examined his prize. After all his adventures, his ordeals and his narrow escapes, he had finally achieved his goal. Here in his hands were the Golden Worms! Now, at long last, he could return to his home and present them to a grateful Meggamole. His quest was over! Little had he expected to find the precious worms in such a dingy place. He had imagined a great palace, with worm-guards that he would have to fight to the death, and with fiery dragons protecting a golden door, leading to a golden room containing a golden casket in which the priceless Golden Worms would be lying, shimmering and glistening magically. He would plunge his arms, dripping with dragon's blood, into the golden hoard, cram his pockets full, and turn to cut his way back through the desperately fighting worm-defenders, and out, out over the palace walls and to safety. That was how he had imagined it. But here he was in a dark, smelly, muddy dwarf's nest, holding a necklace in his hands. A necklace threaded with Golden Worms! He examined them closely. They shone brightly enough. He fingered one of them. It was hard to the touch, and about three inches long, glinting with highlights where its shape was twisted. There were about twenty of them strung round the necklace chain. One thing puzzled him. There was no life in them. They were obviously solid metal. How could the Meggamole eat them?

'Come on, come on. Don't dawdle there gazing at those stupid worms. We'll be killed if we don't get to the dug-outs.'

'These Golden Worms are solid metal,' said Jason. 'I thought you could eat them.'

'Eat them? Eat *them*! Of course not, you featherless fool, they are only replicas. What did you expect, the Sculptor's Originals! You must be mad. Now, come on.'

'Replicas? Copies? What do you mean, what are you saying?' cried Jason, shaking the dwarf by the plumage.

'The Sculptor keeps the Golden Worms, I thought everyone knew that. We had these copies made to wear on Sculptor's Day, to honour the Great One. Now let me go.'

Jason's hands went limp and the dwarf sleeked his plumage and fled. In a daze, Jason followed him outside, threw the necklace on the ground in disgust, had second thoughts, and picked it up. Stuffing it hurriedly into his belt-pouch, he returned as fast as he could to the curved hollow where he had last seen Di-di and Ludo. The place was deserted now, except for the crippled raft, which lay there alone and forlorn. He raced this way and that, searching for some clue as to where the two prisoners had been taken. Around a steep, sloping corner he found himself staring at a huge mud-sphere with a large, round hole in the side. Plunging through it, he fell over in the sudden darkness and lay still. Soft voices could be heard.

'I shall pack them all, or I won't come.'

'My dear, your feather-oils are the scandal of this whole colony. You will leave them behind and that is an order, do you hear, an order. Now hurry, the Strummers will be arriving at any moment and our Galoon will be shot down before we have even passed the coast. If you don't . . . '

'You are too late,' bellowed Jason. 'We are here already. Don't move, or I'll strum you.' To his great relief, the trick worked. There was a nervous silence, broken only by a stifled squawking. 'Now tell me about this Galoon of yours, *all* about it. If you hesitate one second, I'll have you both PLUCKED.'

He roared the last word and it echoed eerily around the interior of the shell-and-mud nest. As his eyes became accustomed to the dim light, he could make out two quivering, feathered figures, laden with a great array of shoulder-bags and cases.

'We . . . I . . . er . . . that is . . . the local government officials and I, their president, have personal Galoons standing by for states of emergency such as this. Galoons . . . Galoons are . . . er . . . are . . . '

'Speak up!'

'Galoons are large, inflatable islanders of low rank with red skin-sacs on their backs. They . . . they take air into them and float up, high into the air, and, with a favourable wind, are blown across to the mainland. In peacetime we use them for Galoon-races, but in . . . '

'. . . but in times of crisis, the cowardly leaders of this wretched race use them to escape and save their own skins, is that it?'

'No, no, no. It is a planned withdrawal, a strategic regrouping, a diplomatically sanctioned, committee approved, politically recognized . . . '

'Stop this craven, dunghill drivel! Where is your Galoon now?'

'Er . . . I . . . '

'Answer me!'

'It is above us, in the roof-cage. Up those steps, there by the entrance. But be reasonable – you and I, we are men of the world, we . . . '

'Silence! You will both be locked up. Take me to your prison.'

Squawking dejectedly, they obeyed. In the prison dungeons Jason quickly found Ludo and Di-di, released them and bundled his protesting captives into their vacated cells.

'No time to explain,' he gasped. 'Follow me.'

They found the Galoon without difficulty. It was delighted to be set free and showed them how to attach to its strong legs the round wicker basket used for passengers. There were only two seats, but somehow the three of them managed to squeeze in. There was one moment of panic when Ludo accidentally prodded the underside of the Galoon with her horns. The creature had already taken in a few gulps of air and was hovering above the basket, ready for take-off. It mistook the prod as a signal to depart and started to fill its huge, red back-sacs, gasping in great gusts of air as fast as it could, for a rapid ascent. Di-di was still struggling to squeeze into the basket, helped by Ludo and Jason, when this happened. Majestically, the Galoon started to rise from the mud roof, and, unmajestically, Di-di slipped over the side of the basket, kicking and struggling, until he was hanging on by no more than his two sets of teeth.

'If you are going to make a habit of this, you should see a dentist,' yelled Jason, peering closely at Di-di's groaning jaws.

Unfortunately, this made Di-di laugh so much that he let go of the wicker-work and Jason and Ludo only just caught his necks in the nick of time. Half-strangling him, they dragged him on board and he collapsed in a heap, still laughing and spitting out loose teeth.

The Galoon, who had remained aloof from these goings-on beneath him, had now risen high above the town, and the sound of strumming filled the air. In the distance the three intrepid Galooners could see the enemy approaching. The noise of battle filled the Grannit sky. Feathers floated up from below and danced around their swaying wicker basket.

'Oh dear,' exclaimed Jason. 'They must have killed the dwarf who helped me. Look, over there, I recognize his feathers. I think the islanders must be losing. The dwarf certainly didn't intend going anywhere near the front. That means the Strummers must have penetrated the centre of the town. If only there was a wind.'

'We are becalmed!' wailed Di-di. 'We'll be strummed! It's all right for you lot, you'll just get a straight strumming and curl up

and die, but I'll get the fancy treatment and I can't stand pain.'
The Galoon looked acutely embarrassed.

'What will they do to you?' asked Jason.

'It'll probably be the bagpipes. Can you imagine anything more hideous? What a terrible way to go — bagpiped slowly into jelly. I can't bear to think about it.'

'But why should they be so angry with you? They only lost a few of their instruments, back at Lo-la-po, and they must have realized that you couldn't have known they were going to invade the town that night.'

'No, they are very attached to their instruments. Being separated from them like that must have been very painful for them. They won't forgive me. You see, when they are very young, they have their instruments grafted on to their bodies, so that they can grow together. Then they achieve a perfect balance and they don't have to think about strumming any more . . . it becomes second nature to them. To become separated from your instrument is as painful for a Strummer as if I were to . . . to tear off your ear-lobes.'

'In that case, perhaps we should all start praying for wind,' said Ludo.

'No, I have a better idea,' said Jason, and he twisted over the side of the basket to catch the Galoon's attention. 'Open your mouth and let some air out,' he yelled up.

'We'll sink!' yelled Ludo. 'You're mad!'

'Yes, we'll sink, but we'll sink sideways. We'll be jet-propelled by the escaping air.'

The Galoon seemed to catch on and belched loudly. They shot sideways and slightly downwards.

'Now fill the sacs up again gently and repeat,' Jason called to it. 'Fill slowly, empty quickly. Keep at it.' The Galoon nodded and set to work. Little by little, it managed to drive them away from the battle-zone without losing too much height, until they reached the Headland coastline, where lake-breezes came to their aid and they began to drift slowly out across the water towards the mainland.

'My legs!' screamed the Galoon suddenly. 'I can't stand it any longer. I am going to faint. I am only a two-seater Galoon and there are three of you. One of you will have to go. Quickly, quickly. If I faint, my pouches will leak and we'll all be drowned.'

Jason and Ludo looked at one another and then at the heavy bulk of the two-headed Di-di.

'Easy come, easy go,' shouted the brown beast, and he went.

They watched his brown body rolling over and over as it fell, and saw it crash into the lake below.

'He *was* the champion pebble-diver of Lo-la-po,' said Ludo, 'but it was a great sacrifice all the same.'

'Humph,' squawked the Galoon, who had been staring at the fast approaching land. 'Perhaps it was – or perhaps he knew which way the wind was blowing. Look!'

They turned their eyes to the shore and gasped. As the Galoon was swept in over the beach below they could now make out quite plainly the ranks of the Strummer reserves, drawn up ready to reinforce their advance troops on the nearby island.

'Why didn't that stupid Di-di warn us?' shouted Jason.

'I suspect,' called back Ludo, 'that he was giving us a final demonstration of his professional skills – as a disruptor and disorganizer. Only this time it seems that *we* are to be the disruption.'

'More likely the disrupted!' snorted the Galoon, as violin arrows began to twang through the air around them.

'If they hit the air-sacs, we're done for,' gasped Ludo, and almost as she spoke there was a sharp hissing sound from above them.

'I'm punctured,' shrilled the Galoon. 'Emergency landing, emergency landing,' and he gaped his mouth wide.

As they spiralled down they could see cheering, waving figures beneath them, celebrating their victory over this secret, flying weapon that was now zooming to its destruction. They yelled and laughed as it crashed with a bump on the fore-shore, hurling its passengers across the sand.

Although the grinning Strummers did not appear to be at all

disorganized by this event, the two Galooners did, as predicted by their Galoon, feel considerably disrupted. They ended up sprawling at the feet of a smiling, beautifully tuned Strum-major.

'Throw the red-pouched thing into the lake and take these two back to Composer headquarters. Hand them over to the Conductor for pacifying,' he ordered, his fixed smile never faltering. 'And strum to it!'

CHAPTER FOURTEEN
The Pacification Orchestra

Jason and Ludo had no time to think, or even to study their captors. They were quickly surrounded by Strummer guards and hustled across the beach towards a fearsome-looking armoured beast with two oval drums growing out of its flanks. The drums were opened up and they were bundled in, Jason on the left flank and Ludo on the right. The lids were slammed shut and one of the Strummers leapt on the creature's back. As it moved off, he began to beat on the drums rhythmically with each step it took. The noise inside the drums was deafening and Jason mercifully soon became unconscious.

When he came to, he found himself trapped in what appeared to be a circular harp. Staggering painfully to his feet, his head bursting, he looked around for Ludo, but she was nowhere to be seen. He was alone, at one end of a long, low room. In trying to squeeze through the wires that surrounded him, he set them twanging, and a door burst open and three Strummers rushed in. They picked up his cage, tipped it on its side, and released him. But before they could grab him, he attacked, kicking and punching wildly, and ran at full tilt towards a double door at the far end of the room. Pushing through it he found himself on a platform, surrounded by a vast orchestra of Strummers.

Jason stopped dead. The three guards he had assaulted ran up behind him and blocked his retreat. Like all the Strummers, including the whole of the orchestra, they had weird-looking musical instruments growing out of the fronts of their bodies, and they started to press these into Jason's back, forcing him forward into the huge concert hall.

There was an expectant hush and from the back of the hall there entered a tall, gaunt, long-haired Strummer dressed in green overalls, with a silver-tipped, ivory baton where his right hand should have been. The orchestra rose to its feet with a clatter as he approached the platform and then sat down again noisily as he mounted it and took up his position.

'I am your Conductor,' he intoned, speaking directly at Jason. 'I regret to say that your furry friend, whose horns are stronger than drumskin, has escaped, but she will be caught, have no fear, and then she too will be dealt with. As violent enemies of the United Strummers, you are both to be pacified, by order of the Composer, but as time is short we will commence with you in her absence. Have you anything to say before treatment is carried out?'

On the principle that it is always better to say something, in case it causes confusion and creates a useful delay, Jason blurted out:

'I plead the Fifth Symphony.'

'Guards, give him a taste of your tuning-forks. I won't stand for this nonsense!'

The guards stuck out their tuning-forked tongues and twanged Jason's ears with them.

'I will repeat my question. Have you anything to say before you are pacified?'

'I . . . '

'Careful!'

'No.'

The Pacification Orchestra

'Good, then sit over there and fasten your seat-straps, the performance is about to begin. When you are asked to speak, you will request one thing and one thing only — namely, that you wish to be pacified.'

'But I . . . '

'Quiet!'

The hall was silent, except for a faint whining sound. As if trapped by this strange noise, Jason sat stiffly waiting. He tried not to hear the whine, to make it vanish by stretching his skin, pulling it tight over his tensed body, but the sound grew and began to throb. Beating louder in persistent waves it threatened him.

The Conductor closed his eyes and began to sway in time with the throbbing beat.

'Enough! We must have an answer. The stranger must speak,' he screeched, swaying back and forth.

'No! I will not answer,' gasped Jason. 'I will not be pacified.' His body shook as he desperately resisted the power of the throbbing pulse.

Now all the members of the orchestra were swaying, their bodies plunging forward and backward as if tugged by invisible nooses around their necks. No one moved from side to side. Each pulse dragged their bodies forward, then back they sagged again, forward and back. With a moan, Jason found himself giving in to the strange, whining power. It was beating faster all the time, so hard now that each wrench forward made him gasp. It was almost unbearable.

'Speak! Answer! Answer!' shouted the Conductor, his hair cascading over his face.

The beat was so rapid now that as Jason's arms flew out in front of him, they convulsed and shook as though they were lighted matches being flicked out by some giant hand. Faster and faster, until his body was first shuddering and then vibrating. Everything became blurred. Jason could stand no more.

'Yes, yes. I'll speak. I'll speak. Let me speak.'

His scream was little more than a whisper, but instantly the pulse vanished and the orchestra all slumped in their seats. The Conductor groaned and, with an agonized expression on his face, rapped his baton on the wooden stand in front of him. Total silence. Then the first faint droning of the whine began again.

'Now, now. Quickly,' he hissed at Jason. 'It will be worse next time. Speak now.'

'I . . . I wish to be pacified.' Jason spoke the words softly but clearly.

'Ahhh!' The whole orchestra let out a gasp of appreciation and tapped their instruments in a strange clatter of ticks and clanks.

'I wish to be pacified.'

'Ahhhhhh!' they intoned again.

The baton rapped.

'Gentlemen of the orchestra, prepare yourselves for the Pacification Chord. Place the young stranger on the couch and grease his face.'

Two attendants led Jason to a green velvet couch, shaped like an open pea-pod, and lifted him into it. From a large jar they scooped a handful of orange jelly and smeared it over his face. Its sweet smell was stifling. The pea-pod began to close. He waited. Through the slit above him he could hear muffled sounds. Suddenly the slit widened and a row of anxious faces peered down at him. Their noses were masked, but the eyes were staring and the mouths open. They said nothing and after a few moments the slit narrowed again.

A great chord rang out, dying slowly and reverberating through every crevice of the vast concert hall. Jason felt the orange jelly on his face grow hot, burning, searing. A mist began to fill the close air inside his velvet shell.

When the mist cleared, the pod was open again and faces, unmasked this time, were circling around his couch. They smiled sadly and every so often one of them leant forward and kissed him lightly on the forehead. The jelly had vanished – dried or evaporated – and his skin was cold and dry. It stretched tight over his head and he found he could make no movements, no expressions. His eyes would not shut. He tried to wink at one of

The Pacification Orchestra

the faces, but nothing stirred, not even an eye-lash.

'It's as if I am embalmed and lying in state,' he said to himself. The idea suddenly filled him with panic. Was *this* what being pacified meant? A frozen, living body unable to move, but fully aware of everything around. Was death itself like this? How long did it last? Forever, like a wax-works, or would he slowly decay?

A tear burst painfully from the rigid corner of Jason's left eye. One of the onlookers screamed. Heads were jostled out of the way and the Conductor's face peered in, a nose-mask hurriedly being strapped into place.

'A tear? A tear! Oh no!' he wailed, and beat the side of his head with a sweating baton. 'Clear the pit. Hurry up, hurry up. We'll have to start again. Quickly, there isn't much time.'

Jason felt himself being lifted out of the couch and placed back in his seat. A soft white hood was pushed over his head, squeezed this way and that, and then removed. He could now sense a little power returning to his muscles. He could move very slightly, but for safety he stayed put and listened.

'It's the only way to do it, start from scratch. No good trying to patch up.'

'You don't get a second chance,' shouted Jason, on the spur of the moment.

'Don't be stupid, of course I do, and a third and a fourth if I need it.'

'There isn't time,' roared Jason, praying that there wasn't.

'There's plenty of time,' muttered the Conductor, but he glanced quickly at the main doorway as he said it.

'As you have made a mess of my treatment,' Jason said, more gently, 'perhaps we should use the alternative.'

The Conductor was busy getting the members of the orchestra back into their places. He paused.

'How do you know about The Alternative?' he asked, genuinely surprised.

Jason didn't. He was frantically trying out anything that might change the ceremony in some way. It was on the tip of his tongue to say: 'I would prefer to be cremated.' He remembered that an uncle of his had put it in his will. 'Better than lying stiff in a box and slowly rotting to pieces,' the old man had gurgled as they wheeled him away. But if Jason tried that here, the result might be even more terrible than pacification.

'You know what I mean,' he replied, as calmly as possible.

'You? You wouldn't be able to, not a weakling like you.'

'Try me. Go on, try me. I'll surprise you.' He was surprising himself.

The Conductor looked at the door again, openly this time, and paced up and down, fiddling nervously with his baton.

'It's a bit risky. I think it's too risky. You're not strong enough.' He leant over and felt Jason's arm, then his leg, then his arm again. Everyone waited. After a few hurried words with the orchestra leader, he tapped his baton again on the wooden stand.

'Gentlemen, you have responded well today, but the chord, the great Pacification Chord, was flawed. We have failed and time is against us. The next concert is due to begin any moment. There is no alternative but . . . The Alternative!' The members of the orchestra glanced sideways at one another. 'Young man, you know what is required of you. You are brave indeed to consider The Alternative.'

'I am not ready to be pacified yet,' said Jason with a gracious smile. 'I have something to do. Something that *must* be done, before I can even contemplate pacification. I will not bore you with the details, but you can take my word for it that it is vital for me to remain active.'

'Active is putting it mildly,' observed the Conductor.

'I am not afraid of action.'

'Obviously, or you would never have chosen The Alternative.'

'How would you like me to begin?' asked Jason, getting shakily to his feet.

'You'll have to be toughened first, then suitably armed, and after that it's up to you. The choice of victim will be yours. It could even be . . .' – he grinned at the orchestra – '. . . one of us!' Some of them laughed nervously. 'As you know, you have to kill your victim within one light-cycle of the start of the hunt and return the

The Pacification Orchestra

body here to take your place on the pacification couch.'

'Kill!' Jason couldn't help blurting out the word. The conductor looked surprised.

'Of course, kill,' he repeated. 'What else? I have been awarded one pacification in your name and I have to have one. You pleaded The Alternative and that is exactly what it will be. It means what it says — you provide an alternative body to replace your own. You kill someone, anyone — the choice is yours — and bring the body here for the substitute ceremony. Then you are free to go. Of course, if *you* get killed instead, then I am in trouble. You could end up anywhere. If you were large and beefy I'd feel a lot better about it, but there it is, time is against me and if these gentlemen flaw another chord, the position could be even worse, so now it's up to you. I am going to have your body pumped up a bit — a little forced protalization and musculation. Then a short but bitter little course of moodivational enragement, and you should be ready to go. I only hope you pick on some gentle, shy fig-brain, who will more or less lie down and let you squelch all over him. Your light-cycle will start at the end of your training course, when you leave these halls. Any questions?'

'I really have to kill?'

'You or them. Them or you. For my sake, let it be them.'

'Them,' said Jason, almost inaudibly.

'Good. The attendants will take you off to the training hall. Good squelching, and remember — blood, lots of blood. Theirs, not yours,' and he swept out to deafening applause.

'Who was applauding?' Jason asked the stooped attendant at his side, as they passed down a mirrored corridor. 'I couldn't see any audience.'

'It's in his ears,' was all the attendant would say.

At the training hall, Jason was given a skin-tight, plain white body-costume. He felt ridiculous in it and sat curled up on a black slab in the middle of a dark red room.

'Muscles!' snapped a voice. 'Muscles are dark red. Like this room. Meat is dark red. Muscles are meat. Meat is muscles. Eat meat and you eat muscles. Eat muscles and you make muscles.

Simple. Simple matter of Transform. I am your Transformer. This is the Muscle Room. Stand UP!'

Jason did as he was told. He did not like the look of the Transformer, who appeared to be made of nothing *but* muscles. Instead of a head, there was a bundle of bulging lobes of flesh, flexing and glistening above his black tunic. Jason could not detect any eyes.

'Follow me,' the Transformer ordered.

'What about white meat?' asked Jason. The muscle-head bulged and reddened even deeper.

'No thinking here,' he shouted, his whole form rippling like a sack of snakes. 'This way, look sharp.'

They paced along into a larger red room with a soft, padded floor.

'Watch me closely, then repeat,' commanded the Transformer. He flung himself on to the floor and bounded up again, flew across to one wall, bounced back into a tall, soft pillar and slewed around it, gaining speed. As Jason crouched in one corner, he saw the great bulk crash and skid from pillar to pillar, from ceiling to floor, until it was flying around the room at a terrifying pace. At last, it crashed to the ground and leapt to attention shouting:

'Hup! Now you. Ready, go!'

Jason hesitated and the Transformer lunged towards him, thrusting him straight out towards the largest of the elastic pillars. It knocked the breath out of him, but from that second he had lost control and took off. Five minutes later he was lying in a bruised heap on the soft padding of the floor. He was heaving and panting and limply allowed himself to be carried into a small side-chamber, where he was fitted into a strange rubber contraption. Tubes were clamped into his mouth and he felt a rush of rich liquid pouring down his throat. He tried to cough, but found it impossible. He tried to struggle, but there was not a muscle he could control. He felt himself swelling and swelling, until his eyes watered and he broke out in a lathering sweat. Then the tubes stopped working and the whole rubber cradle began to quiver.

The Transformer watched impassively as the bloated body of

The Pacification Orchestra

his victim was tossed crazily about. Jason felt giddy and started gulping, but then the tubes began pumping liquid into him again. Then more shaking and more pouring. Then peace. He felt the world around him going from red to pink to white.

When Jason awoke he was astonished to find that he was none the worse for his ordeal. He was lying face down on the black slab in the first red room, apparently still wearing the same, white, skin-tight costume.

'Sit up, stand up. Hup!' a voice commanded. To his amazement, he was on his toes in a flash and marking time on the spot, his feet lightly pressing on the ground and sending his body prancing up in the air.

'Good. Ready. Follow me. Hup! Hup! Hup!'

He jumped along after the Transformer, feeling ready to run ten miles if necessary. As they passed through the mirrored corridor, he caught sight of himself and yelped. Crashing back to one wall, he stared across at his reflection. It revealed a huge, muscular, white-clad figure, arms and legs bulging, chest heaving.

'That's not me!' he cried.

'Not the old. Not the old. It's the new! New approach, new body. Hup!'

'Stop it, stop this insane hupping. What have you done to me? You've turned me into a monster,' and his broad neck muscles bulged as he clutched at his hair. 'Aarghh!' he screamed, as the hairs were nearly torn out of their sockets by his own fingers.

'Steady, New Body, steady. Don't know your own strength yet. Got to run it in gently. Do yourself a damage. Can't have that. Hup!'

'Shut up! Shut up! For heaven's sake stop hupping. I can't stand it. What am I going to do?'

'You are going to be moodivated, that's what,' barked the Transformer, pummelling an invisible punch-bag, 'and hurry up about it. One, two, one, two. Follow me. Hup!'

Like a wounded bear, Jason stumbled after him. In a darkened room the Transformer strapped him in front of a green curtain. A mask was fitted over his eyes to press his eyelids open, and his head was clamped tight so that it was unable to move. Not only was it impossible for him to turn away from the scenes he witnessed when the curtain rose, but he could not even close his eyes to shut them out. He tried to assert himself by making his eyes go out of focus, but the vague shapes were still not vague enough.

What he saw made him more and more angry. Scene after scene flashed by and each enraged him more than the last. Each character in each scene behaved in a more outrageous way than the one before.

'They are wicked, they are evil,' he shouted out loud. 'Stop them, they must be stopped, kill them, kill them!'

At last the curtains closed and the mask was removed. Jason blinked his eyes. The clamp was undone. He shook his head and leapt up.

'Fiends! They are fiends!' he bellowed at the blank, green curtain. He swung round, but he was alone. There were two doors. One was locked, the other only slightly opened. He charged at it and it splintered into small pieces. Stepping outside in huge strides, he found himself in a rocky, pebble-strewn landscape. He ran out, away from the building, and dashed from rock to rock, panting.

'Where are you?' he roared. 'Come out and face me. Where are you? I know you're here. Cowards! Yellow-bellied cowards! Show yourselves, you filthy stinking cowards.'

Saliva was dribbling down his chin, as he picked up a rock and hurled it over the top of a boulder. There was a thud and a sharp cry, followed by the sound of running feet. He flung himself around the boulder in time to see a cloud of dust receding. With great leaps he sped after it, covering the ground so fast that the wind whistled through his hair. The cloud of dust was getting nearer. He was passing now through giant grass-stems, scything them to the ground as he went. In front of him there was a splash and a sound of frantic swimming. In a rush he was in the water, ploughing through it, arms flailing. As the water became shallower, he tried to stand up to see which way his victim was fleeing, but found himself stuck in clinging mud. He panicked and struggled wildly, only making matters worse. Sinking rapidly down into the soft ooze, he swallowed water and choked. The whole world was rising about him as his writhing body sank further and further, down into the stinking, sucking mud. He yelled, spluttering and cursing and punching the surface of the water as if to kill it. Then he went under.

CHAPTER FIFTEEN
The Deadly Alternative

Some time later, perhaps a long time, Jason coughed.

'Are you all right?' The worried voice was one he knew. Ludo's familiar furry body was leaning over him. He gulped. 'Why were you chasing me?' asked Ludo, relieved to see some signs of life. 'Were you trying to kill me? What's happened to you?' She looked nervous.

He heaved himself up without a word, leapt at her, and grabbed for her throat. They rolled over and down the bank into the water again. He roared and flung out his arms to save himself. Ludo jumped clear and stared at his sodden, bedraggled form, coughing water and mud and gasping for breath.

'Jason, it's me, Ludo. Are you out of your mind?'

He dragged himself ashore and glowered at her, preparing himself for his next attack. But it did not come. Instead, he collapsed and began to sob, his back heaving and shaking, his mouth biting the damp soil. Eventually the tension subsided.

'Ludo, Ludo, what have they done to me?' He paused. 'Tie my arms behind me — tight. When I get my breath back I may try to attack you again.' Ludo hesitated, still puzzled and wary, but then did as he asked.

The Deadly Alternative

He awoke in her arms, deep inside the giant grasses, in a rough nest of stems. A confused buzzing of conflicting thoughts stirred in his still half-sleeping brain. He moved to touch her face. Was it to caress her or to tear at her? He could not tell, because his arm did not move. It felt strangely cramped and crushed. Then he remembered the bonds that held it pinned to his body.

Ludo moved and sat up, scratching the base of one of her horns. She licked her lips and sniffed. Her eyes began to open. Jumping up, she started away from him and grunted. Jerking back, bit by bit, she lowered her head and charged at Jason's awkwardly trussed up body. He yelled at her and rolled quickly out of the way. Her horns tore into the nest-stems and she began to root into them savagely, tossing them high into the air. With a snort, she looked up, her eyes blazing, stared this way and that, and ran off grunting.

Jason had never seen her like this before. Struggling to his feet, he stumbled off through the giant grasses, his tightly tied arms sending streams of pain up through his shoulders. After a while, he collapsed to his knees and sank forwards, resting his face on the earth. Tears streamed down his nose and formed little round mud puddles on the dry soil. He lay, humped up like this, for what seemed ages. Nothing moved except for the gentle swaying and hissing of the tall stems. He sat up and tried to think. 'If I am all right, then what was it that startled Ludo? I must smell wrong. She must have scented something vicious, something savage in me. And yet, last night, she — oh, I don't understand — she helped me then. Perhaps the mud masked the smell? I don't know,' and he rolled over on to his side and lay still, exhausted despite his long sleep. 'Where has she gone? Is she going to come charging out of the grasses at me again and gore me with her horns? Or has she gone for help, to find someone who can cure me? But cure me of what?'

The grasses rustled. Voices started to whisper.
'Shush!'
'I *am* shushing!'
'Well do it better.'

'I am.'
'Oh, shut up.'
'Well, really.'
'Come on and keep quiet.'

Jason lay stock still. The rustling came nearer and the voices became more distinct.

'What is it?' one asked.
'Stupid!' replied the other, irritably.
'What's stupid?'
'That question.'
'Why?'
'Because how should I know what it is? I can't see any more of it than you can.'
'It looks like a White Whish to me.'
'How would *you* know?'
'Because I was trained in Whishing.'
'You never told me that.'
'I don't tell you everything I know.'
'Why not?'
'Because then you'd know more than I know. You'd know what *you* know, *and* what I know. I'm not that stupid.'
'Well, you can at least tell me how you eat them.'
'Eat what?'
'White Whishes, of course.'
'Oh, them.'
'Yes, them! Well?'
'Salted.'
'Roast or raw?'
'Alive, with lashings of lemon and salt. Delicious.'
'Are they dangerous?'
'Not really. They have no arms. Look, it *is* a White Whish, and a big one!'
'You'll never swallow it whole.'
'That's a point.'
'And you can't eat it live if you can't swallow it whole.'
'Tricky.'

The Deadly Alternative

'Shall we leave it and look for a smaller one?'

'Seems such a waste. There must be a way of swallowing it somehow. Perhaps we could stretch it out long and thin so that it would slip down bit by bit.'

'It's worth a try.'

Jason's heart sank. The grasses parted and two large hairy objects hobbled into view on rows of tiny legs. Whiskers seemed to sprout from every part of their bodies, even their feet, their toes and their faces. Each had five pairs of glistening yellow eyes. All twenty eyes blinked balefully at Jason's crouching, straining figure. Whisker-one winked five times at Whisker-two and cleared its throat.

'Come along, little Whish, don't be frightened, we won't hurt you.'

Jason spun round on his back and kicked it full in the face, right between its third pair of eyes. The yellow light died in them and blood began to trickle down the long, whiskered head. It shook itself and little drops of bright blue blood spattered out over Jason's white costume.

'Keep back!' he shouted, 'or I'll kill you and wear your whiskers at my wedding.'

Whisker-one, gurgling and snuffling to itself, was slowly curling up into a ball. Whisker-two's eyes glinted, turning from yellow to a deep orange. Like a fork of lightning, two huge pincers shot out from under its shaggy face and pierced its wounded companion, impaling it in a savage grip. Slowly it dragged Whisker-one, still gurgling, under its face and began munching at it noisily, spitting out the whiskers and sneezing.

Jason shrank back. Whisker-one was collapsing like a leaky balloon. Soon it was gone and Whisker-two smacked its lip.

'Lovely. Delicious. A broken Whish-eater, I always say, is a tasty Whish-eater. Devour it while you may.' It gulped and hiccuped. 'No point in wasting good food,' and it turned and hobbled off through the waving grasses.

'I am a savage,' groaned Jason. 'I would have killed them, trampled them, kicked them to death. What have the Strummers done to me? Ludo knew. She sensed it. She'll never trust me again. I must get back to the Transformer. He must help me, put me back as I was. It's my only hope.' Then he remembered the Transformer's bulging head of muscles, his rippling, fanatical body. It was no good. That monster would never help him. He wouldn't even understand.

Jason shuddered and tried to think. He would have to try somewhere else. But where? Who? Stumbling through the long grasses, he crashed stubbornly on until he came to a clearing. In the middle of it there was a sleeping musician. It was one of the double-bass players from the Pacification Orchestra. He woke up with a yelp, saw Jason, screamed, and, in desperation, started to tear himself loose from the bass, to which he was attached down the front of his body. With a terrible ripping sound, he wrenched himself from it, opened the back of the instrument, and leapt inside. Slamming it shut, he crouched, quivering, and waited to see if the killer would go away.

Jason could just make out his panic-stricken eyes peering through one of the curved slits on the front of the bass. He approached the instrument, which stood impaled with its spike in the ground, turned his back towards it, and started to rub his wrists up and down the strings, trying to wear through the bonds that held him. Ludo had twisted some of the toughest grasses into a rope to tie him with, but strong as they were they gradually started to snap. The noise was terrible as he heaved himself up and down, and the captive inside was screaming and wailing. Just as the last strands snapped through, the musician burst from the back of the bass and rolled over and over on the ground, groaning and holding his ears.

'I'm deaf! Deafened! Pierced! You pierced my eardrums, I'll never play again. You monster, you, you . . . cacophonist!'

He was a thin, beaky creature, like a huge insect. He hissed and crackled and twisted about on the earth, kicking up clouds of brown dust. Jason picked up the double-bass, his cramped arms throbbing, and raised it above his head.

'Filthy, screeching, squirming, scaly little scab!' he bellowed,

The Deadly Alternative

and poised the spike of the double-bass above the agonised creature's head. 'You are going to die. You will take my place. You will be my ceremonial alternative. I hate you. I will destroy you.' But tears started to pour down his face. He paused and in that split second the musician scuttled out of range and fled. The double-bass plunged into the ground where his body had writhed a moment before. The spike sank deep into the dry earth.

A bubbling sound came from the spot where the musical weapon stood, stab-upright. Water began to ooze up around it. Jason grabbed the instrument and drew it out like a sword from a wound. As it came away, a great fountain spurted upwards into the air and cascaded down into the clearing. In a few seconds he was drenched.

The water was warm and clear, like a hot spring, and he opened his arms and embraced it. Tilting back his head, he let the liquid fall into his mouth. He felt clean again. Clean and good. Refreshed. He swung his arms back and forth over his head, threw his body forward and rinsed his matted hair free of mud and dust.

'Young man!' It was the Conductor. 'Young man, I must have a word with you.' He was obviously nervous. 'You have wandered into the orchestra's sleeping grounds. We rest here from our arduous ceremonial tasks. Rest is essential. You are disturbing that rest. Worse than that, you seem to be taking my little jest about killing one of us – well, you seem to be taking it seriously.' He smiled weakly and shrugged apologetically. 'I'm sorry, but it is, of course, quite out of the question. We can't possibly play a balanced chord when pacifying your Alternative, if you kill one of *us*. Now can we? Be reasonable. It was a joke, that's all. Merely my way of teasing the players. You must find your quarry elsewhere.'

'My victim', said Jason sternly, 'will hardly *need* pacifying. He will be dead already. It will be a pure formality. Any old chord will do by the time I've finished with him.' He rushed forward and the startled Conductor tripped back over a stone and fell on to the wet earth. Jason snatched up his baton-arm and held the pointed tip of the ivory stick at the creature's own throat.

'You! You will do. You don't play an instrument. If I kill you it won't unbalance the chord, will it?'

'But . . . but that's ridiculous! They won't know when to start. They'll be all over the place!'

'Nonsense, I'll start them off myself. Any fool can wave a little stick, even if it's clotted with ex-Conductor's blood,' and he jabbed it towards the gulping adam's apple.

'All right, all right! That's enough. I'll fix something, give me a minute.' But Jason did not move. 'Look, we've found a bloated Whish-eater over there, stuffed full of something that didn't agree with him. So stuffed he couldn't breathe. Suffocated, poor chap. Dead as a pillow. We'll use him. That's what we'll do, we'll use him. We'll say *you* killed him. How's that?'

'Well, in a way, I did,' said Jason, 'but,' tensing again, 'what about me? You can't leave me like this, puffed up with muscles and hate. I won't have it, do you hear?' and he struck the Conductor with his baton. The creature yelped with pain and slithered up to his knees.

'Listen, I'll fix that. I'll fix it. It's not usual, you know, not done. But I'll help you. Anything to be of assistance. If you'll come with me, I'll get the Transformer to adjust you. Reverse the process and all that — you'll see. It will be easy this time. Quite pleasant, really. Soothing. Lovely. You'll see. Come along. Don't be frightened.'

'The last time someone said "don't be frightened", they were planning to eat me,' snarled Jason.

'Not this time, not this time,' the Conductor whined, as he limped off hugging his baton. Jason followed warily close behind him. At last! At last there was a ray of hope.

Arriving at the room with the green curtain, where Jason had been moodivated with hate, the Conductor sat him down and disappeared to make the necessary arrangements. It was risky to let him go, but Jason felt that somehow he had gained the upper hand. In some mysterious way he had turned the tables and beaten the Strummers at their own game. The hate they had put into him had backfired. The conductor had bungled and would probably now be only too glad to be rid of him. He could relax and

The Deadly Alternative

wait for them to start making him normal again.

As it turned out, the process proved to be a lengthy one. For days he was shown endless scenes of love, harmony and kindness, which helped to blot out his anger, while he was made to lounge around on soft cushions, lazily idling the time away and gorging himself on sweetmeats, creamy pastries, sugared buns, chocolate doughnuts, syrupy waffles and jellied figtarts. At the end of a week, both his hate and his muscles had faded back to normal, and he emerged feeling his old self again.

He was provided with a Drummodile, an armoured beast with an oval drum growing out of each flank, like the one he and Ludo had been bundled into by the Strummers on the beach. This time, however, he was to ride on its back and its drums were to be filled with food and drink for the journey.

Before leaving, he asked one of the attendants if he could say goodbye to the Conductor, but was curtly told that the official in question had been 'replaced'. He was given no explanation and felt it best not to press the matter. As he was riding away, he heard the muffled sound of a great Pacification Chord echoing faintly from inside the Strummer halls, and he wondered who the victim could be. Perhaps it was the Conductor himself, disgraced and now confined in the dreaded velvet pod. Or perhaps it was some new victim of the Strummers, condemned, as Jason had been, to a fate that he would not understand until it was too late.

Jason hesitated. More than anything else, he wanted to get away from the Strummers' headquarters, but he could hardly ride off and leave the Chord to be played through to its deadly climax. He turned the Drummodile back in the direction of the Strummer halls, but the creature had only gone a few paces when a crowd of attendants rushed forward and blocked its path. One stepped forward and pointed stiffly into the distance. There was no expression on his face, but from between tight lips he let out a short whistle and the huge Drummodile obediently spun round and set off in the direction indicated.

Jason felt he should have leapt down and charged through towards the halls, but it was obviously hopeless. And then he heard the muffled Chord reach its climax and knew that, in any case, it was all over.

As the Drummodile plodded slowly out into the sea of tall grasses, with Jason sitting thoughtfully on its broad, plated back, depressed at his failure to help whoever it was inside the velvet pod, there was a disturbance in a thick clump of stems ahead and Ludo leapt into view. She sniffed the air, gave a whoop of pleasure and, running to the Drummodile's side, scrabbled up on to its back behind Jason. Sniffing him again more closely, to make sure he had returned to normal, she flung her arms around him and shouted for joy. They both started laughing and the sound was so infectious that even the Drummodile joined in, without knowing why, giving vent to deep, cheerful, rumbling noises. Jason banged on the drums with his fists and they surged forward at a gallop, shouting gaily and singing at the tops of their voices.

Soon they were exhausted and rode on in a contented silence.

'Ludo,' said Jason, after a long think, 'I'm puzzled. Why do you suppose the Strummers let me go in the end, when they are supposed to be so ruthless?'

'It was because you attacked the Conductor. I overheard some of the musicians talking, when I was hiding in the long grasses. They said it's never happened before and it seems the Composer was rather taken aback by it. He's busy now writing a new hate score, one that will make it safe for the Strummers themselves. You had an all-purpose hate and that was too dangerous, so they're going to change it. But it will take time and they decided that as you'd become an unnecessary risk, it would be best to cut their losses and move you on. From what they said, I gather that the Conductor was to be punished.'

'So it *was* him I heard being pacified as I left. I thought for a moment that it might be you.'

'No. They couldn't catch me. I found I could sniff them a mile off. It was their hate I could smell. I'm afraid you caught it, too, when you were treated. That's what made me attack you. I'm sorry, I couldn't help it.'

'Nor could I. They changed me. It was horrible. I hope you

have forgiven me, too?'

'Of course. It wasn't really you, was it? But that's all over now and behind us. Let's not talk about it.'

'Agreed.'

'An end to Strummers!'

'An end to Strummers!'

And they rode on, smiling quietly to themselves.

CHAPTER SIXTEEN
The Battle of the Snowcocks

Before long, Jason and Ludo had left the Strummers' domain far behind and were passing through pleasant wooded country dotted with low hills. Feeling hungry, they called a halt in a small clearing. While the Drummodile rested, they opened its drums and ate and drank, lying peacefully on a grassy bank.

Jason had been given back his belt and his old tunic, carefully mended, before his departure from the Strummer halls and, opening the belt-pouch, he took out the necklace of imitation Golden Worms. Showing them to Ludo, he told her the story of how he had found them.

'So it is the Sculptor we want, after all,' said Ludo thoughtfully. 'Do you remember that tiny hand, back at the Root Forest, the one they all laughed at?'

'Yes of course, the little one that said the Golden Worms were kept in the Sculptor's helmet. Could that be the answer?'

'It's possible. The Sculptor does wear a sort of helmet when remodelling one of us. It is mostly for face protection, I think, because the bottom part is transparent. But on top there is a

The Battle of the Snowcocks

golden dome, shaped like . . . like an onion-fruit. Do you think . . .'

'It all fits! It *must* be the answer. We *have* to find it, there's no other way,' and Jason punched his fist into the soft turf. Ludo, however, stared into the distance and was unable to share his eagerness. After a while, she said softly:

'But no one ever finds the Sculptor. The Sculptor finds *you*.'

Jason rolled over and looked at her. Perhaps she was starting to tire of the quest. He had to think of something.

'There must be a special place somewhere — a palace, a fortress, a great castle, something like that, where the helmet is kept when it's not in use — when the Sculptor is not travelling. Have you ever heard of such a place, during one of the remodelling visits?'

'No, it is not done to ask such questions,' said Ludo quietly. 'The Great One always has to speak first. We can only answer, so we learn very little.' Jason leapt to his feet.

'Then we must search and go on searching, until we find some more clues. Is there nobody who can help us?'

'We could try the School of Unlearning. Perhaps someone there could tell us what to do.'

'Do you know where it is?'

'Only that it stands on a flat-topped mountain and is difficult to reach because of the steep climb. But many learned people go there. It is an important centre and one of them should know *something*.'

'But I thought you said it was a School of Unlearning? Why would learned people want to go there?'

'To forget, of course. To attend the forgetting classes. That's what it's famous for.'

'I don't understand.'

'Well, as each day passes we learn more and more, right?'

'Right.'

'So our brains get cluttered up with facts until there is no room left for new ideas, right?'

'Right.'

'So eventually we need to be untaught, to unlearn all the rubbish in our brains and get back to pure and simple ideas, right?'

'I see. You mean simple ideas are better than complicated ones?'

'Naturally. All the greatest ideas are simple ones. At the School of Unlearning you start out by writing down all you know — all the thousands of details that are clogging up your mind. Then you are set the task — it usually takes about three years — of reducing all that clutter to one basic, simple original idea. Once you have done that, you are rated as unscholarly and fit to go out into the world again. They say there's no stopping a single-minded person with one clear idea in his head.'

'Why doesn't everyone attend then?'

'Well, you have to be a good climber to get in. And, of course, many are so confused by all their experiences that they can no longer see the value in wanting to forget.'

'I'm afraid I won't have time to stay for the whole course, not if it takes three years.'

'I realize that, but we won't have to. We will only need to question the new arrivals, the learned ones who know a great deal and who haven't yet started to be untaught. They are the ones who may be able to help us.'

'Right. Then we'd better get moving and start our search for a flat-topped mountain. The hills are slightly bigger over there, so we'll try that way. Unless of course . . . '

'Unless?'

'Unless you want to go back? You've come a long way from your village. You were happy there. I have no right to expect you to want to come with me. I can go on alone if . . . '

'After all we have been through, I am surprised you feel the need to ask. Surely you know that sharing a moment of danger with someone makes them more important than others you have known peacefully for years and years. And we have shared so many dangers. I couldn't think of going back.'

'I'm glad.'

They looked at one another silently for a moment, then, feeling embarrassed, turned and started busily repacking their drums.

The Drummodile was well rested and set off with its heavy legs

The Battle of the Snowcocks

swinging and its lumpy tail swishing. As they wended their way through scattered tree-plants, heading towards the tallest hills they could see, the great beast began humming cheerfully to itself and then broke into song. It sang a curious waltz, swaying from side to side as it boomed its rumbling chant:

> 'Oh, please, spill me a pillar,
> Kill me a spiller,
> And draw me a bucket of lines.
> Oh, please, call me a cabbage,
> Ravage a carriage,
> And dig me a grave in the pines.'

Jason and Ludo were puzzled by the words and asked the Drummodile to explain, but it pretended not to hear, and went back to its wordless humming again.

'I expect it's just happy to get away from those Strummers,' said Ludo. 'I am sure they treated it badly. Out here, it must find everything very peaceful after all that fighting and hating.'

'Don't speak too soon,' said Jason. 'I think there's trouble ahead.'

Ludo leant to one side so that she could peer past Jason's arm at the place they were coming to. It was a small cluster of stone-walled houses, surrounded by tall tree-plants. Beyond it reared up a great purple mountain, the tip of which was covered in streaks of yellow and orange. As they came closer they could see that the village was in an uproar. Creatures of all sizes and shapes and colours were running, hopping and slithering frantically about, hissing, muttering and jabbering at one another.

They parked the Drummodile beside a fallen log and left the beast contentedly chewing the spiky bark. No one took any notice of them in all the commotion and they were able to saunter into the village street without causing any comment. Ludo tried to listen to what the villagers were gabbling about. She looked surprised as she turned to Jason:

'They say a Snowcock is coming, but that shouldn't cause all this fuss. Usually, it's a time for a festival. But something odd is going on here. I'll sniff around and find out what it is. You stay over there, by that wall, and don't move.'

She went off, shoving and pushing her way through the bustling crowd. Minutes passed, and Jason was beginning to become impatient when he felt a tapping on the top of his head. He looked up and saw a long rope dangling there.

'Quick, climb up. No questions. Hurry.' It was Ludo, perched on top of the thick wall. Jason dragged himself up. Panting, he lay on his stomach on the smooth stones, high above the village street.

'Sorry about that,' said Ludo, 'but there was no choice. It could break out at any moment.'

'What's up?' gasped Jason.

'There's going to be a fight, a fight like you've never seen before. Something unbelievable has happened. I've heard of it but I never thought I'd actually see it myself. The last time it happened was so long ago that . . . '

'What are you talking about? What's going on? I thought we'd finished with fighting when we got away from the Strummers?'

'No, no. It's not Strummers. Quite different. This is going to be a real fight, a clean fight, a beautiful fight. Completely, utterly different, and great fun to watch . . . from up here, anyway.'

'But Ludo, a fight is a fight, you can't have good and bad fights. If people get killed, it's horrible, whatever sort of fight it is.'

'These are Snowcocks, and it *is* different with them, you'll see. They do it so splendidly. Or so everyone says. But let me explain what has happened. It seems that two, not one but *two*, Snowcocks are heading this way, one from the mountain and one from the forest. They are bound to meet here, in the village, and when they do it will mean a duel to the death. You see, Snowblobs are rather unusual. There are about ten thousand Snowhens born for every one Snowcock . . . '

'You mean each male Snowblob has ten thousand wives? That's fantastic!'

'Well, I wouldn't call them wives exactly. They are brides, but

The Battle of the Snowcocks

they don't have time to be wives, not properly. The Snowcock is huge, a mass of bulging bloblets. He is carried in a great net from place to place by his servants and every day he stops just long enough for a wedding ceremony. He marries a different Snowhen each day. She travels with him in his net during the night after the wedding and then the next morning she is taken out by the servants and buried wherever they happen to be.'

'Buried?'

'Yes, she is in a sort of trance, a deep sleep. It doesn't hurt her. She stays under the ground while the eggs are being formed. When they hatch they eat her, but she doesn't feel it, she's still asleep. Then they scrabble to the surface and scatter. They are nearly all females, of course, and then they have to wait around for a Snowcock to come along and mate with them in their turn.'

'Sounds a crazy system to me.'

'Why? It's been very successful. There are Snowblobs everywhere. They spread like wildfire. The old Snowcocks get pretty exhausted, though – all those ceremonies and being humped along in that great net – but they usually manage to get through about five thousand weddings before they explode. When that happens, you can hear it for miles around. The whole thing bursts in all directions. Poofh!' and Ludo threw out her arms and nearly fell off the wall.

'Now I see what all the excitement is about,' said Jason. 'If there are so few males, it means that by the laws of chance they will hardly ever meet one another.'

'Exactly, but that's what is about to happen here. And when two of them meet, it's a sight to be seen from a healthy distance.'

'Will they both explode?'

'I hope not. If that happens, we'll be blown right out of the village. No, the story goes that most of the real fighting is done by the servants. Only at the last moment, if the servants have nearly all been killed, on both sides, do the Snowcocks themselves go in to the attack. They're not really built for it. In fact, I can't think how they do it – all those bulges and blobs. I suppose they ram one another. Eventually, or so they say, the winner will engulf the loser and absorb him.'

'It means an awful lot of Snowhens will never be brides, doesn't it? I mean, the winner won't be able to mate with twenty thousand females, will he? What happens to the loser's ten thousand?'

'That's a good point. It's the weakness of the system, I suppose. But, then, every system has a weakness somewhere. It has to have, or else it would be the only system — all the others would have to give way to it — and there'd only be one kind of life. Very dull.'

'The weakness in the Snowblob system seems a big one to me, and so wasteful, too.'

'Not really. After all, you've got to remember that two Snowcocks hardly ever do meet. This is a rare event we are about to see.'

Jason was on the verge of asking Ludo about the Snowblob wedding ceremonies, where there was a deep rumbling sound from one end of the village.

'Here we go,' she yelled. 'Hold tight. The first one is arriving now.'

There was a stamping of feet and the advance-guard of the giant Snowcock's armed servants strode into view. They were thin, spindly creatures, covered in shiny armour. The fronts of their bodies were a mass of sharp spikes, pointing straight forward. They would only have to run at someone to impale him and kill him instantly. The long tapering legs marched sullenly along, but no arms swung from their shoulders.

'They've got no arms,' whispered Jason.

'Don't need any,' hissed Ludo. 'Those spikes are moveable. They can make them stab in different directions to spear food as well as kill their enemies. And when they are feeding or fighting, their excitement makes the spikes grow longer and longer, like spears.'

'There must be about a hundred of them.'

'At least. The Snowcock is carried by a special group of four-legged ones, and then there are a few more of the ordinary ones to bring up the rear. About 150 altogether. Look! Look! . . .'

From the other end of the wide village street came a second

deep rumbling, as the advance-guard of the second Snowcock came round the corner. When the rival advance-guards saw one another there was a great clattering roar. Their armour began to crackle and their spikes stuck out from their fronts and grew longer and longer, twitching and swishing as the two opposing groups started to rush headlong towards one another.

They met at full tilt in the village square and crashed together at such speed that all the onlookers could see was a confused, shimmering mass of stabbing, lunging bodies. The clash of spike on spike and armour on armour rent the air and in no more than a few minutes the whole square was littered with impaled, tottering figures. They collapsed moaning into the dust, one by one, until all was still. Having been perfectly matched, they were all perfectly dead. Not one remained on its feet.

'Now it's up to the Snowcocks themselves,' whispered Ludo in a tone of awe and excitement. Jason glanced sideways at her face. She was licking her lips nervously and he felt a pang of disgust flood through him at the obvious pleasure she was taking in the brutal scene below them. She had been so happy before to escape from the hate-filled world of the Strummers, and yet here she was enjoying a display of even greater violence. It was a strange contradiction.

He was about to ask her to explain her feelings, when trumpets sounded at both ends of the street and two huge white shapes appeared, carried in bulging silver hammocks by teams of bearers. Gathering speed and trampling over the scattered bodies of the slaughtered advance-guards, the bearers charged at one another, carrying their two giant masters aloft.

They met head-on in the square, ramming one another with such force that the bearers and the following rear-guards were all smashed together and flung against the walls and houses. The two incredible bundles of bulging blobs that Jason supposed must be the Snowcocks sank into one another and appeared to become one lumpy mass, quivering and rolling and hissing. Like a fat white jelly full of wrestling wildcats, it lunged and twisted, banging into doors and walls, knocking over barrows and tearing down striped awnings. The startled faces of the villagers could be seen staring from every window.

Suddenly there was an enormous explosion that blasted Jason and Ludo clean off the top of the wall and down on to a heap of drying fruits in the garden beyond. The air filled with a million swirling snowflakes, a dense snowy cloud that blotted out everything and everyone. The whole village was submerged in huge drifts of settling snow-banks. Down it came, until finally all was still.

From beneath the shimmering white surface two fruit-smeared figures emerged and struggled to their feet.

'Wow!' said Ludo. 'They must have both gone up. What a fight! What a spectacle! Wasn't that tremendous?'

Jason said nothing, covering his silence by busying himself with cleaning off the sticky fruits. As they scrambled back over the wall and dropped into the snow-bound street, they heard a distant pattering sound, like the scurrying of thousands of tiny paws. As it grew louder, Ludo sniffed the air excitedly.

'Snowhens!' she shouted. 'Swarms of them, attracted by the scent. Look! Here they come.'

A seething mass of small white blobs was converging on the village from all directions, filling the streets and rolling ecstatically in the fast melting snow.

'It's a mass wedding,' cried Ludo. 'They're absorbing the snowflakes. I didn't know they could do that. Where's the weakness in their system then?'

'Over there,' replied Jason, pointing.

Brandishing clubs and waving sticks, the shouting villagers were pouring out of their snow-covered houses. With hoarse yells and whoops of triumph, they started methodically beating to death every Snowhen they could catch.

'Why?' yelled Jason. 'Why?'

'Their favourite food,' Ludo called back. 'Normally Snowhens are extremely difficult to catch — very timid — but the snowflakes have made them bold — and easy prey for the hunters. The village will be able to feast for days.'

The Battle of the Snowcocks

'So the final flaw in the system is that they taste good!'

Ludo laughed. 'Yes, I suppose it is. Let's watch from that stairway over there. We'll get a better view.'

'No, let's go.'

'Go! But it's not over yet.'

'We've seen enough. Let's move on,' and Jason turned his back on the massacre of the Snowhens and trudged through the slush, back the way they had come. Ludo caught up with him and walked reluctantly by his side, every so often looking back longingly over her shoulder.

'They were only non-gumfs, you know,' she said, realizing that Jason had been upset by the slaughter. 'They don't feel any pain.'

'Do you remember the last time someone said that?' asked Jason.

'No,' said Ludo.

'It was the Mha-kee.'

'Oh, yes, I remember.'

'And he was talking about me,' said Jason quietly.

'Yes, but . . . well, I expect he thought you were a non-gumf. He wasn't to know, was he?'

'But you *do* know about the Snowhens, I suppose?'

'Yes, of course. Look, you're making a fuss over nothing. The villagers have to eat, don't they?'

Jason was still trying to find an answer to that when they arrived at the fallen log, where the Drummodile was waiting patiently, still munching the spiky bark as if nothing had happened.

They remounted and rode off towards the purple mountain. Skirting the village, they soon came to a well-beaten path that led them through a pass at the side of the mountain and out into a dramatic new world of peaks and crags, stretching endlessly as far as they could see. They climbed a steep slope to an outcrop of jagged rocks and scanned the horizon, but there was no sign anywhere of the high plateau they were seeking.

That night they sheltered in a small cave and Jason felt compelled to speak to Ludo about her reactions to the terrible

Snowcock duel.

'But it *was* exciting,' she insisted. 'You can't deny that.'

'And yet you hated the Strummers.'

'They were different, vicious, nasty. The Snowcocks were glorious, magnificent. Why can't you see that?'

'Because fighting is only right if you have to defend yourself.'

'Exactly — that's it. The Strummers were unpleasant because they went looking for trouble. They weren't defending anything. And they were cruel, too. But the Snowcocks only did what they had to do. No more. Each was defending himself against the other. It was a fair fight and one that made sense.'

'But why couldn't they simply pass by one another and leave it at that — go their separate ways peacefully?'

'Because they didn't know how to. I told you they hardly every meet, so how could they learn how to behave, how to control themselves? They don't go looking for one another to start a fight. What we saw was a freak accident. And I think they both acted very courageously.'

'So courage is lack of control, then?'

'You are twisting my words.'

They argued on into the night, but never really reached an agreement. Jason decided eventually that it was unfair to expect this strange, furry, horned girl to have the same attitudes and beliefs as himself. They came from different worlds and instead of worrying over their disagreements, he should be marvelling at how well they got on with one another most of the time. Without her, after all, he would never have survived this far. Compared with the other inhabitants of the Inrock he had encountered in his travels, she was almost saintly. And on that thought he slept at last, a deep, dreamless sleep.

CHAPTER SEVENTEEN
The Rock Arena

Jason awoke to a strange noise, like the shuffling of feet on dry gravel. He lay still, trying to recall where he was. Then he remembered the cave in which he and Ludo had taken refuge. They had found a small side-pocket in the rocks, a curved hollow, the bottom of which was covered with soft, dry earth. It made a comfortable bed, just large enough for the two of them to curl up snugly, when they had finally settled down to sleep after their long discussion the night before.

Twisting his head, he caught sight of a bright, narrow shaft of light, cutting down through the lumpy walls of the cave from some opening high up in the rocks. The shuffling noise continued and, as he became more fully awake, he felt a wave of alarm pass through his body. Turning slowly to see if Ludo was also awake, his alarm increased on finding that he was now alone in the small rock-hollow. Next to him, in the soft earth, was the clear impression made by her sleeping body, but Ludo herself had vanished.

Sitting up carefully, avoiding any sudden movement, he peered over the rim of the side-hollow and down at the main tunnel. There, to his amazement, he saw a long, orderly line of creatures moving slowly and patiently into the cave. They were of many different shapes and colours, but had one thing in common — each was carrying a large bone of some kind.

Jason did his best to suppress a small shudder at the sight of this sinister procession and stretched his neck forward cautiously to see a little more. Glancing to the left, he was able to look beyond the cave-opening, to the land surface outside. There, stretching away seemingly forever, was the longest queue Jason had ever set eyes on. Hundreds of figures were lined up, nose to tail, and not one of them appeared to be without a large, white bone.

For what seemed like an hour, Jason watched them shuffling on, into the depths of the cave, and waited anxiously for the end of the line to pass him so that he could run out of the cavern and make his escape. But the end of the line never came.

Sooner or later, he realized, one of the creatures would glance up at him and he would be discovered, so he slid back into his hollow and pondered the problem. What *were* they all doing? The only answer he could arrive at was that they were all taking part in some sort of burial ritual. Perhaps some giant creature had died and his bleached bones had been found in a deserted spot and now, with due ceremony, they were being put to rest in the darkest recesses of a holy cave. If only he himself could somehow acquire a bone, he could join the queue and shuffle along with the rest of the mourners. But how?

At that moment there was a loud commotion from the main tunnel. Jason slid his head over the rim of the hollow just in time to witness a nasty accident. A heavy, armoured creature with sharp spines protruding from its forehead must have tripped forward and plunged its head painfully into the soft, rounded rump of the bulbous form in front of it. A froth of large, yellowish bubbles was now cascading from the punctured rear and its owner was kicking and bellowing and trying to spin round in the narrow cave-passage to confront its assailant. The armoured beast, anticipating trouble, had started to back away, crashing into the figure close behind it.

As Jason watched, the chaos spread down the line, the

The Rock Arena

peacefully patient mood erupting into snarling anger and frustration. Legs were being kicked, heads buffeted, bodies bumped and, he noted with interest, carefully carried bones were being dropped.

At the height of the confusion, Jason spotted his chance. A long, curved bone had been accidentally kicked up the slope in front of him to within a few feet of his face. Rolling softly down out of his hollow, he scooped it up and then crouched on the main cave-floor. Feet and hooves and claws were still flailing in all directions and, like a fallen jockey, he curled up into a tight ball, protecting his face with his arms. He was painfully thumped a few times and then felt the wild movements around him dying away. A trumpet was sounding from somewhere deep inside the cave, its notes echoing eerily around the walls. There were shouts for order from somewhere down the line and, as he stood up and wedged a place for himself in the hurriedly reorganized queue, he sensed an increasing urgency as tightly packed figures pushed forward at a quicker pace.

Shuffling along, feeling like an escorted prisoner, he clung to his precious bone and kept his head lowered. The column twisted to the left, then the right, following the curved shape of the main tunnel. To his great relief no one questioned his presence. The order of the line had been too disrupted for his neighbours to identify him as a queue-jumper.

They travelled on in this way for what seemed an age, until the roof of the cave began to open up into a ravine. The slit in the rocks was still high above them, but more light was pouring down with each step they took and Jason did his best to hide his bone beneath his folded forearms.

Now the ravine was widening into a tall, slender rock valley and their speed was increasing with each bend in the path. Everyone was chattering excitedly and the air of mournful patience was giving way to one of eager anticipation. Perhaps, after all, thought Jason, this is not a funeral ceremony. But if it is not, what is it?

The answer was around the next bend. There the passage suddenly widened out into a broad, flat area at the far end of which there was a vertical rock wall. At the base of this wall were five large holes, each manned by two tentacled officials. The queue was splitting up into five streams and passing through the different holes, the creatures in each line obviously knowing which one to choose. Jason was at a loss. Which way should he go? Then he heard one of the officials shouting out:

'Long-bones in the balcony, far left. Finger-bones, standing room only, near left. Ribs and backbones, straight ahead for the grandstand. Skulls and pelvises, near right for the royal box. Tusks and fangs, far right, please climb to the upper balcony. Hurry along! Muzzle-off in twenty minutes. Keep the lines moving. Hurry along!'

Fingering the bone hidden in his crossed arms, Jason calculated that it must be a long-bone and veered off to the far left. He was almost at the opening when a roar of anguish went up from the creature in front of him.

'My bone! I've dropped my bone.'

'Sorry, you'll have to go back for it,' said the nearest official, casting his four eyes upwards in a mocking gesture.

'You don't believe me, do you?' screeched the boneless one. 'But I had it, I tell you, I had it. Let me through.'

The official's only reply was to kick the unfortunate beast between its knobbly front legs. It sighed and doubled up in agony, toppling over on to one side and groaning on the dirt floor. The official smiled down at it and trod on one of its trembling feet.

'*So* sorry,' he smirked.

'That's enough!' shouted Jason. 'Here, is this your bone?'

'Yes, yes, that's it, that's it. Thank you so much. May all your legs be knobbly ones. Now let me through, let me through, or I'll miss the bone-up.'

'Come on, next,' yelled the irritated official, robbed of one of his small pleasures. Jason moved forward, but was halted by a powerful tentacle, thrust across his chest.

'Bone? Show me your bone.'

'I . . . I gave mine to . . .'

'Yours?'

The Rock Arena

'Yes. You were hurting that . . . '

'That was not *your* bone. You *said* it wasn't.'

'I only said that to stop you. Now please let me in.'

'No bone, no entry.'

'Does everyone have to have a bone?' asked Jason, changing tack. He pointed at the official: '*You* don't have one.'

'Everyone but staff and competitors. And I'm staff. Now clear off.'

'Why didn't you say so? I am a competitor.'

A simultaneous hiss came from all the creatures within earshot and they shrank back a little from the spot where Jason was standing.

'A competitor? You should have been here three hours ago, with the others, for the bone-lazing.'

'I was held up. There was a fight in the cave. I couldn't get through.'

The official beckoned a tentacle at each of his colleagues and they conferred hurriedly.

'All right, inside and turn sharp left down the steps and across the yard. The door straight in front of you will take you to the changing rooms. Move it.'

Jason thanked him and ran inside. Behind him, he heard a great burst of laughter, followed by peals of inane giggling. He found this strangely worrying, but did not dare to turn back. As he ran down the steps, it occurred to him that perhaps only a fool would admit to being a boneless competitor. What else could have made them laugh so hard? As a precaution, he changed direction and, instead of making for the door straight ahead of him, turned to the right and ran down a long curved passage. At the far end he saw a small opening and squeezed through it. The sight that met his eyes took away what was left of his breath.

He was gazing down at a vast, oval rock arena. At its centre, a huge open surface was covered with bright yellow sand, flat and smooth and glistening in the bright light. On the sloping terraces surrounding it stood thousands of excited figures, packed tightly together in a dense, expectant crowd. As he watched, a group of spindly banner-carriers emerged from a tunnel and spread out around the perimeter of the sand. Facing inwards, they stood to attention and waited, their banners held stiffly erect. On each banner was a crest showing an emblem of three tall trees.

The arrival of the banner-carriers was greeted by the terrace crowd with a great roar of excitement. Waving their bleached bones high in the air, they began a rhythmic chant that mounted and mounted as more and more voices joined in until the noise was deafening.

'Bone-throwers, Bone-throwers, Bone-throwers,' they cried, the great wave of sound echoing around the giant bowl of rock.

Jason was about to plunge into the tightly packed crowd and lose himself in the crush, when he felt a long tentacle wrap itself around his neck.

'Lost our way, did we?' asked a sarcastic voice in his ear. 'Can't have that, now can we?'

The official guided Jason back to the changing-room door and with rippling tentacles opened it and pushed him through. As the door slammed behind him, Jason felt the first pang of real fear at the thought of what it might mean to be a competitor here. Perhaps the burst of laughter he had heard when he claimed to be one, and the massed chant of 'Bone-throwers', added up to serious trouble ahead. Perhaps the competitors here were hopeless, condemned prisoners, rather than highly acclaimed athletes.

In the dark passage ahead he could detect pathetic groans and the rattling of heavy chains. Was he in some kind of ancient dungeon, from which he, and the other victims, would be forcibly pronged out into the arena for slaughter?

Groping along in the dim light, he turned a corner and was promptly flattened by a running figure that struck him from behind. They picked themselves up and stared at one another. It was Ludo.

'Oh no!' she moaned. 'They've got you too. I hoped you would stay put. I was going to hide and wait for the games to start and then sneak out and collect you and then . . . '

'Calm down, calm down. Tell me where we are and what is

going on here.'

But there was no time. Tentacles lashed out from nowhere and bound them like coils of rope. They were half-carried and half-dragged along the grim passage and into a large chamber, where they were flung on the floor. All around them were sprawled dejected figures weighted down with heavy chains.

'Two more here for you,' shouted an official voice.

'Right, chain them up and let's get this show started,' bellowed another voice in the semi-darkness. 'It's time for the opening ceremony. Strap their armour on, quickly now.'

A wide door clanked open and their wretched companions heaved themselves up and began trudging towards the intense light that was now streaming in on them.

'Wait, wait,' yelled another voice. 'Those two over there, they don't have their head-bags or their redberries. Quick, fix them up.'

'Head-bags, redberries?' gasped Jason, hardly able to move under the weight of his armour plates. 'Is this some kind of nightmare? What are . . . ' but before he could continue, tentacles lurched towards his head and he felt a soft, hairy bag being pulled down over his head. Glancing across at Ludo, he saw that she was being treated in the same way, but with some difficulty because of her horns. Then, peering around him, he realized that all the other figures were wearing similar bags on their heads. But the hairy tops to the bags and their snug fit made them look like bulbous wigs, as if each wearer had a large shaggy head, with long locks of hair hanging down all around.

By now they were so frightened that all Jason and Ludo could do was to stare at one another in dumb shock. Speechless, they were hustled along and out into the blinding glare of the vast arena. There, they were herded in a forlorn huddle of fifty or so clanking, lurching figures, towards the very centre of the open space, while the crowded terraces screamed and hooted with savage delight.

Then a great hush fell over the arena and all eyes turned to the Royal Box. Trumpets rang out and a tall, lozenge-shaped creature appeared at one side of the box and squealed an announcement:

'Welcome to the court of Rasimondus the Triple-Brutal, Muzzleking of all Canini, Overseer of the Skeletal Games and Supreme Judge of the Bonefire Race. The Great Lord bids you welcome. Raise your bones now and salute him. The Muzzleking!'

As their chant rose, stronger and stronger, a shimmering curtain at the rear of the Royal Box drew back and a glowering, cloaked figure swayed majestically forward. The Muzzleking's satanic face gazed down at the crowded Terraces. His wrinkled snout sniffed the air of the arena. A drop of saliva escaped his sagging lips.

His body was almost completely hidden by the long purple cloak, which was embossed with his crest of three tall trees. It was difficult to make out the shape of his trunk or legs, but out of the top of his head grew a strange, conical, leather crown of straps and buckles.

Reaching the edge of the box, he gazed to left and right, accepting the chants of his adoring populace. After a brief pause, he took from a purple cushion in front of him a single, thin, polished bone and held it in his mouth until a hush had fallen over the crowd. Then, with a disdainfully regal flick of the neck, he tossed it forward into the air. It spun down and down and landed with a soft thud in the yellow sand of the arena floor below. This was the signal for an ear-bursting roar from the terraces and the games had begun.

'Now we're for it,' muttered the crouching figure to Jason's left. 'Now we're bone-aching for it.'

'I don't understand. What games can we play in these chains and this heavy armour? How can we race?'

'Race? Race? You bone-headed twitskull. What do you think this is? A honey party? A flower-plucking? Hasn't anyone told you *any*thing?'

'No, I missed the early part.'

'You missed the bone-lazing? You poor little polyp. You're for

The Rock Arena

it. Suss-jee!'

'What does the bone-lazing do? How does it help?'

'It's special exercising – relaxing – trancing – mind-waving – you know – so that when the bones come you don't feel them. You'll find out. Suss-jee!'

'The bones? But I thought they were like . . . well, like tickets to get in here.'

'Oh, my snout and liver. Why do you think you are wearing armour, and head-bags full of redberries?'

'Redberries, what *are* these redberries?'

'Are you sure you're one of us? When did you join the gang?'

Jason sensed something odd and was cautious with his answer.

'I'm a new member. They had no time to explain.'

'This is ridiculous. They're out of their bone-cracking skulls. All right, listen, it will start in a moment. When the bones come, pull your head down into your armour as far as you can. Your head-bag will protect you and any that hit it will burst the redberries and they will trickle down your face and splash all over you. They want blood, don't they, so we give it to them. Got it?'

'I think so,' said Jason. A dim understanding of what was happening was beginning to dawn on him. It was all some sort of gruesome charade. But why? What was behind it?

While they had been talking, the roaring spectators had been throwing themselves round and round in a twirling dance, pushing and shoving and rotating their crowded bodies, with their bones held high above them. Then, on a shrill blast from a strange bone-flute in the Royal Box, they let fly.

'Jason, Jason,' cried Ludo, 'we're going to be crushed to death. It's a public boning. I heard about them once. They used to do them in the old days, but they have been outlawed for years. I had no idea they had been started up again. We'll be killed.'

'No, it's all right. Trust me, I'll explain later. Pull your head down into your armour, like a tortoise.'

'Like a what?'

'Never mind, do as I say. There's a trick. Redberries in your head-bag, they'll squash. Play dead. You'll be . . . ' but there was no more time . . . The bones were flying thick and fast now.

Whistling and spinning through the air, the arcing, tumbling bones, flung wildly in from all directions, descended like giant hail-stones on the tragic cluster of chained bodies in the centre of the arena. They slammed and bounced against the armour plates strapped to the quaking victims. Jason and Ludo tucked their heads down as far as they could and waited for the bombardment to end. Gradually the jolting and thumping died away and they heard another great roar rise up from the encircling terraces.

Stretching their necks slightly, they managed to squint over the top of their armour and saw the Muzzleking mounting a stone-slab throne.

'The public boning is complete. Remove the bodies of the condemned prisoners. Gather the bones and erect the Sacred Bonefires on the cliff-tops above,' intoned the great king, and then sat down regally on his royal slab. 'Prepare the arena for the Skeletal Games.'

The packed crowd cheered themselves hoarse at this announcement, but Jason hardly heard them. His attention had suddenly become focused on the sprawled figures around him. They were a horrible sight, seemingly crushed to death by the bone onslaught and covered in trickling blood. But as he peered closely at his neighbour, he saw his eyes open. One eye winked at him, then they closed again and there was no movement except for the tip of a tongue that darted out and licked up some of the red juice that was trickling in such a sinister fashion over the fleshy lips. Jason stuck his own tongue out and tasted the redberry juice. It was delicious and it was all he could do to stop himself from licking more of it from his face.

Several large beasts with stumpy legs and wide shovel-mouths then entered the arena and began scooping up the apparently dead bodies and carrying them off to one of the exits. Other, tall, many-tentacled creatures, like gigantic versions of the arena officials, started gathering up the scattered bones and placing them into huge skin-bins. These were then dragged away through

The Rock Arena

another of the dark exits.

Scooped up along with the other victims, Jason found himself tumbled in a clanking heap inside a dark exit tunnel. Although a little bruised, he felt surprisingly fit, considering his ordeal, and hoped desperately that Ludo had managed a similar escape and had not been caught by an awkward bone.

As the arena exit doors slammed shut, there was a moment of terrifying darkness. Then hidden lights flashed on and, to Jason's astonished gaze, the whole scene changed. Where there had been silent awful carnage, there now erupted a busy babble of instructions, sighs of relief, and friendly laughter. Although he had guessed there was some deception, he found the transformation hard to take in.

'Well done, Snouts, let's get moving,' urged a hidden voice. 'That was a great show – tremendous. Even better than last time. Get those bags off your heads. Hurry up. Stack the armour by the walls. Let's go now, let's go. Into the baths, as quick as you can. Wrestlers and bone-jumpers first, please. You're on next. Bonefire racers to the cliff-tops as soon as you can.'

'Jason, Jason, over here.' It was Ludo's voice, and Jason dragged himself gratefully through the mass of scrambling figures to reach her side. Her face was matted with dried redberry juice.

'What a trick,' she gasped, as they struggled together to a quiet corner and began removing one another's armour. 'The crowd thought they'd killed the lot of us, but it was all an act, a sham.'

'I wish someone had told me before we went out there,' muttered Jason. 'That entry into the arena was one of the worst moments of my life.'

'Same for me, but isn't it a marvellous feeling now. The relief is almost worth it.'

'What do we do next?'

'Let's follow them to the baths and try to join the cliff-top racers. There's a better chance of escape that way. I only hope someone doesn't discover we are not part of the act. They might stop acting with us then, and do something for real.'

'Why do you suppose they let us take part at all? We have

discovered their secret. That could be dangerous for them.'

'I don't think those officials — the ones with the tentacles — are in on it,' replied Ludo. 'They must have thought we were simply two more useful victims to improve the spectacle. And the others were too involved by that time.'

'I said I was a new recruit.'

'Good, let's stick to that, and hope that someone high up doesn't spot us.'

They removed the last of the armour plating and found that the chains on their feet could easily be unclipped. Shaking themselves free, they followed the other figures that were now moving off to a circular hole in the far wall. Through it, they found themselves in a large, communal, rock-cut bath of warm, flowing water. Jumping in, they splashed about with the others and eavesdropped on their chattering.

'Bones, bones, bee-utiful bones. Roll on the bone-feast.'

'Bigger than last time. I can't wait to get at all that lovely marrow.'

'You'll have to run in the marrow-thon first.'

'Dunk him, somebody. His jokes are as bad as my bruises.'

'It was rough out there this time. Those head-bags aren't thick enough. One good squelch and the protection's gone.'

'Might knock some sense into you. Get off!'

General mayhem erupted and Jason and Ludo were nearly drowned in the floods of water that swirled around the playfully fighting figures. Then, one by one, the contestants left the bath and disappeared into another changing-room nearby.

'Did you notice something about them?' asked Jason, as he and Ludo floated quietly in a corner of the rock-bath. 'Although they were different shapes and sizes, they all had a sort of doggy look. Heavy snouts and pointed ears, shaggy fur and tails.'

'As they are all part of the trick, I suppose they must all be secret members of the Muzzleking's court, and *he* is rather snouty, isn't he? But who cares? All we need is a way out of here. Let's join the bonefire racers and get to the cliff-tops.'

They managed more easily than expected. By the time they left

The Rock Arena

the bath, most of the others had gone and from the terraces outside they could hear the roar of the crowd, urging on the competitors in the games that were already taking place on the arena floor.

Along with the small group that remained, they donned special racing tunics of blue and yellow and then filed obediently out into a corridor and up a long, spiral rock-cut stairway. After a tiring ascent that seemed to last forever, they found themselves lined up high on the cliff-tops near a huge pile of twigs and branches. A tentacled official fussed about with torches and rags. Far below lay the arena with its packed, noisy terraces and its leaping, jumping athletes.

'I don't understand,' whispered Jason to Ludo. 'They haven't used bones to build the fires, only old bits of wood.'

'Must be another trick.'

'Well, if it *is*, then these officials up here must be in the know.'

'Perhaps these officials have been bribed. Who knows? Nothing is what it seems here. This whole event is a joke, a bad joke at the expense of all those spectators down there. It's disgusting.'

'Personally I think it's the spectators who are disgusting. They thought they were boning us to death. They loved that blood-bath or what they thought was one. They're monsters. Serves them right if they *are* tricked.'

'It's still a cheat. And what's the point of it all? Why bother?'

'I've been thinking about that. The secret must be to do with the bones. Perhaps they have some magical properties.'

'Nonsense. They are any old bones, picked up out on the desert, or wherever.'

'Yes, but it would take an age to collect them all together like this, if you tried to do it on your own.'

'But who would *want* thousands of bones? It makes no sense to me,' muttered Ludo, staring down at the arena as the last of the athletic events came to a resounding conclusion.

An idea was beginning to form in Jason's mind and he was on the verge of pinning it down when a fanfare sounded from below and the cliff-top official shouted:

'Quick, quick, attach your torches and stand by.' Each of them had a burning torch of wood strapped on top of their heads and then they lined up again along the very edge of the cliff. A loud bang was heard from the direction of the distant Royal Box.

'Go!' shouted the lanky official, his tentacles writhing wildly and changing colour with excitement. 'Go-go-go!'

CHAPTER EIGHTEEN
The Bonefire Race

The Bonefire Race began. Watching the other runners, Jason and Ludo saw that they had set off at a steady trot around the great oval of the cliff-edge, stepping perilously near the rim. One slip and they would be bouncing down the rough rock wall and on to the heads of the spectators below, who were all craning their necks to see the race high above them.

'If this is a race,' panted Jason, 'how do we win and what do we do with these torches? There are fires built all around the cliffs and we have passed two already. Why don't we dip our heads and light them up as we go?'

'The others must know what to do. Follow their lead. Don't try anything odd, but keep your eyes open for a good escape route,' called back Ludo.

Escape did not look as easy as they had imagined, however. There were tentacled officials everywhere, positioned at regular intervals like watchful prison guards. If only Jason knew how the race would end, it might help him to plan something. After a full circle of the cliff-edge, his curiosity overcame him and he steadily increased his pace until he came alongside one of the big-snouted racers.

'Where's the winning-post?' he panted. Big-snout cast him a suspicious, sidelong glance, but said nothing.

'How do we know when someone's won?'

'He'll be the last one standing, won't he,' snapped Big-snout from between clenched teeth.

'Of course,' said Jason, 'just testing you. Carry on.' Big-snout's response was to spit on the ground in front of Jason's running feet. His action made Jason pause for a moment and he heard a gasp of alarm from Ludo just behind him.

'Sorry, did I nearly trip you?' he asked, without looking round.

'No. It wasn't that,' spluttered Ludo, coming up alongside Jason. 'It's — it's much worse. I have discovered the secret of this race and it is bad news. Very bad.'

'Spit it out.'

'Yes, exactly, that was it. When he spat in front of you, you nearly stopped for a moment.'

'Yes?'

'And — well — the flames on your torch burned in a different way. They crept down the stick, towards your head. There must be a strong down-current of air, all around the edge of the rock-bowl, and the slower you run, the nearer the flames come to your head. If you stopped altogether, out here on the rim, the flames would soon set fire to your hair and burn your head off!'

'I could put it out with my hands,' shouted Jason.

'Don't try. I went to touch the flame a moment ago and it is white hot. I couldn't even get my fingers close to it.'

'So the longer we keep going fast, the longer we survive. That is what he meant by the winner being the last one standing. And I suppose the winner then lights all the fires, on a final lap of honour.'

'Brilliant!' shouted Ludo. 'What a race! What a spectacle! What a . . . sorry, I forgot.'

'Why are you so cheerful?'

'I'm the best racer I know. I'll win easily. No problem. But I forgot that by then you'll be . . . '

'Thanks very much. I suggest we keep a steady pace and try to

The Bonefire Race

think of some way out of this.'

As he spoke, one of the other racers lowered his head and made a desperate sprint, trying to put out his flame altogether. The crowd below roared him on, pointing and laughing.

He failed, and collapsed in a heaving, panting heap. As the others ran past him, they saw the flames of his head torch burn quickly lower and lower. Just as they were about to singe his shaggy fur, he leapt up and ran wildly round in circles, to the crowd's delirious delight.

Twisting his head, Jason saw the hapless figure run on one last, big circle, right behind a tentacled official. When he emerged from the other side he was a rolling ball of flame that crackled and spluttered and finally flickered out on the very edge of the cliff-top. The crowd below went wild with prolonged applause and the Muzzleking bowed stiffly from his regal slab.

Jason was horrified and racked his brain for a solution. As they ran on, he saw one figure after another running in circles and finally exploding into a flaming mass on the cliff-edge. But there was something strange about the way this happened. Each time the final circle took the racer behind one of the tentacled officials. Once again, perhaps all was not what it seemed to be.

Changing direction slightly, Jason ran closer to the next official and there, as he sped past, he was just able to make out the silent form of one of the supposedly dead racers. Crouching in the official's shadow, the figure looked up at him briefly and grinned.

So it was yet another trick. As Ludo had claimed, the whole horror-show was a great fraud. As before, the victims were all actors, playing out a huge deception for the crowds on the terraces.

He was about to catch up with Ludo to explain it all to her, when he felt the flames on his own torch burning painfully close to his head. Following the lead of the others, he circled wildly and plunged behind the body of the next official. Sure enough, there, hidden in the shadow, was a ball of dry twigs and he dipped his head onto it and ignited it, kicking it round towards the cliff-top. As it burst into flames and the crowd roared once more, he felt a large, wet tentacle snuff out his flames and he lay still and silent, crouched down on the hard, rocky surface.

A few minutes later, Ludo was the last racer left and a great blast of trumpets from below told her the moment must have come to perform the climax of the race.

'Bone-fires, bone-fires, bone-fires,' chanted the crowd and Ludo, hoping desperately that she was doing the right thing, touched her torch to the nearest pile of branches. It burst into flames and she ran on to the next and the next, until all were burning wildly, a great ring of flaming beacons, circling the huge oval cliff-top like a fiery necklace. The timing was perfect, for darkness had now fallen and the games were over. The Muzzleking had risen, bowed stiffly to his ecstatic followers on the terraces, and withdrawn behind his royal purple curtain.

The terraces erupted into waves of celebrating figures, spilling out over the arena and running madly in all directions, bumping into one another and flattening smaller figures underfoot.

While this pandemonium was going on below, the crouching figures behind the cliff-top officials were sneaking away towards a beckoning form near a hole in the rocks. Jason rushed over to a forlorn Ludo, sitting sadly by the cliff-edge, her torch still burning and creeping dangerously near to her fur.

'I'm all right, I'm all right. Quick, get to an official. He'll douse your flames.'

'Jason? How did you manage to . . .'

'No time now. Hurry,' and they stumbled across to the nearest official who doused Ludo in a second and pointed all sixteen tentacles towards the exit hole. They were the last in, and ran down the long curving slope in front of them with a new burst of energy. After a while they slowed down and Jason explained to Ludo how he had joined in the deception.

'You might have told me. I was . . . I was . . . ' Ludo faltered and stared down at the sloping floor of the rock tunnel.

'There was no time. You were racing so fast.'

'Yes. I did well, didn't I? I am the winner, the champion of the Bonefire Race. I wonder what the prize is?'

The Bonefire Race

As they turned a sharp corner a cheer went up and they found themselves looking down from a stone balcony on to a scene like some medieval court. Happy figures sprawled everywhere and they all howled their applause as Ludo appeared on the balcony.

'Quiet, Snouts, quiet now,' said a deep voice. Ludo turned to see the regal figure of the Muzzleking, lying lazily across a large, raised slab.

'First, let me welcome the winner of the Bonefire Race. Following the ancient tradition her reward is to become my Muzzlebride until the running of the next race. So come and sit beside me, my dear, and bring your servant with you.'

As they descended from the balcony, Ludo and Jason exchanged worried glances.

'This is crazy,' whispered Jason, 'what if *I* had won the race? *I* couldn't be his bride. And those other racers, they weren't all females, were they?'

'Couldn't you smell them?'

'Smell them?'

'Yes. They were all females. My nose twitched them.'

'Then pretend you broke the rules somehow, and the real winner is the last one to burn out before you. I'm sure the rest of them here are all dying to be his bride. Look how envious they are.'

When Ludo reached the Muzzleking's side, however, he roared for silence before she could say anything.

'Now then, Snouts,' he boomed, 'I am sure you would like to know today's take. It's bigger than we ever dared hope. 2,348 bones, not counting gristle, splinters and small teeth.' There were yelps of delight at this news and a great deal of tongue-slobbering and leg-nibbling. 'You all performed brilliantly. Not one slip-up. You will be pleased to hear that the bones have already been shipped out to our private pleasure grounds beyond the Rock-bowl, and we will be able to start gnawing on them at our leisure, as from tomorrow morning. I should add that forty-three of the fans were killed in the crush and the celebrations, and they are being shared out between our tentacled friends, so *they* will be happy for a while. Any questions? No? Well, thank you again, Snouts, you were great. Now enjoy yourselves.' And the king stretched himself beneath his long purple cloak and licked his black nose.

After a few moments he rose and coughed. Silence fell immediately.

'I shall now retire for the Bone-jumping Bride-night. Come, my dear, and bring your lackey with you to stand guard over our bed-chamber.'

He swept out, followed reluctantly by Ludo and Jason. At the end of a rock passage they passed through yet another heavy purple curtain and into a circular bed-chamber, the floor of which was scattered with some of the largest bones Jason had ever seen.

'King-sized,' drawled the Muzzleking, as he followed Jason's gaze. 'My special treats. Wow! I'm pupped. What a day. What a charade. I don't know how I keep it up.'

Jason was eyeing the walls for possible escape routes, but could see none. And he was not sure whether he and Ludo, even between them, would be able to overpower the Muzzleking and get away without him raising the alarm. As he silently pondered the problem, he was startled to hear a howl of laughter from the robed figure lying across the vast circular bed.

'Cringe before me, you flat-faced slave, you naked skin-bag, you tailless twerp!' And to Jason's bewilderment the Muzzleking began howling with laughter again, rolling from side to side and wagging his stiff tail.

'Oh dear, it's no good, Jason,' gasped the Muzzleking, 'I can't keep this up any longer either. Forgive me for teasing you. Who is she, by the way? Rather nice, really — but I suppose she's yours?'

'Yes. I mean . . . What? I don't understand.' Jason sat down, looked at Ludo and shrugged helplessly. Nothing was as it seemed, not even the Muzzleking himself.

'No, you wouldn't, you poor old thing. You're too bone-shaken and bone-shocked. Never mind. Perhaps this will help,' and, taking his robe in his teeth, he removed it with a flourish. Beneath it lay, not one of the unfamiliar creatures Jason had come to

The Bonefire Race

expect in the Inrock, but the ordinary, friendly body of a large dog.

'Satan?' asked Jason softly.

'Right in one, old boy. Right first time. But steady on with the Satan, that was only an old nickname. My real title, as you may recall, was Rex, or, as we say down here, King!'

'But you can talk, and your head — it's different. I didn't recognize you.'

'Talk, yes. Great, isn't it. And the Muzzlecrown — rather fetching, don't you think? But I had better explain from the beginning. Sit down. Make yourselves at home.' And he began to recount his adventures since the day of the Mad Meggamole's arrival in Avebury.

It seemed that, on the day in question, the dogs of the village had been driven nearly mad by a jarring vibration in the air. They all started whining and running frantically about in a large pack. The villagers were so frightened by this that they barricaded themselves in their cottages and refused to come out, even when there was a knock at the door.

Then the vibrations grew stronger and stronger, as a great meteor rushed overhead, and the whole pack of dogs fled in terror, leaving the village and sprinting off into the countryside. Most of them were too scared to return and agreed instead to go hunting for rabbits on the nearby downs. Rex, alias Satan, was unable to join them because of his leather muzzle and had plucked up courage to return to the vicarage for his evening meal. As he was passing the stone circle, he noticed one of the largest stones glowing and vibrating and went to investigate.

'That,' said Rex, warming to his story, 'was when my adventure really began. The stone had a funny smell, so I went over to sniff it out. It was an unfamiliar smell, a cross between a baker's oven and a dead hedgehog. So I cocked my leg on it, to protect myself from evil spirits, and then it happened.

'The earth under my feet began to shiver and grow warmer, and I noticed there was a great gaping hole in the middle of the stone. That was new to me, so I sniffed a little deeper, and the *smell* inside that hole, you've no idea what it did to my poor old snout. It was like the garbage-pit of heaven. It drove me insane. I started digging down to find out where it was coming from. Then suddenly I felt everything go soft under my feet. My paws sank in so quickly I couldn't pull them out.'

'Like pushing your finger into a fruit-jelly?' suggested Jason.

'If you say so. Anyway, there I was, rolling over and over down into some sort of cave. I was so bruised that I simply dragged myself off into a dark corner to recover. Then I heard another crash and there *you* were. But when I went to stand up, my legs gave way and I couldn't follow you. I tried to bark, but my mouth was full of earth. By the time I had my legs working again I saw you, ahead of me, being attacked by some strange animal that I didn't recognize. So I hid and watched as they took you away. After waiting for a while I sneaked out of the cave and ran off as fast as I could.

'I wandered for days until I was nearly starving. I saw many juicy meals hopping and slithering about, but my muzzle made it impossible to eat anything. Eventually I fainted from hunger and I have no idea what happened next. But when I came round I found that my muzzle had been removed and there was food and water in front of me. I was in some kind of enormous kennel, and I slept and ate until I had regained my strength. Then I decided it was time to move on so I dug a tunnel out under the wall and pushed through it. But I was in another kennel-room and there was a dazzling light and someone said, "The Sculptor is ready for you," and I was lifted up and placed on a circular platform. Bells rang and spots of light flashed in my eyes. I felt drowsy and fell asleep again.

'When I awoke my first sensation was of a great thirst. I went to drink at a long trough of water. Seeing my reflection in the water, I found it hard to believe my eyes. The Sculptor, whoever that was, had fixed my muzzle so that it was growing out of the top of my head. Not strapped in, you understand, but actually growing out of my skin. "It looks like a crown," I said to myself. Then I realized with a shock that I had spoken out loud and

The Bonefire Race

I howled with delight.

'I slurped up the water, yelping and snapping, and made such a commotion that attendants came running in from other rooms. "I can talk," I shouted, "I can talk." They looked puzzled and whispered among themselves. I realized something was wrong and kept my council. I discovered later that here in the Inrock everyone can talk and that I had, in fact, been able to speak from the moment I accidentally broke through. It had nothing to do with the Sculptor's operation. All that had done was to put my muzzle on top of my head, as a growing part of my body. I suppose they thought it was an improvement. Or perhaps they imagined it had slipped down over my mouth by mistake, and were putting it back where they guessed it belonged. The attendants became so suspicious when I started singing and shouting at the water-trough that I decided to take off at the first opportunity.

'Three days later I managed to escape and I ran for miles and miles, hardly pausing until I came to this place, where I have been ever since.'

'I thought I caught a glimpse of you once or twice,' said Jason, 'but you were travelling so fast and were so far away.'

'It's a pity we didn't meet up again,' yawned Rex. 'We would have made a great team. But I can't complain. I've done well here. And wild horses wouldn't drag me back to the Outrock now. Think of all this,' and he waved a jewelled paw in the direction of his festive court.

'But that savage crowd out on the terraces – how can you stand them? And the show you put on makes them even more bloodthirsty,' protested Jason.

'Well, you know how I love bones. I was always in trouble back in the old village – remember the graveyard scandal? – and it took me ages here to collect just a few together. But I met these Snouts who were after the same thing. I organized them, using my old Outrock experience, and we set up shop here, convinced the local population that we were reviving an ancient tradition, and away we went. Who says you can't teach an old dog new tricks?

'It succeeded beyond our wildest dreams. We always have

enough bones to chew ourselves silly. It's a doddle. A dog-eared doddle. And for each occasion we think up something new. The more horror the better. We know what they want now.'

'Aren't you afraid you may be found out and attacked by the angry crowd?'

'Little chance of that, dear boy. Listen, my muzzle may be on at a strange angle, but my head is straight. All you need in life is a clear idea of what you want. Then everything else is easy. I want bones, mountains of bones, and I don't care how I get them. Off the flesh if I have to, but this way is so much easier. And if the crowd does turn nasty one day, they'll take it out on the officials, poor tentacle-suckers, not us.'

'How did you get the officials to work for you?'

'They lived here before we came. It's their foothold. So we did a deal with them. We have the use of the Rock-bowl and they get to clean up the mess at the end of the day.'

'And they agreed to that?'

'Sure. Dry-cleaning is their passion. They feed on anything left over. Before we came, the place was so clean they nearly died out. Now we guarantee them a regular mess and they are in heaven. So everyone's happy. Our Bone-gang and the Tentacle-boys and those screaming idiots out there on the terraces. And, as you've seen, our Snouts don't really get hurt. So where's the flaw? It's neat enough to satisfy even a Ministry Vet.'

'A what?' asked Ludo.

'Nothing — just an Outrock dog-joke. Forget it. Now, what are we going to do with you two?'

'Well, I have to get back to the Outrock as soon as I can . . . '

'You're crazy! You can't be serious, old boy. All that collar-and-lead stuff. No thanks.'

'Yes, I am serious. But first I have to find some Golden Worms for a friend, and Ludo here is helping me. We are trying to locate a place called the School of Unlearning. Have you heard of it?'

'Yes, I've heard of it. Full of fools trying to get through to the Outrock. If you go back through the ravine to the cave, then out of the cave entrance and turn left, that is the direction. But I can't be

The Bonefire Race

more precise than that.'

'Thanks. That will be a good start.'

'But it is too late now. Stay the night — rest and drink and howl a little. Every dog has his day and this is mine. So share it . . . Agreed?'

'All right. And thank you for letting us go,' said Jason.

'Listen — back there in the Outrock you scratched *my* chest, now I'll scratch yours. Fair deal?'

'Fair deal,' Jason replied, with a smile.

'But not a word about what you have learned here. That is part of the bargain.'

'Of course, but I wish you'd give it up and come with us. I'm sure you will be caught out one day, whatever you may say.'

'Enough of this Outrock nonsense,' boomed the Muzzleking, bounding to his feet and resuming his regal role. 'Let us return to the Snouts' Den. This is a time for celebration.' And celebrate they did until, exhausted, they collapsed together on the great king's huge, circular bed.

In the morning, refreshed, they bade their farewells and made their way back to the cave entrance, past the now deserted Rock-bowl, where the tentacled officials were greedily sucking up the last of the left-overs. Once outside the cave, they both heaved a great sigh of relief and looked around to see if their Drummodile was still there. Happily he had not deserted them and was snoozing contentedly in the shade of an overhanging rock. They woke him up, climbed aboard and set off once more on their search for the flat-topped mountain and the mysterious School of Unlearning, where, with luck, they would find a clue to the whereabouts of the elusive Sculptor and the magical Golden Worms.

As he stumped cheerfully along in the direction suggested by the Muzzleking, Jason was surprised to hear the Drummodile muttering to himself:

'Great game, great game. At the end of the day that's what it's all about.'

'What did you say?' asked Jason.

'Nothing,' replied Ludo, 'I was day-dreaming.'

'No, not you, the Drummodile. He said something.'

'I was remarking,' drawled the Drummodile, 'that it was a great game. All that lovely noise. Made my drums tingle, it did.'

'How did you get in? You didn't have a bone.'

'Yuddle, yuddle, yuddle,' gurgled the Drummodile, being the nearest it could manage to a laugh with its mouth full of cave-gravel. 'Said I was part of the fanfare. Had the best view in the place. Yuddle, yuddle.'

'Then aren't you surprised to see me?' asked Jason. 'You must have seen that I burst into flames during the Bonefire Race.'

'Yuddle, yuddle, beat the other drum. Didn't fool me. You took a dive behind that sucker-head. I saw you.'

'But you still thought it was a great event?'

'Of course. I don't mind pretend-blood and pretend-fire, but I don't want anyone to get really hurt. Have a heart.'

'You see,' said Ludo, after a long pause, 'we're not *all* blood-thirsty savages. We're not so different after all — Inrock and Outrock.'

'Are you saying that those other spectators back there knew the whole thing was a trick? That they were only enjoying it because they knew it was an act? I don't believe you.'

'No, well, some did and some didn't, I expect. I bet it is the same in the Outrock — some are vicious and some are not. I agree that the younger ones believed it all, but then the young really *are* vicious. Natural to them, I suppose. It takes time for them to mellow.'

'That's rubbish,' shouted Jason. 'It's the other way around. The young ones *hate* violence. It is the older ones who . . . '

. . . And they were off again on one of their interminable arguments which they enjoyed almost as much as their agreements, and which helped to pass the time on their lengthy travels.

CHAPTER NINETEEN

The School of Unlearning

For days Jason and Ludo journeyed through valleys and ravines, down canyons and narrow passes, over hill-tops and past rushing streams, until in the far distance they saw the great black shape of a high plateau, surrounded by steep, jagged cliffs of rock.

'That must be it,' cried Ludo. 'You remember, I told you the School of Unlearning was on a flat-topped mountain. We'll soon be there.'

As they drew closer to the foot of the mountain they could just make out some sort of building high above them, but it was too far up for them to see any details. Arriving eventually at the base of the steep, rocky slopes, they bade farewell to the faithful Drummodile, which stumped off singing mindless bone-chants and swaying its oval drums. Then, eagerly, they turned to the rock-face and began their arduous climb.

About half-way up, they came to a wide ledge and paused to rest. The air was thin and crisp and clear, and they breathed deeply as they lay back against the rocky wall and stretched their aching limbs, gazing out at the sea of peaks below them. Jason had taken off his shoes and was rubbing his blistered feet, when he heard a sharp, twanging sound.

'Eeunk, eeunk, eeunk.'

'What's that noise?'

'Eeoink, EEeoink, EEEoink, EEEEoink!'

'What is it?'

'Grannits above! It's a pair of Gruntles. Mind your toenails.'

'My what?'

'Your toenails. They love them. As a matter of fact, domesticated Gruntles are rather useful. They're used as trimmers.'

'What exactly do they trim?'

'Toenails, what else? Claws, too, of course. But there won't be any tame ones in these parts. These must be wild ones, so watch out for them. They burst out of hiding — they live in cracks in the rocks — make straight for your feet, and clamp on.'

'Why on earth do they want to eat toenails?'

'It helps to harden their shells.'

The twanging-grunts rose to a squeal.

'Sounds like trouble. They pair for life, but they hate one another. Miserable beasts, really. No one likes them.'

'If they hate one another so much then why do they stay together?'

'Only because they hate being alone even more than being together. But sometimes it does get too much for them and then they separate. Then they are really miserable. Being dis-Gruntled makes them permanently depressed. That's where we get the word "disgruntled" from.'

Jason grabbed his shoes and hurriedly pulled them on again. The grunting faded slightly but did not die away altogether.

'They're still there. I think we'd better move along the ledge, round that corner. It gets narrow there, but I think we can make it.'

Squeezing carefully round the sharp bend, their bodies pressed tightly to the rock-face, they noticed a small, dark hole in the cliff-wall slightly above their heads.

The School of Unlearning

'A Gruntle-hole?' asked Jason.

'No, it's too big for them. They prefer narrow crevices. Here, let me climb on your back and look inside.'

Jason got down on all fours and Ludo clambered up and slithered into the hole. Turning round, she grabbed his arm and helped to drag him up and into the tunnel beyond. It was a tight fit at first, but soon began to widen out until they were able to pull themselves to their feet and straighten up. Jason tried whistling and the echo told him that they were standing in a vast cavern, but as yet their eyes could pick out no details.

'Are you registered?' said a bored voice.

'No, we are climbers,' said Jason.

'I know that, but are you registered climbers?'

They peered into the darkness, but could see no one.

'Up here,' said the voice. 'Above you. I'm the Registrator.'

They craned their necks up and were just able to distinguish the shape of the speaker, hanging from the roof.

'What are you doing up there?' asked Jason, trying to change the subject.

'Painting. What are your numbers?'

'Er . . . 53,' said Jason, inventing one quickly.

'47,' said Ludo, following his lead.

'Hold on, I'll check that,' said the bored voice. He could be heard scratching about. 'Where did you get those numbers?' he asked after a while. 'I can't find any record of them here.'

'The Sculptor gave them to us.'

'Who else, who else? Are you trying to be funny? I didn't ask who, I asked where. Nobody listens to me any more. I don't know what the Inrock's coming to. You are supposed to be educated when you come here — you must be, or you wouldn't be so anxious to become uneducated, would you? Eh? No. Exactly. But you're not educated enough to listen to me, are you, what? What did you say? Eh? Eh? EH?'

'We were given the numbers locally, quite near here, but it was some time ago, and . . .

'Then what kept you? Eh? Dawdling about learning a load of

rubbish, I suppose? Don't understand you, simply don't understand you. The Sculptor gives you your numbers and sends you on here to the School of Unlearning, so that you can be prepared to go on through to the Testing Grounds, and what do you do? Eh? Eh? Dawdle about, that's what you do. It's . . . it's preposterous. You don't know when you're well off.'

'Did you say the Testing Grounds?' asked Ludo.

'Of course, of course. When you have been successfully untaught and completed your course of unlearning in all subjects, you are then qualified to proceed to the Censor's Gateway. If you get past the Censor, you're allowed through into the Testing Grounds.'

'And the Outrock,' said Ludo, half to herself.

'What was that? What? What? Speak up! Eh?'

'I said, and on to the Outrock.'

'Yes, yes, once you have been tested, if you are lucky you should get a through-rock ticket to the Outrock. But it's not so easy these days, they say. Too crowded out there already. Getting harder and harder to find an unoccupied niche for a new arrival. Still, there's always hope, once you get past the Censor. Now, I can't keep hanging about here all day answering your fool questions. You should have been briefed by the Sculptor's assistants, anyway. Suppose they are becoming dawdlers, too, eh? It's the same everywhere, my hooks it is. Now, those numbers, local you say?'

'Yes, local.'

'Hmmm. Well, in that case they should have a nought in front of them, shouldn't they? Why couldn't you say that in the first place? Save all this trouble, eh? Eh? What? What? Speak up!'

'Ah, yes, well, we took that as read. I am 053 and she is 047.'

'Wait there, don't go rushing on. I'll have to check first. Always in a rush, everyone in a rush. I don't have time to rush. Not like all you unlearners. You dawdle away outside and then have the gall to think that you can rush through here without so much as a "by your leave". Yes, here they are, 053 and 047. That seems to be in order. I have your bookings here. But you weren't due in until next week. I'm not sure your rooms will be ready yet. Just a

The School of Unlearning

minute, I thought you said you were given these numbers some time ago? They are new numbers, brand new, part of the latest batch. There's something fishy here.'

Having invented it on the spur of the moment, Jason could hardly remember what he *had* said, but obviously he had made a mistake.

'Did I say that? Ah, well, it depends how you measure time. I live from minute to minute myself, so it seems a long time ago to me, but for others I suppose it was only yesterday.'

'Yesterday?'

'Yes, yesterday.'

'Hmmm. Well, that's better. That fits. Very well. You can go through then. But I don't think that you, 053, will have much to unlearn about time, will you, eh, eh? Go on then, up those stairs.'

Still unable to see the speaker clearly, except for a bundle of flaps and folds hanging from the roof, they clambered across to a flight of rock-cut steps and started climbing. The Registrator watched them go and then returned thankfully to his painting.

The rock staircase seemed to go on forever, winding and twisting, spiralling and steepening, then straightening and flattening out, only to curve and rear up in front of them once again. When they were almost too tired to mount another step, they were suddenly startled by a light flashing on above them.

'Numbers?'

'053.'

'047.'

'Did the Registrator let you through?'

'Yes.'

'He's mad. It's all that cave-painting of his. Why can't he keep his mind on his job? You're not due yet. Didn't he warn you your rooms aren't ready?'

'Yes, but we don't mind that. We are keen to get started. We have a lot to forget.'

'Yes, I can see that. Well, come on up. Here are your badges and your keys. It's most irregular, but I can't have you cluttering up the stairway. Others want to use it too, you know. Follow me and I'll show you the way.'

They dragged themselves hurriedly up after the bobbing light, anxious not to lose the advantage they had somehow managed to gain. With the glare in their eyes they could see little of their new guide until, with a clatter, he flung open a door and they stepped through into a beautifully decorated and brightly illuminated hall, lined with thousands of books. Their guide led them over to a huge desk covered in papers and files and sat down importantly behind it.

'My name is Mulu-mulu, called Malee-malee, and I am the book-keeper. Empty your pockets, pouches, flaps, fringes and bags.'

'We have no books.'

'Papers? Diaries? Backs of Snittle-packets with lists scribbled on them? Nothing like that?'

'No. Nothing.'

'Strange. I find that nearly all the new unlearners try to cling on to some last scrap of information. Are you sure?'

'Positive.'

'Very well, then. You can go to your rooms. They won't be cleaned yet, mind you, but don't blame me. It's your own fault for arriving early. Your course doesn't begin for four days, so you'll have to keep yourselves amused. Over there, through that exit, turn right, then left, then left again. The numbers are on the doors. Ring for room service if you are hungry. You'll be told where to report later.'

Instead of looking for their rooms, Jason and Ludo began a systematic search of the maze of corridors and passage-ways. Nearly all the doors were locked and those that were open led only into large empty halls.

'The place is deserted,' said Ludo. 'Somewhere there must be some other unlearners, but where? We've got to find them and question them, before the real 053 and 047 turn up and they find out that we are impostors. We only have a few days.'

'That should be long enough. We're bound to find someone soon. Unless . . . '

'Unless what?'

The School of Unlearning

'Unless we can make *them* come to *us*. Like this . . . ' and he cupped his hands around his mouth. 'Fire!' he shouted at the top of his voice. 'Fire!'

There was a scurrying sound from behind one of the nearby doors that they had tried to open, but had found securely locked. Chains clanked and bolts rattled and a key could be heard grating in the lock. The door swung slowly open and a long pimply hand emerged, followed by a thin warty wrist, followed by a lean spotty arm and a knobbly mottled elbow. A slender scabby forefinger curled upwards and beckoned to them to enter.

Inside the room the even spottier owner of the spotty arm ushered them to two empty seats and eased his hunched, podgy body down into a sagging basket and sighed. His spindly limbs flopped out on either side as he cleared his throat and summoned up the energy to speak:

'Greetings. Greetings. You must be the fire inspectors? Good of you to come. Would you like to start it here, or do you have somewhere else in mind? It's all the same to me.'

'Start what?' asked Jason.

'The fire.'

'But fire inspectors don't start fires.'

'Of course they do. How can they inspect the fire drill if they don't? Are you sure you're the fire inspectors? That was you calling outside a moment ago, wasn't it?'

'Yes, we wanted to attract attention.'

'Well, now you have mine. Undivided. What are you going to do with it?'

'There are some questions we would like to ask you.'

'Questions, is it? I don't know about that. I'm only an unteacher here, I don't answer questions, I simply put them out of people's minds. But we could try, I suppose. My course isn't due to start for several days yet, so I've nothing to do but wait. It might help to pass the time. What sort of questions did you want to ask me? My name is Snit, by the way, B. Snit. Bibbling Snit. Bibbles, the unlearners usually call me. Cheeky spicklers.'

'We'd like to interview some of the unlearners, find out . . . er

'... find out what they are doing about reducing fire risks in the school. That sort of thing.'

'That's not a question.'

'No. Well, the question is: where are they? The place seems completely deserted.'

'Not completely. I am here, aren't I? So are the other unteachers. We've nothing to do but wait. I am not sure which is more boring, the waiting or the unteaching. You can't call it living, can you? We were all promised research posts in the Sculptor's studio when we came here, and now look at us! It's a swindle, a rotten swindle. Frankly, I wouldn't mind if you set fire to the whole place, burned it to the ground. It would suit me fine, except . . . well, I don't suppose I'd get out in time. My legs seem to have withered. All this sitting around in classrooms unteaching, that's what does it. What was your question, then?'

'Where are the other unlearners?' said Ludo patiently.

'Hmm. Well, some of the advanced ones are here, on the upper storey. Perhaps you'd like to try those?'

'How do we get to them? There don't seem to be any stairs.'

'Stairs? No, there aren't any stairs. My class, for instance, is unmathematical, and higher unmaths is immediately above us. When I've finished with them here, they are so light-headed they simply float up to the ceiling and through that funnel, there. See it, in the middle of the ceiling? I'd give you a bunk up, but I don't think my legs would take the strain. Sorry, and all that, but there it is.'

'Don't worry. We'll manage,' said Jason, and he and Ludo quickly began piling desks and chairs on top of one another in the middle of the room.

'Goodbye, goodbye, and don't forget, if you do see your way clear to burning the place down, please try and give me a half-term's warning, so that I can drag these withered old limbs out into the Grannit-light again. Ah, what it must be like to step into the real world once more, no classes, no scorn, no ink-stains, no unruly abuse, no reports, ah, what bliss . . . bliss . . . perfect bliss . . .'

CHAPTER TWENTY

The Sculptor's Den

The forlorn unteacher's voice faded beneath them as Jason and Ludo struggled through the circular funnel and heaved themselves up on to the floor above. They found themselves in another classroom identical to the one below, except that there were windows looking out over the school grounds, beyond which they could see the sharp edge of the mountain's flat top, and the sheer drop beyond.

'I thought Snit said we'd find advanced unlearners here, but it's as empty as the one below,' complained Ludo.

'Listen,' whispered Jason. 'Someone's coming.'

'Bumble-dee-dum, bumble-dee-dee, bumble-dee-bumble-dee-dum.' The door opened and a tall, thin unteacher popped his head in. He had wide red cheeks that hung down over his jaws, a long, bristly moustache of nicotine yellow, and small, twinkling eyes with blobs of sticky white in the corners. His skin was the texture of ripe strawberries, pitted, red and glistening, as if the blood inside it was feeling overcrowded. 'Ah, there you are, there you are,' he crackled, in a throaty, jovial rasp. 'Heard your fire call down below. What's the routine?'

'Fire drill,' said Jason.

'Oh, I say, dash it all, not those ghastly capers with buckets and sand and Mud-merks getting their knickers caught in the canvas chutes! We went through all that, let's see, it must have been, oh, about seven years ago. Surely that's good enough, old boy, isn't it? I say, wouldn't you rather quiz some of the advanced unlearners, they're a very unstudious batch, I'm sure you'll find they've forgotten practically everything. Should be very reassuring for you, what? Fair do, eh?'

'Very well, we'll see them now.'

'Jolly good, jolly good. I'll hand you over to old Rippleflog then, if you don't object. Fact is, he's just about to give them their final going-over, so he'll have them all together in one place for once — that's not so easy, either.'

'Of course. Rippleflog will do. Where is he?'

'Through here, my dear old boy, through here,' and he flung open a large frosted-glass door with such force that one of the panes shattered and burst all over the striped head of a sleeping figure on the other side. 'I say, sorry, what?' chortled the intruder, tweaking first the left end of his nicotine moustache and then the right. 'Two inspectors here for you, Ripple, old sport. Over to you, over. Bye-bye, bye-bye,' and he marched gaily off down the corridor, whistling the theme from the Spattle-catcher's parade march.

'Blast that Rasfin! Now he's woken up one of my best unlearners, and at the very second when, if my diagnosis is correct, the poor boy has reached the final moment of unclogging. I do believe his last fragments of cluttered fact were about to dissolve away in that dream he was having. Now look at him, restless, listless, dreamless, sleepless and blissless, all due to that wretched Red Rasfin. What a clumsy brute he is! Inspectors? Ah, yes, come in, come in. Now, what can I do for you? First of all, are you fire, flood, theft or general?'

'General,' said Jason quickly, thinking this would prove more useful if they were to find out where the Sculptor might be. Ludo frowned at him. She had obviously enjoyed the thought of starting a fire and was rather sad at the idea of no longer being a fire

The Sculptor's Den

inspector. But Jason shook his head firmly at her and turned towards the unteacher. Rippleflog was pondering as only Rippleflog could. One of his ponders involved shifting his weight from one striped water-pouch to another, the pouches sagging down and then shrinking up again as his bulk wandered around his loose-skinned body. He was shaped, in general, like a tall bunch of grapes, but each grape-lobe was capable of stretching into a long, droopy, wobbly bladder-finger, or contracting to a mere bump on his surface. His face was as blank as a face can be without ceasing to be a face altogether. Presumably to conceal this fact as best he could, he wore a bright green eye-shield.

'General, eh? Well you are lucky, lucky indeed. Even fortunate. I was about to hear the advanced class give their final sentences. If you'd care to sit over there, we'll begin.'

'Thank you, Rippleflog, thank you. Most satisfactory,' said Jason, as pompously as he could, trying to assume the authority of a general inspector. 'Perhaps you'd care to give us a little background?'

'Of course, of course. Well, this class has now completed its three-year course of unlearning. They have carefully and painstakingly written out all they knew — written it right out of their systems, we trust, and totally uncluttered their brains. They should now, with any luck, have reduced it all to a single sentence — a solitary idea with which to go on through to the Censor and, ultimately, we hope, to the Testing Grounds beyond. If you're ready, I'll take roll-call and then we can hear their sentences.'

'Ready.'

'Good, good. Wake up, everyone, wake up and pay attention. Klaggit?'

'Present.'

'Scrunt?'

'Present.'

'Sipple, Ursitter, Looge?'

'Present.'

'Present.'

'Present.'
'Graggle, Sput, Fissett and Flumpit?'
'Present.'
'Present.'
'Present.'
'Flumpit, where's Flumpit?'
'Present.'
'What's wrong, Flumpit? You heard your name?'
'Yes, but . . . but . . . I was thinking.'
'You were *what*?'
'Thinking.'

The unteacher's body rippled furiously. He yelled towards the doorway and, after a few moments, Mulu-mulu the book-keeper rushed in.

'Flumpit, over there, stand up! Now, perhaps the book-keeper can tell us whether there is an explanation of your — your thinking. Well?'

'I fear so, I fear so. I have done my best to keep him out of the library, but he sneaks in when I am greeting new arrivals. I have done my best, Rippleflog, truly, but . . . '

'Take him away. He is not fit to be a senior forgetter. He will never unlearn well enough to pass the Censor. He is wasting our time. Take him and have him retrained, then send him back. He can be de-gumfed and breed in the Inrock, for all I care.'

Mulu-mulu took the jibbering Flumpit away and shut the door. Rippleflog relaxed and beamed at his class. 'Now we are, let me see, one, two, three . . . eight. Not bad really. Can't complain. Right, we'll begin. Klaggit, you first, come forward and give us your sentence.'

Klaggit stepped forward, cleared his throat nervously and spoke in a high, piping voice:

'The articulate fool is doubly blessed.'

'Good, next. Scrunt.'

'The short and rich must pay the tall and poor to go on their knees.'

'Excellent, next. Sipple.'

The Sculptor's Den

'Each year is more important than the next.'
'Very subtle, Sipple, very subtle. Next. Ursitter.'
'He who stands still has time to itch.'
'Good, next. Looge.'
'Work is the failure of play.'
'Good, next. Graggle.'
'It is dark inside my head.'
'Hmmm. No. I don't think so. I fear we have gone too far with you, Graggle. Never mind. You did your best, but I'm afraid your best was a little too much. I'll speak to you later. Next. Sput.'
'The fading of a smile tells more than the smile itself.'
'I'll think about that one. You wait behind with Graggle afterwards, Sput. Next. Fissett.'
'The facts of death are more important than the facts of life.'
'Good, next. Flumpit. Oh no, of course, he's no longer with us. Pity. Can't help wondering what his sentence would have been.'
'There is a piece of paper over there,' said Jason, pointing. 'I think Flumpit left it behind. Perhaps it's his sentence?'
'Ah, thank you, inspector. Read it out, Fissett, you're nearest.'
'It says: "May heaven protect us from dreams of heaven."'
'Amusing. Most amusing, but I think it's as well he went. Never really entered into the spirit of the thing. Now, inspectors, what do you feel? A good batch, eh? The Censor should be pleased, don't you think?'
'Yes indeed, Rippleflog, you have done well. A great discredit to the school, I'd say. Would it be possible to follow them through, by any chance, to accompany them to the Censor to see how well they are received? Then we could report back to you and let you know the results. I appreciate that this may seem unusual, but . . .'
'Not at all, not at all. A pleasure. Delighted to see that you are taking such a keen interest. Most inspectors these days seem to spend all their time testing the water in the showers. Can't imagine why, but there it is. Yes, if you can be at the Censor's Whiskers in two days' time, I'll arrange for you to go down with this batch and see them through. How's that?'

'Two days, you say?'

'Yes, that's when they are booked out. In the meantime you might like to look around the place. Have you seen the different departments yet? We have a very strong Anti-sociology department, and then there's Unathletics, old Rasfin's lot, and Uneconomics, Irreligion, of course, and general Pseudology, not forgetting Unmining, Deforestry and, above all, the Coarse Arts. The Mystery department is closed, I fear, but you should have plenty to keep you unoccupied.'

'I'd rather like to see the retraining section, where Flumpit was sent. Would that be possible?'

'I suppose so. A strange request, but I imagine it can be arranged. I'll call Mulu-mulu. Mooooo! Ah, here he is. Take the inspectors to retraining, will you. Thank you. See you at the Censor's Whiskers then, in two days, at the cliff-top. Don't be late, will you? Can't keep the Censor waiting. Goodbye for the present. Good hunting.'

Jason and Ludo followed Mulu-mulu down countless corridors, across courtyards, up steps, down steps, and through passage-ways until they came to a broken-down little shed in a remote corner of the school.

'In here,' said the book-keeper. 'Excuse me, but I must dash now, the new batch is starting to arrive from below,' and he vanished around a corner.

'The new batch! I'd quite forgotten,' exclaimed Jason. 'Supposing our numbers come up? They'll be on to us.'

'But they think we are inspectors now.'

'Luckily they don't think very clearly. At least, the book-keeper doesn't. He welcomed us as new arrivals, then accepted us as inspectors. I suppose he is as forgetful as the rest.'

'I expect that's how he got his job here.'

'Yes, but if the real 053 and 047 arrive, even he is going to start wondering about us. After we have had a look in here and tried to question Flumpit about the Sculptor, I suggest we go into hiding until it's time to go to the Censor's Whiskers, whatever they are.'

'Right, but do you think it's worth wasting time with this

The Sculptor's Den

Flumpit? Shouldn't we hide straight away?'

'No. He is the one who was having trouble trying to forget. He is still thinking and he may have some information on the Sculptor. We can't afford to miss that. Come on.'

They entered the shed and found themselves in a ramshackle room, full of junk and jumble. The wretched Flumpit was sitting dejectedly on a pile of dusty rubbish, being shouted at by a tiny, scruffy, cucumber-shaped re-thinker.

'You are, without a doubt, the most inter-laceranting, fumi-galvanizing, throttleated, pamplemoosogenized calcicephalite it has ever been my misfortune to bandy words with,' yelled the re-thinker.

'Nit!' spat Flumpit.

'Saprophyticized, bladderomerated pifflebuccalator!'

'Twit!'

'Pappoflagotolic, slaggerinching, anti-fiscatomaphile!'

'Git!'

'It's no good. I can't communicate with you. It's like talking to an anvil — clang, clang, clang!'

'Excuse me,' interrupted Jason, unable to control himself any longer, 'but if you didn't use such long words, perhaps he would be able to understand you better.'

'Who are you? What are you doing here? You're not on my list,' snapped the re-thinker.

'We are inspectors, touring the school for the Sculptor,' replied Jason, with great dignity.

'Well, there's nothing to inspect here, so go away. I'll use long words if I want to. I'm in charge here and I do as I like. Besides, if I used shorter ones this inferior being would know what I was talking about and that would be intolerable.'

'Then why are you bothering to speak to him in the first place?'

'Because I want to re-educate him, naturally.'

'But if you succeed, then you'll *have* to talk to him.'

'That is precisely why I am re-educating him so badly. Otherwise he might try to take over from me. What kind of fool do you think I am?'

'May we have a few words with him in private, please?' asked Jason, losing his patience.

'Oh, very well, but don't give him too much encouragement,' snapped the re-thinker, and stalked over to the door, slamming it hard behind him.

'Now, Flumpit, perhaps you can help us?' said Jason, squatting on the floor in amongst the piles of junk. 'What can you remember about the Sculptor?'

'The Sculptor? That gormless old gold-bags?'

'Yes,' said Ludo. 'Can you recall the time when you were last altered? The time before you came here, to the School of Unlearning. The Sculptor must have been pleased with the new version of you, pleased enough to send you on here to be prepared for the Censor and for passing through to the Testing Grounds. Tell us what happened.'

'Well, they came to my village and I was selected. They had me put in their travelling studio and . . . '

'And?'

'And, well, the Sculptor worked on me. Gave me more joints and an extra pair of fins and said I'd do. It didn't hurt much, because of that stuff they spray over you. Makes you go fuzzy, then you wake up and there you are, remodelled. Nothing much to it, really, after all the fuss they made.'

'What happened then? Where did the Sculptor go?'

'Came back here, I suppose.'

'Here!'

'Yeah. I was the last one, they said, on that trip, and they were coming back to the Sculptor's Den for a bit of a rest-up. Gave me a number and told me to report here later. And that's what I did, but I wish I hadn't. It's all a load of cods-waddle if you ask me. I'll be glad to get back.'

'This Den, have you seen it?'

'Course not, no one has. It's on top of the school, high up. You can't reach it, except up the middle of the tower, and that's guarded all the way. Wouldn't want to, anyway. Gormless old gold-bags.'

The Sculptor's Den

'Thank you, you've been most helpful. How do we get to the tower from here?'

'Don't know, but if you get on the roof you'll see it. Can't miss it. Dead centre of the school, it is.'

Jason and Ludo hurried outside, leaving the sullen Flumpit kicking at the piles of dusty junk and sneezing noisily. Ten minutes and fifteen corridors later, they had found their way up some fire-escape steps and on to the flat roof of the School of Unlearning. The view was breathtaking. All around them was the sharp edge of the mountain's flat top, with the sheer drop of the cliffs beyond. At one point they could see a set of what appeared to be curly-ended wires, clamped into a row of strong masts.

'Those must be the Censor's Whiskers,' said Ludo. 'We must remember where they are. It sounds as though they'll be our escape route later on.'

'And there is the Sculptor's tower,' cried Jason, pointing at a tall pillar of smooth rock, soaring up from the centre of the roof. They ran their eyes up it, higher and higher, until their necks nearly snapped. Gazing almost straight up, they could just make out a bulge at the top, where the tower widened out and changed colour.

'That must be the Sculptor's Den,' said Ludo. 'It's covered in gold — a great knob of gold, towering over all the Inrock. Almost touching the Grannits.'

'Fantastic!' said Jason. 'This is it. We've found it at last.'

'Now all we have to do is get up there!' snorted Ludo. 'That won't be so easy.'

They made for the base of the great pillar of rock and walked all around it, but could find no way in. Its surface was smooth and completely unbroken. No doors, no cracks, nothing.

'There must be a way in from below,' said Jason, and they clambered over the edge of the roof again and down more steps, through more doors and along more passage-ways until they were standing in a circular corridor immediately below where they guessed the pillar must be.

'This is the first circular passage we've been in,' said Jason excitedly. 'It must run around the base of the pillar. Come on, let's go right round it. There has to be a door somewhere.'

When they were about half-way round, their path was blocked by a bright, golden screen. There were no handles or catches on it and no visible means of opening it. It covered the whole of the passage-way, from wall to wall and ceiling to floor. Ludo sniffed it and Jason tapped it. It rippled slightly at his touch.

'I don't think it's very thick,' he said. 'Let's charge it,' and they walked back a few paces and ran full tilt at it, bursting through in a shower of gold-dust, and falling in a heap at the feet of a row of gold-clad guards.

The guards surrounded them and hustled them into a hollow golden sphere which shot up at terrifying speed, through the centre of the giant tower. Their ears were bursting with the changing pressure and their heads reeling and their stomachs sinking and their fingers prickling and their eyes smarting, as they were tumbled out and rolled across a golden carpet to crash against a golden couch on which was sitting a golden figure. Shimmering and glinting as it straightened up, the figure raised a golden hand, and spoke in an echoing, golden voice:

'Welcome. This is an unexpected pleasure.'

CHAPTER TWENTY-ONE
The Censor's Whiskers

Jason and Ludo sat up and blinked. The whole of the huge, circular room was shining bright with gold. Everything was golden, even the silver. They themselves were covered in gold from the moment when they had crashed through the screen in the corridor so far below. From big windows, set all around the edge of the room, they could see the distant peaks and crags of Inrock spread out like mole-hills on a lawn.

   The thought of mole-hills jogged Jason's buzzing mind into action. The Meggamole! The Golden Worms! This was his chance. He was here at last, face to face with the Sculptor. And what a face! He blinked again. The Sculptor was not a man, as he had always imagined, but a beautiful, golden-haired, golden-eyed, golden-lipped woman, tall and slender and immaculate in a long, glowing golden gown. She was smiling down at them and beckoning them to stand up. They followed her across to a golden table, sat with her in golden chairs and ate a meal of golden food. No one spoke. The air was filled with the notes of golden music plucked from unseen golden strings. Golden droplets floated in the gentle breeze that wafted through the open windows, billowing the golden curtains and making them dance a gentle, flowing rhythm. Jason felt drowsy, unable to gather his thoughts again. What was it he wanted to ask? Something . . . something important, but — no, it was gone. He would remember later . . . another day . . . it could wait. Ludo's golden horns winked at him and he smiled softly and fell gradually, deeply, totally, utterly asleep.

He awoke in a great golden bed with Ludo at his side. The Sculptor was gazing down at him, still smiling. He sat up.

'I thought you would be a man,' he said.

'Why?' echoed the golden voice, singing through the air and gliding off the walls. 'Why did you think that?'

'Because . . . well, if you are really a woman, you wouldn't be a Sculptor, you'd be a . . . a Sculptress.'

'Like a Paintress?' laughed the golden figure, rising and waving to her guards. They staggered forward, carrying a huge, circular mirror in a golden frame. 'Here, look at yourselves in this. See how I've improved you.'

Jason sat up and stared. Ludo propped herself up beside him, rubbing her eyes and yawning. Then she, too, looked into the mirror, and gaped.

'You've . . . you've change me!' gasped Jason. 'I'm all covered in golden fur and . . . and you've given me horns, golden horns!'

'You look just like me!' yelped Ludo. 'Exactly like me. We're a pair!'

'Yes, you are a pair now,' said the golden voice. 'I know I should have punished you for breaking through my screen, but I feel lenient today. It has been a good day and I feel well rested from my labours. I have therefore pardoned you and you may go. But you will not, I fear, be continuing your journey to the Testing Grounds. You know, better than I, that your presence here in the School of Unlearning is highly irregular. You will have to be returned to the Inrock without delay and there, I am sad to say, you must remain for the rest of your days. That is why I have made a pair of you, so that you will be able to breed and multiply and live full Inrock lives.'

'But that means we'll be non-gumfs! That means we will be

hunted and persecuted by the gumfs, and we will lose the desire to pass through to the Outrock,' wailed Ludo.

'I fear so.'

'We'll do it!' said Jason, suddenly.

'What!' cried Ludo.

'We'll do it on one condition. That you give us some Golden Worms.'

'It is not for you to make conditions. In any case, there is no point in your having the Golden Worms if you are returning to the Inrock. If you ate them there, you would shrink to nothing. They are to prevent growing for those who pass through to the Outrock. It would be disastrous if you ate them here. I cannot agree.'

'But they're not *for* us.'

'No. You have heard my last word. Now go and start a colony in some pleasant corner and give up your wild thoughts of Outrock and Golden Worms. Go.'

They were taken by the golden guards and placed inside the golden sphere. As it sank at giddying speed to the base of the great pillar, Ludo asked Jason why he had agreed to stay, even with the condition he had made.

'Because there was no point in arguing. We were powerless. It was a last chance to get the Golden Worms, that's all. I didn't intend to stay and I don't now. Worms or no Worms, we are going through to the Testing Grounds with the next batch of unscholars. Somehow, when we get below, we must lose our guards and make for the Censor's Whiskers. We don't know how long we were asleep up there. It may have been for days. We may even be too late — our batch may have left already.'

'And we may not escape the guards, either,' muttered Ludo to herself.

As they were released from the hollow sphere, Jason shouted, 'Now!' without warning, and made a dash for the golden screen. It had been perfectly repaired, or a new one had been installed while they had been aloft with the Sculptor, but it shattered exactly like the first one as he and Ludo crashed through it, leaving a stream of gold-dust behind them. Struggling up from the floor, they saw that their bodies had lost the golden sheen of a moment before.

'I'm back to my old colour!' shouted Ludo, running fast.

'I'm back to your old colour, too,' moaned Jason.

'What? I couldn't hear.'

'Nothing. Look. Behind us!'

The golden guards were pouring through the broken screen, but as they did so they lost their golden glow and started to melt, wilting away to nothing.

'They must have been solid gold!' shouted Jason. 'They have vanished – completely vanished. We are safe! Now, let's get to the Whiskers, over by the cliff-top. Hurry.'

Outside the atmosphere was thin and cool and light and they swelled their chests and opened wide their mouths to drink in deep draughts of the pure, crisp air, and laughed and ran and waved wildly to the group of figures they could see gathered around the masts ahead. As they came nearer they were able to identify the familiar faces. There was no mistaking Rippleflog and his small band of successful unlearners.

'Wait for us! Wait for us! We're coming.'

'It's those two inspectors,' muttered Rippleflog, scratching one of his many body-pouches. 'Now, I was told something about them. Something not right there. Something definitely wrong. What was it now? Oh dear, I forget. But then, that's my job. Ah well. Come on, you two, we're just getting harnessed up for the trip.'

He was busily supervising the final preparations for the journey to the Censor's Gateway. Jason and Ludo joined the others and were each given a complicated set of yellow straps and a bright yellow back-pack. They struggled quickly into them, helping one another with the stiff buckles, fastening them as tight as they could.

'All harnessed up? Good. Good. Now, in our final selection we have Klaggit, Scrunt, Sipple, Ursitter, Looge and Fissett, and, of course, the two inspectors who will accompany you to watch your progress. As you can see, there are six masts here – one, two, three, four, five, six – and to each is attached the end of one of the

The Censor's Whiskers

Censor's remarkable Whiskers. These, as you will find out for yourselves, are truly extraordinary appendages. If you look over the edge of the cliff, you will notice that they stretch like mountain cables as far as the eye can follow – further, in fact, much further – for the Censor's Whiskers are no less – no less, mark you – than 300 miles long. In your descent you will travel at an average speed of 60 miles per hour, making a total journey of about, let me see, five hours. Light refreshments will be served during the trip and the flying stewards will hover beside you from time to time to tend to your needs. Any questions? Yes, Klaggit?'

'These packs on our backs. When do we . . . ?'

'Ah, yes, the back-packs. A word of warning about those. Do not touch them whatever you do. They are for emergencies only. Each one contains a safety-bladder, made of dried Galoon-skin. It is self-inflating and, if you come off your Whisker, blows itself up into a sort of parachute. Or, it can act as a life-jacket, in case the Censor is thirsty and his Gateway has become flooded. It opens automatically if you become submerged, so you have nothing to worry about. Yes, Scrunt? What's your problem?'

'How exactly do we slide down the Whiskers? Five hours is a long time to hold on with . . . '

'No, no. You don't have to hold on. Gracious, no. That large clip hanging from your harness – see it? Yes, that one – in a moment you will each stand under your allotted Whisker, reach up and snip it on. You will then leap from the precipice when I give the word and slide the entire way down hanging comfortably in your harnesses with your harness rings slipping smoothly along the Whiskers above your heads. Very simple. No effort. The greatest joy-ride in earth. Sipple?'

'How do we detach ourselves when we reach the Censor's Gateway?'

'Automatic, my dear Sipple, automatic. Nothing to worry about. The Censor's Whiskers become thicker and broader as they reach his Gateway and the clips on your harnesses are pressed open. This both slows you down and finally releases you as the rings snap apart. Ursitter?'

'How do we pass through the Censor's Gateway?'

'You are flung through at some considerable speed. Not 60 miles an hour, of course. The widened base of the Whiskers will have slowed you down, as I have already explained. Looge?'

'Where do we go if we fail to pass the Censor?'

'If he doesn't like the feel of you as you slide down – that is, if you give off bad vibrations – he simply twitches the Whisker you are on and flings you off. Your parachute opens and you drift down on to the rocks below. After that, you're on your own, and you can kiss goodbye to any Outrock dreams you may have had. If he likes the feel of you, but doesn't like the *look* of you, when you finally sail into his range of vision, then he shuts his Gateway with a bang and all you can do is jump for it at the last moment and hope for the best. Can be very nasty, that, and I'd rather not talk about it. Now, Fissett, hurry up, time is passing and I still have to make my farewell speech.'

'What does the Censor's Gateway look like?'

'His Gateway, Fissett, is his mouth – quite big enough to accommodate you, I can assure you of that. It is set in the great rock-curtain at the edge of this central section of the Inrock. If you are fortunate enough to pass the Censor's Gateway, you will be taken into his mouth, down his throat, through his stomach and on round his winding gut until you emerge into the Testing Grounds. Once there, you will be set a task to perform and if you succeed you will be duplicated for breeding and awarded a through-rock ticket to the Outrock. Now, finally, do the two inspectors have any questions?'

Ludo shook her head, but Jason raised his hand:

'The Golden Worms? We will need them to stop us growing when we – that is, *if* we reach the Outrock. Can you . . . ?'

'Yes, yes. All in good time. But first, today is Speech Day and, whether you like it or not, I have to give my farewell speech. After that, you will each be given your casket of Golden Worms. You will keep it close and guard it at all times until you reach the Outrock. Once there, you will immediately break the seal, open it and devour the contents. If you fail to do this the Outrock food will quickly make you swell and grow until you burst. Now, if there are no more questions, I will deliver my farewell speech and then see you safely on your way.'

Moving across to a small platform, Rippleflog laboriously took out some prepared notes and began to read:

'This is a proud day at the School of Unlearning, and pride, they say, comes before a fall. Your fall, my forgetful ones, will be great indeed, a fall of 300 beautiful miles, your minds uncluttered, your bodies streaming through the winds of Inrock, down, down to the Censor below. As I look at your unlearned faces before me, I think of others who have slid the long slope before you, and I shed a tear for friends departed, beautiful brains all, pure and simple, cleared of the clutter of facts and the rubble of memory that for so long had festered inside their overcrowded skulls. We, at the School of Unlearning, rejoice in our vast achievements over the centuries, at our sustained ability to send out into the world beyond, brains as thoughtless and as . . . and . . . '

'He's going to sleep,' whispered Ludo.

'I heard that!' shouted Rippleflog. 'It's all right for you — it's new to you — but I have had to listen to this mushy rubbish a thousand times. Now, where was I?'

'You were just about to present us with the Golden Worms,' said Jason hopefully.

'No I wasn't. Was I? No. No, of course I wasn't. I was about to give you some Golden Words of advice. Words, not Worms. Please pay attention. If you reach the Outrock you will find that three things become important to you and three things only: love, friendship and success. Nothing else matters, so heed my words carefully. First, one never needs love more than when one is at one's most unlovable. Second, the best friends are those who appear beautiful to others, but ugly to themselves. And third, success is like a desert — you can move in any direction, but there are no signposts. These are my Golden Words and they are really . . . really rather lovely, don't you think?' and he shed a few sticky tears of embarrassed self-admiration. Then, stiffening, he scowled at the small group in front of him: 'And anyone who says I stole

Inrock

those Golden Thoughts from my pupils is a filthy, stinking liar,' he shouted, quivering with rage, while his audience shuffled and fidgeted and tried to avoid his gaze.

'Now!' boomed Rippleflog, more cheerfully. 'It is time for the School Song. Where's Bibbling Snit? Bibbles, ah, there you are. Heave his basket up here on to the platform beside me. That's it. Now, you all remember Bibbles from your early days here at the School of Unlearning. He is the only one who can remember the School Song, so he will lead us. Are we ready?' And Bibbling Snit started to moan out the words of the dreary, meaningless, graceless song:

'Snoggle-yaps are sent to try us,
But we'll neigh their whine.
Prazzle-taps are spent to buy us,
But we'll pay their fine.
We will not decline.

'Grottle-snaps are bent to tie us,
But we'll fray their spine.
Niggle-flaps are tent to guy us,
But we'll say their line.
We will not define.

'Spattle-scraps are pent to fry us,
But we'll clay their shrine.
Pottle-wraps are rent to dry us,
But we'll spray their vine.
We will not refine.

'Bandle-saps are lent to dye us,
But we'll grey their shine.
Bootle-traps are meant to spy us,
But we'll lay their mine.
We will not resign . . . not . . . reeeeee . . . signnnnn!'

The effort was too much for Bibbling Snit and he subsided saggily into his creaking basket and fell instantly asleep. Rippleflog cleared his throat:

The Censor's Whiskers

'Follow these melodic instructions,' he intoned, 'and you will never set a foot wrong. Now, if you will step up this way I will present you, one and all, with your own, your very own, genuine bedouine, double-wrapped and triple-guaranteed, individually hand-carved caskets of the original, the magical, the utterly, totally, indispensable . . . Golden Worms. Here you are, Klaggit, you have excelled in Overtaking and Unbalming, I see. Well done, well done. The School is proud of you. Take your casket, secrete it about your person, clip to your Whisker and await my signal.

'Scrunt, you have shown great promise in Crimination and Repravity. Keep up the bad work. Here is your casket. Now, clip to your Whisker. Sipple, ah subtle Sipple, how I shall miss you. Follitics and Paraging were your strong points, were they not? Take your casket and go. Clip to your Whisker. Ursitter, the specialist in Mortifaction and Denudity, I do believe? Splendid lack of concentration, splendid. Here is your casket. Clip to your Whisker. Looge, dear Looge, your work in Misplay and Uncommercial Art will long be forgotten. Stout chap, well done. Take your casket and clip to your Whisker. Hurry along. And finally the remarkable Fissett. Well played, Fissett, the great all-rounder, as strong in Turbance and Volt as you were in Smudging and Subministration. Take your casket and clip to your Whisker.

'There we are, then, the big moment has come. Stand to attention, everyone, while, as a final gesture, we will forget the School motto.'

'Excuse me,' said Jason, in an anxious voice, 'but you seem to have overlooked us.'

'Oh, my ripples, yes! The inspectors. Oh dear. Oh dear me. I fear there are no caskets left and no spare Whiskers, either. I'm not sure I can help you after all. Oh dear, this is most awkward.'

'We shall have to report this matter to the Sculptor,' said Jason sternly, nodding at Ludo, who nodded seriously back.

'Oh, come now, that won't be necessary. Let me see. It's never been tried before but, yes – Sipple, unclip and double up with

Ursitter, and Looge, you double up with Fissett. Re-clip, both of you, and stand by. Now, there you are, inspectors, two spare Whiskers for you. Clip up and we'll be away.'

'But the caskets?' asked Jason.

'Sorry, can't help there. But surely you won't really need them, will you? I mean to say, it's not as if you are going right on through to the Outrock, is it? I mean, you'll have to report back here eventually with your findings, won't you?'

'Yes, of course,' said Jason, worriedly.

'But . . . ' Ludo started to protest.

'That's all right. We are ready,' interrupted Jason, turning to whisper to Ludo: 'We'll manage somehow — one of the other caskets — don't argue — we can't afford to delay.'

He was proved right almost immediately. As they all lined up ready for the take-off, an alarm bell sounded in the main school building.

'Hallo, hallo. What's that?' muttered Rippleflog, as running figures came pouring out of the school doorways, shouting and waving their arms. 'Hold on, everyone, stay where you are.'

'Ready to jump!' roared Jason, trying to drown out Rippleflog's words. 'Go!' and they all flung themselves over the precipice.

Rippleflog's gesticulating figure shrank behind them as they rapidly gained speed, sliding faster and faster down the cable-like Whiskers that stretched tautly away into the far distance. The wind whistled through their fur and stung their eyes. They gasped for breath — 30 miles an hour, 40, 50, 60. They were screaming through the air, dangling from their yellow harnesses, their Whisker-clips hissing and humming above them. Down and down and down they flew, on towards the great gaping mouth of the Censor's Gateway and the long-awaited challenge of the Testing Grounds beyond.

CHAPTER TWENTY-TWO

The Journey to the Gateway

Jason and Ludo had been travelling down the Censor's Whiskers for over an hour, without incident, when they heard a faint twanging noise. At first, it was no more than a murmur above the rushing of the wind, but then, quite suddenly, it grew and became so intense that it began to set their teeth on edge.

'Look!' cried Ludo. 'Look at the Whisker to your left, the one carrying Sipple and Ursitter – it's starting to twitch. The Censor must be rejecting them.'

'Help! Help!' yelled the two unscholars who, having been forced to double up to make room for the two 'inspectors', were sending bad vibrations down the line to the Censor's Gateway. But before anyone could come to their aid, their Whisker gave a final vigorous, twanging twitch, and their clips snapped clean through, sending them whirling and wriggling out into space, their balloon-like parachutes popping open above their heads.

'It must have been the extra weight,' shouted Jason.

'Listen,' cried Ludo, 'the twanging is starting again. What about Looge and Fissett? They are riding double, too.'

'Yes, look, it's their Whisker that's starting to twitch now. Quick, Looge, Fissett, lighten your load, or you'll go the same way as the other two.'

They stared helplessly at one another as the twanging and twitching continued to grow.

'Your caskets,' shouted Ludo, 'throw them over. We'll keep them for you.'

Reluctantly, they did so, but Looge threw badly and his precious box of Golden Worms fell like a stone until it was no more than a mere golden speck and was then, finally, lost to sight. Jason tensed himself for Fissett's throw and, by some miracle, managed to catch it and thrust it safely beneath one of his yellow harness straps. If he could only remove one – just one – of the worms before giving it back to Fissett, when they reached the Gateway, that might be enough to save the Meggamole, and it surely couldn't make so very much difference to . . .

'Fissett! Looge!' screamed Ludo, as their Whisker gave a final savage twitch and they, too, were flung out into space and floated slowly down to the rocks below.

Now, apart from Jason and Ludo, only Klaggit and Scrunt remained, and the four survivors listened intently for further twanging, but none came and eventually they managed to relax a little and hang limply and gratefully in their harnesses as they sped on their way. Jason said nothing to Klaggit or Scrunt about the fact that he had kept Fissett's casket of Golden Worms. They made no comment, apparently blissfully unaware of anything other than the delicious absence of any twanging on their respective Whiskers. So now he had them! The real thing – the real Golden Worms. And what was more, he was on his way to the Testing Grounds and home. After searching so far and waiting so long, Jason could hardly believe that it was true. But what a price had been paid to save the Mad Meggamole, a creature he hardly even knew. There had been a trail of disasters, starting with the pathetic Red Warty in the Display Prison and ending with the tragedy of the four twitched unscholars. Had it all been worth it? Should he have given up? Or would it have been unforgivable to

The Journey to the Gateway

desert a friend, even a new friend you have only just met, no matter what the cost, once he has asked for your help and you have agreed to give it?

Jason was still wrestling with this problem when a strange new voice crackled unexpectedly by his side, and twisting his head he saw the gliding shape of a skinny, long-legged bird-creature, with rather grubby wing-tips, grazed knee-caps, and a long, grinning mouth full of chipped, yellow teeth.

'I am your simmering steward,' it was saying, 'and I am here to serve you with a smile, cheap perfume, dark and light refreshments, and Whisker-bags in case anyone is feeling too heavily Censored. I will also make inane, fuzzy and more or less inaudible remarks about the landscape below, such as: We are now passing over the Great Plain of Pearls. To your right is the Wilderness of Burning Ice-cubes, and on your left you should be able to see the Coast of Frozen Flames, and beyond it the Reef of Knotted Scapegoats. That, I need hardly tell you, is where the Scapegoats retire when they are told to get knotted. Outside the reef is the Bay of Biscuits, where you may be lucky enough to spot one of the floating pollution-slicks of discarded ship's-crackers, and the famous Islands of Brow, noted for their Lids and Sties. As we move on around the Cape of Bad Omens and enter the Gulf of Understanding, you will clearly see the great curtain of rock that marks the end of your journey. In it is embedded your much envied destination, the gaping gate-mouth of the illustrious Censor.'

'I hate to admit it,' said Jason apologetically, 'but, after a while, I find scenery rather boring.'

'Then how about some refreshments? I can offer you folk stories, legends, fairy-tales, myths, presidential addresses . . . '

'They're not refreshments!'

'I find them refreshing. They refresh *me*. Therefore they are refreshments.'

'Where do you get them from?'

'I make them up to amuse my friends.'

'All right, we'll try one, then.'

'Which would you prefer?'

'Er . . . we'll have a myth, I think.'

'Certainly. Now let me see. Yes. How about this: Once upon a time there was a three-legged King who was riding his four-wheeled tricycle with a five-speed gearbox along a six-lane foot-path at seven o'clock in the afternoon, on his way to the local slave-market, with his fat daughter, the unlovely Princess Podgipa, perched on his handle-bars, when he spied a Secret Agent of a foreign power, lurking in the bushes. Ringing his royal bell, he deafened the Secret Agent with a single, sharp trill, and the wretched brigand, whose child and three wives would live forever in ignorance of his terrible fate, fell squirming and unhearing beneath the silver spokes of the royal-foot-propelled carriage.

'Feeling the unseemly bump beneath her handle-bars, the unlovely Princess Podgipa opened her fat-lined eyes and pouted a double pout. This gesture, so trivial on a more slender form, was sufficiently gross to unbalance the regal vehicle and hurl its lofty passengers into a pose less elevated than that to which they were accustomed by right of their aristocratic birth. Feeling herself slighted by the intrusion into her sheltered life of this untitled personage, the unlovely Princess set about punching the deaf Agent in the ear-lobes. The lobes in question were uncommonly large and, in so being, were, to be truthful, the only uncommon feature of an otherwise thoroughly common ruffian. The right ear-lobe, having recently been pierced by a foreign ear-piercer of limited practical experience, was already badly swollen even before the regal fisticuffs assailed its tender flesh, and stuck out sideways at an alarming angle, giving the impression that its owner was indicating an urgent desire to make a sharp turn to the right.

'The protrusion of this exceptional, if damaged organ exposed the gold ring that hung from it to the forceful finger of the enraged and unlovely ear-boxer in such a manner that, by the time her wrath had subsided, she found herself engaged to be married to this unknown commoner, the ring having torn loose and become firmly lodged on her fat wedding finger, resisting all attempts to remove it, short of regal amputation.

'Since the ill-mannered stranger had been so bold as to permit this betrothal to occur without a formal introduction, the King was in a quandary as to how to proceed, there being no court protocol available to deal with such an event. Being a wise King, in addition to possessing an extra lower limb, the Princess's father promised to recognize the match if only the deafened scoundrel would first make the unlovely bride-to-be thin enough to pass through the doors of the Royal Chapel, so that the marriage could be solemnized in the eyes of the church and, above all, in the crossed eyes of the dreaded Archbishop Nog, whose twisted gaze, it must be said, saw little that was solemn enough for his liking in the ungodly times of which I speak.

'Are you still with me?' asked the flying steward.

'Yes,' replied Jason, 'but I am not finding it very easy to follow. What happened next? Did the Secret Agent manage to make the Princess thinner?'

'Oh, lord, yes, they always do, but in a high class myth that only leads to more trouble.'

'How?'

'Well, the Secret Agent was a part-time dabbler in the Black Arts and so he was able to cast a spell over the Princess's fat and banish it on to the body of a slender slave-girl he knew, who was coming up as lot 27 in the auction at the slave-market that day. The slave-girl was delighted to have it because it made her so ugly that she failed to reach her reserve price and had to be bought in. Instead of ending up in some filthy harem, she was then able to turn to social welfare and charity work and hold her chins high again in respectable society. But the newly lovely Princess was not so lucky. Stripped of her fatty layers, she became so terribly thin that the gold ring refused to stay on her wedding finger, slipped off and fell into the mouth of a passing toad who was about to snap up a crunchy cockchafer which happened to be in season at the time.

'Now, you see, the lovely Princess could get through the doors of the Royal Chapel, but the wedding ring was gone and the marriage had to be postponed until the toad could be persuaded to co-operate. To assist in this matter, the Secret Agent turned himself into a toad of the opposite sex and conversed with the lumpy amphibian in its own tongue. By a stroke of luck, the ring-swallowing toad turned out to be something of a flirt and had soon coaxed the Secret Agent into eloping with her to the nearest spawning-pond, where, I am sad to report, she was promptly eaten by a large toad-fish that was shortly afterwards caught and cooked for the King's table. The lovely Princess, being so thin, was by this time ravenously hungry and gobbled down the fish so fast that the gold ring slid down her royal gullet without so much as causing her a regal hiccup. Have you noticed how it's always the finicky feeders that get the fish-bones? No? Well, anyway, soon the Princess became fat again and one fine day was riding on her father's handle-bars to the next auction sale at the slave-market.

'Do you want me to go on?' asked the steward.

'Is there much more?' enquired Ludo.

'Oh, yes, as much as you like. That's the great advantage of myths — they can go on for ever and ever.'

'Well, I suppose it helps to pass the time,' said Jason.

'Precisely. Now, as the royal tricycle approached the clump of bushes where the Secret Agent had been hiding on their last trip, it hit a bump in the road and the Princess was once again thrown to the ground. She struck it with such force that she coughed up the gold ring, which sailed through the air and landed at the feet of a handsome Prince, who happened to be hitch-hiking to a minstrel song festival, where he hoped to make some loot with his lute. Picking up the ring, he graciously handed it back to the Princess who promptly swooned away into his manly young arms, thinking that it must be her betrothed returned to her.

'Recovering as rapidly as custom permitted, she congratulated him on his success at finding the gold ring, not to mention the improvement in his appearance and bearing. Not appreciating her Highness's error, the young Prince drew the hasty, if understandable conclusion that she was in immediate need of care and protection, and handed her over to the aforementioned social

The Journey to the Gateway

welfare lady, who was glad of the work, since she had begun to lose her fat and was returning to her earlier, more appealing shape that she knew would once more attract the attention of the local slave-traders.

'She was installed in the Royal Palace to watch over the Princess and one sunny morning happened by chance to stray near the King's private fish-ponds, where she met her old friend, the Secret Agent. He was still searching desperately for the ring-swallowing toad, unaware of its fishy end. When she told him what had come to pass, he quickly used his magic powers to change himself back into human shape. Unfortunately, he had been a toad for so long that he had lost the knack and accidentally turned himself into a beautiful, stately woman. The King saw this vision of loveliness splashing about in his private fish-ponds and lost his heart without delay, having recently buried his Queen, who, with proper respect for matters of state, had died shortly before her funeral, rather than shortly after it, as is sometimes unhappily the case.

'As soon as the King's new love had passed the required Christmas-speech and balcony-waving tests, he married her with due pomp in the Royal Chapel. There was only one unusual feature in an otherwise highly conventional ceremony, namely that the wedding ring, borrowed for the occasion from a reluctant Princess, was slipped, not on to the new Queen's finger, but instead, at her own request, into a pierced hole in her right ear-lobe. The Princess thought that there was something decidedly sinister about this strange departure from the usual marriage ritual, but on this particular occasion was unable to put her finger on what it was. Her step-mother arranged with the palace cook to provide her with a special diet that soon reduced her to a more appealing shape and then banished her to the slave market, where she was bought by a second-hand Princess collector, with whom she lived happily ever after.

'How does that cling to you, leech-wise?' asked the fast-talking, myth-making, flying steward.

'What happened to the social welfare lady? The one who

became the Princess's nurse?' asked Ludo. 'I suppose she lost her job and was kicked out of the palace?'

'No, no. Good heavens, a beautiful girl like that? Never. Well, not in a myth, anyway. No, she was taken on by the new Queen as an ear-lobe masseuse. And sometimes, or so the story goes, when the King was away on the royal hunt, her Regal Majesty would turn herself back into the Secret Agent again for a few hours, transmit secret messages to the enemy via the miniature device concealed in his gold ring, and dally with the beautiful masseuse in the palace steam-rooms. But personally I don't believe that part of the story. I think it was simply added to lend the tale spy-appeal.'

'But if you make it up as you go along, how can you doubt yourself?'

'That's my trouble. I am full of self-doubt. That is why I am still a steward.'

'Is there any moral to your story?' asked Ludo.

'Of course not. Myths don't have morals.'

'What do they have?'

'Enough stupid double-talk to keep a lot of big-brained mythology professors arguing until they are senile enough to write their memoirs.'

'I must confess,' said Jason, 'that it sounded to me more like a fairy-tale than a myth.'

'You wire-gliders are all the same. I clap my beak out passing the time for you and what do I get? Quibbles! Nit-preening quibbles. But I'm used to it. You can't freeze *my* in-flight smile.'

'I'm sorry. It was a very good story. May I ask you a question?'

'Certainly. Go right ahead. I'm *your* steward. Bugfly's the name. Fly by name, fly by nature.'

'Bugfly? I was going to ask if you were some sort of stork.'

'Stork! Stork! Oh, not that old gag about storks delivering babies down chimneys again. We're always getting that one. No, I'm *not* a stork.'

'But you look storky to me.'

'I don't know who you are, but I have news for you. You

couldn't tell stork from heron!'

'You're a heron, then?'

'No, no, no! I told you — I'm a Bugfly. Oh dear, I'll have to explain. You see, we look like storks because that's our disguise. You noticed how I worked a Secret Agent into that myth of mine?'

'Yes.'

'Well, that's because I'm one myself and I like to have someone in a myth I can think of as me. It helps to keep my interest.'

'That's why you came off so well in the end, then?'

'Of course — you catch on fast.'

'And I bet you did dally with the ear-lobe masseuse at the finish of the story, *and* send those secret messages, didn't you?'

'What do *you* think, pal? It was my myth, wasn't it?'

'What sort of spying do you do? In real life, I mean.'

'Well, when I'm not checking security on this Whisker-run, I'm off planting bugged babies on the Outrock. Risky business. Tricky if I get shot down, see. How'd they explain a dead Bugfly in, say, Northern Wiltshire, if up there I don't even exist yet? Get the picture? So I fly by night — always fly by night — and I use this stork-rig as a cover. Works a charm. Those poor, stupid, bird-brained storks upstairs have to put up with a lot of coarse jokes, but that's their funeral.'

'Who bugs the babies?'

'That's classified information. Top secret, sorry.'

'All right, but why take them? There are far too many babies up there already, arriving in the usual way — horrible, wet, smelly things.'

'Well, I guess it's O.K. to tell you this much — you see, we need a regular feed-back of information from the Outrock, to see how our latest models are making out. So the Sculptor gets out the old magic hammer-and-chisel and knocks up a baby, we have it bugged, and I get a special twelve-hour pass to whisk it upstairs — no details, sorry — then I make the switch, and get back here fast. Occasionally I'm spotted and then that fool stork story starts up again. But mostly, no one notices.'

'I won't ask what happens to the real babies you take away.'

'That's wise. I wouldn't tell you anyway — security again. Have to think of our public image. It's a rough job, mine. Can't cry over a few spilt milk-bottles, though, when Inrock freedom is at stake.'

'How do you get the bugged babies back? Are you allowed to tell me that?'

'Yeah, why not. They're great crawlers, the ones we make, and they always end up falling down disused mine-shafts, old wells, that kind of thing, and we bring them back to base and de-bug them, check the information and feed it through to the Sculptor. Neat, huh? Keeps us up to date on everything that's going on up there. No one thinks twice about shooting his mouth off in front of a baby, so we get it all, the whole works. Hey, I've been chatting away here and look at this, we're coming down to the Gateway already. I can see the Censor starting to open his eyes. You'll be in visual range any second. Good luck! I hope he likes what he sees. Bye now,' and the mysterious Bugfly soared away into the Grannit-sky, intent, no doubt, on some urgent government business.

The Censor's Whiskers were beginning to thicken out slightly and the four surviving travellers felt themselves slowing down. The great face in the wall of rock, staring up at them like a giant, gaping codfish, was easy to make out now, as they came skimming in at the end of their long journey. Its heavy-lidded eyes, each of which must have been at least a yard wide, blinked several times and opened to their full extent. The huge black pupils dilated, then shrank to pin-points. The open jaws seemed to be closing a little now, or was it their imagination? No! They were definitely shutting. The Censor's Gateway was going to be blocked.

'He doesn't like the look of us!' cried Ludo.

'Slow us down, somebody slow us down!' screamed a frantically struggling Scrunt.

'No! Faster, faster!' shouted Jason. 'We'll make it if only we can speed up.'

'No, no! Slower, slower!' yelled Klaggit. 'We're too late. We'll be splattered all over the Censor's face,' and he and Scrunt started twisting wildly in their harnesses. They managed to turn the clips

The Journey to the Gateway

slightly to one side, then slightly to the other, making them jam on the Whiskers and reducing their speed of descent by several miles per hour. They both started to lag behind Jason and Ludo, who raced on desperately towards the closing mouth of the great Gateway, bunching their bodies up into tight balls to reduce wind resistance.

The base of the Whiskers broadened out, as they had been told, and the clips snapped open, first on Jason's harness and then, a split second later, on Ludo's. They were both flung at great speed through the nearly closed mouth, only a few moments before its lips met with an echoing crash. As they tumbled into the long, deep mouth, they could imagine all too vividly what must have happened to the unfortunate Klaggit and Scrunt – tragic victims, like their friends before them, of the sudden and violent whims of the ruthless Censor.

Now Jason and Ludo alone remained, spinning and slithering down a long, slippery tube that could only be the Censor's throat. They nearly stuck in it when their yellow back-packs, reacting automatically to the dampness, flew open and inflated, but with a few jerks and twists they slid on down and dropped with a plop into the pond of the Censor's stomach.

Lights flashed at them as they floated there, and voices were calling from somewhere nearby in the dimness.

'Over here, you two. Swim for it. This way, this way. Stop dithering about, you're giving the Censor indigestion. We want you out, out of there, *out!*'

CHAPTER TWENTY-THREE
The Zoobore Collection

When Jason and Ludo were dragged from the swirling waters of the Censor's stomach, they were hustled through a long, winding, orange tunnel by a group of hooded guides, their lamps flickering eerily on the corrugated walls. They emerged into a large, curved chamber, stacked high with thousands upon thousands of discarded harnesses and yellow back-packs, where one of the guides told them to remove their equipment, clean themselves and wait. Then they were left alone.

'If only Klaggit and Scrunt hadn't slowed down. They so nearly got through,' said Ludo, shaking her fur dry and wiping her horns.

'I wonder why the Censor tried to reject us?' muttered Jason. 'There must have been something wrong with us.'

He was interrupted by a loud, disembodied voice which shook the walls, roaring:

'You have failed to pass the Censor. You should not have been allowed through. You will be sent back immediately.'

'But why? Tell us why,' shouted Jason, turning this way and that, not knowing where to look.

'Because you have already been duplicated. You are a pair.

The Zoobore Collection

This is not permitted before you have proved yourselves in the Testing Grounds. There has been an error. You should not have been despatched. You will be returned.'

'Of course,' Jason whispered to Ludo, 'that must have been what upset him when we came in range of his eyes.'

'Wait!' shouted Ludo. 'I have a suggestion. If we can make ourselves different from one another, will you let us through?'

There was a long pause.

'It is possible,' the voice boomed. 'You may try, but there must be no delay. I will give you five hundred heartbeats, no more. It is up to you.'

'Five hundred heartbeats,' cried Jason, 'but that's . . . that's only a few minutes. What can we do in a few minutes?'

'Give me the casket,' said Ludo, holding out her hand.

'Why? What good will it do?'

'It may not work, but do you remember what the Sculptor said? We were not to eat the Golden Worms here in the Inrock because they would make us smaller. It might not work on you because you come from the Outrock, but if I were to take the smallest possible bite — no more than a nibble — of one of the Worms, I might shrink enough for us to cease to be a pair. We'd be such different sizes, they'd have to let us pass.'

'It's too dangerous.'

'We can't go back. Imagine what would happen to us. Imagine what the Sculptor would do. We'd be scrambled, for sure. Now give me the casket. If it doesn't work, we are no worse off, and if it works too well and I shrink to nothing, at least you will be able to go on through.'

'I won't go without you.'

'Of course you will. You *must* get back with the rest of the Golden Worms, or everything we have done together will mean nothing. It will all be wasted. We can't let that happen. Now, give it to me!'

'One hundred heartbeats,' boomed the great voice. 'Only one hundred left. No more.'

Jason hesitated. Little more than a minute remained to them.

Ludo and he stared into one another's eyes. Then, with a heavy heart, he handed over the small golden box. Ludo tore open the seal and lifted the lid.

A blaze of shimmering yellow light filled the curved chamber, flooding their faces with a rich golden glow. Inside the casket lay a pile of tiny, undulating, rippling Golden Worms, glinting and glistening as they moved. Jason was hypnotized by their unbelievable beauty, but Ludo quickly broke the spell as she snatched one up, held it for a second wriggling in her furry hand, and then bit a minute piece off one end. The rest of the worm continued to move after she had bitten it and she dropped it back in the box, shut the lid and handed it swiftly to Jason, smiling up at him as she gulped the golden fragment down.

They waited. The heartbeats passed like hours and nothing happened. Then Jason frowned as he saw Ludo's body slowly begin to dwindle in size. Down it went, until her head only reached up to his waist.

'Ludo!' he cried. 'Ludo, stop!'

'It's too late,' called Ludo, her small voice growing fainter. 'I ... I ... good luck, Jason. You'll make it. You'll ... ' But he could no longer hear her.

She shrank down and down and down and began to curl up into a minute ball. As Jason sank to his knees in front of her, he saw her change gradually into a small egg. The egg itself then began to shrink until it was no bigger than a small, brown bean. Only then did it stop. Carefully, tenderly, he picked it up and held it in the palm of his sweating hand. He could just see two little bumps where her horns had been, but no other features of the Ludo who a few seconds earlier had stood before him remained.

'Your time is up!' boomed the voice, and the hooded guards returned. They saw at once what had happened, whispered amongst themselves and left without a word. After a while, the deep voice spoke again:

'All is well. You have satisfied the Censor. You may pass. Go through and you will be told the Test that is required of you, so that you may prove yourself worthy of a through-rock passage. Go now, the board is ready for you.'

Placing the brown bean carefully inside his belt-pouch, Jason stepped sadly through the doorway and out of the curved chamber. He had lost his greatest friend, the brave companion who had left her village, abandoned her home, and risked her life for him so many times, now, finally, to give it up completely, so that he could return to the Outrock and fulfil his promise. And there was no way he could repay her. Nothing he could do. It would be hard indeed to live and laugh again with this huge debt unpaid.

In his sadness he hardly noticed the scene around him. He was passing through what appeared to be a vast graveyard, spreading in all directions as far as the eye could see. Two hooded figures walked in front of him and two behind, as he was marched along a narrow yellow path that stretched in a perfectly straight line towards the horizon.

After an hour's non-stop march, Jason tried to slacken the pace, but was nearly knocked over by the feet of his guides – or were they guards? – whose speed seemed to be completely fixed and unalterable. They were moving too fast for him to be able to read the names on the tombstones, but the inscriptions appeared to cover an enormous period of time, some being very ancient and almost illegible, while others looked virtually brand new.

'Who is buried here?' he asked the backs of the guides marching in front of him. But there was no reply, no acknowledgment, even, that he had spoken.

The march continued in silence for what seemed like another hour. Jason was passing the time by working out how many heartbeats there were in one hour and was on the verge of arriving at an answer when, without warning, the guides suddenly halted and made a smart turn to the left. Leaving the path, which still showed no sign of ending, they struck off into the graveyard and came to an abrupt stop in front of a pink marble tomb of unusual design. It was shaped like a gigantic snail-shell, surmounted by a strange, tapering mast at the top of which was a great bronze circle, divided into two halves by a stout, upright bar.

The four guides clustered around the entrance and it was clear from the way they were standing that they expected Jason to proceed inside without delay. Taking a deep breath, he stepped over the threshold and waited for them to follow. Instead, he saw them line up across the entrance space, firmly blocking his exit. He stared defiantly at them for a few moments and then, when it was obvious that they were not going to move or speak, he shrugged and left them to it.

Walking into the interior of the tomb, he found his footsteps spiralling down and round, round and down, until he emerged into a vast, low basement area, dotted with big slabs of marble on each of which lay a motionless body. Each body belonged to a different kind of creature, but they all appeared to have one thing in common – they were all dead. Very, very dead.

At the four corners of each slab stood short pedestals, like squat egg-cups, and on each pedestal stood a large, painted egg. One was brown, one grey, one black and one white. He was about to reach out and touch one of them, when he heard a sound close behind him.

'Name?' asked a voice at his elbow, and he spun round to see a slender form, like a large splinter of wood, perched on four spindly legs.

'Jason.'

'Follow me. The Board is waiting.'

As he was led past slab after slab, his curiosity got the better of him.

'Who are all these?' he asked, waving his arm out in a wide arc, hoping that his new companion would be more forthcoming than the hooded guides who had brought him to this sinister place.

'These? Oh, they are Zoobore's collection. He only collects mistakes.'

'Mistakes? You mean rejects?'

'No. Rejects never get to the Outrock. These have been there, failed, and become extinct. The last few of each kind are brought here to the Yard for reference purposes.'

'Like a museum?'

'No, more like a zoo. They're dead, aren't they?'

The Zoobore Collection

'Yes, but . . . '

'Well, then, it's more like a zoo, isn't it?'

'If you say so.'

'I just did.'

'I suppose,' said Jason, squinting at the low ceiling, 'that each of the tombstones up there matches a slab down here. There must be thousands of them?'

'Millions. It is a very fine collection.'

'But why these large eggs on each slab?'

'Those are the Mystic Eggs of Porus. They contain all the vital statistics of the bodies on the slabs, all we need to know about them. From the contents of the Mystic Eggs it would be possible to reconstruct in detail the precise kind of Outrock life they led in any particular case. The brown one is the Egg of Location. It contains fingernail-dirt, circus-sealed fingernail-dirt. Careful analysis of this dirt can tell us exactly where the creature in question was scratching around when it became extinct. The white one is the Egg of Mastication. It contains supper-guts, sound-proofed supper-guts — the left-over innards from the last supper eaten on the Outrock.'

'Why are they sound-proofed?' enquired Jason, who despite the great depression that was hanging over him, was beginning to take an interest in the curious rituals of this bizarre, deathly place.

'To stop them rumbling, of course. They are rather empty, as guts go. Then, the grey egg, that is the Egg of Vocation. It contains skin-maps, face-lined, rustic skin-maps. By studying these we can deduce the lines on the creature's face and from those its facial expressions when it perished. This tells us what kind of role it played, what sort of job it did, and so on. Suppose, for example, that it was a middle-class martyr by profession, then you'd find the bland face-lines of soft-centred sacrifice. That kind of thing.'

'And the black egg?'

'Ah, yes, that's the most important one of all. That is the Egg of Generation, containing the mate-pods, starch-reduced mate-pods.'

'Mate-pods?'

'Yes, pods of shrunken mate-beans. Placed in male-blood, they swell up to full-sized females. The creatures lying in state on the slabs are all males, naturally — being more colourful — and they need a small group of females standing by for breeding purposes, in case we ever decide to start up any particular line again.'

'But these are all Outrock failures. If they have become extinct once, why would you want to revive them?'

'Oh, we get occasional requests from the Sculptor, who wants to try out some experiment or other. Checking why they failed, mostly. Once in a while, once in a very blue Grannit, a minor alteration is made and back they go for a second attempt upstairs. But that's rare. Last time it happened, as I recall, it was some ugly old fish-thing. Can't remember its name, but the Sculptor had some crazy idea about sticking its fins on some sort of legs. Wasn't worth it in my opinion, but the mate-beans are . . . '

'Beans! Did you say beans?' shouted Jason, interrupting his spindly, splintery companion, who jumped back, startled and quivering.

'Yes. We shrink them down from the full females with a little dust from ground-up Golden Worms. It's rather fun . . . '

'Fun!'

'Well, yes, like pricking balloons at a party. Great fun. We always enjoy that bit. Er . . . although I shouldn't say so, it gets a little monotonous here sometimes. Even silly things like female-shrinking can help to relieve the tedium. And it's harmless enough fun, you must admit.'

Jason's mind was racing. Perhaps, after all, there would be a chance of getting Ludo back. But he would have to tread carefully. This was not the time for it. Much as he hated the idea of delaying, he would have to wait until he was alone somewhere.

'You use male-blood?' he asked casually.

'Yes, a few drops from the male is all we need. They keep very fresh down here, you'd be surprised. Zoobore is an expert in these matters.'

'Tell me about Zoobore,' said Jason, changing the subject.

'His full name is Spiral Zoobore of the Split Circle. I expect you saw his emblem up above. A bit showy if you ask me. No, I mustn't say that – very impressive it is really. His rivals call him Twisted Zoobore and that drives him berserk. As a matter of fact I can tell you in strict confidence that one or two of these slab owners aren't failures at all, never were. Old Zooby can be nasty when he's roused. When he gets to hear he's being called Twisted, he gets his hood-boys into action and wham! – there's an extra slab where there shouldn't be one. But you've no need to worry, he'll be all fairness and pomp when you meet him. Sitting on the Board he has to show off to the others. He is the President of the Board, you see, being one of the few, the very few great-gumfs in the Inrock. The other members are only super-gumfs and he has to show them how dignified and detached he is. Great phoney. No, I shouldn't say that. You know the old saying: Walls have ears and potatoes have eyes, he who keeps quiet is the last one who dies. Well, I've said too much already.'

'Who will I meet, apart from Zoobore?'

'I'm not sure. They take it in turns. But you're lucky. I happen to know that there are very few here today. It's a slack time – I gather you are the only candidate. Some trouble back at the Whiskers, they tell me.'

Jason was about to ask his splintery companion what he was expected to do at the Board meeting, when they came to a curved, pink marble door.

'There you are,' said the spindly creature. 'In there,' and he sloped off between the rows of slabs, whistling to himself and twitching.

Jason entered. Behind a low table were three chairs. The centre one was empty, but to his surprise the other two housed familiar figures. On the left slumped the great bulk of Lord Ten-chin and on the right, to Jason's horror, sprawled the massive, scaly form of the Mha-kee of the Root Forest. He was puzzled to see that Ten-chin's bloated face was scowling angrily, while the Mha-kee, in striking contrast, was beaming down at him in a most friendly way.

'Do sit down, do sit down,' hissed the Mha-kee warmly. 'Make yourself at home, make yourself comfortable. The President will be here shortly.'

Jason lowered himself nervously into a small seat facing the table. After a few moments there was a scuffling noise and both Ten-chin and the Mha-kee heaved themselves to their feet. A yellow curtain behind the table was thrust aside and a tiny, misshapen figure entered and climbed with difficulty into the central chair. The Zoobore was, indeed, a twisted creature, with a soft, spiral body of yellow skin, covered in round, brown patches. It was impossible to see his face because he had eyes in the back of his head and was forced to speak through a U-shaped megaphone, which he clapped over his hidden mouth and pointed menacingly at Jason.

'One Jason?' he asked with a metallic cry.

'Yes, I am Jason.'

'I have your record here. I will read it to you and ask you to confirm that it is a true and fair description of your past activities. It states:

1. That you did fail to present the necessary name-papers and love-papers when requested to do so by a Polizesti in the normal course of his duties.
2. That you did cause the death by shock-puncture of one Red Warty, housed at that time in His Lordship's Display Prison.
3. That you did falsely present yourself to His Lordship as a member of the Sculptor's personal staff.
4. That you did impersonate a missing person, namely one Meggamole, called Mad Meggamole, during the ritual of a village flag ceremony.
5. That you did cause the death of an infant Night-slopper by taking its place in its mother's back pouch and leaving it at the mercy of roaming Sabenites.
6. That you did assault the tender nasal organ of the great Mha-kee of the Root Forest, violate his sacred skin-tomb, impersonate his supreme being without his prior permission and stir up rebellion amongst his hand-servants.

7 That you did steal a golden necklace from a feathered dwarf, imprison the President of Headland in his own dungeon and make off with the presidential Galoon.
8 That you did brutally assault and thereby cause the death of a Whiskered Whish-eater, mutilate a Strummer musician, and cause the downfall and disgrace of a distinguished Strummer Conductor.
9 That you did obtain illegal entry to the School of Unlearning, improperly assuming the role of an official inspector.
10 That you did effect a forcible entry into the private quarters of the Great Sculptor and did subsequently disobey a strict order to return whence you had come, making your escape instead down the Censor's Whiskers to the detriment of six legitimate Unscholars.

Tell us now, one Jason, is this a true and accurate statement of your recent Inrock activities?'

Exhausted by his long speech, Zoobore slumped back into his chair and awaited Jason's reply. Ten-chin scowled, and the Mha-kee nodded, smiling even more warmly than before.

'Yes,' said Jason finally. 'Yes, I am afraid it is.'

'Excellent, excellent,' shrilled Zoobore. 'Your ingenuity, coupled with your obviously violent nature, will fit you well for life on the Outrock. You will now be set a task to perform here in the Testing Grounds and, if successful, you will be granted a through-rock passage. Now, to choose the task. Mha-kee, any suggestions?'

'Yes, something simple, I suggest. This creature has done me a great service.'

'Have I?' Jason blurted out. 'Have I really?'

'Of course. You started that rebellion in the Root Forest, didn't you? I shall always be grateful for that.'

'But why?'

'Why? Why? Because it gave me the chance to take the most *hideous* revenges, the most terrible reprisals. Delicious, quite delicious.'

'Very well. Something simple then,' said Zoobore. 'Now, my Lord Ten-chin?'

'I cannot agree,' rumbled Ten-chin angrily. 'When this creature lied to me about his spying for the Sculptor I believed him and he made me look a fool in front of my whole court. I propose a full-force task. Something *special*.'

'Any ideas, gentlemen?' asked Zoobore in his best detached manner.

'Yes,' growled Ten-chin. 'There is a herd of wild Tricorns I have in mind. Nasty brutes. The original Tricorn had been passed by the Board, proved itself on the Testing Grounds, and had been duplicated into a small breeding herd ready for a through-rock passage, when the whole bunch of them cut loose and took off for the Undersea. I suggest that the task for this Jason should be to round them up and take them with him to the Outrock where they belong. No Tricorns – no passage. Simple, you said, my dear Mha-kee? Well, what could be simpler?'

'But Tricorns are Mark III Unicorns! They are as swift as they are vicious. It is an impossible task,' retorted the Mha-kee.

'Good!' grinned Ten-chin, smiling for the first time since Jason had arrived at the board-room.

'I agree,' said Zoobore. 'We have been getting slack lately. But this is a fitting task, for I note that this creature, Jason, has horns, too. It is apt. I give my consent.'

'You are both much too severe,' hissed the Mha-kee, 'but as it is two against one, I withdraw. Tricorns it is, then. And very good luck, my dear Jason, you will certainly need it. Oh, and by the way, an old friend of yours, the mayor of Lo-la-po, asked me to give you his warmest regards, if ever I bumped into you again.'

'The mayor of Lo-la-po?'

'Yes, you must remember him – a large brown beast with two heads.'

'Di-di!'

'I believe that is his name, yes.'

'But he flooded the town. They were furious with him. They can't have made him the mayor.'

'They can and they did. He told me about that little spot of bother. It seems he did them a good turn after all. Apparently they had been suffering from a plague of the Dreaded Punies, filthy, oozing little pests that had infested the walls of their houses for years, causing rising damp and giving them all Galloping Puny-fever. When the mayor – er, Di-di – flooded the town, the Punies, seeing all that spectacular dampness, imagined they were up against a superior rival and abandoned the town overnight in a blind panic. The walls have been bone dry ever since the flood subsided, and Di-di returned to find himself the hero of Lo-la-po. They installed him as mayor and now, I gather, he has retired and lives peacefully there, presiding over banquets, tending his pet Water-knots, and sailing on Long Lake. He told me you might like to know about all this – thought you might be worried about him.'

'Thank you. I was worried, I must admit. But I should have known better.'

'When you two have finished nattering,' boomed Lord Ten-chin, 'perhaps this test we have set can get under way?'

'Of course, of course,' hissed the Mha-kee. 'Goodbye, my dear Jason, and once again may I say . . . '

'No you may not!' shouted Ten-chin, changing colour alarmingly. 'Jason, get out and get on with it. Zoobore, get your Hooded Cronies to give him a shove in the wrong direction.'

'Patience, patience, my dear Ten-chin. There is no time limit in the Testing Grounds, as you know full well. Jason, you will proceed from here to the space below, where you will go at your own pace to the Undersea. This is a vast Inrock area covering the whole of the land beneath the oceans. There you will find a runaway herd of creatures called Tricorns. You will capture them and take them to Through-rock Bridge. Then you will go to the Ticket Officer and obtain your official pass to the Outrock. That is all I . . . '

'Can you give me some idea of . . . '

'That is all I am at liberty to tell you. Now go, and may Grannits light your way. Goodbye,' and the Spiral Zoobore, Lord Ten-chin and the Mha-kee of the Root Forest all rose, bowed solemnly three and a half times, and withdrew.

CHAPTER TWENTY-FOUR
The Valley of the Hearties

The moment had come for Jason to prove himself. Leaving the board-room, he was ushered by hooded guides down a long, spiral staircase and out into a fantastic landscape of what looked like multi-coloured pillars of flesh. They loomed up all round him, pink and blue and mauve and crimson, indigo and viridian and sepia and vermilion, rearing over his head, twisting and curving away up into space, up towards the Grannit-sky.

The hooded figures disappeared like silent ghosts as he gazed, open-mouthed, at the scene before him. When he turned to seek their guidance, he found that he was alone. For a moment he wondered whether this was the time to prick himself and soak the small brown bean that nestled in his belt-pouch with the male-blood that would bring Ludo back to life once more. But feeling that it would be safer first to get right away from the Censor's domain, he set off through the sloping pillars of flesh and headed for an open space he could just make out in the far distance.

After he had been travelling for a few hours, the light began to

The Valley of the Hearties

fade. As night fell, he took refuge by the curved base of a huge magenta-coloured pillar and, totally exhausted, sank into a deep sprawling sleep. The soft pillar sighed and breathed deeply, as Flesh-pillars do when they are pleased, but having no face, she was unable to smile down as she would have liked to have done, at the tiny, slumbering figure with its head resting on her soft curves. But she was contented enough simply to know that she would be able to offer a night's comfort and peace to a weary traveller. Flesh-pillars are like that, although hardly anyone ever realizes it. Unhappily, a beautiful trunk and exquisite limbs are of little interest to others if there is no face attached. A face by itself, on the other hand, or one with a perfectly revolting body, all scrawny and scabby, or bloated and blotchy, can rule the world. It is most unfair to Flesh-pillars, but there is little they can do about it, having no voices with which to protest.

Blissfully unaware of these long-standing problems, Jason slept soundly on through the night. When he awoke it was already broad Grannit-light once more. Sitting up, rubbing his face, he had the distinct sensation that he was not alone, but no one was in sight. The only object he did not remember seeing before he lay down to sleep was a tall, rippled shell, standing in the ground about ten feet away from him, but it was motionless and showed no sign of life.

'Will you love me always?' said a tiny, tinkling voice.
'Will I what?'
'Will you always, always love me?' repeated the voice.
'Who are you?' asked Jason drowsily, looking all round the strange, multi-coloured landscape, but still seeing no one.
'I am only a humble Plod-wig. Say you love me.'
'But I don't even know you.'
'If you knew me, you'd despise me, so say you love me now, before it's too late. Please!'
'Where are you? I can't see you.'
'Promise you won't laugh, and I'll come out.'
'I won't laugh.'
'Promise?'

'I promise.'

There was a faint creaking sound behind him and he turned round in time to see a lid lifting from the top of the delicate pink cone of the rippled shell he had noticed a few moments before. So it was alive after all. It looked remarkably like an overgrown ice-cream cornet, except that where the ice-cream itself should have been there now emerged a sad little face.

As the lid opened further, the face was followed by a slender neck and a pair of needle-thin arms. The arms shrugged helplessly and the face screwed itself up into a sad, sickly smile.

'I'm a failure, a dismal failure. They set me such a simple test, but I failed and now I'm stuck here forever. Will you help me?'

'What was your test?'

'That's just it — I can't remember. I don't move very fast, you see — only about $3\frac{1}{2}$ inches a year — and by the time I got this far I remembered that I had forgotten the test. I'm hopeless. Say you love me and then we can live here together and hurt one another.'

'Hurt one another? But I thought you were supposed to be kind to those who love you?'

'Oh no, it's the people who *don't* care about you that you have to be kind to — to stop them ignoring you. Those who love you are the only ones you can afford to hurt, because they are the only ones who will put up with it and stay with you afterwards.'

'So it pays to have lots of enemies?' asked Jason sarcastically.

'Only if you want to live politely all the time, but a completely polite life gets awfully dull after a while.'

'I'm sorry, you must excuse me, but I must be going. I have a test to . . . '

'There you are, I told you. You despise me already. I knew it.'

'I don't despise you. You have some funny ideas about love, but I don't despise you.'

'And you promised, you promised,' wailed the Plod-wig, tearing at its long, droopy hairs.

'I promised not to laugh, and I haven't.'

'Yes you have, you have. You said my ideas were funny. That's laughing with words — you know it is.'

The Valley of the Hearties

'You are beginning to irritate me,' said Jason, exasperated, and he stood up and stretched himself.

'You can irritate *me* if you like,' whispered the forlorn Plod-wig, 'and if you'll only say you love me, you can hurt me, too.'

'But I don't want to hurt you. It's against my principles to hurt anyone — except in self-defence, that is. And even then I don't enjoy it.'

'Principles? Don't tell me you have principles? How awful!'

'Of course I have principles. We all have to have some sort of general principles to live by.'

'Oh no, you're so wrong, so very wrong. My old shell-maker always said "Never have any general principles — they ruin you, make you thoughtless and ruthless." You see, if you have them you have to apply them, even when they don't apply. They make the intelligent look half-stupid and the stupid look half-intelligent, and they level everyone out, which pleases the fools, who, being in the majority, carry the day. Then everyone is stuck with their ludicrous principles when what they should be doing is treating every problem they meet as a special case.'

'If you are so clever,' snapped Jason, who was finding this pathetic, pink-shelled creature increasingly annoying, 'then why are you such a terrible failure?'

'It takes a failure to understand these things, to know how things go wrong. What do the successful know about life? They only live it. They don't stop to think, they're too busy succeeding. You only see things clearly when you are deeply depressed, like me.'

'You are certainly beginning to depress me.'

'Am I? Am I really? Oh, how wonderful. Then perhaps we will be able to fall in love after all, and start hurting one another in our own little love-shell.'

'No thank you, I'm leaving.'

'I'll kill myself if you go.'

'That's blackmail.'

'Scrumptious, isn't it? Does it hurt a bit?'

'If you don't stop this drivel, I'll kill you myself.'

'Ooh! Delicious. Now you really do want to hurt me. Go on, go on. I love it.'

'You disgust me.'

'Oh, wonderful, wonderful. You are filling my poor shell with an agony of pleasure.'

Unable to stand any more, Jason stepped forward, grabbed the pathetic Plod-wig's lid and, ramming its head down into its cone with his other hand, slammed the hard, round disc of hinged shell on top of it. Muffled cries of delight seeped through from inside the cone, and only increased when Jason gave the lid a parting thump with his fist. As he was walking angrily away, the tiny, tinkling voice called after him:

'Thank you, thank you. That was lovely. You hurt me terribly. Now I know you love me. Is there anything I can do for you in return?'

Pausing, Jason tried to collect his thoughts. The wretched Plod-wig had made him so cross that he had almost forgotten his own test.

'Yes,' he said, turning reluctantly, 'you can tell me where to find the Undersea. Which way is it?'

'Straight on the way you are heading. You can't miss it. Through the Valley of the Hearties and down into Joy-poloy's Tunnel. But wouldn't you rather stay here and be a failure with me? We failures have much more fun than the successes, you know. We can feel sorry for one another, and tell one another all our troubles, and share our miseries. It's lovely, really, when you get used to the idea. You'll find it gets very lonely being a success. And dangerous, too. I'd forget it if I were you. Stay here and say you'll always love me.'

'That is where I came in,' said Jason. 'Goodbye, and thank you for your helpful directions.'

'There you are, now you're being polite. I knew our love couldn't last. I'm hopeless. Helpless and hopeless. I think I shall have to catch a terrible disease, perhaps then someone will come along and nurse me. Being nursed is almost as good as being loved, really, once you get used to the idea. I'm good at getting

The Valley of the Hearties

used to things. Hi — where are you? Where have you gone? Come back. I haven't finished. I have some complaints for you. Wouldn't you like to hear my complaints?'

But Jason was already out of ear-shot and the wretched Plod-wig, sighing heavily, subsided once more into its delicate pink shell, to wait for the next passer-by.

The landscape changed as Jason strode on through the curving, bulging, coloured pillars of flesh. The land began to dip away more and more steeply in front of him until eventually he was running at full tilt through a sharply slanting ravine. Slipping, he rolled over and over and, like a kicked ball, went crashing down, faster and faster, into a deep valley. He ended up sprawling at the feet of a group of surprised figures who were vigorously washing a large, smooth boulder of rock.

''Allo, 'allo, 'allo!' said the biggest. 'What 'ave we 'ere? Har yew a membah of the club?'

They were broad neckless creatures, the colour of raw bacon-rind, with stout bandy legs, thick hairy arms and anvil-shaped heads. Noticing that their hearts grew out of their chests on short stalks, Jason realized that he must already have arrived at the Valley of the Hearties.

'I fell,' he said, rather lamely, getting painfully to his feet.

'They all do!' roared the biggest Heartie, and his companions all laughed uproariously, slapping one another on their broad backs and punching one another playfully between their piggy eyes.

'Har yew down-'arted?' they cried in unison.

'No, only winded,' said Jason.

'Then where's your heart? It seems to have gone down to me,' snarled the big Heartie, suddenly becoming serious and dropping his funny accent.

'Down? Down where? It's inside my chest where it ought to be, not stuck out in the open like yours.'

'Oh-ho! We've got a joker here. Definitely not a club member, this one. Heartless too,' and they all started roaring with laughter again.

'Is this the way to the Undersea, please?' asked Jason, as politely as he could.

'Yes it is, my old salt. But stay a while and we'll put a heart on your chest — fix you up in no time — then you'll feel more one of the boys. What do you say to that?'

'I'd say . . . I'd say . . . why are you washing that rock?' replied Jason, who did not like the way they were clustering round him, leaning on one another's shoulders, licking their lower lips, and grinning with anticipation.

'Got to keep it spick and span. Got to have everything tidy. And look at that grass — look at it — not a blade over half an inch high — not one blade in the whole of the valley. How's that for neatness? We never rest here, I can tell you, up with the Grannits every morning, snip, snip, snip. It's a great life. You'll love it. Now, about that heart of yours — let's get it out into the open where we can see it, shall we? Hold him, you two, hold him firm.'

'Stop!' shouted Jason.

'What!' roared the big Heartie. 'What's this? Shirking it, are you? Don't want to be one of the boys, eh? We'll soon see about that,' and he spat on his hairy hands and rubbed them vigorously together, winking at his smirking friends.

Held firmly by his arms, there was little that Jason could do, but as the broad figure approached him with brawny fingers outstretched, he kicked out with both legs, thumping the big Heartie in the chest. With a bellow of rage, the bulky figure toppled backwards and sat down grunting and snorting on the neatly clipped grass. His exposed heart began to beat wildly and turn a deeper shade of red. All the other Hearties began to redden in the same way and their grins faded rapidly from their hard, anvil-shaped faces.

'Little blighter,' growled the big Heartie. 'I've a good mind to de-horn him, scalp him and skin him alive. Grab him, you lot, and bring him to the club-room. We'll fix him.'

Singing a hearty song and carrying the struggling Jason aloft, they marched off towards a small hut on the far side of the immaculately tailored lawn. Inside, they threw Jason down in a

The Valley of the Hearties

corner and held a hurried conference, bending over in a tight circle with their anvil heads almost touching one another.

Straightening up, the big Heartie swaggered over to Jason and spat on the floor.

'We don't like trouble-makers here. Gives the club a bad name. If you won't wear your heart on your chest like the rest of us, how can we tell what you are thinking, eh, what you are feeling? How would we know you were one of us, hated the same outsiders, sneered at the same ideas? Answer me that if you can. You might be a black-hearted villain yourself, for all we know.'

'I am,' shouted Jason, searching for anything that would help him to escape from these odious creatures. 'That's exactly what I am — black-hearted. You wouldn't want to see a black-heart throbbing at you all day long, would you? And I'm big-hearted, too — a big, black, throbbing heart. Huh! You'd have to cover yours up, you'd be ashamed to show them alongside mine. Now you'd better let me go, or I'll tear your hearts off — piffling little pink jelly-bags, that's all they are, so get away from me, I'm dangerous.'

'You're black-hearted?' gasped the big Heartie. 'I don't believe it,' and they held another hurried conference. 'If you are as you say,' he roared, straightening up again, 'we don't want you in this club. The sooner you are out of the valley, the better. But before you go, we have a little treat for you. Okay, boys, get him!'

They pounced on Jason, who soon disappeared beneath a heaving pile of heavy bodies.

'The scissors,' someone shouted. 'Get the scissors.'

Jason felt the breath being squeezed out of him as they pressed down harder and harder to stop him moving. It was like being packed in a suitcase when the lid won't shut. Arching his neck back, he heard a scream as his horns dug into bulging muscles, then a large fist landed in his face and everything went dark.

When he came round, he ached all over. Trying to prop himself up on one elbow, he sank into something soft. It covered his face and he rolled gently over on to his back so that he could gasp for air. Sitting up slowly and carefully, he found that he was lying on a huge pile of rubbish, mostly rotting grass clippings and old rags worn thin from rock-washing, that had been heaped up at the far end of the valley.

Looking down at his smarting body he was astonished to see that the coat of fur the Sculptor had given him was gone. The Hearties had snipped him clean. Apart from his horns, which he could still feel firmly in place on top of his head, he was now back to his old, hairless self again! He could hardly believe his luck. He was sore and stiff and bruised, but apart from that, and a slight buzzing in his head, he was better off than he had been before. In their own stupid, brutal way, the Hearties were even bigger failures that the pathetic Plod-wig. He almost laughed out loud, but then he realized something was wrong. His belt was missing, and with it, the belt-pouch and its precious contents. Grabbing a long, tattered rag and wrapping it round himself, he staggered to his feet. In the distance, he could see the Hearties doing exercises on the trimly cut lawn and busily scrubbing another of the large boulders that littered the valley floor.

'My belt,' he gasped, 'they've taken my belt,' as he started searching frantically through the pile of soft rubbish. At last he found it, flung down amongst the litter, but when he opened the pouch his face fell. The crystals he had kept from the pink desert and the gold necklace of imitation Golden Worms were gone. The large pebble he had traded with Di-di when they were drifting down the river to Lo-la-po was still there, the Hearties obviously considering it worthless, and beneath it when he took it out was, to his great relief, the tiny object he was looking for – the small brown bean that was Ludo. He put her gently back in the pouch, snapped it shut, and fitted the belt around his waist.

Holding the pebble in his hand, he was about to throw it away when he remembered the casket – the golden casket of real Golden Worms. That had gone, too! He had been carrying it crammed tightly between the belt and his fur and now it had been stolen by these idiotic, grotesque Hearties. His anger rose in him like a tide and he gripped Di-di's pebble tightly in his fist. Striding towards the busy group of exercising figures on the lawn, he roared at them:

'You great, hairy fools, give me the casket, or I'll blow you to pieces.'

They paused in their exertions, looked up, and started laughing at the pathetic, naked-skinned figure advancing towards them, his tattered sheet held in place by his frayed leather belt, and his right arm held back above his head.

'Ho, ho, ho. Blow us up, would you? And with what, may I ask?' sneered the big Heartie, bouncing to his feet.

'With this magic pebble,' shouted Jason. 'It's a bomb, you simple-minded fools, didn't you realize that? No, you're too stupid, so you threw it away, didn't you? Now give me back my casket, or I'll destroy the whole valley and blast a great hole in your stupid, useless lawn. It won't look so tidy when I've finished with it.'

'Here's your little box, poor little black-hearted nudie,' taunted the big Heartie. 'Come and get it, little plucked chicken. Cluck, cluck, cluck,' and he threw the casket through the open window of the small hut.

The trick had failed. His bluff had been called. There was nothing for it but to throw the pebble and run. He would be lucky to get out alive this time, but if he made a dart for it, he might just get to the end of the valley before they caught up with him. The Golden Worms would be gone — there was nothing he could do about that now — but at least he still had Ludo. Pointing straight at the big Heartie, he took aim.

'All right, you asked for it,' he bellowed, and threw the pebble as hard as he could, turning and running the moment it had left his hand. Behind him he heard peals of laughter and then, to his immense surprise, there was a huge explosion which hurled him through the air and on to the soft pile of rubbish at the end of the valley.

When he dragged himself up, half-stunned, he was astounded to see that his bold words had come true. Di-di's pebble had lived up to its reputation. It really had been a special pebble after all — one of the dam-cracking kind — and there was the proof of it, a vast gaping hole where a moment before there had been a neat, trim lawn.

The broken Hearties lay groaning and whining on all sides. Jason picked his way past them and entered the small hut through what had once been its side wall, but was now a ragged, open space. The building was little more than a skeleton of splintered wood and on its rubble-strewn floor he could clearly see the glint of gold that had caught his eye from outside. It was the casket, but when he threw aside the broken planks that half-covered it he found to his horror that it had been torn open by the blast. It was empty. The Golden Worms had vanished, scattered by the explosion. Kicking aside the rubble that littered the twisted floor of the hut, he hunted for any survivors. In a dark corner, beneath some shattered poles, he found one and with trembling fingers placed it safely inside his pouch. He went on searching and searching, throwing fragments of wood this way and that, but without further success. The rest of the Golden Worms were lost without trace. Finally, sadly, he gave up.

Outside, the stunned Hearties were trying to sit up and console one another, their stalked hearts thumping heavily. Jason walked straight past them, ignoring their groans, and strode on to the end of the valley, whistling to himself to keep his spirits up, but secretly feeling rather sick at the chaos the pebble had caused. Well, at least Di-di would say it was for the best — a giant disturbance that would keep them talking and lawn-patching for weeks.

With that thought comforting him slightly, Jason left them behind and set out for Joy-poloy's tunnel, hoping against hope that a single Golden Worm would be enough to save the Mad Meggamole from disaster.

CHAPTER TWENTY-FIVE
The Tunnel of Joy-poloy

As there was only one obvious way out of the valley, Jason did not hesitate over which route to take. The path sank down and down, the high banks on either side getting steeper until they were upright walls, hemming him in. Little by little, they started to curve over, so that he was soon entering a tall, slit-shaped tunnel. It was getting darker and he had to step warily. When it finally became pitch dark, he had to edge his way forward inch by inch feeling the walls on either side with his outstretched hands.

After about ten minutes of this awkward progress, he was on the verge of giving up, returning to the valley and finding another way out, when, with a thump, he banged into something blocking the tunnel in front of him. Feeling it carefully, he discovered that it was flat, hard and cold. Deciding that it must be a door, but finding no lock or handle, he knocked on it loudly with his fist. The sound echoed fiercely back down the tunnel behind him.

In front of his eyes a small slot slid silently sideways. A red and black eye blinked at him three times and the small slot slid silently shut once more. After a few seconds the door opened inwards and he stepped cautiously through.

'Who sent you?' rasped a deep, wheezy voice.

'Zoobore,' replied Jason, not knowing quite how to answer.

'Listen, skin-baby, that shell-less screwback couldn't send his own shadow. Now pinch the other claw — who told you about this place?'

'Oh, yes — er — it was — er — Plod-wig, that was the name. Back there, on the other side of the valley.'

'Okay, that's better. Now move it,' and an unseen hand thrust open an inner door, blinding Jason with a gash of harsh, flashing light.

Shielding his eyes as he entered the space beyond, Jason tripped and felt himself sliding down a soft, furry chute. Wild music filled the air and dazzling lights flashed and spurted all around him. As his vision cleared he saw a long, bright, gaily decorated cavern filled with pink and yellow puffs of smoke, with holes and tunnels dipping and twisting in every direction. Crowds of dancing, leaping figures jostled and swayed, plunging and gliding in and out of the strange burrows, like rabbits in a gigantic warren. Before he knew what was happening, he was picked up and whisked into the throng, handed from one lurching figure to the next, swinging and curving with the deafening rhythm of the blaring music. Almost breathless, he arrived eventually at the far end of the cavern and was thrown headlong into a gaping blue hole. Inside it, he felt the soft, rubbery walls of the tube around him pulsating with the same rhythm and, as they did so, slowly shifting him along.

As he progressed in this way, bumping and plunging against the beating lobes of the tube, the texture of the walls began to change. The rubber feel gave way to creaky leather, then slippery silk, then light downy feathers and finally warm flowing hairs. Finding himself unharmed by this peculiar mode of travel, he was beginning to relax and enjoy the changing sensations when, in a rush, he was tipped down into a narrow pit and fell softly into a round nest of dense creamy wool. The nest began to rotate, slowly at first, then faster and faster, until he was spun out through the

The Tunnel of Joy-poloy

loose mass of wool and on to a huge bed of thick padded velvet.

'How does that toss you, skin-baby?' rasped a deep voice similar to the one he had heard at the entrance door.

Looking up, he saw that the owner of the voice was floating lazily in the air several feet above him.

'It was . . . it was pleasant — whatever it was — really rather pleasant,' gasped Jason, 'but how . . . how do you stay up there, floating like that? And who are you? Are you Joy-poloy?'

'That's me. I'm a drifter.'

'I can't think how . . . '

'Don't think, skin-baby, don't think. We don't do that here. Never, never, never. It's bad for the complexion — brings you out in spots. No, all we do here is *feel*, feel, that's the style, skin-baby, touch and feel. It's the only way to live.'

'But how can you feel anything if you are floating up there? You are only touching the air.'

'That, skin-baby, is to keep the nerve-endings fresh and free — so that when I *do* touch — wow! — it's a feast of pure, slithery skin-joy.'

'Can anyone do it? Could I float?'

'Simple as oiling a cheek, nothing to it. Just do as I say. Ready? Hold your nose, shut your mouth, close your eyes, waggle your ears and press your stomach. All at once, now go! More, more — squeeze your eyes tight, that's it, now blow, try to blow your nose open, but hold it tight, keep it shut, blow harder, harder, harder, feel your ears popping, you're rising now, don't look, squeeze those eyes, make them water, that's it, that's it, now swing your head, roll it round, round and round, like a ball on your neck, press your stomach harder, flatten it down, blow, skin-baby, blow. Okay. Let it go, relax. Relax. Okay, now open your eyes and take a squint.'

'I'm floating!' cried Jason. 'I'm floating — I don't believe it.'

'Simple, wasn't it?' grinned Joy-poloy, swaying and tilting his body luxuriously in the air. Jason imitated him and laughed out loud with pleasure at the novel sensation.

'Say, why don't we take a trip?' suggested Joy-poloy. 'I could do with a change of pressure. Where would you like to go? Somewhere skimmy?'

'Yes, somewhere skimmy. How about the Undersea?'

'Wow-wheee!' rasped Joy-poloy, his smooth, soft skin glowing at the thought. 'That's a real touchy trip, baby. Sure you wouldn't rather slip through the oil-spouts, or ripple in the rice-piles?'

'Er — no — I think the Undersea will do, thank you. I want to rub horns with a herd of wild Tricorns there.'

'Tussle with thundering Tricorns? You're out of your mellow, melting mind, skin-baby. You been in some kind of accident? Spilt your skull-juice, maybe?'

'Well, it's true I had some trouble with a bunch of Hearties, back in the valley, but that's not . . . '

'Those early-rising, loud-mouthed, lawn-lopping louts. Say, why don't we float over and toss their turfs?'

'I'm afraid there isn't much left. I blew it up.'

'Oh steamy creamy — you're dreamy, skin-child. Weee!' and Joy-poloy spun off through the air, twisting and rolling his smooth, rounded form.

'Excuse me asking,' said Jason, 'but you don't seem to have any hands or feet, just long lobes of flesh. Have you always been like that? I mean — do you change when you're down on the ground?'

'Of course, what do you take me for? I can change shape like anyone else. But I hardly ever settle these days, just flop down for a skin feast once in a while when the mood takes me. Most of the time, though, I ooze around up here. It's the only way to go, you'll see,' and he floated off up through an oval space in the soft ceiling. Jason followed with an ease that surprised him.

'Say, I have a great idea,' said Joy-poloy suddenly, hovering in a wide blue cavity that gaped around them. 'Let's skip this Tricorn lark and go on a haunting trip instead. What do you say?'

'Haunting? What sort of haunting?'

'House-haunting, of course. Listen, we'll skim out of here and slide up to the big roof — it's strictly against the rules, but who cares. Up there, where the Inrock meets the Outrock, there are old stone houses, thousands of them, and we can take a glide

The Tunnel of Joy-poloy

through the walls, you'll love it. When we see some old Outrock bag of nerves, we can wail and moan at them and watch them jump. It's a scream. How about it?'

'You mean we can float through the walls and into the rooms of the houses? Like ghosts?'

'That's it, you've got it — the ghost game. Only we don't go right through into the Outrock, we'd blow up if we did. There's no need — all we have to do is float around inside the walls and make groaning noises. Drives them wild — so wild that sometimes they actually believe they can see us. In fact all the stones are one-way, like the rocks — we can see them but they can't see us — so I guess it's just their imagination. Unless the one-way screen breaks down sometimes, but I don't see how it could. Anyway, whatever happens, it's perfectly safe, and very, very funny.'

'I'm sure it is, but . . .'

'We have to pick old houses, naturally. The new ones are so badly built. Only the really old ones have thick enough walls for us to glide around in comfort. They're knocking a lot of them down, but there are still plenty left. Let's go.'

'Joy-poloy, wait. I'm sorry. It would be fun, I'm sure, but I don't have the time. I simply must find those Tricorns. If you won't help me, then please tell me the way to the Undersea and I'll float there on my own.'

'You'd never find it, skin-child, never. Okay, okay, if you're set on it, I'll take you there, but you'll never know what you've missed. Everyone should go on a haunting trip at least once in their lives. Okay, then, follow me — this way to the Undersea,' and he skimmed gracefully off to the right.

Soon they were soaring through the air, along hollow green funnels and out round pink and purple spiral tubes, past hovering, star-shaped blobs of shiny black and crimson. Before long they were rushing down a gaping cavity lined with shimmering white slabs and then out into a magnificent blue arena bathed in a pale, gentle, blue light.

'There she is!' called Joy-poloy. 'Let's cruise awhile.'

Lying on his back and drifting slowly along in the buoyant air,

Inrock

Jason's lazy gaze revealed to him a scene of unbelievable beauty. Above him lay the ocean, the great swirling waters of the sea, full of a galaxy of every imaginable kind of fish and marine life.

'We are under the sea,' he gasped. 'It's fantastic!'

'That's what you wanted, isn't it?' called Joy-poloy, rocking his curving body gently back and forth, like an infant in a cradle.

'Yes, of course, the Undersea. But it's so much better than I imagined. How can we see it so clearly?'

'You're in the Testing Grounds now, skin-baby. It's all one-way rocks here. That's why there are so few Grannits in these parts. Of course, if there was a break-in from the Outrock, the place would be swarming with them in seconds and we'd be in trouble. We'd get fossilized in the rush. But that hardly ever happens, so no need to worry.'

'So there's enough light coming through from the Outrock? We're in day-light, real day-light. I can't believe it, it makes me quite home-sick.'

'Say that again, slowly, will you?'

'Well – er – I was once in the Outrock for a while, on a special mission – er – I can't tell you any more – it – er – it was top secret.'

'Boy oh boy oh boy oh boy! You poor melting skin-child. Those Hearties have done you a mischief. First you want to hunt Tricorns and now you have been on a mission to Outrock. Oh, baby, you're sinking!'

'Don't say that,' cried Jason, looking nervously down at the ground hundreds of feet below them.

'Just a figure of speech. Relax. Where was I. Oh, yes, I was telling you about the rocks here. Well, like the stones in the old houses we were talking about before, the rocks, which we know from this side are hollow, look solid from the other side. In the Outrock you can't see through them, but here in the Testing Grounds you can float up and look through them like . . . like a sheet of glass. Didn't anyone ever tell you about this, skin-baby? Where have you been all your life?'

'Yes, of course,' said Jason, 'I think you're right about those

The Tunnel of Joy-poloy

Hearties — it was quite a bang!' Privately, he was remembering the moment, long ago, when he had entered the Inrock through the growing-stone at his home village of Avebury. The second the stone had snapped shut and he had stood alone inside the great slab of rock, it had become transparent. He had been able to see the village world through it, as though he had been staring at a shop window. Now he could see the underside of the ocean in the same way. This meant that, after all his travels in the interior of the Inrock, he was at last back near the surface again. For the first time since his journey had begun, he had the feeling that he was on his way home. He still had no idea exactly how he was going to get there, but he could *see* it and that made him feel good. His thoughts were interrupted by his floating friend:

'Dreaming about upstairs, are you?' enquired Joy-poloy, drifting over beside him.

'Yes, I was,' admitted Jason.

'Forget it. Not worth the hassle. Stay here, relax. Float a little, trip a little, skim a little — it's a great life. I gave up worrying about upstairs a long time ago.'

'Did you fail your test then?'

'Sure, we're all failures here, but we learn to live with it. Poor old Plod-wig, the horrible Hearties, those Niggle-pickers of mine back at the cavern, all of us, we're all failures. But who wants to blast off through the rock anyway? It's a drag, skin-baby, forget it. Float free, baby, let it sag, let it flop. There's no winning-post, so stop racing, skin-child, flake out, flip over and flap along with me. Scan that scene, baby, isn't that something?'

'It's certainly very beautiful, but I *have* to find those Tricorns. I'm sorry. I'd like to stay, but I must start looking for them. Do you know anything about them that would help?'

'Okay, if that's the way you're drifting, it's your scramble. Tricorns? Yes, they're large, white and wicked. About six or seven of them altogether. They keep in a tight bunch and Grannits protect anyone who tries to close in on them. They can smell you a mile off and come charging straight at you.'

'I was told they are Mark III Unicorns.'

'Yes, the original Mark I was useless, couldn't resist young girls. Used to go and lay its head in their laps and get its horn cut off. Then it got put to work, pulling chariots and giving rides on the sand, or so the story goes. Hopeless thing. It soon dropped out. The Mark II never got off the drawing-board. Even before it could be started, the Sculptor came up with the Mark III version – made it much fiercer and gave it three horns, one behind the other down its forehead. It would have been a winner upstairs, with two spare horns, but it was so fierce that it nearly killed the Duplicator after he'd finished copying it into a herd, ready for the Outrock, and the whole gang of them made off here for the Undersea. No one could catch them, or get near enough to tell them the good news.'

'What good news?'

'That they are free to go through. The whole herd can go through to the Outrock any time they like. They were told this when they were being duplicated, but they wouldn't believe it. They were convinced that they were going to be sent back to the Sculptor for another horn. They'd had enough of that already, so they kicked their heels in the air and rushed off here. No one's been able to approach them since.'

'But why wouldn't they believe that they were going on through to the Outrock? I don't understand.'

'It was the Duplicator's fault. He made a stupid remark about "another horn should do it", meaning the third horn the Sculptor had already given them, but they thought he was hinting that they might have to have a fourth one and that was that. They were off! If only someone could tell them, maybe they'd go through and stop charging around down here, scaring the life out of us.'

'Thank you,' said Jason, 'you have made my Test much easier. Now all I have to do is to get close enough to tell them the truth. How fast can we float, if we really try?'

'Flat out? About . . . hey, hold on a minute. Hold it right there. I'm not chasing after those crazy beasts. What kind of a floating freak do you think I am? Listen, baby, I'm an easy drifter, see, not a screaming dragster. You're on your own, skin-child. If that's

The Tunnel of Joy-poloy

your scurry, count me out. I'll flop along for the lazy look-see, but once we eye-spot those horny killers, I'm skimming off back to the furry fun-tubes, and that's a floating fact, baby, that's a floating fact,' and with a graceful twirl of his soft lobes, Joy-poloy went into a steep dive towards the open plains below.

Jason zoomed after him. Clearly, once they had sighted the Tricorns, he would have to meet the challenge on his own. It was a daunting thought, but nevertheless he was grateful to Joy-poloy for having helped him this far. Now it would be up to him.

After several hours of criss-cross floating over the landscape beneath them, searching every detail with their eyes, they detected a small cloud of orange dust in the far distance.

'There they go!' shouted Joy-poloy. 'And here, too, go I. Farewell, skin-child. Float free, baby,' and he was gone, skimming into the air above them and drifting gently away, back in the direction they had come.

'Goodbye!' called Jason, 'and thank you,' but Joy-poloy was already out of ear-shot.

On the distant plain below, the orange cloud was growing smaller every second. There was no time to lose. Jason aimed himself at it and went into a full-speed float, soaring after the vanishing herd. The air whistled through his horns and tugged at his skin. Gradually he began to gain on them. The orange cloud was getting bigger now, instead of smaller, and already he could faintly hear the thunder of angry hooves. Soon, soon he would be over them, and his Test would begin in earnest, the Test which, if he was successful, would eventually lead him back to the Outrock and home. He *had* to succeed, he had to, he had to.

CHAPTER TWENTY-SIX
The Tricorn Herd

For seven days and nights Jason pursued the galloping herd of savage Tricorns. Relentlessly he floated along above their backs, hovering over them like a jockey who has died and almost gone to heaven. The cloud of orange dust kicked up by their pounding feet filled his mouth and nose, making him choke and cough, but he never gave up. Every so often he shouted to them, telling them to stop and listen, but they either ignored him or were unable to hear above the thunder of their hooves.

On the eighth day the pace was as fast as ever and Jason marvelled at the incredible stamina of these magnificent white beasts. Apart from the three sharp, pointed horns on their heads, they looked for all the world like sleek, powerful race-horses, but no horse, not even the champion of the Outrock, would have been able to keep up with these magical beasts. The Sculptor had produced a truly miraculous new creature. But how in earth was Jason ever going to capture them? The Mha-kee had been right – it was an impossible task. Then, as he was racking his already over-racked brains yet again to find a solution, he was shaken to discover that the ground beneath him was empty. The herd had vanished! Skimming to a halt, he twirled round in

The Tricorn Herd

mid-air and looked back the way he had come. There, to his utter surprise, were the Tricorns, calmly sitting in a circle on the ground. They must have stopped dead without a second's warning when his attention was relaxed for a brief moment, as he pondered on how to solve his problem. Slowly, gently, he floated back towards them, until he was right in the middle of the circle, only a few feet above their savage-looking heads. The ring of haughty faces stared at him, unblinking, expressionless. There was no trace of exhaustion, not even slight tiredness. Jason was duly impressed, but tried not to show it. Taking a deep breath, he spoke softly to them, terrified that his voice might send them galloping off for another seven days and nights.

'My name is Jason and I have good news for you.'

The tallest Tricorn, the one with the longest, most beautifully spiralled horns and the thickest, most flowing mane, heaved a sigh.

'If', it said, in a lofty, bored tone, 'you have the audacity to inform us that we misunderstood that dithering, doll-handed Duplicator and that really — truthfully, faithfully, sincerely, honestly — we can proceed to the Outrock without delay, then, like the other nine feeble little filly-busters who came before you, you will be pronged into a fork supper with our compliments.'

Jason was so taken aback that he simply stared in dumb astonishment at the haughty face in front of him. The tall Tricorn waited a few moments for an answer, then sniffed contemptuously and spoke again:

'Your face is your reply. Words would be superfluous. The herd and I therefore invite you forthwith to be our fork supper. Tails will be worn, of course.'

'I'm afraid that counts me out. I have no tail.'

'Don't be droll. Augustus, skewer him from behind.'

'Wait!' cried Jason. 'Before you convey me to your noble mouths, answer me this. If the Duplicator's words did not startle you, then why did you bolt? There must have been a good reason, something truly awe-inspiring, to alarm a breed as fine and brave as yours. Tell me what it was and I shall die content in your aristocratic jaws.'

'If you are mocking my manner of speech, young floater, I shall devour you feet-first instead of head-first, a much more painfully gradual demise.'

'I spoke in a manner befitting your auspicious presence. That is all. But perhaps you are ashamed to impart the information I so humbly seek?'

The tall Tricorn neighed softly to its companions, shook its heavy mane and answered:

'The explanation is simplicity itself. While we were being duplicated we met a small Gook, one of the gobbling kind, a tiny, triangular, lemon-coloured, foul-smelling, sticky-haired, lozenge-shaped creature of lowly origins and lowlier feeding habits. Under normal circumstances we would not, of course, converse with such a . . . thing. But there was something odd about this particular Gook. It kept pointing up at our horns and laughing. When pressed to explain itself, it admitted that it had heard a rumour, supposedly emanating from the Outrock, a rumour . . . '

'Go on,' said Jason, 'I am listening.'

'A rumour that horns like ours were selling at a rate of five gold bars per inch . . . *per inch*, not per foot, mark you, but per inch . . . on the Outrock markets. Naturally we refused to believe such nonsense, but he was so insistent that we took the trouble to ask the Ticket Officer at the Through-rock Bridge if there was any substance in this extraordinary rumour. From his face, without a doubt, we saw that it was so. Taking rapid council, we made a herd decision and, as you rather crudely expressed it a moment ago, bolted. We have never regretted our decision. According to the Gook, we would have been killed within days of our arrival at the Outrock and our horns hacked from our carcasses, to be sold to medicine men and ground down to a powder, in this form to be disposed of at vast profit to ageing politicians, supposedly to give them a more vigorous body to impress their close followers. That, I need hardly say, was a fate too nauseating for us to contemplate, and we took the only choice open to us. Now perhaps you understand and we can proceed with the pronging. Augustus?'

The Tricorn Herd

'Wait!' cried Jason a second time. 'If that is your only worry, I can solve it for you without delay.' The Tricorns murmured amongst themselves at this bold statement.

'Explain your audacious claim immediately,' snorted the tall leader of the herd.

Jason had to think quickly. 'I, too, have horns, as you can plainly see, and . . . '

'You insult our intelligence. Your horns are a pair. Paired horns are of no value. There is no comparison.'

'Please let me finish. My horns may not be worth five gold bars per inch, like yours, but even so, for reasons I cannot explain, I do not intend to enter the Outrock wearing them on my head. I shall arrive hornless and so, if you follow my instructions, will you.'

'Hornless! But that is unthinkable. Even our Mark I, the Unicorn, had a single horn.'

'But you are far superior in strength and nobility. Masquerading as great white horses, you would dominate the equine world. You would race before kings and queens, you would be royally treated as champions of the Outrock world. There would be nothing to fear. I speak as one who knows the ways of the Outrock and you may trust my words.'

'Perhaps it will be as you say. We are indeed a strong, swift breed. The Sculptor was proud of our bodies. But pray, how do you propose to dissolve our noble horns?'

'That should not be difficult. We will travel together to the Through-rock Bridge and lie in wait. As travellers arrive to obtain their through-rock passes from the Ticket Officer, I will question them. Sooner or later one will arrive who has it in his power to remove our horns without otherwise harming us.'

'But why should such a one pause to perform such a service? They are always in haste at the bridge. We have seen the way they hurry to cross its span and meet the Overtaker who will guide them through to the Outrock. They will brush you aside without a moment's hesitation.'

'Not when I tell them of the vast wealth they will carry in their arms. Not when I tell them that the horns we are offering them are worth five gold bars for every inch.'

'But surely they will wonder why we ourselves do not transport this treasure? They will be suspicious.'

'No. I will simply tell them what you have already told me, namely that if we carry the horns on our own heads we will be killed by hunters before we can offer them freely. But if they are taken through in bags, dissolved or powdered, this fate will be avoided. The horns' new owners will be able to trade them for great wealth. It cannot fail. Do you agree?'

'We will take council. Leave us for a while to consider the matter.'

Jason floated a short distance away and watched as the circle of Tricorns discussed the problem, snorting, neighing and tossing their great manes of flowing white hair. His hopes were high. His only fear was that they would be unable to find a through-rock traveller with the necessary powers to remove their horns. He had made light of this, but secretly had some doubt as to how easy this would prove to be. But if the Tricorns agreed to go with him, it would mean that the first battle had been won. They would no longer be looking upon him as an enemy. It would be a beginning, a beginning to what had previously seemed an impossible task.

The council was ended and the tall leader of the Tricorns approached him.

'My herd and I have debated your ingenious proposal at some length. We have grave misgivings, but we have reached an agreement. We will accompany you to the Through-rock Bridge. There we will make a camp in the nearby woodland while you attempt to find a suitable traveller. We will not show ourselves at the entrance to the Bridge, but will remain in hiding to await your return. You will bring the traveller with you and if he fails you will both be pronged and eaten without further discussion. If he succeeds, we will all journey to the Outrock together. Is that understood?'

'Perfectly. It is understood and agreed.'

'Very well then, we will depart for the Bridge. You will cease to float and will ride instead upon my back, so that I can throw you and trample you should you seek to betray us.'

'I agree to that also, and I am ready to depart,' replied Jason.

'Together we will solve our problems.'

The magnificent herd reared on to their hind legs and with a great snorting and neighing set off at a gallop for the Through-rock Bridge, with Jason riding boldly on the leader's broad, strong back. They travelled through many strange landscapes, the scenery around them changing constantly. Occasionally they passed a small group of mumbling failures who jumped screaming from their thundering path. Jason felt like a great conqueror, charging through a defeated land, but his mood was marred by a nagging fear that he might fail to find the traveller he sought when they eventually arrived at the Bridge.

At nightfall the herd stopped and they all fed and rested, but at dawn they were on their way again immediately and by the afternoon of the following day they came to the vicinity of the Bridge. Jason dismounted and the Tricorns left him for a small cluster of trees nearby, where they made camp and waited. He approached the Bridge openly, without stealth, and marched straight up to the Ticket Office at one side of the entrance. A sharp blast sounded from inside it and a trumpet-shaped creature with six long, thin legs rushed from a side door and blocked Jason's path, hooting loudly.

'Excuse me,' said Jason politely, 'but can you tell me if any travellers are expected today?'

'Travellers? Travellers?' trumpeted the Ticket Officer. 'Of course there are travellers. Always travellers, nothing but blasted travellers. And what about my holidays? What about that, then? They never give that a moment's thought, do they? No, never. When did I last get a day off, answer me that? It's been so long I can't remember. And where's my relief officer, I'd like to know. Where is he, eh? Answer me that if you can. And now you come along here asking me if there are any travellers. It's pathetic. And what are you doing here, anyway? You haven't been duplicated yet. Go back to the Duplicator's this instant and stop wasting my time. For all I know you haven't even done your Test. How would

I know that, eh? Go and report to the Duplicator, prove to him you have completed the Test that was set for you and he will duplicate you. Then you can come back here and worry me for a pass, but not before. Do you hear, not before? Now be off with you and leave me in peace,' and he started hooting and trumpeting into Jason's face again, blowing himself up into a frenzy of bleeps and trills.

'If you'll stop that for a moment, I have something to tell you,' shouted Jason.

'Tell me, tell me? What could you possibly have to tell me? Where's my relief, that's all I want to know.'

'That's what I wanted to tell you,' said Jason. 'I *am* your relief.'

'You are? You *are*? No, no, I don't believe it. It's too good to be true. Wait there, no, come in here, no wait there, oh dear, oh dear. My relief has come, at last, at last,' and he dashed this way and that, in and out of his Ticket Office, scurrying round as if demented. Finally he gave a great blast on his trumpet mouth and scuttled off into the distance. The Ticket Office was empty. Jason sat himself down at the desk and peered out of the small window where the passes were issued. He sorted through the papers scattered on the desk and arranged them neatly into piles. Then he waited.

Before very long there was a sound of pattering feet approaching the office and peering out of the window he saw a pair of travellers approaching. They were tripping gaily along hand in hand, which was no easy matter, since they had sixteen hands apiece. Their bodies where shaped like hour-glasses and were covered in a sort of green floss.

'Papers?' said Jason, who imagined it was what was expected of him.

'Here you are, sir,' they giggled, and handed over documents to say that they had been passed by the Duplicator. Jason stamped them and clipped a through-rock ticket to each one. As he was handing them back, he paused, holding the papers in mid-air, just out of reach.

'One moment,' he said, in a serious tone.

The Tricorn Herd

'Yes sir, what is it, sir?' they asked anxiously.
'What de-horning experience do you have?'
'De-whating, sir?'
'De-horning.'
They looked at one another blankly and their hands began to tremble. Obviously it was useless, and Jason took pity on them.
'Never mind,' he said. 'Here are your papers. They are all in order. Proceed across the Bridge and report to the Overtaker.'
'Oh, thank you, sir, thank you,' they gabbled, and pattered off as fast as they could go.
'This is not going to be easy,' Jason muttered to himself, and started to wonder how long the Tricorns would wait for him before losing their patience and galloping back to the Undersea once more.
In the hours and days that followed, Jason kept up the same routine, always asking the same question and always getting the same blank look of astonishment and fear on the faces of the hopeful travellers. There were Clod-snappers and Hooting-lubs, Nottol-bibs and Bongey-tongues, small hairy Flopsies and big shiny Steeple-clingers, but none of them had the faintest idea what he was talking about. A trio of Coffin-borers seemed to show a glimmer of interest, but it soon emerged that they were merely showing off and he had to let them go through like the rest.
He was beginning to despair when, on the afternoon of the fifth day, the Ticket Office was approached by a pair of hunched up Dibble-runts. They waited patiently and silently while Jason dealt with a sinister family of Stinging Starhorns, nasty poisonous creatures that he would dearly have liked to refuse, but he was frightened that if they went back to the Duplicator and complained, there might be questions asked. The Outrock would have to put up with them, that was all there was to it.
'Next?' he called out, as the Stinging Starhorns slithered off across the Bridge.
'Ugh, don't they make your scales creep?' said the latest arrival, pointing after the disappearing Starhorns. 'I'd like to dibble their horns into their horrible heads, wouldn't you?'

Jason stiffened at the words. Perhaps it was just a figure of speech, an idle threat, but all the same he could hardly control his excitement.

'Let me see,' he said, trying his best to speak in a casual tone. 'One pair of Dibble-runts. Good, yes, everything seems to be in order. As a matter of interest, what is your speciality? How exactly do you dibble? If you have a moment to explain, I'd be most grateful. Haven't had a dibbler through here before. At least, not in my time.'

'Oh dear, I'm sorry, we have to hurry,' spluttered the first of the Dibble-runts. 'We can't stop talking here, we must get across. Please give us our papers.'

'Take my advice,' whispered Jason in a confidential tone, 'and hold back a while. Let those filthy Stinging Starhorns go through first, otherwise the Overtaker may put you in the same batch and, well, you never know, it might be rather dangerous. If you get my meaning?'

'Oh dear, do we go in batches? I didn't know that. Yes, thank you, I think we will wait a little then. Dibbling? You want to know about dibbling? Well, we dibble people's feet, you see. So many people get hard skin on the bottoms of their feet these days, or so the Sculptor assures us, that they'll do anything to get it dibbled off. We hope to become highly successful domestic pets. People will want to keep us in their bedrooms so that, when they are asleep at night, we will be able to creep out and dibble their corns away. I suppose you could say a dibble is a gentle nibble, really. A nibble so gentle that you don't even feel it. It doesn't wake you up or disturb your sleep, but in the morning all that hard skin and those horrid corns, they're all gone, like magic. The Sculptor thinks we'll prove to be very popular, very popular indeed.'

'And I completely agree. A splendid idea. There's only one problem. Hold on a minute, will you, while I check the records.' Jason had decided that these Dibble-runts were far too humble to become involved in big-time horn-dealing, but a new idea had occurred to him. He shuffled the piles of paper on his desk, pretending to inspect one of them with great care. 'Ummmm,' he

The Tricorn Herd

said, as thoughtfully as he could.

'What is it? Is there something wrong?'

'Well, I must admit to you now that my question about dibbling was not a matter of idle curiosity. I had a special reason for asking. You see, about a week ago, before I came on duty here, a pair of travellers, calling themselves Dibble-runts, presented themselves at this Ticket Office and were issued with tickets. They have already gone through to the Outrock.'

'They were impostors!' shrieked the two hunched up figures. '*We* are the true Dibble-runts and we demand to be let through.'

'I agree that a trick has been played,' said Jason slowly, stroking his chin, 'but who are the culprits, that is my problem, you or them. You see my difficulty, don't you?'

'Them, them,' cried the frantic Dibble-runts in unison.

'But can you prove it?' asked Jason blandly.

'Prove it? How? We *are* the Dibble-runts. How do you want us to prove it? Go on, tell us. We have nothing to fear.'

'Perhaps if you gave a demonstration . . .'

'Yes, yes, anything, anything. How, where?'

'If you'll come with me, I think we can clear this little difficulty up in no time at all,' said Jason in a more friendly tone, leaving the Ticket Office and setting off in the direction of the Tricorns' camp. The Dibble-runts dragged their hunched up bodies along as fast as they could, anxious to keep up with him as he strode towards the small clump of trees. Jason explained to them as they went that in the woods there was a group of large white creatures who, as chance would have it, were extremely worried about three long, horny growths that had sprouted out on top of their heads. The poor beasts, he confided, were so ashamed of their deformities that they couldn't bear to show themselves at the Ticket Office to get their passes for the Outrock. If the Dibble-runts could help them, they would not only be proving their own identity but would also gain the undying gratitude of these wretchedly afflicted, but otherwise magnificent beasts. The Dibble-runts, to be honest, seemed to care little for gratitude, but were desperate to prove that they were who they were, and set to work with a will.

The Tricorns, whose patience, as Jason had feared, was on the verge of running out, were delighted to see him and almost lost their natural dignity and restraint when the two Dibble-runts went to work on them with such a gentle touch that they hardly felt their horns crumble and vanish. Their haughty faces positively beamed.

'There!' said the Dibble-runts proudly. 'Now perhaps you will believe us?'

'Hmmm,' said Jason. 'Those horns were soft. Softer than mine, for instance. I doubt whether . . . ' but before he could finish, the Dibble-runts were nibbling away at the top of his head and in a few moments his own horns had been dibbled clean away.

'Astonishing!' exclaimed Jason, unable to control a broad smile. 'It didn't hurt a bit.'

'Of course not. *Now* are you satisfied?'

'Oh, yes, completely. Here are your papers. You can go on through now. Obviously that other pair must have been the impostors. Thank you for . . . ' but the Dibble-runts had already sloped hurriedly away to the Bridge.

'You have done well,' intoned the leader of the Tricorns. 'Mount my back again and we, too, will cross the Through-rock Bridge.'

At the very moment the Tricorns emerged from the clump of trees and headed towards the Ticket Office, there was a loud trumpeting sound. Rushing headlong towards the entrance to the Bridge and cutting them off was an angry, excited crowd of jabbering officials. As the herd reared to a halt, Jason could see that in the centre of the group was the outraged figure of the original Ticket Officer, blowing his trumpet as if he were going to burst. Next to him stood a tall, gaunt figure with seven noses and two chins, one on the left and one on the right of his haggard, wrinkled face. He had no body, his long, tapering legs disappearing into his withered neck.

'Hi there, stop!' called the gaunt figure. 'I am the Duplicator and I demand that you give yourselves up. The Ticket Office has been violated and you are all under arrest. You will be scrambled

The Tricorn Herd

for this. Polizesti, guard the Bridge. No one is to cross. No one, do you hear?'

Jason was pleased to see the distant figures of the helpful Dibble-runts scurrying safely across to the far side of the Bridge. He was glad they had escaped. But what were he and the Tricorns going to do now? It was hopeless to attempt to rush the Polizesti. They'd all be spiked and stunned and carried off to be scrambled. There was only one thing for it — they would have to go back the way he had come. Somehow they would have to find the route to the side-passage that led off the main assembly area of the Inrock and up to that huge growing-stone in his own village of Avebury. It was a slender chance, but there was no alternative. He whispered in the leading Tricorn's ear and with a neighing snort, the great beast reared up and pawed the air with his front legs. The others followed suit and then together they wheeled and galloped off, away from the Through-rock Bridge, the gaunt Duplicator, the trumpeting Ticket Official and the angry, twitching Polizesti.

A cloud of dust rose around the thundering hooves and the noble, magnificent herd sped swiftly away, a long, hazardous journey ahead of them. Even if they succeeded in completing the trip, they still had to face a secret and difficult climb, up into the magical growing-stone of Avebury village. The prospect was poor, but their spirit was strong, and even the withered old Duplicator had to shake his head in admiration at the sight of them as they pounded away and rapidly dwindled to a small, dusty speck in the far, far distance.

CHAPTER TWENTY-SEVEN
The Muzzleking's Sacrifice

After travelling for several months and enduring many more adventures, Jason and the noble Tricorns had still failed to find the side-passage they were seeking, which would take them up and through to the Outrock. They had almost given up hope when, one evening, they heard an eerie, baying sound, coming from a hill-top just beyond the hollow in which they were resting.

The Tricorns pricked their white ears and fell silent. Jason put his forefinger to his lips and then crawled stealthily to the rim of the hollow. There, high above, he could see a small silhouette and, as he watched, it threw back its head and emitted another long, mournful howl. At this, the Tricorns sprang to their feet, nervously shaking their manes and flaring their nostrils, ready to bolt, but Jason called down to them:

'It's all right! I know who that is. It's an old friend of mine. He won't harm us,' and, cupping his hands, he shouted, 'Satan! Rex! Satan! It's me – Jason. Over here. Over here.'

The howling stopped and the hill-top shape disappeared.

'I've frightened him away. Quick, let's follow him. He can help

The Muzzleking's Sacrifice

us. He knows the secret passage. He came in that way. Perhaps *he* can remember.'

But the old dog was not fleeing as Jason imagined. As soon as he had heard his friend's voice in the distance, he had given a soft yelp of relief and started off down the hillside. Sliding and rolling and cursing, he reached the bottom and sprinted headlong towards the hollow. He arrived just as the herd came galloping out and, unable to stop, crashed into the leading Tricorn's chest. Sprawling in the dust, the old boxer lay panting and gasping. He tried to drag himself to his feet, failed and sank back again. Jason ran to his side.

'Satan, Satan, are you hurt?' As he hugged his old friend, the only part of the dog that moved was his tail which slowly thumped the ground in an apology for a wag. Looking closely at him, Jason frowned.

'What's happened? Where is your muzzle-crown? What have they done to you?'

The old boxer covered his face with his paws.

'They nearly killed me,' he snuffled. 'Savage brutes. Murdering monsters. They said the games were getting boring. Not vicious enough for them. Not enough blood. We did everything we could. Kept on adding new horror-shows, but it was never enough. Then, one day, one of the spectators discovered the truth. Hid in the changing rooms and found a bag of redberries. Overheard the fight manager's instructions, and told the others it was all a sham. They went wild. Tore the place to pieces. Ripped my muzzle-crown out by the roots.' He winced at the memory. 'And trussed us up for a ceremony of their own. Only *this* time, for real. As far as I know, I was the only one to escape – gnawed through my bonds and dug myself out while they were arguing about the most horrible way to destroy us. It was terrible, terrible – and they are still after me. I have been running for days.'

'But if you are hiding from them, why did you howl like that? It might have drawn them to you.'

'I know, I know, but I couldn't help it. This is something I could never explain to you up there in the Outrock, where dogs can't talk, but, you see, the howl of a dog at night is like a human prayer. We call to the Great Moondog to protect us. We appeal to the mercy of Dog the Father, Dog the Pup, and Dog the Holy Werewolf. Some breeds even pray to the Great Mother Bitch when times are really bad. People don't realize how devout dogs are. They see us making our daily offerings to the Sacred Tree-spirit, but they never understand. They are very self-centred, people,' and the old boxer subsided again, laying his head mournfully in the dust.

'I had no idea,' said Jason. 'I promise never to call you Satan again. That must have hurt. From now on, it will always be Rex. Come on, cheer up. We'll help you. The Tricorns will protect you. And in return you can help *us*, help us to find the place where you and I entered the Inrock. Do you remember the side-passage where we . . . '

'Of course, that's easy. Dogs don't forget their tracks, do they?'

The Tricorns eyed one another, snorted and pawed the ground in eager anticipation.

'But first I must rest. I'm nearly done for. Does anyone have a juicy bone to spare? There's a question for you! I had millions and now I am begging for just one. No? Oh well, some sleep then, some sleep. Will you keep watch for me?' And in an instant the old dog was snoring noisily, his wrinkled face vibrating with each heavy breath.

The Tricorns formed a circle around him and stood staring into the distance, scouring the landscape for signs of danger. Jason sat down beside the slumbering dog and patiently waited for their guide-to-be to recover his strength.

The next morning they started out once more on their quest, with their hopes much higher than they had been for many weeks. Rex ran ahead of the trotting Tricorns, his nose low to the ground, sniffing, pausing and changing direction again and again. Then, at last, he let out a yelp and took off at a gallop, closely followed by the excited, neighing herd.

'There it is,' shouted Rex, and in the far distance they caught sight of a small, dark smudge that was the longed-for entrance to

The Muzzleking's Sacrifice

the secret tunnel. As soon as they came close, Jason recognized it immediately. Unfortunately, the Polizesti guarding it also recognized him at the same moment, having never enjoyed the luxury of spiking anyone else. His one great moment of power had lived on in his nasty memory, the moment when he had spiked that peculiar, naked-skinned stranger and presented him to the Interviewer so proudly. He had told many a tale about the incident at the annual Polizesti Ball, and it had become considerably embroidered in the retelling. Now here was that strange creature once again, heading straight for his tunnel on the back of a huge white beast, and accompanied by a whole herd of possible spike-victims. It was too good to be true. He rushed from his hole in the wall and waved his spike bravely at them as they thundered towards him.

As soon as they saw the quivering spike, the Tricorns shuddered to a halt and reared up in fright.

'Hold your ground,' shouted Jason, 'I will try to talk him round. Don't move. Stay still.'

'It is no use trying to reason with one of *those*,' snarled Rex, his fur bristling and his teeth glistening in a savage snarl. 'Leave this to me,' and he advanced slowly and menacingly towards the spike-brandishing figure blocking the tunnel entrance.

'Now listen to me,' he growled, 'I am the great, the all-powerful, Rasimondus the Triple-Brutal, Muzzleking of all Canini, Overseer of the Skeletal Games and Supreme Judge of the Bonefire Ceremonies. You will kneel to me and sheath your slimy spike, you wall-eyed whiner!'

The Polizesti stiffened and reared himself up, his eye-stalks dancing and his sinister spike shimmering with rage.

'I know all about you,' he hissed, 'I've got papers on you here. You two-faced Boner-Fido, you Skulldoggerer, you Redberry Sham, you Slurp-worrying Fraud, you Chomping Charlatan, you, you, you Mangy Mutt-stray. I'll spike you into oblivion. You'll get death for this, and no time off for good behaviour.'

Rex responded to this verbal onslaught with a deep-throated growl and began edging towards the defiant Polizesti.

'Take care,' shouted Jason, leaping from his Tricorn and running to the dog's side. 'Please, Rex,' he whispered into the animal's ear, 'please, let me talk to him. I'll try to bribe him in some way. Don't fight him, he'll kill you with one touch of that spike, or stun you at the very least. I know. He stunned me with it. You don't have a chance.'

Without taking his fixed glare off the body of the Polizesti, Rex replied:

'It is good of you to care about me, but it is no use. He will never listen. I have to do this. While he is dealing with me, you can all rush past and escape into the tunnel. If I survive, I will follow you. Now remount, my mind is made up.'

'Rex, you are my friend, I . . . '

'Don't whine for *me*. I have lived the life of a king, these past months. A glorious life of untold pleasures. They say that every dog has his day but sadly that is not true. Many do not. But I, I have had my day, many, many days. During them I have fooled all of the people all of the time, but now it is the moment to atone. Do not rob me of this moment, or I shall despise you. Now go! That is the Muzzleking's last order.'

Jason could find no words to answer this. He hugged the old dog, patted his tense, bristling back, and slowly remounted his Tricorn. There was a silent pause and then Rex crouched and leapt, snarling and growling at the figure in front of him. He went straight for the spike, snapping down hard on it with his powerful jaws.

The Polizesti let out a fearful shriek and changed colour several times in quick succession. Clinging tightly, the dog was whisked this way and that in the air as the spike writhed furiously in his grip. Then, as the Tricorns watched in horror, Rex's body suddenly went limp and fell to the ground.

'Spiked! Spiked! I have spiked him,' screamed the Polizesti. 'That Triple-Stupid Tyke, I've spiked him dead.' But then his tone changed to a whimper. 'Oh, my spike, my smarting spike, he won't let go. He's dead, but he won't let go. Get off, you filthy flea-bag. Oooh! Aaow!'

The Muzzleking's Sacrifice

'Look,' cried Jason, 'his jaws are locked on the spike, the Polizesti is helpless. He has killed poor Rex, but he is trapped. Now, charge, charge the tunnel together, go!' and the whole herd thundered forward.

The last thing the wildly jerking Polizesti saw, the last thing he *ever* saw, was a mass of huge white hooves pounding down on him, as the herd crashed over him and up the long, winding passage.

As the tunnel narrowed the startled Tricorns neighed and whinnied in panic, their flanks tearing against the sharp walls.

'Don't stop!' shouted Jason. 'On! Keep going, don't stop!' and they thundered up the jagged pathway, falling into single file, slithering and slipping on the uneven floor, their huge white haunches rippling with immense power.

Realizing that he had no idea exactly where the growing-stone was situated, but merely that it was somewhere up there, above them, Jason drove the herd on with shouts and yells until, rising higher and higher, they came face to face with a dead end, a wall of soft, crumbling earth. There was nothing for it but to plunge straight in and pray that they would burst out through the other side.

'Charge!' bellowed Jason. 'Charge!' and the valiant Tricorns, their hooves flying, hurled themselves at the wall of earth. Into it they crashed, kicking and writhing, sweating and neighing and thrashing about with their great, muscular legs. The earth began to tumble around them, cascades of yellow and brown particles showered over them and then, with a final surge, they were through.

All around stretched the Outrock, the green landscape of hedges and rolling fields that Jason knew so well. He was home! There in the distance nestled the village of Avebury, as quiet and sleepy as ever, but instead of having come up through the growing-stone, they had burst through the steep side of a nearby hill. The Tricorns, vigorously shaking the soil from their bodies, were wandering over its grassy slope and bending their necks to taste the fresh, green grasses that grew there in such profusion.

Dismounting from the tall leader of the herd, Jason patted its neck and thanked it. Its answer was a wordless snuffle.

'Where will you go now?' asked Jason, as the great beast lowered its head and began to munch at the grass like its companions. 'Will you stay in these parts, or will you travel on?' But again the reply was no more than a snort, and it dawned on Jason that up here, in the Outrock world, the Tricorns would probably lose their power of speech, a thought which made him sad. But he had other matters to attend to now. Somewhere nearby, the Mad Meggamole was waiting for his Golden Worms, and one, at least, was on its way. Jason started to run off down the hill, then braked himself to turn and wave farewell to the valiant Tricorns. As he raised his arm in salute, he saw to his horror that they were changing in front of his eyes. Each one was swelling and swelling, growing to huge proportions and drifting off across the hillside, floating through the air, whinnying pitifully and thrashing its legs in the air. Like great white balloons, they spread out across the landscape, growing larger and larger all the time. Then they started to descend, one after the other, and crashed into the hillsides all about, some nearby, others miles away in the far distance. The leader of the herd collided with the earth not far from where Jason was standing and he rushed wildly through the long grass to be by its side. Stumbling and panting, he finally arrived at the spot where it had landed. As he watched, horrified, he saw it collapse and sink into a vast, flat white shape on the side of the hill. Staggering over to it, disbelieving, he bent down and touched its surface. It was already no more than a chalky white patch etched on to the once grassy slope of the hill. From head to tail, the great white shape of the Tricorn must have stretched at least a hundred feet.

'Of course!' gasped Jason. 'The Golden Worms. They ate the grass and exploded. They had no Golden Worms. What had they done with them? Why didn't they tell me? They must have known this would happen. Or did they forget? But now I'll never know.'

Sadly, he trudged down the hillside and into the road. It was the main road that ran from London to Bristol and passed right by the outskirts of his village. As he walked along it, his head down,

The Muzzleking's Sacrifice

thinking about the terrible fate of the brave Tricorns, another awful thought crossed his mind: 'If they blew up as quickly as that, then there was no hope at all for the Mad Meggamole. He must have exploded almost as soon as I left for the Inrock. So I am too late, weeks, months, years too late. The Meggamole will have long ago plunged screaming into the earth, searching desperately for giant worms to fill his giant belly, and digging himself the biggest mole-hill in the world.'

As the words formed in his mind, he stopped in his tracks and gasped in amazement. There at the side of the road, between him and the village, was a vast, towering mole-hill, taller than a cathedral. Like a huge Christmas pudding it stood there looming above him, a monument to the late lamented Meggamole.

'Poor old Mad Meggamole!' muttered Jason, as he stared up at the great mound. 'Forgive me. I did my best, but I was too late.'

Climbing slowly up the steep slope of the hill, he clambered on to its flat top. The wind whistled through his hair and through the tattered remains of the sheet he had so long ago picked up from the rubbish dump in the Valley of the Hearties. How strange and remote that all seemed now, and how unreal!

He was about to leave and return to the farmhouse, which he could almost see across the other side of the village, when he remembered the single Golden Worm in his belt-pouch. If only he had thought of it in time he could have given it to the leader of the Tricorns. Perhaps he could have saved him. But it was too late now. Perhaps, though, down there, deep in the soil of this strange, round, flat-topped hill, the Meggamole was still lurking, munching his way through a million worms a day to keep himself going. The Golden Worm had been brought for him, and he should have it.

'Here you are, Mad Meggamole,' shouted Jason, moving to stand in the very centre of the top of the giant mole-hill. Opening the pouch, he drew out what he thought was the Golden Worm. Holding it aloft, he glanced up to see its golden glitter for the last time, before dropping it on to the soft grass, only to find that he was grasping a small, brown bean.

'Ludo!' he screamed. 'It's Ludo! I forgot, I forgot. At least *you* are still with me.'

Placing the bean carefully back in the pouch, he saw the Golden Worm still there, glinting in a corner, but he left it where it was and snapped the cover shut. He was not taking any chances this time. If he was able to bring Ludo back to full size by pricking himself and soaking the bean in his male-blood, then there was always the risk that, here in the world of the Outrock, she might swell up and burst like the Meggamole and the Tricorns if she did not have a Golden Worm to devour before eating her first Outrock meal. But with the worm, the bean, and a drop of his blood, gladly given, he should be able to bring Ludo back to him and keep her the way she was meant to be. At last, something was going to go right.

With a whoop of delight, he ran at full tilt down the side of the circular hill and all the way back through the village, along the farmhouse path, round the farm building and into the old barn. Picking up a sharp knife from a bench, he climbed excitedly up the rickety ladder and into the hay-loft. Now, the great moment had come, the moment when Ludo would once more stand before him, as his hot male-blood trickled on to the tiny brown bean into which she had shrunk trying to save his life.

There was, of course, the problem of how to explain her strange horns and her peculiar coat of fur to the villagers when they first met her, but that could wait until tomorrow. For now, there was only one consideration — to bring her out of that bean and back to full size again.

'It has been a strange journey,' said Jason to himself, as he lifted the knife and held it against the skin of his arm, 'but this, this will make it all worth-while,' and he jabbed the point of the blade into his flesh.

As the blood dripped down on the small brown bean, lying where he had gently placed it on a bed of hay beside him, he saw it move. As he watched, smiling, fascinated, the bean became an egg and then slowly started to grow . . . and grow . . . and grow . . .

Postscript

No one knows for certain what became of Jason, for, by the following day, he had vanished from the village and was never seen again. I was fortunate enough to come across him shortly before he left. It was late at night and, hearing a noise in the cow-shed, I went to investigate. I discovered him milking one of the cows and greedily gulping down the milk straight from the pail. He was startled at first, having never set eyes on me before — you must remember that he had been away for a very long time — and tried to hide, but when I offered to fetch some food for him, he calmed down and we spent much of the night there, sitting on two wooden milking stools, while he ate and told me his strange tale. I have tried to write it down exactly as he told it, but I fear there are many who will not believe it. Certain facts, however, speak for themselves. The giant growing-stone of Avebury still stands by the side of the road that runs from the village towards Swindon. On the surface of this stone, in certain lights, it is still possible to detect the faint line of the crack where the Meggamole broke through into the Outrock. On the hillsides nearby, the remains of several of the Tricorns can also be seen to this day, although they are commonly referred to merely as 'white horses'. Naturally enough, no one has been able to explain their existence. Nor, too, has anyone found a plausible explanation for the giant mole-hill, the huge, 130-foot-high mound of earth constructed by the Meggamole in his last desperate hours. If ever you

Postscript

are travelling past Avebury on the main road from London to Bristol, you will be able to see it for yourself. They call it Silbury Hill, arguing that it was the burial mound of an ancient king called Sil, and that it contains his fabulous golden treasure. Several times they have tunnelled into its interior, downwards, sideways, and at all angles, but needless to say they have found no trace of either the king or his treasure.

Perhaps, one day, far below Silbury Hill, they will discover the sad remains of a giant mole-like creature and wonder at its peculiar anatomy. Perhaps not — for the Meggamole must have burrowed very deep to have thrown up such a huge mound of earth. I wonder, could he have returned to the Inrock and be lying snugly now in the sleep-dip in his home-tower at Ludo's village? It is a possibility, but somehow I doubt it. Time was against him.

Probably we shall never hear what finally happened to him, nor, I fear, will the mystery of Ludo's recovery ever be solved, unless Jason returns. He refused all my requests to visit the loft with him that night, and when, the following morning, I went there alone and climbed the ladder, there was no trace of either of them anywhere, except for a sharp knife lying on the hay and a small patch of dried blood. But really, they proved nothing.

And there my story must end. Whether you believe Jason's tale is up to you. Personally, I know it is true because I saw the light in his eyes as he described the journey to me, and as we all know, faces speak louder than words. But you did not have this chance, and so, if, in the end, you think that I have been a gullible fool, why then of course I shall forgive you.